Praise for *Hand Me Down Husband*

"At once tender and compelling, *Hand Me Down Husband* illustrates so beautifully the power of love to make all things new. I look forward to reading more by Rosanna Huffman!"
—Ann Tatlock, award-winning novelist and children's book author

"This book has it all: heart, community, and characters who will remain with you long after the book ends."
—Mary Ellis, author of *The Last Heiress*

"Soon after Rosanna had a conversation about this story, she let me know she had a book contract. Since then, I have eagerly awaited the novel. The characters immediately grabbed my heart and pulled me into their lives. I had a hard time putting the book down when I needed to. I loved the satisfying ending. I know these characters won't leave my mind for quite a while."
—Lena Nelson Dooley, multi-award-winning author of *Maggie's Journey, Mary's Blessing,* and *Catherine's Pursuit*

HAND ME DOWN HUSBAND

Rosanna Huffman

Abingdon fiction

a novel approach to faith

Nashville

Hand Me Down Husband

Copyright © 2015 by Rosanna Huffman

ISBN-13: 978-1-4267-7028-9

Published by Abingdon Press, P.O. Box 801, Nashville, TN 37202

www.abingdonpress.com

All rights reserved.

The persons and events portrayed in this work of fiction are the
creations of the author, and any resemblance to persons
living or dead is purely coincidental.

Macro Editor: Jamie Chavez

Published in association with Hartline Literary Agency

Original cover design by Jotham Yoder; final design by
Rick Schroeppel.

Library of Congress Cataloging-in-Publication Data has been
requested.

Printed in the United States of America

1 2 3 4 5 6 7 8 9 10 / 20 19 18 17 16 15

To my mother, who taught me by example that
sometimes reading is more important than sleeping.

Acknowledgments

A thank-you is the norm for a paragraph acknowledging all the people who made this book possible. You know who you are, and I thank you. I could make a list, but it wouldn't be complete and I've already used up my page count. So if you played a part in this book, your name is here in spirit, and I thank you from the bottom of my heart.

1

The *thud, thud, swoosh* outside the classroom window lulled Suzanne Bloomer into a trance as she graded English compositions. She recorded the last paper and scanned her desk. Math homework to check for the ninth and tenth graders, biology quizzes to grade, and a chemistry test to write. Poems from the juniors and seniors to read. She wouldn't be out of here before seven tonight.

Today's impromptu lessons hadn't gone half bad, but she couldn't risk that two days in a row. Tomorrow had to be planned. Her stomach growled, a reminder that breakfast had been nonexistent and lunch skimpy. Propping her head in her left hand, she closed her eyes and listened to the rhythm of Jacob Sanderson's basketball on the concrete.

A gruff throat clearing interrupted Suzanne's micro-nap. The other teachers and the high school students who stayed for tutoring had left, and Jacob's ride should have come and gone by now. Then a distant whoop from the playground told her the sixth grader was still out there. Of all things, here was his aunt—who shouldn't even have had to get out of her car—. Wait . . . *gruff?* Amazing what all could zip through her mind in the split second it took to lift her head.

The person at her desk was not Jacob's aunt. It was his grandfather, Mitchell.

Thank the Lord it wasn't Marissa. She didn't need that woman catching the teacher asleep. Even after all these years, she had a way of making Suzanne feel foolish and inferior. Thankfully, none of her kids were in high school yet.

Flames shot up her cheeks. Talking to the elder Mr. Sanderson didn't thrill her either. Besides being related to Marissa, he was recently widowed. There are probably nice, proper, comforting things to say to the bereaved, but she couldn't think of a single one.

"Uh, hi." She stood, tucking her hair behind her ears. "You're here for your grandson? I'll get him." Raising the screen in the window behind her desk, she called to the NBA wannabe, then turned back to her visitor. "He's coming. Sorry about that. I told him to watch for you."

"No problem." Mitchell Sanderson strolled around as if he had all the time in the world. One hand in a pocket and the other clutching a *Stine Has Yield* cap, he hardly resembled the busy, all-important businessman farmer whose youngest teenager she had taught years ago. Not that she ever saw him back then. His wife had come to parent/teacher conferences alone. Suzanne couldn't recall ever having a conversation with him in the two years she'd taught Marci.

He didn't offer any more comments, and she had no idea what else to say, so she checked to see that Jacob was on his way. In a sense he was. He must have sent the ball out into the grass and was now retrieving it in that slow, deliberate way Suzanne had once admired so much in his dad. The screen was still up, so she rapped on the siding to get his attention and returned to her mountain of grading.

"You're the high school teacher, right?" Mitchell materialized beside her desk.

She flinched and instinctively turned over the paper on which she'd marked a dozen red X's. "Yes. I'm sorry, I told Jacob to watch for his ride. He was supposed to be ready." She should smile. Everyone knew Sanderson money kept New Vision Christian School going.

"No problem. We had to stop running beans when the combine's auger chain broke. Marc and Martin have everything covered. I'm in no rush."

Jacob bounded in at that moment and grabbed his backpack. "Hey, Grandpa. I'm ready to go, come on." At the door he turned, crossed his arms, and tapped a foot. "Let's go. I'm hungry."

"Hold on, Jake." Mitchell laughed and held up a hand. "Did you tell your teacher thank you?"

"For what? I didn't want to stay, Mom made me. And she ain't my teacher." The outside door slammed and he was gone.

"I'll thank you for him." Mitchell twisted the seed corn cap in both hands. "Thank you. I'm sure you're not doing this because you're bored. I'll get out of here now so you can get your work done."

With the roar of the heavy pickup heading east on Chicken Bristle Road, Suzanne stretched her legs and did the evening school chores. When she was sure all the doors were locked, she settled back in her desk to finish her work.

No, she didn't tutor because she was bored, but she was glad to fit it into her schedule and help these kids. Haley and Jacob truly needed the help—Spanish and math, respectively. Not Tina. Suzanne had convinced her to stay after school on Mondays and Thursdays to practice vocabulary with Haley.

Tina was as much a genius in all things academic as she was a dunce in all things social. Suzanne hoped that as Tina helped Haley master Spanish, she would gain at least a modicum of self-confidence. Not that either girl had been clued in on their teacher's motives.

At six o'clock Suzanne washed down a granola bar with Pepsi. She brushed away the crumbs and stepped on the empty can readying it for the recycling bin on her way out—hopefully in the next hour.

"Hey, let me in!" Knocking accompanied the hollered words. Karen Young popped in when Suzanne opened the door. She was headed to her night shift at Miami Valley Hospital. Karen had roomed with Suzanne for almost a year. The eighth or ninth young woman to fill the position of boarder, and undoubtedly the most annoying. If Suzanne hadn't needed help with the rent so badly, she would have sent Karen along months ago. But with monthly payments that took half her teacher salary, Suzanne couldn't afford to live alone.

Karen's stopping in like this was not unusual. She always needed something, and because she paid part of the rent, she believed Suzanne owed her whatever she asked.

"Hi there. What do you need?"

"What? Oh, nothing. I'm supposed to tell you that Trevor's dad has to talk to you. He left a message on your answering machine this morning, and then Trevor told me to have you call since you hadn't called back yet. Plus, we're out of milk. You used the last yesterday and forgot to get more. I had to drink water." She tossed the reproach over her shoulder and slipped back out into the lengthening shadows.

Trevor's dad. Bob Hopkins, Suzanne's landlord and Karen's soon-to-be father-in-law. What was the problem now?

Suzanne had been renting his little house for a dozen years. It wasn't much, but it was the best she could find in her price range. And then only if she took in a paying boarder. When she first moved away from her parent's house, she had tried to live in the rental alone and loved it. She didn't mind eating beans and rice and the garden produce she could grow in her small garden. Then Bob raised the rent and Suzanne hardly had enough money left each month to buy gas. She bicycled to school until the days got too short and the weather too wet.

If she had gotten the expected raise, it might have worked. However, several families dropped out of the already-small private church school, and Suzanne accepted a cut in pay instead. But the Lord provides. About the time she started packing to move back to her parents' house, Sheila Brubaker asked if Suzanne had a room to sublet while she finished up her nurse's training. First Sheila, then Anne, and Lori, and Colleen, and Abigail who-wouldn't-answer-to-Abby, and Jessica. Seven times she'd lived through wedding plans as these girls moved in from other states, supposedly to go to college or work out their chosen careers, but more obviously to snag a husband.

Suzanne should have seen it before she agreed to let Karen take the room. But she noticed it too late—from day one Karen was after the landlord's son.

Eight more months. Suzanne could live with that. Then Trevor and Karen would be married and living their own luxurious life. Maybe with her recently added responsibilities and the school not having to pay a principal's salary anymore, Suzanne would get a raise. Then she could swing the rent alone and reap the added benefit of privacy.

Daylight was a faint memory when she opened the creaking screen door at home with tomorrow's lessons planned, a budget that could accommodate her anticipated single living strategy, a throbbing headache, an empty stomach.

And a red six blinking on the answering machine.

"Suzanne, this is Bob Hopkins. Give me a call as soon as you can."

So Karen was right. He did want to talk to her.

"Aunt Eva calling, darling. Checking to see you got the chair. I'll try back later."

The fancy new desk chair her aunt had had delivered to the school. With no possible way of knowing how welcome it was.

"Hey, it's Bob. I'd really like to talk to you. Call me."

Give me a minute, sir.

"Bob here, call me when you get in."

Okay, okay!

"Miss Suzanne? This is Jackson. What's our assignment for tomorrow? Can you call me tonight?"

Comforting to know that Jackson hadn't undergone a personality change.

"Suzanne? Suzanne! I need to talk to you. Maybe your phone's not working. I'll come over when I get the next load of beans hauled." Bob's voice ended on the final message as his trademark knock sounded at the door.

Mitchell Sanderson drove through the countryside marveling at the beauty of the golden fields. "Look at that cornfield, Jake. How many bushels you think we'll get from that one?"

"I bet at least two hundred an acre. What's your guess, Grandpa?"

"You might be right. That field is one of our best, and this year it'll probably break some records. Going to keep us busy, that's for sure." That field and the rest of the multiple hundreds of acres of corn and soybeans either rented or owned by Sanderson Farms. God had certainly blessed them with a bountiful harvest here in southwest Ohio. For the second year in a row.

His sons had been right in encouraging him to buy the new S-690 John Deere combine last summer. His dad would have swooned at the outrageous price of the giant machine with its sixteen-row corn header and forty-foot bean header. But another year even half as plenteous as the last, and it would be paid off.

Two turns and as many soybean fields later, Mitch stopped his tan Silverado beside Marc's garage and watched Jacob disappear into the house. Four-thirty. Enough time to drive out to the combine and see if Martin needed help. Then he better hightail it to Marissa's house for supper.

He couldn't be late. That would make three times in two months, and Marissa might have a stroke. Supper with Marissa and Layne tonight. Tomorrow at Marc and Kelly's, then on to Marci and Abe's house, and finally to Martin and Janelle's before starting the routine again.

In the year after Marilyn died, he had appreciated and enjoyed how they took care of him. Especially he'd liked being with his grandchildren, who remembered their grandma and asked questions. They hadn't stayed around to hear all the stories he yearned to tell about her, but their existence and presence had kept him going.

Now they were growing past that. Nobody wanted to hear about his childhood sweetheart anymore. His sons' wives and his younger daughter obviously fixed supper out of a sense of obligation. Marissa insisted they cook, but he longed to escape her increasingly suffocating control.

At fifty-four Mitch was far from being an old man. An episode of chest pains a month after Marilyn's death had scared them all, but his physical heart was fine. The combination of stress and indigestion had sent him to the emergency room. His four grown children panicked and to hear them talk were still ready to banish him to a nursing home. Maybe when they heard the doctor's report from this morning, they'd back off. The report that didn't vary from the past three physicals.

"Hi, Daddy." Marissa greeted him with a wooden spoon wave from the stove. "Hope you don't mind spaghetti again tonight. I talked to Janelle after I thawed the beef. She said she fixed it last night."

"You know I'm not picky." He hung his cap on the closet doorknob and started to set the table. "Where're the kiddos? It's about dark. They're not still outside, are they?"

"You bet your bananas they are. After last week's rain, I'm making them play outside every daylight hour that's dry. This house is way too small for all that energy."

"How many places tonight? I assume Layne will be here?" Mitch stood at the cabinet, ready to count out plates and glasses.

Marissa heaved a drastic sigh, planted her left hand on her left hip, and continued stirring. She looked so much like her mother, he almost grabbed his chest at the sight. He set down a stack of glasses and caught his breath and the last of her words.

". . . to set up a tree stand to be ready for bow season. But he promised to be here by seven for dinner."

The four children, Layne and Marisa, himself. He arranged the plates and glasses, added the napkins and flatware, and pulled the extra chair from the closet.

After supper Mitch stacked the dishes beside the sink and turned on the hot water. Before he got the sink filled, his shirt pocket vibrated. Text from Marc. *Bring gas for grain truck. asap.*

Stifling a sigh of relief he handed the dishwashing off to Marissa and gathered his leftovers in a plastic grocery sack. The tension from their supper conversation hung thick in the air.

"Dad." Her hand went back on the hip. "This is your night with us. Marc knows that. You have to stop letting him jerk you around."

Mitch hooked the sack over his arm and hugged his firstborn daughter. "Chill out, honey. I'd soon be leaving anyway. If you don't want to wash dishes, get Layne to do them. Or Merry, she's old enough to help, isn't she?"

"Just try not to be late Monday, remember we need to eat at five-thirty so I can take Landon to guitar lessons." Marissa sighed and ducked from under his arm.

"That reminds me, I probably won't be here Monday night."

Her cheeks tightened and her eyes narrowed. "Why?"

Must he explain his every move to his kids? Good grief, she grew up on the farm. What else would he be doing besides harvesting this time of year? The boys would likely chase him away once again, but he *might* be running the combine. Marissa couldn't go on thinking she ran the show.

He let her stew as she followed him out to the truck. He replaced his cap and slid behind the wheel.

"Why, Dad? What are you doing Monday night?"

"Check your calendar, it's October. Remember that season called harvest? Well, I'm still a farmer with crops out there to bring in. I hope to be on the combine or in a grain truck Monday night."

The wrinkles in her forehead smoothed for a moment. "Oh."

"If you're really desperate, I'll come over after dark and wash up the dishes."

"Dad! It's not that. I just worry about you. What will you have for lunch on Tuesday?"

"Probably this." Mitch lifted the bag from the seat beside him.

"No way. That's five days from now, it'll be spoiled. I'll bring something Tuesday morning and you can microwave it."

"Don't. I'll put this in the freezer and thaw it if I need it. Or I can get something in town. Better run. Thanks for supper, honey."

She turned to go, but not before getting in a parting shot. "You think about what we want to do for you."

He left the graveled drive and pulled onto Chicken Bristle Road. As he passed the school, he noticed lights still on. For years he'd passed it multiple times each day and never noticed a thing. Now twice in the same day his mind was drawn inside. How late did those teachers work anyway? Teachers? There were more than one, weren't there? He'd only seen one when he picked up Jacob. And there was only one car there now—the same one he'd seen earlier.

Who was that woman, anyway? Oh sure, he knew who she was. What's-her-name Bloomer, Jim and Connie's girl. She'd been there forever it seemed. Hadn't she been Marci's teacher?

In the dusty darkness Mitch fueled the grain truck from the tank on his pickup bed. With the roar of the combine on the far side of the field, conversation with Marc was impossible. Martin had repaired the chain, and the harvesting operation was up and running. Without Mitch.

At quarter to ten Mitchell Sanderson stacked a Glad disposable plastic bowl of spaghetti and meat sauce on top of a gold Tupperware microwave container of spaghetti and meat sauce. Spaghetti and meat sauce for Wednesday night supper, Thursday breakfast, lunch, and supper, and now enough for breakfast and lunch the next three days.

It was high time to visit the library and find some learn-to-cook books. If he could show her he could cook for himself, maybe Marissa would back off a bit.

2

Bang, *bang, bang.* Suzanne plodded to the door. For no one else would she unlock after sunset, but she had to keep on the good side of Bob Hopkins. He had a reputation of evicting tenants from his dozen or so rental houses at the slightest provocation.

"Evening, Bob. Come in?" She held the door and shooed away the beetles that swarmed around the bare light bulb.

"Nope. Just gotta talk to you a minute." Bob dragged a crumpled red handkerchief from his back pocket and scrubbed his nose. He flipped his straw hat onto the railing.

She stepped onto the porch and down the steps to the grass. There wasn't room for both of them at the top, and Bob always got along better if he was looking down on her. Thankfully he didn't beat around the bush. "You gotta be out of here by the first of the year. Trevor wants me to remodel before they move in after the wedding. I'll check New Year's Eve and return your deposit if I need to."

Mission accomplished, Bob Hopkins replaced his hat, stuffed the hankie in his pocket, and sauntered into the darkness. At his truck, he paused. "You been a pretty good renter. Thanks." Then he peeled out the lane, satisfied, she figured, that he'd done the right thing by coming to tell her instead of leaving a message on the phone.

An eviction *without* the slightest provocation.

She sank onto the crumbling concrete steps. How could Bob's timing have been any worse?

The ringing phone and her grumbling stomach called her back into the house. After giving Jackson the algebra assignment, she heated a can of chicken and stars and called to thank Aunt Eva for the luxuriously comfortable chair.

"Now, I know you don't sit down very much through the day, but when you get off your feet at the end of the day, you ought to be comfortable."

"And now I am, thanks to your thoughtfulness."

"Thank *you* for returning my call, but I'm not going to let you run up your phone bill, darling. Plus, I know it's a school night and you need your sleep."

Suzanne returned to studying trigonometry, but she couldn't focus. The end of December was less than three months away. She didn't have as much to her name as most thirty-seven-year-old women in America, so packing her things wouldn't be an enormous job. But moving to who-knows-where looked daunting. Especially at bedtime. She had to turn her mind off the subject if she wanted to get any sleep tonight.

If she knew her best friend Joy was still up, Suzanne would call her. Joy was the only one she could talk to, but not with a late-night non-emergency call. She dressed for bed and watched the clock turn eleven, then twelve. At quarter past midnight, she gave up and curled up in a corner of the couch with her journal and Bible. Before she finished the first paragraph of pouring out her frustrations on paper, the phone rang. Its rude bell sent her pen skittering across the page.

"Suzanne? What are you doing up?" Joy's voice skipped across a patchy cell phone connection.

"Me? What are you doing? Where are you?"

"Don't panic. We're on our way home from the hospital. I saw your light come on but didn't see Karen's car. Why are you up so late?"

"Oh, no. You first. You mention the *H* word and you finish it. What happened?" According to her tone of voice it couldn't be too bad, but a trip to the emergency room easily trumped an unexpected eviction.

"You know my kids, if somebody don't get stitches or a cast at least once a month, they think they're shunking their duty. Amber broke a glass in the dishwater, so we took her in. Jason thought since it was on her right hand we better get it stitched. The ER done a quick job."

Don't? Shunking? Suzanne convinced her teacher brain to overlook the grammar and mispronunciation. "You should've called me. What'd you do with the rest of the tribe?"

"I tried, but you were at school. Mrs. Adams across the road sent her oldest girl over. We done that before. Hey, we're pulling in the garage now. Hold up a minute."

Doors slammed in the distance and then Suzanne heard running water. "Okay, I'm back. Got her off to bed, and Jason's going to crash. I need a bubble bath before I can even think about sleeping. Your turn."

Joy did a lot in the background while Suzanne recounted Bob's visit, but she didn't miss a word. "Man, that makes me mad," Joy said when she finished. "That kid's been working and making money for six years. Good money too, for not having a college education. I don't know why he's gotta have his daddy's rental."

"My word, girl, what in the world are you going to do? It's not like you have time to go house hunting or anything with all the extra time you're packing in at school. I could just take Bob and Trevor and that quitter Erik and braid their necks together."

Suzanne laughed at the thought. If anyone could do just that, it would be Joy. Tall and big-boned with plenty of padding, her midnight caller was everything Suzanne was not. But Joy's dark, stick-straight hair and Suzanne's curly dishwater blond didn't contrast as much as their marital and mommy statuses. Joy was a wife of seventeen years and a mother of six kids.

Another major difference was their temperaments. While they might both experience the same emotions, Suzanne tended to hold hers inside. Let them fester and grow. Not Joy. If she thought it or felt it, she said it. Jason often said he'd like to mix the two women's personalities together and divide the result in half. Suzanne needed to learn to share her feelings, and Joy needed to learn not to say everything that crossed her mind.

Her friend's aggression, while not a surprise, caught Suzanne off guard and struck her funny bone, as Joy would say. Their guffaws blended across the airwaves.

"Shh, Joy. You'll wake the kids and it'll be my fault." Suzanne staggered to the kitchen for a drink. She thought she had her laughter under control until Jason's voice rumbled in the distance.

"Knock it off, shug, I'm trying to get some sleep here." Like he never thought anything he didn't say.

His tone set her off again. Then her laughter turned to tears. She grabbed a wad of tissue from the bathroom.

"What's going on, Zanne? Are you crying? What else?" A couple of glugs from Joy's bathtub reminded Suzanne of the years she'd sacrificed bubble baths—baths at all—for a house near the school. The concern straight from her friend's heart to Suzanne's ear reminded her what a valuable friend Joy was.

"Joy, what will I do? I need to find a place to live. And today I ripped my school outfit. I don't have time to sew before next Thursday."

"You're stressing over that? Wear something twice. Wear a Sunday dress. Those kids'll never notice. If it's that big a deal, I'll get you some of Amber's clothes."

"Forget I mentioned it. Sorry. It's just been one of those days. I'm starting to feel sleepy, so I better see if I can catch an hour or so before the alarm. Thanks for letting me dump on you."

"Watch it girl, or you'll be dumping all over everyone all the time. You've almost reached your yearly quota of twice."

"Enough, goofy. Save the sarcasm for your family. Good night, and thanks." Suzanne hung up and returned to bed and yet another attempt at sleep. At least this time her brain was stuck on the wardrobe problem.

Funny how a rogue compass claw ripping the skirt of her Thursday dress could derail her thoughts from the eviction problem. Because her scrawny frame and discriminating tastes didn't fit well with the sizes or styles of ready-made clothing, she couldn't—or wouldn't—shop just anywhere for clothes, and her closet held exactly enough outfits for each day of the week. No more, no less. Except now it *was* less. And no way would she take Joy's offer of a teenager's castoffs.

She didn't mind using the back side of a piece of paper discarded by someone else. She didn't mind reading a used book or driving a pre-owned car. She didn't even mind the old couch she'd saved from the dump. But she hadn't worn secondhand clothes for two decades, and she didn't plan to start now.

She had her reasons for accepting neither hand-me-downs— nor hand-me-ups—when it came to clothing. Or to husbands, she had told Joy. Although thinking about marriage, secondhand or otherwise, was certainly a waste of good time.

Most women married but a few didn't, and God obviously wanted Suzanne to be single. Not that God had told her so Himself, but plenty of church people kept her posted. We need some people like you to teach and babysit our kids. It's a gift God reserves for special people.

If that were true, she wished she weren't so special, and she really didn't appreciate the gift. But so far she'd refrained from exploring those feelings with herself, let along sharing them with the all-knowing church folk.

She plumped her pillow and searched for a cool place to lay her cheek.

"Make it decaf this morning, Phyllis, if you don't mind." Mitch nudged his cup to the edge of the Formica table and smiled at the server. "Please. Guess I'm getting old enough that caffeine keeps me up of a night. Thanks. The guys are almost here, you can put in our regular orders when you get to it."

Mitch Sanderson and his two sons had started meeting in Farmersburg at Betsy's Diner for Friday morning breakfast right after Martin got his driver's license. More than a decade of coming here, it was one of the few constants that hadn't been ripped away that awful January almost two years ago.

Phyllis limped off as Marc strode through the door and slid into a chair across from Mitch. "Morning, Dad. You order yet?" He crooked an index finger toward the server and raised his voice. "Hey, Phil, regular here."

Minutes later Martin joined them. "Hey, Dad. What'd the doc say yesterday?"

They leaned elbows on the table and inched their noses toward Mitch.

"He says I'm in better shape than most thirty-year-old men he sees. Nothing wrong at all with the old ticker."

"Good deal. You check the bean prices this morning?" Martin tapped his iPhone screen and handed it to his brother. "Show Dad. See? Didn't we say you shouldn't have contracted all those beans last winter with Farmersburg Grain and Long Enterprises?"

Mitch shrugged. You win some, you lose some. His years of agonizing over the loss of a few cents a bushel were past. He didn't mention that corn futures were looking like he'd made the right call there. Course you couldn't be sure from one week to the next.

"So . . . we move back to Eagle Road after we finish up at Lenk's on Hemple, right?" Mitch formed the statement as a question.

Both sons agreed without seeming to hear the words. Phyllis brought their orders, refilled the coffees, and commented on the weather. After she left, Mitch nodded at Marc, who proceeded to voice their thanks to the Lord before picking up his bagel sandwich.

"Uh, Dad?"

He widened his eyes in answer to his younger son. The look between the two boys was clearly conspiratorial and the tone vaguely familiar.

"You think any more about what we said last Friday?" Martin speared a bite of pancake and spoke around it.

Yes, and there was nothing more to say. They had started running beans Monday. He wasn't going to leave his grain farm in the middle of harvest. Neither would he argue week after week. Driving a combine or a tractor or a truck was no more a health risk to him than it was to them. He said all that last week and now he had the doctor's words to back him up. "Drop it, son. Please?"

Marc flagged down Phyllis for a coffee refill. "Just hear us out, Dad. I know we hit you pretty hard last time with all that about your heart and all, but it's more than that."

Hear them out. Okay, he could do that.

They didn't want him to think they were pushing him out because they thought he was an old man. But he deserved to slow down after all the years he'd worked so hard for his family. Besides, when he was their age he managed the entire business. Shouldn't they have a chance at it now? They both had two sons who needed to learn a work ethic like he had taught them.

Of course they would still need him. But wouldn't he appreciate more time to devote to his agricultural financial consulting clients? Maybe he could even go back to teaching those agribusiness classes—full-time instead of just the winter quarter.

Right now they just wanted to get everybody talking about the possibility. Didn't expect him to drop out of the game in the middle of harvest. Just start the ball rolling. Go through this season with them making the decisions instead of him being in the driver's seat. Let them take the reins while he was still there to see how it went. See if they could get along as business partners instead of the boys doing what Dad decides.

"That pretty much covers it," Marc concluded, tipping his seventh cup of coffee.

"What'cha think?" Martin pushed his chair back and rubbed a palm against his stubbly chin.

Mitch closed his eyes and shook his head. Was that how they perceived it? Did he treat them like little boys instead of business partners? He hadn't meant to. He tried to make them as much a part of the business as he was and felt the effort he put into it had paid off. Goes to show how much he knew.

He was tired of the whole mess. Why did everything have to change? Just because Marilyn died, why did the rest of his life have to be rearranged? He didn't want to spend his days in the office while someone else farmed his fields. The ebb and flow of the seasons—spring planting, summer spraying, autumn harvest, winter planning—it's what he knew best. A rhythm that for fifty years had been as much a part of himself as breathing. A rhythm that had held him together for the past twenty-one months.

"Give me some time to think about it, okay?" A decade maybe. Mitch fiddled with the last corner of toast, drizzling it with honey.

His sons nodded.

"This your night to eat supper with us, Pops?" Martin asked.

Mitch wadded his napkin and drained the last of his coffee before responding. "According to the schedule . . ." He concentrated on not emphasizing *schedule*. "I go to your brother's tonight. But you know how meals are this time of year, Marc. Tell Kelly not to worry about me. The fridge is full of stuff I need to get eaten up. And—"

"I know," Martin broke in, "don't tell Marissa."

Mitch looked at his watch. "At the risk of sounding like I'm the boss and you're the underlings, shouldn't we get moving? I want to grease the combine before the elevator opens, and I know you like to stop in at home before the kids leave for school."

They scattered, each man to his pickup. As Mitch headed north on Farmersburg-Johnsdale Road, he replayed last night's conversation with Marissa.

"I'll be over with the kids tomorrow to clean, Dad. I'll do your bedroom and bathroom too, so leave the door unlocked."

"When I want you to clean in there, I'll leave it open." Same reply he'd been giving for a year and a half.

A year and a half, and Marissa was still coming to clean and do laundry? In the last six months, he had tried occasionally and half-heartedly to stop her. He could run his own washer and dryer and vacuum cleaner and dust mop. Couldn't he? And this coddling was getting on his nerves.

He didn't know how to convince Marissa that he was ready to move on with his life. He would never stop grieving Marilyn's death. Part of him had died too. But not *all* of him, and what was left needed to go on. Everything he had tried so far set Marissa off on a repetitive and completely unrelated tirade, "Nobody wants to remember Mom, but I won't let you guys forget her."

The kids had eaten and left, and Layne retired to his recliner with a hunting magazine. Mitch leaned across the table and laid his hand on Marissa's wrist. "Rissa, we need to talk."

"You're right. Me and Layne've been talking about how much time I spend cleaning and doing laundry at both our places. We have a fantastic solution. Think about this, Daddy."

So it was *Daddy* now—he recognized the tone. "You bounce around in that big old house and I'm cleaning two houses every week." She stopped talking and studied Layne's iced tea glass carefully before picking it up and dumping the shrunken ice cubes into her own glass.

"You know I don't mind. But you and Mom talked about building something smaller, even had plans drawn up, didn't you?"

His daughter, the bloodhound. She had seen the blueprints after sweet-talking her mother into sharing the not-yet-public documents. What did she want now? Him to build that house?

"Well, that tells me you thought about selling the farmhouse. Do you know how hard it is to sell real estate these days? I don't want you to have to go through that." She launched off into a long and detailed story she heard in town the other day about an elderly couple trying to sell.

"There's a point to this?" He sneaked a glance at his watch.

The glare she gave him could have been inherited only from her mother. "I'm getting there. You just have to know where I'm coming from."

"If you don't mind, I'll go ahead and take care of these." He nodded at the supper dishes spread all over the table.

"What I'm saying . . . actually, do you think . . . well . . . okay, Daddy, it's like this."

Her half-finished attempts suddenly clicked in his brain. He raised a handful of spoons and forks. "Let me guess. You want me to move in with you? Forget it, Riss, I'm too old to sleep on a couch every night."

"No, we'll move in with you."

"Yeah, right."

"Seriously, Daddy. You won't have to sell the house, and we've been looking for something bigger anyway. You can keep the same bedroom. We'll add another bathroom upstairs. It's the perfect solution—you won't get lonely and I'll only have one house to clean."

With free rent and a full-time babysitter and dishwasher? He cleared his throat to flush the irritation from his voice. "Sounds like you have it all figured out. Now all you have to do is convince me and your brothers and sister. You know—" He had wheeled around and grabbed the last bowl from the table. "I think you're going to have a pretty hard time getting that past all four of us."

Mitch whizzed back to today, signaled his left turn onto Zehring Road and waved as the other two Sanderson Chevrolets roared past in the rural Ohio daybreak.

3

After three hours of sleep Suzanne disarmed the alarm clock an hour before it was set to ring. Every time she turned over her troubles to the Lord, they somehow boomeranged back. She blamed herself, not her Savior.

Finding another place to live currently led her troubles list, but school pressures came close behind. Since New Vision Christian School's principal Erik Angle left, she had been teaching all the high school classes. After a dozen plus years of teaching, she had the routines pretty much memorized. In all, the high school class had only twenty-eight students. She had made a science of combining classes, but still there were fifteen classes scheduled each day. Always before, the principal had taught several classes, as there was no way for her to fit them all in adequately.

Now it was up to her to make a way. To teach all of them with a semblance of adequacy since the beginning of last week when Erik left for a better-paying job.

The school board had shown up at school two weeks ago on a Friday evening. All five of them. All looking like they'd rather be anywhere else. All checking their watches and smart phones frequently. Erik had already left for the day, and Suzanne had been the only teacher called into their meeting.

Her heart pounded like an efficient typist. She scanned her mental files for an altercation with a student in the four weeks since school started and found nothing remotely suspicious.

The board chairman, Gerald Cook, began the meeting with a short prayer and got right to the point. "You probably know what this is all about?"

She willed her heart to slow its pace. "No."

"Mr. Angle didn't tell you about his plans?"

"No." He'd acted odd all week. More so than usual. Not that she took time to accurately rate the oddities of her superiors.

"So you didn't know today was his last day here?"

What?

"No." She folded the green Post-it note into sixteen three-eighths inch squares. Her responses were starting to feel quite negative.

Gerald laughed and for a second she hoped he was going to say it was all a joke. Then he got serious. "Okay, here's what's happening. Mr. Angle called me yesterday morning and said that he is quitting. As of today. Something about a job opportunity somewhere else. Sounds like a done deal. So now we need to talk about where we go from here."

An hour later they all left, and Suzanne wanted to leave too. For good. Like Erik Angle had. Only she couldn't. What would happen to her kids if she left? Instead she pulled out her plan book and Erik's plan book and designed a way to do the work of two people for the rest of the school year.

That they would find someone to replace him was unthinkable. Erik had taken the principal position after Mr. Garber retired the year before last. Following in Mr. G's steps had to be difficult, but Erik's heart was never in it. From the beginning he made it clear that he took the job only because he couldn't find anything else more glamorous.

Nine school days had passed since that surprising meeting, and Suzanne was surviving. With a nearly nonexistent social life, she didn't mind giving up an extra couple of hours in the evenings.

She'd made sure everything was ready before she left last night so she didn't have to leave for school at five a.m., but she was awake with nothing else to do. She stopped by the freezer to grab a granola bar from the box she'd hidden there last week. But *someone* must have discovered her stash—the empty box sat on a bag of peas. She grabbed her lunch bag and steamed all the way to the car.

On the way to school she passed the diner in Farmersburg. Her stomach growled at the smell of bacon wafting into the street. She hit the turn signal and the brakes. Plenty of time to eat this morning.

Breakfast. One of the issues that had driven her to find a place of her own. Her mother practically forbade her to leave the house in the morning without eating. Preferably something hot and lots of it. Suzanne's stomach rarely woke as soon as she did, and eating early in the morning had proved disastrous more than once. Mother took it as an insult. To no avail, Suzanne had tried to explain that if at twenty-five years old, she chose to go to work on an empty stomach, Mother's parenting reputation was not at stake.

Her digestive system still had an attitude and she seldom ate breakfast. Especially if she had to fix it. But she loved breakfast food. Problem was, by the time her system would accept it, the restaurants had quit fixing it.

Pulling into a parking spot—the only car in a sea of pickup trucks, Suzanne looked through the windows. Betsy's Diner had fewer than a dozen tables, and inside the nearest window sat the Sanderson men.

The smell of bacon and pancakes coming through her open window made her retch. She backed out and sped on to school. She would starve before going in alone to order takeout or eating by herself at a table if Marc Sanderson might see her.

The hours between eight-thirty and three o'clock flew by relatively interruption free. Mrs. Bower, who taught grades seven and eight, came to Suzanne's room only three times. Miss Lana, the first grade teacher, kindly saved her requests and brought them during the high school lunch break. Oh well, Suzanne's stomach had grown weary of growling hours earlier. That meant more to eat after the last carpool left. Miss Kortney of the second and third grade classes didn't show up at all. Instead she dispatched students—two at a time during every class—to borrow books from Suzanne's shelves. None of which they could find without help.

It seemed Mrs. Miller in the fourth, fifth, and sixth grade class must have taken a field trip when Suzanne hadn't seen her by lunchtime. But then she showed up with two misprints in a teacher guide as the bell rang for Phys Ed.

The stack of books and papers to grade towered over her after-school snack of lukewarm ham and cheese with stale crackers. She eyed the workload and estimated she could be done before eight if she hurried.

She popped two ibuprofen and hummed, "We'll work till Jesus comes."

———❦———

Mitch and Martin drove the grain trucks while Marc ran the combine. On Mitch's first trip to the elevator he got stuck talking to Gerald Cook. He made himself small in the seat when he saw the guy pull in a couple of trucks back. Other experienced drivers did the same, each hoping, Mitch guessed, that Gerald would catch some greenhorn without the wisdom to go invisible. Despite Mitch's best efforts, he made a beeline for the Sanderson truck.

Mitch sighed and rolled down his window. "Morning, Mr. Cook."

"How you doing today, Sanderson? Can you believe this weather—and they say we ain't gonna get any rain for another week. It sure is great to be getting all this harvesting done in good time, but I'm starting to worry about how low the water table's getting."

The truck ahead of Mitch moved and he eased his foot off the brake, silently inviting Gerald to find someone else on whom to bestow his wisdom.

Gerald whipped out his Nextel. "Gerry, you move our truck up if you need to."

"Got him out here learning how to do it." Gerald nodded back the line. "The teachers squawk some at how much time he's missing, but I say a boy's gotta learn while he's young. He don't take too well to book learning anyway. Like his old man. Good thing I'm smart in other ways to make up for it. I thank the good Lord for giving me common sense. I guess that's what got me on the board over there at New Vision." He looked back at his truck and sent another command to his son.

"Speaking of school stuff, I was wanting to talk to you, Mitch. I'm chairman of the board over there?" He spoke in questions, but didn't wait for an answer to continue.

"We kinda got us in a pickle over the principal we thought we had. Probably the best person we've ever had in there, and now he's gone and quit on us. Look, it's your turn on the scale. Good talking to you. I'll catch you later. I still need to talk at you some more."

On subsequent trips to the elevator, Mitch managed to steer clear of Gerald. But just as the sun set, the loose-lipped farmer pulled in the Sanderson lane. He ambled over to Mitch's work table in the shop, hands in pockets. "You guys stop running after I saw you this morning?"

Mitch paused his welding and shook his head. What had he done to deserve this kind of punishment?

"Anyway, I gotcha now. You think any more about what I said earlier?"

"About the low water table?" What else had the man talked about? "You don't need to worry too much about that. You know how it is around here, start worrying about drought this time of year and we get a big rain that won't let up. Then we start panicking that we'll never get the rest of the crops in."

"Not that. You been thinking about our little school problem? Like I said, our principal quit. Up and took off without no notice. See, most of us on the board, we don't think it's that big a deal. I mean, we got Miss Suzanne, she's been there pretty much forever and a day. She'll do whatever we tell her."

Suzanne. That was the Bloomer girl's name.

As Gerald talked, he wandered around the work bench. He grabbed a wrench from its carefully marked spot on the pegboard, inspected it, and laid it on the table.

"So, anyways. We're getting along fine without a principal, I'd say. And goodness sakes, we're saving a pile of money. You know how much we had to agree to pay Erik to get him to take the job? Way too much if you ask me."

Mitch hadn't been involved in starting a school in the church basement thirty-how-ever-many years ago, but he had known the men who were. They surely never imagined a goon like this as head of the school board. He finished his task and turned back to his uninvited visitor. "I'm sure there's a point to all this, but I'm not getting it. I have to leave now. If you need something, Gerald, just ask."

"Like I said, if it was up to me, we don't need nothing. But them other teachers are complaining, and some of the parents are squawking about how much Suzanne has to do. Some of their spoiled brats not getting enough attention, probably."

This man was getting on Mitch's last nerve. He picked up the repaired part and headed toward the door. "Got to get this out to the field. If you have something to say, you'd better come along." He flipped off the light and lowered the overhead door.

Gerald followed Mitch to the pickup and made himself at home in the passenger's seat. "Nice truck for a Chevy. You got any trouble with the brakes sticking? Us Cooks, we're Ford men. Never could figure out why someone would waste good money on a Chevy."

"Don't tell me you've chased me around all day to criticize my choice of motor companies." Mitch ended his sentence with a chuckle so Gerald might think it was a joke.

"Shucks, no. What I'm trying to tell you is we need to find somebody for that principal job over at school. And I'm asking you to do it."

"Asking me to find the school a principal? Wouldn't that be the school board's job?" It was almost fun pushing Gerald's buttons. "Hey, pal, with all your wisdom, if you can't find anybody, I wouldn't stand a chance of getting you a replacement."

"No, no, no. You got it all wrong. I'm asking you to take the job."

"Me? What in the world makes you think I would do something like that. I mean even if I were qualified, which we both know I'm not."

"I hear your sons are taking over more of the farming, so what else do you plan to do with yourself? That line about you not being—what'd you call it, qualified? Baloney. I remember that you never put in any time on the school board like most of the dads, including mine, did. My dad said they were smart never to elect you, cause you didn't have time for anything but your farming, that college stuff, and your con-salting business."

Mitch's mouth dropped open. Figuratively if not literally. Way to lay a guilt trip on a man. That was undeserved. He had put many dollars into the school even in the years between Marci's graduation and when the first grandchild started first grade.

The two-mile drive between the shop and the field where Marc waited with the combine stretched into twenty, with no way of getting rid of Gerald short of shoving him out the door.

"Your dad didn't know the whole story, Gerald. But that's not the point. I'm still very much a part of this farming operation. We're smack dab in the middle of harvest. Qualified or not, I cannot abandon my fields. Go look somewhere else." Mitch steered across the bumpy field and stopped beside the combine.

A head emerged from the hood of the giant machine. "Don't say no without thinking it through, Dad." Marc reached for the part. "Thanks. I'm going to put this back together and we ought to call it a day."

Mitch plodded back to the truck, Gerald dogging his steps. *Change the subject.* "So, tell me, Gerald, how many acres do you have out this year?"

Bingo. Gerald's chest puffed out and he counted for a while on his fingers, muttering under his breath. "Four hundred some in beans, about four fifty in corn. And I bet this is gonna be the best year yet for yields. We're getting more per acre on the corn than anyone around. It must be that new fertilizer I tried and that new seed. No offence, I know you're a Stine man."

When Gerald's door closed, Mitch had the engine started. Before Gerald finished explaining why this new seed corn was so incredibly better than anything the world had ever seen, and how he knew the return would justify the higher price he'd paid, Mitch parked at the shop and jumped out.

"See you around, Gerald. I have evening plans and I'm already late. Good luck hunting." He sprinted to the shop without listening for Gerald's reply.

What a coincidence that just yesterday Mitch had set foot inside New Vision Christian School for the first time in a decade. No wonder the teacher seemed busy. She may have been there for close to forever, but he bet she was thankful bumbling old Gerald hadn't been on the board all those years. Speaking of forever, what about Clarence Garber? Hadn't he occupied the principal's office most of that time? Mitch didn't remember much about his kids' school days, but Mr. G was unforgettable. Garber must have retired. Maybe Gerald and his underlings should consider dragging him back to finish off the year. He couldn't be much older than seventy-five, and pretty spry at that. Mitch didn't intend to retire until long past the end of his own eighth decade.

That Cook guy didn't have the sense God gave a gnat. Mitch would never consider walking off the field in the middle of harvest.

4

Suzanne awoke before daybreak on Saturday. Of course the only morning she could sleep in, she was wide awake at six a.m. She luxuriated in the pleasure of lying in bed for another hour, recalling a recent conversation with Aunt Eva. She had to be careful how much she told her favorite aunt. Okay, her only aunt, who'd been after Suzanne for years to take a stand for her financial well-being. "Make those people pay you more, or go find a job that you can live on."

But Suzanne didn't want another job, and not just because it would require returning to college for a teaching credential to tack onto her bachelor's degrees. She loved her students—how could she ever abandon them? So maybe the pay wasn't the greatest. Maybe the parents and other teachers did take advantage of her. Maybe she did complain sometimes. Just maybe this wouldn't have been her first choice of a life, but second choice had its rewards. The most important one being the peace of knowing she was right where God wanted her for now.

When she returned from her shopping expedition, Karen followed her in the drive. The bride-to-be might see through it, but Suzanne didn't want to be viewed as resident slave and milk shopper. So she left her car running, ran into the house, grabbed the first thing she saw—her plan book—and dashed back past a surprised and sleepy-looking Karen. "I left the door unlocked," Suzanne called. "I'll be gone most of the day."

She backed out the lane and drove to Joy's house where, after ten minutes of rearranging, she made room in the refrigerator for a gallon of two percent.

"Here, have some with Ovaltine," Joy offered. She dug in a drawer and produced a jar of chocolate drink mix. "Jason came home with this last month after he went to Kroger on an empty stomach." She rolled her eyes. "Men. They make the absolute worst grocery shoppers. He knows none of us—and that includes him—need stuff like this."

She hurled it to Suzanne, who caught it like an expert football player and screwed off the lid. "Thanks, but I already had steak, egg, and cheese on a flatbread and a large OJ."

"Yeah, yeah. If I didn't love you so much, you'd make me sick." Joy broke eye contact and looked toward the bathroom door. "Elliot James, get back in there and don't come out until you get your shirt on.

"You actually ate breakfast for once?" Joy held the bathroom door open and monitored her son's dressing. "Good for you. I'm going to throw a party for you when you break a hundred and five. But then you ran off and took poor little Karen's milk? Shame, shame. I suppose I'm an accomplice for letting you hide it in my fridge."

Elliot re-emerged fully shirted. "Hey, Aunt Zanne!" He grabbed Suzanne's legs and held up a hand. "Gimme five . . . up high . . . down low—too slow." When she missed his hand, he dissolved in a puddle of giggles at her feet.

Coming here was so much fun. She loved to hear Joy and Jason's kids say *Aunt Suzanne*. When her own four nieces and nephews called her anything it was simply *Suzanne*. But in this household she was a cherished aunt, and loved on—for at least the first hour of each visit.

Joy grabbed Elliot and set him on a stool at the counter. "Raisin Bran or Honey Bunches of Oats?" then to Suzanne, "So, what'cha gonna do with the rest of your day? Don't tell me you have to go back to school to work."

"I should, but I'm not. I've seen enough of that place for the week. What I really need to do is find somewhere to live." Suzanne grabbed a handful of cereal from the box, rolled the bag down, clipped it, and tucked in the box flap. "You don't happen to have an extra room I could rent, do you? Or maybe you have an empty rental somewhere you haven't told me about."

"Don't I wish. I told Jason we could fix up the basement and let you stay there."

"Really? Would you really do that?" Suzanne's heart accelerated.

"Fixing up the basement is something we really could do. However . . . the reason we've never done that has to do with Jason's lazy, shiftless brother."

"Aaron?"

"None other. He gets out of rehab in December—for the third time. If we had any remotely spare space, it would be our responsibility to give him a place to live. I could be strong enough to finish the basement and let you live there instead. But my dear hubby still hasn't learned how to stand up to the Moore clan, so he refuses to finish it."

"If nothing else turns up, I suppose I could try paying Mother and Daddy room and board again." Suzanne helped herself to a glass from the cabinet and poured a glass of milk, adding Ovaltine and stirring absently. Please, Lord. Anything but that.

"Man. I'll never get it." Joy wiped the counter and waved her dishcloth emphatically. "Your parents making you pay to live with them. Denise has always lived with Mom and Dad and they'd never take a penny from her. She tried, but they say that's one way they can make up to her all the dollars they've spent on the rest of us kids' weddings and showers and in-laws' birthdays. Not to mention the stuff they give the grandkids. They always say Denise's singleness has saved them a lot more money than they've lost in rent payments."

What would it be like to have a relationship like Joy and her sister had with their parents? Suzanne drained her glass and nudged the dishwasher. "These clean?"

"Yeah, just set it on the counter. Hold on." Joy sprinted to the stairs that led upstairs. "AMBER," she hollered at a decibel level that mowed off a couple dozen cochlear nerve cells. "Time to get up." She paused, and a low moan sounded, followed by the thump of feet hitting the floor. "I'm giving you twenty minutes. You be down here, or I'm taking your phone for the weekend."

Then in a normal human voice, "You wouldn't believe how effective that threat is. Don't tell me it's not a big deal for you to move back to Philipsburg with your folks."

"My folks? Come on, you're showing your age. Nobody calls their parents *folks* anymore."

"You didn't answer my question."

"I didn't know I needed to. You know me well enough to know the answer. Of course it's a big deal and not just the distance."

"But wouldn't it be cheaper in the long run? I mean, they wouldn't make you pay near as much as that skinflint Hopkins does, so even with the added travel costs, you'd have more bucks left over at the end of the month."

"You've never had to live with my parents, Joy. I hoped their relationship would improve after I moved out, but every time I'm around them, I see that it has only gotten worse."

"Come on. Every married couple fusses from time to time." She squinted and affected an exaggerated tone. "Even me and Jason find something to disagree on almost every year."

"At least that often, I'd say." Suzanne punched her shoulder playfully. "Let me remind you, Miss Smarty Pants, I may not be married, but I've certainly seen enough 'real life—'" She made finger quotes. "—to know that all couples have their differences. Never mind. Just believe me when I say I'd rather live in a shack in Drexel than with my *folks*."

"I think you're crazy, but I'll say I believe you just to get you to shut up about it. Now, on to the next question. What are you doing first in your search?"

"I have no idea. That's another reason I'm here. For your advice. When I moved here, it was something that just kind of happened. Uncle Raymonds had heard that Bob was looking for new tenants. But to start out, basically from scratch, I don't know where to begin."

"Oh really, Suzanne. You're too smart to be so dumb. I've never seen you in a situation yet that you couldn't just take by the horns and figure out. You're always so confident."

"AMBER! AMBER JOY!" Without warning she must have decided twenty minutes had passed. Suzanne nearly fell off the stool where she'd perched after rinsing the glass.

"Yes, Mother?" Amber appeared in the bathroom door, faux-angelic expression fixed on her thin face.

"You watch the kids. I'm leaving with Aunt Suzanne."

"Mother." Amber turned the word into seven syllables as only a fourteen-year-old can. "You know I can't keep El and Fran from fighting. Don't make me watch them. At least take Elliot, he's the brattiest." She grabbed an apple and polished it on her sleeve.

"Am not, you are. Mommy, take me. Amber's mean. I wanna go with Aunt Zanne. Where are you going?" Five-year-old Elliot jumped to action. He dragged out his blue Crocs and put them on the wrong feet.

Suzanne gave Joy a wink and a nod. She loved this kid. Somehow the two of them clicked. She liked to tell people that he was "my little boy." To which he would reply, "I'm not a little boy."

"Okay then, Amber. Brandon, Carlie, and Denee are already out in the garden with Dad. Listen for Francine, she should be awake soon. Help her get—"

"I know, *Mom*. Get her dressed, take her potty, and give her a bowl of cereal with soy milk since she's allergic to cow's milk." She rolled her eyes dramatically. "I'm not a child. Go on, have fun. Don't forget to bring me a diet Mountain Dew, and I won't charge you by the hour for the babysitting." She ended with a grin that assured them she liked being treated like a grown-up. "And, oh yes, I know, call Dad's cell phone if I need help."

"He's in the garden, Amber, a stroll across the yard works just fine." Joy grabbed her purse and Suzanne's arm and walked toward the door through which Elliot had already disappeared. "For the record, young lady, we are not headed out just to have fun. We have work to do. I do not plan to return until we have found a new house for Aunt Suzanne to live in. I'll call you by eleven-thirty if I need you to fix lunch for the crew. *Adios, muchachas.*"

At five-thirty Suzanne begged Joy to admit defeat and go home. Only Amber's fifty-sixth phone call convinced her determined mother to acquiesce.

By Saturday noon the rain had moved in and unpacked. That put an end to the harvest operation for the week, so Mitch came home and showered and got comfortable in sweats and a t-shirt.

He started to throw his jeans and chambray shirt on the pile on the laundry room floor, but an image of Marissa standing here loading the washer with her family's clothes stopped him.

How did this machine work anyway? Could he have lived here for thirty years without learning how to wash a load of clothes? Marilyn had prided herself on keeping up with the laundry, even when the kids were little.

Years ago Mitch had thrown a pair of pants and a shirt into the washer and started turning dials when his wife appeared. "Honey, I'm sorry. I didn't know you needed these clean. Go on, I'll take care of them." She snaked her way between him and the machine, plucking his fingers off the dial and deftly changing the setting.

He would have forgotten the incident if not for what happened next. He let her finish before he turned her around to face him. "Don't think you can get away so easily, my beautiful laundry queen." He wrapped her in his arms. They were lost to the world until Marc's squeaky man-boy voice interrupted them with his opinion of how gross it was to find his parents making out like teenagers.

That was when Marilyn asked Mitch if he had added any Tide to the load. Of course he hadn't and neither had she. She laughed and raised the washer lid. "It's half finished now, so we'll have to start it over. This time with soap. Like this." She poured in a capful of detergent and closed the top. "Push it in and turn it around to the first black ten."

That was only one of the many everyday intimate encounters they had shared in their thirty-three years together. He'd had no way of knowing how to appreciate them to the fullest. Now he wanted to follow his sons and sons-in-law around and tell them to appreciate their time with their wives. Instead he had been a zombie for the past twenty-one months. Letting his girls feed him and clothe him and clean his house.

What a helpless baby. He looked again at the clothes hamper. "Push it in and turn it around to the first black ten." He heard Marilyn's words so clearly from the past. If he could remember that, why couldn't he do his own laundry?

Bingo. He would spend the rest of the afternoon taking care of his own clothes, and then if he had time, clean the house. Mitch turned to the two machines. The one wearing a dial with a black ten—and a lid on top where a beautiful wife could sit—was the washer, of course. Except, neither of the contraptions parked in his laundry room had lids on top, and neither had a ten-digit dial. Both opened in front and sported millions of buttons around a tiny computer window.

An hour and a half later Mitch returned from the library with a tidy stack. Six books about cooking and one from the new release section: *The Twenty-first Century Bachelor's Guide to Home Appliance Operation.*

He read the guide and figured out how to operate the front-load washer. Then he sat at the kitchen table and read through the cookbooks. Next he moved to the kitchen counter. He opened all the cabinet doors and all the drawers, taking inventory of stuff he'd never seen before. He could find plates and glasses and silverware, but what was with three sets of measuring cups? Or six paring knives?

While he learned to know his late wife all over again in the perusal of her kitchen gadgets, he couldn't get his mind off Gerald's request from yesterday. Time after time, he caught himself thinking, "I need to ask Marilyn when she gets in."

Marissa wants to move into my house and banish me to a single bedroom. Marc and Martin want me to let them do the farming. New Vision needs a principal. *Are you trying to tell me something, Lord?* Mitch looked at the clock. Four-thirty. Supper at Marci's was scheduled for six. He picked up the phone.

"You aren't going to any special effort on the meal tonight are you, Marci?" She usually didn't.

"No, I don't know what to fix. Abe could run for a pizza."

"Sounds good, except, I'm going to cancel for tonight. If you want to take the kiddo and go out somewhere, I still have a couple of Applebee's gift cards. You can have it on me, just the three of you."

"That'd be awesome, Dad. Maybe I'll call Marissa and have her keep Kaylee and call it a date night. Thanks, Dad."

It took a couple of phone calls to track down Mr. Garber and his wife in their cottage at the Brookhaven Retirement Community. Mitch decided to take Clarence up on his invitation to eat supper with them. Mitch would rather visit the older man in his home on the farm, but this would be interesting. He had no intention of going into assisted living any time soon. But he could have a lot of fun pushing Marissa's buttons telling her he was checking out the facilities at Brookhaven.

After following Clarence and Ethel into the dining hall at the Brookville facility and then back to the cozy living room of their small house, Mitch waited until they were seated comfortably in their recliners and he on a new-looking couch. They had already discussed the loss of his wife, how they had decided to move here, and the blessings of grandparenthood. If either Garber wondered why he had come visiting out of the blue, they hadn't expressed it.

"Let's see, how long did you work at New Vision, Clarence?"

"Twenty-five years," Ethel answered. "He started the year the school did and retired the year before last. We like to say he served rather than worked."

"You were some of the school founders, weren't you?" Mitch recalled a handful of families wanting an educational choice besides public school.

"Could say that." This time Clarence got the answer out first. "Remember how we started out with only about a dozen students and two teachers in the church basement?"

Nope, the numbers had slipped his mind over the years. He did know that by the time his kids were school age, the school had blossomed and out-grown the basement. They operated for at least two years from Chester Miller's remodeled tractor shed. Finally, they extended enrollment beyond just the children of Farmersburg Grace Church and built the present structure on Chicken Bristle Road.

The clock had struck nine before Mitch tore himself away from his gracious hosts. He ran his windshield wipers the whole way home and didn't even look at his iPhone. What had ever possessed him to go see Mr. G? As the grandkids liked to say, TMI. Way too much information. Enough to make him feel like a total loser and selfish brat if he refused to try the principal position. It wasn't his responsibility, that much he knew. But did he?

He had to quit saying he wasn't qualified. He was—or had been—the brash, young farmer who couldn't sit still between harvest and planting. He'd powered through college classes every winter until he held a degree in agricultural business management. With his education Mitch became the local farmers' consultant, working at first through a local credit union, and finally on his own. For a few years he had even agreed to teaching an adult agribusiness class at the community college.

When he unlocked the door and entered his empty house, a crippling longing for Marilyn assaulted him. Along with the persistent beep of the answering machine.

Six messages. Five from Marissa, demanding to know where he had gone and why he wasn't answering his cell phone. Sure enough, the cell showed about a dozen missed calls, all from his eldest daughter.

The last message was from Marci. "Call me, I have to talk to you about something."

Mitch called Marissa and assured her that he was fine. He was sorry she spent the evening calling all the Dayton hospitals to see if he was in their emergency room. No, he didn't have to account to her for his every move. He had been running errands.

Which reminded him, he'd forgotten to pick up a long list of grocery items on his way home from Brookville.

The phone rang in his hand as he took a breath after practically hanging up on Marissa. "Hi, Marci, what's up? How was Applebee's?"

"Fine, Dad. Did Marissa get ahold of you? She interrupted our date three times."

"Didn't you talk to her when you dropped off Kaylee?"

"Rissa wasn't home, so I called Joy Moore. Her girl Amber's a good babysitter and Kaylee loves her. Can I tell you what Joy said about the school needing a principal?"

Mitch had seldom shopped on Sunday. Only for medicine in emergencies and forgotten items necessary for some recipe Marilyn was fixing. So it felt funny to be strolling through the Kroger Marketplace with a cart full of groceries on a Sunday afternoon.

From the beginning of Marissa's plan for him to eat evening meals with the children, Mitch had insisted on Sundays off. It evolved into everyone without other plans showing up at his house on Sunday evenings. They brought snacks and popped corn, and Mitch supplied the soft drinks.

Tonight his kids all had other plans, so after rereading all six cooking books, Mitch updated his list and headed to the supermarket. On a whim, he asked for a pound of chipped ham and a pound of sliced baby Swiss at the deli. On the day-old rack he found a pack of soft potato rolls, which he laid on top of the other items. These were for a sandwich to take for lunch tomorrow when he visited New Vision Christian School.

5

A sore throat woke Suzanne Monday morning. She swallowed repeatedly and tried to convince herself it was nothing but a reminder of her recent sleep deprivation. Apparently the two-hour nap yesterday afternoon hadn't made up for the previous restless nights. Tonight she *had* to go to bed early.

She emptied a packet of EmergenC into a small glass of water and gagged it down. On the way through Farmersburg she stopped by the quik-mart for a Pepsi. Not in the least healthy, but the fizz soothed her scratchy throat. She should've finished planning today's lessons yesterday instead of taking a nap. By getting to school at five-thirty, she had plenty of time to work before the interruptions began. School policy required teachers to be at school by seven-forty-five, and the rest of the staff were pretty good at being on time.

School started at eight-thirty, but Suzanne needed at least an hour and a half at her desk before she felt prepared to meet the school day. More than that if she didn't have everything ready the night before.

She finished the lesson plans and took out her devotions-for-teachers book and her Bible. Her throat throbbed, her head and limbs ached. She crossed her arms on the desk, laid her head on them and prayed for strength to make it through the day.

Then the students started coming and nobody had done home-work. Half of them had forgotten their lunches and the kids in Suzanne's room weren't her students. She looked down and real-ized she wasn't dressed for school. Her pajama tops didn't match the pants, and she was barefoot.

"Suzanne?" A voice boomed beside her head.

She jerked awake and looked at the clock. Quarter till eight. A blink, a swallow, and a glance at her fully-clothed and shod self. Relief that it was only a dream eclipsed the embarrassment of sleeping in school.

"Uh, yeah?" With a sharper mind, she could have covered with a reverent *amen* before raising her head. With a sharper mind, she wouldn't be in this predicament.

The other teacher didn't seem to notice. "I've got to work with two of my slower second graders this morning. Can I send the rest of my students in here for a while? That's what we used to do at my school when I was a kid. We loved it. The big kids love helping the little ones with their lessons."

Why was it so hard to say that two-letter word? Suzanne had her morning planned. The classes had to fit in tighter than jigsaw puzzle pieces. This would totally upset her schedule.

Kortney widened her big brown eyes into a pathetic and for-lorn look. "I don't know how else to get Damon and Andre and Denee caught up in their reading."

All the teachers asked Suzanne to do things like this because she was such a softy. Her inability to say *no* was well known. She tried to swallow away the scratchiness and started coughing. While she struggled for control, she assessed her classes. This was the eighth week of the quarter and they had managed to stay on schedule every day so far. Even with Erik's work. What would it hurt to relax for a day? Her students could afford to miss a few classes. And it would be fun to have the contact with those little people. Since she started teaching high school, she had missed the everyday exuberance that students lose by the time they reach the teen years.

"What time?"

"Thanks. If I didn't get them caught up today, I was going to have to keep them after school this week. And Forrest and I have dates planned for every afternoon. He goes back to Virginia on Friday, you know."

Suzanne ignored the date comment. Kortney didn't miss an opportunity to remind Suzanne of her active dating life. The current boyfriend, Forrest Bowman, spent nearly every weekend in Ohio.

Suzanne could still see Kortney's retreating figure when first grade teacher Lana walked in.

"She in here flaunting her boyfriend again?"

Lana took Suzanne's silence for affirmation.

"Just so you know, I don't approve of what she's doing."

"You're the only one who should ask favors from me?"

"That's not what I mean. How do you stand having all these girls come in here every year to teach and parade their boyfriends past you?"

"Why wouldn't she share with me about her life? You do."

"Doesn't it bother you to hear about everyone else's dating life? I mean, have you ever dated?"

No, she had never dated, and Lana knew it. Maybe bringing up the question made her feel better about her own lack of the same. Suzanne uncapped the lukewarm pop and drained the last flat inch, which did little to soothe her throat. Honestly, Lana was more irritating than Kortney, who bared her heart as if Suzanne were a normal person. She hated feeling so defensive over Lana's question, but she was too tired to keep it out of her voice. "Probably about as much as you have. Why? Need some advice?"

Even if Lana's neck and face hadn't darkened a dozen shades, Suzanne would have recognized the look. She'd felt it on her own face so often in the past. Shame flooded her being.

Lana turned away, but not before Suzanne saw the tears.

She dismissed her irritation, her weariness, her pain, and caught Lana's arm. "I'm sorry, Lana. I was totally out of line. Can you forgive me for being such a crab? What an awful way to start a week."

Lana followed Suzanne back to her desk and left smiling ten minutes later. After lunch, Suzanne would send two senior girls to watch Lana's class while she went to the orthodontist for a wire replacement. The high school schedule was already in shambles, one more twist couldn't hurt. She could sleep off this stuff tonight, and tomorrow they'd get back on track. A day like this would be good for all of them. Without break duty, she could catch her breath between class periods.

Suzanne barely got the thought out of her brain when Mrs. Bower strode in. "Just so you know, Ronnie's coming to pick me up at first break, and Carol's going to take my place the rest of the day. I told her not to worry about monitoring the playground, if you wanted somebody out there, you'd go yourself." She plucked the empty bottle from the waste can and waved it disapprovingly. "This could go in the plastic recyclables." She set the offending vessel on the closest student desk. "What's wrong? You look terrible. Anyway, yesterday was our anniversary, so Ron wants to take a little Cincinnati trip. If we don't get back in time for school tomorrow, I'll just have Carol come in again." She didn't wait for a response, but pointed again at the rescued trash and left.

Linda Bower's nineteen-year-old daughter, Carol, a substitute teacher? What was Linda thinking? The girl was a high school dropout who couldn't keep a steady job.

Please, Lord, no visitors today.

6

Mr. G had suggested arriving at the school in time for devotions at eight-thirty. So at twenty-three minutes after eight Mitch pulled in the gravel drive, waited behind two vans and an SUV unloading kids, and parked his truck beside a rusted green Toyota. His door opened automatically and he looked down to see Jacob and Merry Lyn standing there grinning.

"We saw you pull in," Merry said with a giggle through her missing front tooth. "Come see my room, Grandpa."

"No. He's coming to mine first." Jacob pushed his cousin aside.

"Hey, hey, I'll be here long enough to see them both." Mitch took his oldest granddaughter's outstretched hand and followed Jacob.

They led him through the front door and disappeared into their respective classrooms. Mitch tucked his hands in his Dockers pockets and stood in the entryway beside the drinking fountain, looking around with what he hoped was a look of nonchalance. Not counting the few minutes he'd been inside last week, he could count on one hand the times he'd been inside this building. Not a fact he was proud of, now that he thought about it.

They'd had children attending here for fourteen years. He counted it up last night. Fourteen years and he didn't know his way around the school. Not even since the grandchildren attended had he taken the time or interest to show up.

Now that he was here Mitch didn't know what to do. To his right was a small room marked OFFICE. He sauntered toward the open door where a middle-aged woman sat inside at a desk busily moving her fingers over a laptop computer. He cleared his throat, but she didn't look up. Beyond the office was the room he'd seen last week. The sign beside the door said Room 3. Two girls and a boy pushed past him. High school students, he surmised from the attitudes on their faces. He couldn't help looking into the classroom to see their teacher.

A pale, slump-shouldered young woman sat at the teacher's desk wiping her nose. Not the perky, competent woman he'd seen last week. She looked up and saw him in the doorway, and an unreadable look crossed her face.

He moved quickly on and down the hall. Past the library door, to Room 4 where Merry Lyn popped out and dragged him in. She introduced him to her teacher, Miss Kortney, and to all her little friends. Merry's cherubic face as she proudly showed her grandpa around wrung his heart. Why would he want to be anywhere else?

The introductions were scarcely made when a rude, jangling bell sounded. Mitch jumped and tried to cover how startled he was. He looked around at the kids, expecting to see hands over ears, but nobody else seemed to hear the awful noise. Most of them didn't even pause in their talk.

"Come on, Grandpa, that means we have to go to our desks." Merry wove her arm through his and pulled him along.

Miss Kortney awarded him with a broad, open-lipped smile and came over to Merry's desk. "Are you here to visit all day, Mr.—" She emitted a fluttery laugh. "I guess I don't know your name. I can't call you Grandpa, can I?"

Was the little twerp flirting with him? He kept his voice even. "Mitchell Sanderson."

"Oh, yeah. I know who you are. I remember hearing they got a day off school for your wife's funeral. People always think it's the kids that welcome a snow day or funeral day, but let me tell you, the teachers appreciate it even more."

This girl is teaching my granddaughter? Surely she had redeeming qualities, but he wasn't sure he wanted to stay around long enough to find out.

Again the bell rang, nearly lifting him off the floor with its intensity. Merry grabbed his hand. "Don't be scared, Grandpa, you'll get used to it. I used to think it was loud too, but now I don't hardly even hear it. I believe you'll get accustomed to it."

Mitch hid his grin. She was so much like her mother. He and Marilyn had often covered grins as their first daughter started speaking in multi-syllabic vocabulary almost before she could walk.

Miss Kortney gave them a disapproving look and called roll. When she finished, the children lined up soundlessly at the classroom door. Mitch risked another visual scolding and leaned down to Merry's ear. "What are we doing now?"

"Going to devotions. Are you doing them this morning?" Merry lifted up on tip-toes and whispered loudly back.

His heart skipped a beat. "What do you mean, am I doing them?"

"Usually when somebody's daddy or grandpa's here, they do devotions for us. I couldn't wait till you came."

"Merry, do you remember our rule about talking in line? Maybe you could teach it to your grandfather too." Miss Kortney's tone belied her words. She showed her teeth as she smiled and surrounded each word with a breathy pause. Merry's face fell and she dropped her chin to her chest. The teacher's voice trilled gaily, "I'm joking, I just—guys, it's time to go. Andre, lead the way."

Mitch lifted Merry's chin with his right thumb until she looked up at him. He rolled his eyes the way he always did to make her laugh. Then he winked and fell in line behind her. She turned around and talked as she walked. "So are you doing the devotions?"

"I don't think so, honey. Not that I know of, anyway."

"Well, you could sit with me, but you might block the kids behind us's view. Usually the visitors sit back there." She motioned to a row of chairs in the back, and Mitch slipped into one of them.

Merry's class took seats near the front of the large almost-but-not-quite-gymnasium style room. Behind them sat the older students in graduated rows. A queue of slightly smaller children followed the third grade, and finally the teachers filed in and stood facing the room.

For a long moment the entire room remained silent. Mitch felt the eyes of all five teachers on him. A few students turned and looked toward the back, and his face went hot. They weren't waiting on him, were they? He had told no one of his plans to visit, and he had no idea what these devotions were supposed to consist of. His palms grew wet and his neck itched.

Then Gerald Cook walked in the door beside the teachers. He carried a large Bible and cleared his throat importantly. Mitch's heart returned to a near-normal rate, but he missed the point of the story Gerald told. He joined in the singing but didn't fail to notice the looks of amusement on the high school students' faces. Well, they weren't asking him to teach music. He stood with them and in unison the whole group prayed the Lord's Prayer.

Afterwards one of the teachers stepped to the wooden podium and made a few announcements. "You're dismissed," she said, and the children exited in perfect order. Many of them waved and grinned at him as they walked past, and the teachers walked up to him and greeted him with a handshake. He recognized all of them except that Miss Kortney character.

"It's so great to have you here, Mitch. Be sure to come see us," said Linda Bower, who had been a good friend of Marilyn's. "We're in Room 6." She lowered her voice. "*How* are you *doing*? I *still* can't believe she's *gone*. We *miss* you at Bible study." She still spoke in italics, a trait that he and Marilyn had often noted.

Mitch looked beyond her to the next teacher standing as if in a receiving line. He put out his hand. Anything to get away from Mrs. Bower. "Patrice Miller. Good morning."

Mrs. Miller extended a warm welcome to her fourth and fifth grade room, as did the first grade teacher with the well-wired smile. Mitch couldn't think of her first name, but he knew she was Dirk and Monica's daughter.

Merry's teacher took the opportunity to greet him again. "Okay, you told me your name, Mitch—it's okay if I call you that, right? In case you didn't know, I'm Kortney Root. My parents are Phil and Brenda, we . . ."

Mitch tuned her out without turning off his hopefully polite smile. He nodded and inserted a few *uh-huhs*, but his attention was elsewhere. Elsewhere being on the high school teacher who obviously wasn't coming to shake his hand.

Instead she went to a Kleenex box on a shelf between two chalkboards, sneezing daintily all the way. She blew her nose, discarded the tissue, and pumped hand sanitizer from the bottle beside the box. As she walked past the verbose Kortney Root, Mitch couldn't help noting her red eyes and tired look. It looked more like she was wringing her hands in despair instead of rubbing in lotion.

Kortney stopped rambling when a student appeared at her side. "Miss Kortney! Damon's getting in your desk. I told him to stop it, but he won't."

"Hey, good talking to you, Mitch. Stop back in. I know Merry will be glad to see you." Kortney took off at a run.

Then Mitch was alone in the enormous room. With forced casualness, he hooked his thumb in his back pockets and walked the perimeter of the room, studying the student art displays. From there he wandered into the hallway. A row of photographs lined the west wall, and he couldn't resist a look. There were group shots of the whole school through the years. Each framed print had a year written below it, and he perused the earliest shots until he found Marc and Marissa, and a couple of years later Martin, and finally Marci.

"Hi, Grandpa!" Merry's voice dragged him from his reminiscing. He looked up to see her in a line of small students that meandered from Room 4 to Room 3. He waved back and she disappeared into the high school classroom.

He couldn't remember which grade Jacob said he was in nor which room. So he headed to the closest door, which turned out to be Mrs. Miller's room. Drew and Landon, Marc's second son and Marissa's oldest, waved shyly from their chairs lined up in front of the large dry-erase board. Kids. They could come from the same parents and be so totally different. Mitch calculated the list of differences between Jacob and his brother Drew and between Landon and his sister Merry as he listened to the students recite the times tables up to seven times thirteen.

Must be math class, but only half the children were participating. The rest sat quietly and busily working at their desks. He walked around and looked over their shoulders. Each one was reading from a hard cover reader. One little girl—the label on her desk read *Annie*—apparently sensed his presence and turned around to reward him with a freckle-framed smile. "Are you going to be our new principal?" she asked.

"Annie." Mrs. Miller's voice raised in warning at the end of the word. "You can show Mr. Sanderson what you're reading. Or you can read to him if you want to. But you need to stick at it."

"Okay. Mr. Sanderson, do you want to hear my story?"

Mitch smiled and nodded, relieved that he didn't have to answer her principal question. Annie stood and crooked an index finger in invitation. She led him to a hammock in the corner. "This is our reading corner," she whispered proudly. "You sit there." She pointed to a small chair at one end of the swaying seat. "We can't share this unless we're both girls," she explained. "Or both boys."

Annie was in no hurry to read, and Mrs. Miller had her full attention on the math class. "What would you like to read to me, Annie?" Mitch asked, trying to get her back on task.

She looked up, startled. "How did you know my name?"

Okay, so she wasn't quite as bright as Mitch's grandchildren, but this little girl had won his heart in the space of three minutes.

He smiled and winked. "You can learn a lot if you keep your eyes and ears open. Go ahead and read to me, please."

Ten minutes later she had labored through only a page, and Mitch understood why Annie would rather chat than read. He took pity on her and offered to read the last half of the story for her. She accepted without hesitation. It probably wasn't the best way for her to learn, but he couldn't spend all day in this corner.

"Annie, are you in fourth grade or fifth grade?" he asked when they'd finished the reading.

"Fourth. And I know I'm not a good reader. Everybody in our whole class is better than me. Probably Miss Kortney's class too. I'm just dumb."

The despair in her voice and on her ruddy face tugged at Mitch's heart. "Listen, not reading well doesn't make a person dumb, Annie. I can tell already that you have really good people skills. That's important too. I heard about a lady who had a hard time reading when she was in school, but she grew up to become a famous author. You know what an author is, don't you?"

"Yeah, somebody that writes books." Wonder and awe dawned on the narrow face. "Really? That's what I want to do. I think of so many wonderful stories. So much better than what I can't read in here." She thumped the reading book. "You think I could do that?"

"I think you could surely try. Now I know you're not dumb, Annie, so you're not going to say that anymore, right?"

She nodded somberly.

"You have a good teacher. Keep doing your best, and someday I expect to see your name on books in the library."

Annie jumped from the swinging hammock and wrapped her arms around his waist. "Won't you be our principal, please?"

The thin, freckled face was the first nail in his coffin. No, scratch that analogy—too gruesome. A straw on the camel's back. A weight on the other side of the balance. And added to it was Jacob's overflowing joy when Mrs. Bower gave permission for him to give his grandfather a tour of the school. Plus the sweet, clear voices of the first graders, the sweetest of whom were Martin's twin sons who nearly burst with pride at Grandpa's presence.

Neither did it help any to stand at the high school room door, unnoticed by the teacher, and see her orchestrating three classes at once. One of those classes included Merry Lyn, who was definitely not in high school. Why was this teacher, whose room overflowed with teenage energy and apathy, teaching the students from Miss Kortney's room?

"Wanna see the library, Grandpa?" Mitch's grandson bumped his elbow. "Let's go up there before we see Miss Suzanne's room." Jacob held the heavy door and pointed up the stairs.

The library was . . . well, a library. Books, books, and more books. Exactly what he expected. He feigned interest for Jacob's sake, but tried to hurry him along. "You probably need to be getting back to class, don't you? What are you missing by showing me around?" Mitch started back down the steps.

"Aw, not much this morning. She always does history first on Monday. It's so easy. I already read the whole book last year. I bet if she let me teach it, I could make it fun. It's like she don't know those guys were real people. Or they did real stuff—" Jacob stopped midsentence when the bell rang—this time only a foot from Mitch's head.

Jacob didn't seem to notice how Mitch nearly tumbled down the last few steps. "I have to go, Grandpa. That's for the little kids' break, but it means I only got fifteen minutes to get my history seatwork done so I can have break." He sprinted down the stairs and through the door at the bottom.

Mitch watched Jacob disappear around the corner and caught the door to keep it from slamming. He stood there on the next to bottom step and watched the high school room through the library door window. The same meandering Merry-containing line of students stood at attention by the door of Room 3. A bell tinkled in the distance, and the children marched by, nine bundles of pent-up energy, bursting at the seams. Mitch slipped out behind the last one and followed them. They maintained their decorum until they reached the short hall that led to the playground. There they erupted. "Which team are you on?" "What are we playing today?" "Tag, you're it."

A gust of their youthful vigor fanned sparks in his. He followed them through the hall and stood watching as Miss Lana blew a whistle and brought everyone into lines. On the other side of the wall, a strident voice sounded from Room 4. "No, Damon. You can't go to break until you get that page done . . . What, Denee? What do you mean, do you have to carry? Of course you have to carry. I thought you learned that in first grade."

Mitch couldn't help it. He retraced his steps in the short, narrow hallway, lined with coat hooks and rounded the corner to that classroom door. Closed, but it had a small window at Mitch's eye level. He looked in just as the teacher looked up, stopping mid-sentence in another scold.

Her expression morphed from irritation to fake pleasantness. She motioned him in, and when he shook his head and stepped away, she opened the door and propped it open. "Break time, guys."

Three teary-eyed, but now smiling urchins, blasted past him toward the playground. He stepped into the room, suppressing a frown.

Kortney rolled her eyes and turned both palms upward. "*Kids.* They can be so dumb sometimes. I had to send the rest of the class over to the high school so I could work with them to get them caught up. I don't know why I even try. Denee might be getting it, but the other two are like hopeless cases. Well, sorry to take off, but I need to go. Be right back." She giggled and patted his shoulder as she left the room.

Without the teacher in it, the room improved immediately. He checked out the bulletin boards and the student work displayed around the door. He had to give her credit for her decorating sense. And for her neat handwriting on the chalkboard—he guessed she wrote the assignments herself. Maybe she had another teacher do it for her. He stopped himself—she was out of place considering her students a hopeless case, so he shouldn't do the same for her. She could soon return, so he hastily exited the room and entered Miss Suzanne's domain.

Mitch counted twenty-eight student desks in the high school room. In the far corner of the room three white poly banquet tables each held two computers, in front of which sat six teenagers. Eight more lounged—at least half with chairs tipped back—around what looked like a conference table in the opposite corner, deep in discussion. From his distance, Mitch couldn't hear everything, but he picked up both serious tones and friendly banter. He surveyed the rest of the room. A dozen or so students sat at desks, and a folded paper made its way, supposedly unnoticed it seemed, under one foot to another.

A feminine figure at the far end of the conference table raised her head and her voice. "Leon, please put that paper on my desk. The one you just picked up from under your shoe." The teacher. She had blended in with the students. Her words held a twinkle of amusement beneath their authority.

Leon apparently responded favorably and Suzanne lowered her gaze, but only for a split second. Her head shot back up and she looked directly at Mitch, eyes not twinkling. Her back straightened as she broke eye contact. She continued leading the discussion as if the interruptions had never happened.

Miss Suzanne appeared to be an outstanding and efficient teacher, and if he was any good at reading body language, the students respected her—liked her even. Mitch had no way to prove it, but word on the tractor-lined roads was that New Vision grads with college ambition scored exceptionally high on their SATs. That alone spoke volumes about the high school teacher. But was she this unfriendly to all visitors? And did she have to come to school when she was sick?

7

Only prayer—fervent, minute-by-minute prayer—got Suzanne through that awful day. At lunch she called and cancelled the tutoring session. Since her lesson schedule had been scrapped, she could use it for tomorrow, and she let the students trade papers and grade the day's makeshift assignments. So for the first time in eight weeks she found herself at home before four o'clock on a Monday afternoon.

On her way in, Suzanne passed Karen heading out the drive and breathed yet another prayer of thanksgiving. Karen didn't have to work, and that could have meant hearing her voice drone on and on into the phone, making sleep nearly impossible. Suzanne didn't know who all Karen called, but she had a long list of faithful phone buddies. And a voice that could penetrate the heartiest earplugs. Usually it wasn't a problem, as—thankfully—she worked nights and Suzanne worked days.

All Suzanne could think about now was taking a painkiller and snuggling into bed. She emptied the milk jug, shaking the last drops into a glass a quarter full—including the ice cube she added to bring it to optimum drinking temperature. At least it was enough to wash down the remainder of her lunch. Lunch on a normal day was hard enough to eat without that annoying Mitchell Sanderson sitting there asking all kinds of nosy questions. Mrs. Bower wasn't even there to take control, and Carol had eaten in the classroom so she could talk on her cell phone the whole time. Suzanne had hardly choked down half her sandwich.

She finished it now along with the stale potato chips and three baby carrots. She took two generic ibuprofen and turned off all the phone ringers.

The distant roar of a combine reached the bedroom window, and Suzanne drifted off, expecting it to get nearer and disrupt her sleep. When she opened her eyes, the room was dark and she sat up, disoriented, and found the alarm clock. 9:02. She stumbled to the bathroom and back, bringing a glass of water along.

The next time she regained consciousness, it was six o'clock. In the morning. She leapt from bed and raced to the kitchen, turning on lights as she went. The microwave and stove and Karen's state-of-the-art coffee maker all agreed with Suzanne's alarm clock. She flew into action.

Not until she was half way to school and past the quik-mart did she remember to check her health. No throat pain, no headache. Sure enough, all she'd needed was a good night's sleep.

Gerald Cook's begging hadn't moved Mitch. Clarence Garber's description of the job had come closer. An overloaded high school teacher beside a flirty, irresponsible second grade teacher and a beaten down little Annie. Now, there was the kicker. The first challenge that had snagged Mitch's emotions since Marilyn died. As he drove away from the school, the challenge taunted him. And if there was one thing Mitchell Sanderson couldn't turn down, it was a challenge.

A merciful rain made fieldwork impossible the next evening. Mitch cancelled his supper plans at Marc and Kelly's and invited everyone to his place instead.

"I'll take care of the food," he said.

They would all expect take-out pizza. But Mitch cooked the meal himself. He turned to his library books, following detailed instructions for herb rolls, gourmet potatoes, barbeque meatballs, tossed salad with homemade croutons, and fresh green beans in cranberry almond sauce. Ice cream and toppings for dessert.

Nobody seemed surprised to arrive at six-thirty to a bare kitchen table. Marissa and Marci started pulling napkins and paper plates from a cupboard. "Someone get the ice," Marissa called.

Martin walked to the oven and peeked in. "That doesn't look like—" The rest of his words were cut off by Mitch's hand.

"Wait." Mitch said it louder the second time to be heard over the din of the eight adults and eleven children. "I want to eat in the dining room tonight." Everyone stopped in their tracks. "So if you would all go there now and find your places."

He had used the good china, the good flatware, the good crystal, the cloth napkins. With such a beautiful table, he'd always wondered why Marilyn covered it up with a tablecloth that had to be spot-treated, laundered, and ironed after each use. This time he was in charge and the table was visible.

"What in the world?" "Dad, this is beautiful," and "Who helped you do this?" erupted as they gradually obeyed him. When all were seated, he silenced them, and they joined hands for prayer.

Several times throughout the meal Marissa tried to get an explanation from Mitch, but he was firm. "We'll talk business after we eat."

"Business? What do you mean, Dad?"

"Just eat and don't worry about it."

So they discussed other subjects as Mitch brought in the rest of the food.

After dessert and coffee, he stood. "Ladies, sit still. We men will take care of the dishes."

Mitch could hear the girls as they cleaned up. "What in the world is he up to?"

"Do you really think he fixed all this by himself?" Janelle's voice.

Marissa let out a shriek. "What do you mean?"

"I *mean*, do you think he has a *friend*?"

They loaded the dishwasher and hand washed the crystal. Then eight curious adults squeezed around the small conference table in Mitch's office.

"Okay, Dad, spill before the girls blow a gasket." Marc's feigned indifference fooled no one.

Mitch had planned his words all day. "You know it's going on two years since your mother died." He cleared his throat. "I want to start out by saying that I have not forgotten her. I will always love her. Whatever happens please remember—"

"No!" Marissa jumped up and crossed the room to stand beside him. "You promised Mom."

He caught her hand. "You don't even know what I'm going to say."

"Well it sounds like you're telling us you're seeing someone else. You can't do that, Dad. Remember, you promised Mom . . ." Her words got lost in a sob.

"Sit down, honey. Let me talk." He tried to use the tone of voice that allowed no arguing. "I want you all to know how much I appreciate your taking care of me the past twenty months, two weeks and five days. Thank you. You know how I relied on your mom to take care of the house stuff. After she was gone, I was pretty helpless. However . . .

"I don't like the sound of that *however*," muttered Marissa.

"However, I've been thinking a lot lately that it's time for me to move on." He raised both hands in a stop gesture. "I don't mean leave this house. Though the grief is still here." He put a palm over his chest. "It isn't as fresh and sharp. It's time for me to learn to live on my own.

"Marissa, all this time you've been coming here to clean and do my laundry." Mitch nodded at the others. "You've all been cooking for me. I know it's been a burden at times, but I've never heard you complain. I expect you've noticed how often I've cancelled out lately." He watched Marissa's face, which showed she didn't know this. "Not the nights at your place, Rissa. I knew better than that."

The other three siblings snickered, and she glared at them. "What? So I was the only one responsible enough not to shirk my duty? That's funny?"

Mitch ignored them. "Three of you have come to me with suggestions for change in the past week. Marissa, you told me of your plan to move your family into this house."

Marc rocketed to his feet. "Hey, I'm the oldest. If anyone gets this house, it's me. I mean, maybe not, but wouldn't that be a family decision? Are you planning to rent it? Buy it? Mooch off Dad while I do all the farming work and live miles away?"

"Calm down, Marc. Wait for the rest of the details. Marissa and Layne are not moving here. The day after Marissa shared her idea, Marc and Martin laid out their hopes to take over my farming business."

"Wow, Marc, that's thoughtful. Treat Dad like he's an old man. Much better than me keeping house for him, huh?"

"Cool it, guys. Do me a favor and hold the comments until I'm finished. Please?" Mitch hadn't heard them go at it like this since they were teenagers.

"Around the same time, I got a job offer. Something completely different from anything I've ever done. My first thought was absolutely not. But I couldn't get the idea out of my head." He scanned their faces for a reading. "In fact, I lost a night's sleep thinking and praying."

Marci tapped a fingernail on the table. Martin twirled his hand as if to say, come on, spit it out.

Mitch paused for effect. "It seemed that if everyone seemed to think I'm so helpless, at only fifty-four and a half, maybe I was the only one who didn't see it. So . . . last Saturday night I spent some time at Brookhaven." He looked at their incredulous faces shaking right and left. "Seriously, I did. I ate supper in the dining room. Later I toured one of the cottages."

"Dad, that's absurd. I know you said zip it till you're through, but that is not what Martin and I meant when we talked last Friday morning. You are not old. A nursing home is not the place for you. Are you crazy?"

"Retirement community, not nursing home." He waited as they sputtered. "I didn't go with any intention of living there. I visited Clarence and Ethel Garber." Mitch saw the light come on in a few sets of eyes.

"Mr. G spent a couple of hours answering my questions about the principal position open at New Vision. Since then I've been considering the ramifications of stepping down from farming, and taking on a new challenge. I have also started a new hobby, the results of which you sampled in the dining room.

"Marc, you and Martin had a point. I've given it a lot of thought. When I was your age, circumstances made me the head honcho. You need the opportunity to work with your own sons like I worked with you. I can continue with my farm consulting and management clients, but I'm willing to discuss selling out my share of the crop farming."

Marc sent Martin a fist pump. "Yes!" he whispered a little too loudly.

"Marissa and Marci, did I prove to you tonight that I can cook for myself?"

"The food was great, Dad. Probably better than I fix," Marci shoved her husband's hand away from her mouth. "Stop it, Abe. You know I'm a disaster in the kitchen. I take after Mom. She cooked, but we all knew it wasn't her thing. Come on, Marissa, she didn't like it, and you know it. She cooked because that's what mothers and wives do."

He prided himself on his poker face, but this time it was pretty hard to keep. He had never known this about Marilyn. He couldn't remember a single dish she'd ever made that he couldn't eat. The surprise of Marci's revelation kept him quiet for a long moment.

"Daddy, you don't have to do this. Maybe they don't want to cook for you, but I will. And just so you know, Mom was an excellent cook, wasn't she, boys?" Marissa looked to her brothers for support.

Both raised their hands in surrender. "I'm staying out of this," Martin said. Marc nodded his agreement.

"That has nothing to do with my next point. I have discovered that I like to work in the kitchen. I can run the washer and dryer and vacuum, and I will be doing so." He touched Marissa's shoulder. "I know part of your plan for me to rotate among your homes for supper was to prevent me from being too lonely. Taking the principal position will keep me out of the house during the week days. And out of the Sanderson fields and machinery." He nodded at his sons.

"At school I saw a stark contrast between the picture Mr. G painted and what Erik left behind. You know I like a challenge. I haven't nailed down my decision yet because I wanted to talk to all of you first.

Mitch leaned back in his desk chair and looked into each face. "That's my story. What do you say?"

Silence.

No predicting this group. When he wanted them quiet, they interrupted. When he gave them the floor, they were speechless.

Finally, Marissa's husband Layne spoke up. "Sounds great, Dad. I mean we loved having you, but it'll be good to get back to normal. Right, hon?" He pulled Marissa's hand down. "Aw, come on. It will. You've even said it." She pushed him away, shaking her head, but uncovering her face.

"Thank you, Dad," Marc said. "We'll be talking."

"Yeah. We can work out the details later when it's just us guys," Martin said. Janelle sat beside him nodding and grinning.

"Cool, Dad. You should've done that when we were in school." Good old Marci, he could always count on her for support.

Marissa abandoned her sulk. "I don't know, it doesn't seem like you've thought this through very far. You've only known about this for less than a week. Spent one day in the building. You don't know anything about running a school. The principal has always taught some of the upper grade classes. You haven't ever done anything like that. Never even helped us with homework. Even if you insist on going through with this hare-brained idea, you'll still need us to fix dinner for you after being gone all day."

He laid his hand over hers. "Number one, even if it is different than teaching agribusiness to adults, when have I ever let inexperience prevent me from taking on a project? Number two, after a day at school, I'll be ready for some peace and quiet at home. Last of all, I'm sorry I was never available to help you with homework. Now I have grandchildren there, and I'd like to do my part to make up for all those years. This is a decision I can make without my children's permission, but I would greatly appreciate having your blessing." He sat back and took a deep breath.

All eyes turned to Marissa.

"Okay. You have my blessing. I'm not happy about it, but I guess it's your life. At least it's better than hearing that you were going to break your promise to Mom."

His promise to Marilyn? Did she think he was still bound to his promise not to run the washing machine? "Would you tell me your version of that promise, Rissa?"

"You know. That you would never marry someone else if she . . . if you . . . I mean if . . ."

"If Mom died first. Come on, Rissa, we all know she died," Marci said.

"Yeah. If that happened. Mom was always saying that."

"I have no intentions of breaking any promises. Your mother was the only woman I ever loved like that and I'm not looking for another wife.

"Well," Marissa muttered, "at least the school is a safe place for you to spend your time."

8

The remainder of the week sped by on schedule. Mrs. Bower made it back in time for classes Tuesday morning. Suzanne only babysat the second and third graders mornings through Thursday. And they didn't have any more nosy visitors.

After missing their Monday session, her tutees seemed ready to get to work after school and their snack. From the beginning, Jacob and Haley showed up with prepackaged treats to fuel their afternoon studies.

"Want some beef jerky?" Jacob had graciously offered the first day.

Tina shook her head without looking at him. "Nah, I'm not hungry."

Haley held out a bag of Cheetos. "I don't like that stuff either. Here, these are better."

"I said, I'm not hungry," Tina snapped.

In the next session Haley opened her lunch bag and extracted two granola bars, two bags of grapes, and two bottles of juice. "Since you're helping me study, I bring the snacks for both of us." And when Tina tried to protest, "My mom said so. You know we have to listen to my mother, right?" She finished with a warm laugh that effectively brought down Tina's defenses.

Tina's dad was known in the community as a poor manager, and her family fell much lower on the economic scale than any of her classmates' families. Suzanne empathized with her. She had gone through school under many of the same conditions. She wondered now if her own classmates ever tried as hard to reach out and be her friend as Tina's did. Had she pushed them away and wallowed in self-absorption like Tina seemed intent on doing?

Every week seemed to reconfirm Suzanne's belief that putting the two girls together outside the normal classroom setting had been a genius plan. Every day she prayed that Haley wouldn't push too hard and that Tina would see the truth.

Friday afternoon with an hour's worth of grading and an hour or so planning Monday's classes awaiting her, she took a moment to bask in her unrushed evening. She was ravenous, but a student's mother—bless her heart—had packed Suzanne's lunch, and most of it sat in the refrigerator, an afterschool snack. She organized her work and started for the kitchen and her food and the soft drink that came with the lunch.

Voices filtering through the closed metal kitchen door stopped her. She cocked her head and tried to recognize the speakers without eavesdropping. One voice sounded like Gerald Cook. The other was familiar, but she couldn't place it. More voices joined them. She stood on tiptoe and peeked through the slightly-above-eye-level window. Four school board members. *Now what?*

Suzanne ducked, praying they hadn't seen her, and slinked back to her room, stomach growling. She kicked out the rubber stop and the door closed behind her. Why were they here again on a Friday afternoon? Didn't they have work to do in the fields, or at whatever their jobs were? *Lord, please don't let them need to talk to me, and get them away from the refrigerator before I starve.*

"Miss Suzanne?" Gerald walked in without knocking.

She looked up from her grading and raised her eyebrows.

"We're headed up to the library?" It wasn't a question, but he asked it with his usual inflection. Of course they would meet in the library, it was the only air-conditioned room in the school and the Indian summer day had become uncomfortably warm.

She nodded.

"We need to talk to you in a half hour?"

She waited until the last footsteps faded. Then she raced to the kitchen to grab her nourishment. She had only about twenty-nine minutes to eat. And a considerably diminished appetite.

The sandwich that had sounded so good minutes ago turned to Styrofoam in her mouth. The few swallows of cola she managed to sip wrestled with the bread and sliced turkey. Finally she gave up and returned it to the fridge.

Only twenty-one minutes of the thirty had elapsed when a tap sounded at Suzanne's door, obviously not Gerald. The newest board member stood there, arms folded. "Um, I guess we're ready for you." He held the library door open and followed her into the frigid air.

At the top of the stairs she raised her eyes to see five men sitting around the library table. There were only five board members, and one of them was on the steps behind her. She looked farther and recognized the face of Mitchell Sanderson.

"Well, have a seat, Suzanne. Don't just stand there with your teeth in your mouth." Gerald stood and motioned her into the empty chair. "Meet our new principal. We just hired him fifteen minutes ago. He starts a week from Monday, and he'll be here some every day next week and after three o'clock those days you can show him the ropes."

Forgive her, but she couldn't mimic the looks of joy on the other six faces in the room. She hadn't even known they were looking for a replacement for Erik. Maybe they didn't think she was handling all the work well enough, but how would they know? Secondhand, no doubt. She liked secondhand news even less than she liked secondhand clothing.

"Say something, Suzanne. I'd think you'd be glad to have less work to do."

She spent sixteen hours a day being a good teacher, striving for excellence in an effort to keep her mind and heart from fixating on her unfulfilled dreams. Now she had to take more time to train this haughty rich farmer who had lived a storybook life, that included a handsome son and a self-centered daughter who had so wounded her spirit years ago.

Lord, pardon this less-than-truthful answer. "Welcome, Mr. Sanderson. I'm sure you'll be just the person for the job." She put a smile on her lips, fully aware that it came nowhere near her eyes.

Saturday morning Suzanne searched her cupboards and found they all resembled those of Mother Hubbard.

Go to school and get all of next week's lesson planned? Or let the work wait, so she could honestly say she had no time to train a new principal? She decided to head to school but changed her mind halfway there and went to Joy's house. Where there was always food.

Joy met her at the door. "Ready to go house hunting again? Come in, we're making applesauce. Pardon the mess."

When some people say their house is a mess, they're fishing for compliments. But when Joy said it, Suzanne expected to see the path left by a tornado. From the looks of it, this twister was an F-5. At least.

It would have driven Suzanne crazy to work in such litter and disarray. Apple peelings carpeted the floor. The sink overflowed with food-smeared bowls, plates, and utensils. The tabletop was hidden from sight, and amid the clutter and Ziploc bags in all stages of fill-dom, sat three-year-old Francine with a wooden spoon, tasting some from each bag, box, and bowl. Under the table lay Rusty, Amber's St. Bernard dog with a cat sleeping between his paws.

Suzanne had actually seen it look much worse. But she knew that before Joy went to bed tonight, the kitchen would be spotless and sparkling clean.

Normally Suzanne wasn't obsessive about cleanliness, but her empty stomach roiled at this picture. "You know, Joy, I think I just remembered that I need to get a tooth pulled this morning. Without Novocain."

"You haven't had breakfast yet," Joy said. "That green tint on your face gives you away. I warned you it was a mess, didn't I?"

Suzanne nodded, afraid to open her mouth, waved weakly, and turned to the door. *Get me out of here. Fast.*

"Wait, Zanne." Joy took her shoulder, steering her into the formal dining room. As far as Suzanne knew, they never used the room, but Joy was immeasurably proud of it. Mostly proud of the table that always stayed immaculate—in stark comparison to the kitchen table that caught everything that came through. "Sit. Orange juice or grape juice with your omelet?"

"Anything except apple, but really, you don't have to do this. I'll just get out of your hair."

"Right." She waved a finger at Suzanne and backed out of the room. "Don't move. It's the least I can do for you after all the hours you slave away for our children. Speaking of which, I think you have some news to tell me."

Ten minutes later Joy returned with a mushroom, ham, and Swiss omelet and a tall glass of juice. "I know, you're going to say that's way too much, but do what you can do with it. I lay awake nights figuring out ways to put some meat on your bones." She set it on the table in front of Suzanne, and Denee followed with a handful of napkins.

"Amber and Brandon are taking their turns peeling apples right now. You do the eating, I'll do the talking." Joy shooed Denee from the room and pulled out a chair. She sat on the table, resting her feet on the chair. "Before you tell me your news from school, I have to tell you what I found out yesterday about Trevor and Karen."

Of course by "your news" she meant the new principal. Joy would know—probably knew before Suzanne did and had more details. Joy had contacts who kept her posted on neighborhood news and often heard more about what was going on in the school community.

"We knew Bob wanted you to move out so Trevor could rent the house." She waited for Suzanne's nod and continued. "And we knew they're going to remodel the whole house. Now Janice says Trevor had Grant draw up plans for a new house they're going to build on some property down on Hemple. But obviously the McMansion won't be done by the wedding, so Daddy's wedding gift is your place, completely refurbished, and rent-free for as long as it takes to finish their new one." Joy watched her expectantly.

That certainly made Suzanne feel much better about her eviction. She tried to squelch her sarcastic thoughts. Joy meant well, but sometimes she came up with the worst information. Should Suzanne be furious at the Hopkinses or irritated at her friend for telling her? She took a few more bites of egg and sipped the juice, thinking of a sarcasm-free reply.

"Wow, that's a new incentive for finding a husband with a rich papa."

"It makes me mad, Suzanne."

"Yes, but it doesn't make me need to find another place to live any more than if they were going to live in it as is for more rent than I pay." Suzanne finished the breakfast and patted her stomach. "Just what I needed. Thanks."

"You're right, and Jason said the same thing, but the principle of the thing just makes me steam. Yeah, it's the principle of it. Hey, leave those dishes set, one of the kids can take care of them later."

Suzanne ignored her command and carried the plate, glass, and fork to the kitchen. The dishwasher was full of dirty dishes. There was no room in the sink, so she stacked them with the rest and heeded Joy's command to come back and finish their conversation.

"As I was saying, it's the principle that bugs me. Hint, hint. Don't you get it? That's your cue to tell me about the new principal at school."

"I should ask you. You always hear more than I do."

Joy sighed and slid from her table perch onto a chair. "We better make this quick. Those kids will soon be done with the apples. Okay. Mitchell Sanderson has agreed to take Erik's place as principal. He's a math and science whiz, so he'll teach that to the high school and for Mrs. Bower. He's probably a computer genius too, so he'll teach computer lab and typing. Right?"

Suzanne was right. Joy had increased Suzanne's information database by fivefold. "You're the expert."

"Stop it. You knew, didn't you?"

"The first part, yes. The rest about his abilities and what classes he'd take, I haven't heard yet." She suspected Joy didn't know all of that for sure either.

"I wondered if you'd let him take your math and science without a fight."

"It's not like I have a choice. That was one thing I liked about Erik—his wanting the classes I didn't. I *can* teach the English and social studies even if they're not my favorite. At least I have been for the past three weeks."

"What is it, Suzanne? Something's bothering you about this. Come on, spill."

Suzanne shook her head. "Just a lot to process. You know my load won't be any lighter if I have to train the new principal. He comes in after school every day next week for *training.*"

Amber called to her mother for the dozenth time and finally Joy stood, pushed up her chair and wiped the table with the microfiber cloth she'd folded and refolded during their conversation. "Back to the mess. Maybe you can stand it now that you're not starving. Mitchell's a busy farmer—why do you think he's coming to work at school, and in the middle of harvest, to boot?"

"I'm no expert on farmers, much less on men. Don't ask me." Back in the kitchen Suzanne grabbed a broom and dustpan and started scooping up apple peelings and seeds. "Do you want these in the trash, or do you have a garbage pail?

"Compost bucket's full, see if there's room in the waste can. I can tell something's bothering you. It's that family, isn't it? You don't like the Sandersons, do you? You always bristle at the sight of any of them or the mention of their names."

"I . . . I . . . I think you have an overactive imagination. They're not my favorite people, but I wouldn't say I don't like them. Have I ever said anything bad about them?"

"No, but a friend can tell. I don't get it. They're the nicest people I know. I mean, they're generous. Popular. Good-looking. I never met them till after we were married and I moved down here, but I'd say they are my ideal for a family. The ones I compare my life to and try to imitate. Did you know they started the first home Bible study all those years ago? And . . ." Joy leaned down to where Suzanne was sweeping a pile onto the dustpan and dropped her voice. "I'd never tell Jason this, but Marc and Martin are the best-looking men around, don't you agree?"

Suzanne snorted. "When do you think I'd have time to check out men's looks?" Of course they were, but wild horses couldn't drag it out of her.

"Now that you have everything under control here, I better run along and get my laundry done. I'm going to stop by the gas station and pick up a village newspaper. Maybe there's something new in the rent section."

The weekend passed without her finding a suitable rental. But she did cut out and sew up a new dress for Thursdays. She also ran the washer and dryer, praying all the while they would both wait until the end of December to break down. They came with the house and were decades old when she started using them. Bob had promised long ago that he wouldn't be replacing them when they died.

Aunt Eva caught up with Suzanne on Sunday evening. "How are you, my dear girl?"

"I'm fine, Aunt Eva. Busy, as always."

Their opening lines didn't vary from the years-old script.

"Tell me what's new in your life since we talked. How's that girl doing? Tina—isn't that her name?"

Monday began the final week of the first quarter. A busy week, with all the teachers trying to tie up the first fourth of the year's lessons. Finishing all the records and getting ready for report cards.

When the dismissal bell finally rang, the usual hunger reared its rumbling head. The normal reasons. No breakfast and only a few bites of a dry bologna sandwich at noon. The rest of her lunch didn't sound at all appetizing, but it would have to do.

Suzanne had cancelled the week's tutoring sessions, so she was alone when Kortney followed her into the high school room after the last carpool left. "I need you to help me make a special exam for Andre. There's no way he can pass the one in the book."

The next ten minutes passed with Suzanne questioning Kortney and helping her understand that she needed to administer the same test to all the second graders. Suzanne had worked enough with Andre to know what he was capable of. He might not pass with a perfect score, but if she gave him an altered version—or worse yet, let him see it ahead of time—it would not be an accurate assessment of what he'd learned.

"But he'll bring the whole class's average down. That makes me look bad," Kortney wailed.

At least she was honest. Suzanne sighed for the days when they had a principal who could adequately deal with these issues. Dare she hope that Mitchell Sanderson would be any better than the last one?

A throat cleared at her classroom door. The next project had arrived. And Suzanne hadn't even begun her snack.

Kortney looked up too, all smiles. "Hi, Mr. Sanderson. It's so exciting you're going to be our principal. I'd show you around, but my boyfriend'll soon be here. I better run." She took off, her messy stack of books and papers abandoned on Suzanne's desk.

Mitchell crossed the room as Kortney skipped out. In one hand he carried a McDonald's bag and in the other a drink carrier with two large cups.

"Good afternoon, Miss Bloomer. I hope this is a good time for me to come. Gerald said after school, but I should have checked with you to find out what would be most convenient for you." He waved the bag toward her and her stomach growled. "I didn't get around to eating lunch, so I hit the drive-thru on the way over. Okay to set it here?" He nodded at the conference table.

She shrugged. "Sure."

Lovely. She'd smell hot food while she trained the new principal. However, if he was eating, surely she could too. "I'll be right back." She sped to the kitchen to retrieve the rest of her lunch and fill her water bottle.

She returned a minute later to find two meals set out on her table. Who else was coming? She looked away and tried not to smell the fries.

Mitchell was across the room studying a bulletin board. He turned around as Suzanne reached her desk. "Uh, Miss Bloomer, I hope you like Big Macs. That's what I got and I brought one for you too. Didn't want to eat here if you didn't have something too."

"I don't have to eat your food. I have some here."

He laughed. "I hope it's something that'll keep. I won't eat two burgers and two large fries." He stopped and frowned. "I'm sorry, you don't like them, do you? I wondered if I should get chicken. I should have called and asked you."

"Oh, well . . . thank you." One part of her brain wanted to split her face with a smile and gush shamelessly. Who didn't like Big Macs? The other part of her brain—the dominant one—demanded caution. There's no such thing as a free lunch. She shook her head and formed a lips-only smile. "No, a burger's fine, but you didn't have to do that."

His eyes cleared. "Then, what are we waiting for? Those fries aren't getting any warmer. Do you like iced tea? I got one sweet and one unsweet. Take your pick, or we can mix them. They make it too sweet for me."

While they ate, he pulled a notebook from his shirt pocket. "I have a few questions here, if you don't mind." He held the pad at arm's length and flipped a couple of pages. "Should've brought my glasses . . . How many students are in each of the high school grades?"

Suzanne swallowed a fry so she could answer, but he continued without pause. "What classes are you currently teaching? Which of those did Mr. Angle teach? Do you mind if I sit in on classes a few days this week? Could you help me find Erik's schedule?"

After the third question she didn't attempt to answer the barrage of questions.

Two pages later, he looked up. "Sorry, go ahead and eat, I'm just reading the list I made last night." He closed the book and laid it on the table.

As much as she hated to admit it, the food brightened her day. She'd be able to concentrate for the next two hours without her stomach interrupting. But that didn't mean she could let down her guard.

When he'd discarded the food trash, Mitchell went outside and returned with a professional-looking briefcase. Probably real leather. He pulled out a portfolio and opened it to a yellow legal pad filled with more illegible scribbles. "So . . . maybe we should talk first about which classes I'll be teaching and which ones you'll keep." He looked at her expectantly and turned to a blank page.

"I'm familiar with them all. I understand you're somewhat of a science enthusiast and a mathematician . . ."

"Don't believe everything you hear." He made a few notes. "Which are your favorite subjects to teach?"

"It doesn't really matter that much, but I guess I'd have to say I enjoy math and science most. Not that I dislike the language arts or social studies—" She stopped. Not entirely true. "Well, history, geography, and government are my least favorite. But I—"

"Then I can take those. Okay? But, if you're willing to keep on with the language stuff, it'd probably be best. Grammar and I never hit it off too well. Same with composition, spelling, and literature."

In the end, they agreed on a division of labor. Mr. Sanderson would take all the history, government, and geography classes along with the science classes—biology, chemistry, and physics. The rest were hers: literature, composition, grammar, algebra 1 and 2, geometry, trig, and Bible. The elective classes were taught by volunteers and didn't go on either list.

He left before six with a mountain of books. "I'll be back tomorrow to observe teaching techniques around the school. And when the students leave, I'd like to get a professional tour of the facilities."

Mitchell was nicer than she'd expected him to be. Maybe too nice.

9

Mitch left school Monday evening, head spinning. That this job would be a challenge was a colossal understatement. He fastened his seat belt then checked the rearview mirror, reaching to tip it up. Marilyn must have adjusted it to—no, of course not. He chuckled at how frustrated she'd always been to get in the Lexus after he drove and have to change the mirror. It never occurred to her that he had to do the same after she'd driven.

Of course she had not been the last one to drive the Silverado.

It took Mitch a few seconds to figure out the difference in the mirror's position. It was his own posture. He could feel it, the lift of his shoulders, the straightening of his back. Even the set of his jaw. That once familiar, but now foreign lilt in his thoughts. *Look out challenge, here I come.*

Even the grief-pain in his heart felt duller today. She would want him to live—not drift—the rest of his life. The challenge of managing New Vision Christian School might be just what he needed to feel alive again.

Halfway across Chicken Bristle Road Mitch slowed behind a wagon-pulling tractor and waited for an oncoming car. As he accelerated to pass the obviously empty wagon, he recognized the driver. Gerald Cook's son—what had he called him? Gerry. Gerald Alden Cook the Third. Mitch waved at the boy and made a mental note to see if he was in school tomorrow. If he wasn't, were the Cooks expecting the teachers to send home catch-up work?

From Mitch's vantage point, the high school teacher didn't need extra work piled on her just because Gerald wanted his son's help in harvest.

Safely back in the right-hand lane, Mitch straightened the stack of books on the seat beside him. He picked up the biology text but put it back unopened. Years ago, after a close call on the road as he unwrapped a granola bar, he had promised Marilyn he'd never eat and drive. Reading and driving was probably worse. Wait until supper, then he could eat and read.

Four hours, two fields, and three wagon-moving trips later he did just that over a plate of microwaved leftovers. His very own meatloaf, scalloped potatoes, and herbed green bean leftovers. He sniffed almost proudly. Who knew cooking would be so fun? He should have tried it years ago, given Marilyn a break occasionally. He skim-read the first few chapters in all the science and social studies textbooks, closing the last one long after a crust had dried on his empty dinner plate. He scrubbed the plate and leaned it in the drainer. Then he made a sandwich from the last of the meatloaf for tomorrow's lunch.

Mitchell Sanderson fell asleep with the New Vision bylaws handbook open across his chest and the nightstand lamp still burning.

Because he'd forgotten to ask what role he should play in morning devotions, he took the easy way out Tuesday morning and arrived at school twenty minutes after the eight-thirty bell had rung.

Mrs. Bower bustled down the hall as he gently closed the front door. "I suppose I should tell you I have to leave staff meeting early this afternoon. I told Suzanne we should just skip it for this week. It's not like we ever have anything really important to discuss. But you know how she is about that kind of thing." She rolled her eyes dramatically. A piercing shriek came from the direction of her classroom and she sighed. "Can't turn my back for a minute without a ruckus."

Mitch threaded his way through the outer office to the inner office and his newly inherited desk. He slung Marci's old backpack onto the floor and laid his briefcase on the chair. Then he visited Linda Bower's sixth, seventh, and eighth grade class for the next hour and returned with a page of notes.

At lunch he learned that staff meeting was held weekly on Tuesday at 3:20 p.m. "Sometimes very weakly," Miss Suzanne concluded with a sniff. Mitch caught a glimpse of dry humor beneath her taciturn exterior. *Taciturn.* There was a word he didn't use often, and even less often to describe a woman.

He had hardly begun extracting more staff meeting details when the first grade teacher appeared at her elbow with an inquiry. Something about how to get gum out of hair, yes she'd asked Donna in the office first, but Donna was on the phone— long distance with her new daughter-in-law, and couldn't be bothered—so if Miss Suzanne didn't mind coming in to help . . .

Suzanne stuffed her mostly uneaten lunch back into a blue and green plaid insulated sack and followed Miss Lana from the room. Mitch snatched a pen from his shirt pocket and added to his notes.

At quarter till three he called the Village Pie and ordered a large meat lover's pizza to be delivered to the school in half an hour. With a two-liter of Pepsi.

Four of the teachers gushed and raved over the unexpected treat while mourning loudly that it would ruin their diets. And Miss Kortney had to go to Weight Watchers at six o'clock. Miss Suzanne thanked Mitch and ate as she presented a list of items for discussion.

On Wednesday Mitch left school before lunch and hauled two loads of beans to the Farmersburg elevator. He booted up his laptop on the passenger seat and wrote lesson plans for next week's biology and chemistry classes while he waited his turn on the scales. At three he returned to take more notes from the high school teacher.

So went the rest of his week, seesawing between school and the farm as he worked to ease out of harvesting and into school management. It was both harder than he'd hoped and easier than he'd expected. He nurtured an increasing pride in his sons as he watched them take over the grain operation and an increasing fondness for the children he saw each day at school.

Harvest had always been a busy and tiring time, and Mitch had impressed himself with how well he handled the stress. Now he was deciding that, compared to the stress these teachers faced on a daily basis, farming twelve hundred acres was a piece of cake.

Monday morning he left for school at five-thirty, having wakened at four. He would be the first one there and spend some time strolling through his new domain before it became occupied for the day. He wanted to put some notes on the chalkboard in the classroom he would use and print out the new syllabuses he'd created on his laptop.

But the school was not vacant when he arrived. An old Toyota sat in the parking lot and the high school room was lit up like a Christmas tree.

The clattering of the front school door broke the stillness of Suzanne's early morning preparations. For years she'd been the only morning person on staff at New Vision and she liked it that way. In the past five weeks she had needed every minute of the time to get all the classes ready. Starting today her class load was reduced, so she was enjoying time to relax and savor the stillness.

She slipped to the other side of a deep set of shelving, out of view of anyone entering her room. Who could it be? It wasn't Lana or Kortney. They weren't morning people, even less so on Monday. Mrs. Miller and Mrs. Bower had both bragged Friday afternoon how they had everything buttoned up and didn't need to come in until eight this morning. That left . . .

"Good morning, anyone in here?" Mr. Sanderson's voice confirmed her hypothesis.

She stepped from her hiding place, waved, and grabbed a random book from the shelf, flipping pages arbitrarily. "How can I help you?"

He laughed and walked toward her. "You sound like a retail greeter. Nothing I need right now. Just wanted to say hello. You're here early, Miss Suzanne. I expected I'd be here alone for a while. But . . . don't let me bother you." With that he spun on his heels and left the room, his cologne hanging in the air.

She didn't recognize the scent, but it smelled a lot better than what Erik had worn.

After school Jacob, Tina, and Haley were back. Suzanne should have stopped their conversation when three-fifteen arrived, but she was learning a lot.

"Your grandpa's cool, Jake."

"Really?"

"Yeah, he made biology class fun."

"I hope he stays till I'm in high school."

"He's gonna be real good with the guys. They always goofed off so much in Mr. Angle's class, we never hardly learned nothing. But your grandpa made them pay attention."

"Good. I told him he should be principal." Jacob's tone indicated that he took full responsibility for recruitment.

Suzanne bent her head over the desk and let them talk until it degenerated into silliness. Then she called them to order, set the girls up with a list of vocabulary words and guided Jacob in checking his math assignment.

"My dad says this is stupid. He never understood casting out nines either, when you can use a calculator."

Suzanne ignored his remarks, which were as unexpected as tomorrow's sunrise. If there was one thing she'd learned over the years, it was not to challenge what a boy's dad said.

Mr. Sanderson announced his presence with a clearing of his throat. How long had he been standing there? Now she was doubly glad she hadn't responded to the outburst.

"Casting out nines? Some kind of exorcism going on here?" Jacob's principal grandfather stepped up to the desk, caught Suzanne's eye, and winked.

Her gaze dropped as quickly as her hackles rose. How dare he make fun of their lessons? Jacob didn't need to add another person to his list of those who thought what he was learning was stupid. She counted to nine before she could speak without sounding indignant. This was, after all, her boss, and no matter her annoyance, she would show respect. "That's one way of looking at it I suppose. It is a handy little system once you figure it out."

Mr. Sanderson stepped around to the other side of his grandson and dropped to one knee. "Show me how it works, Jake."

She left them and began a Spanish conversation with Haley and Tina, keeping an ear tuned to the family scene. "So I have to go through each addend and take out all the nines, add what's left and write it over here. Then you do that to the sum . . ." Jacob explained.

Jacob's mother picked him up right on time and the girls left shortly afterward. Suzanne settled in to finalize tomorrow's lessons, nibbling at her remaining lunch. Why was she not surprised when Mr. Sanderson ambled into the room? He'd probably run into some tangles and needed her help to unravel them. She finished writing a sentence and looked up with raised eyebrows. Actually, she shouldn't be complaining. Another half hour and she'd be finished with her work. Two hours earlier than usual, and probably thanks to the man whom she was struggling not to sigh about.

He sat on the corner of her desk, and she instinctively pushed back to restore a larger personal space. "We had a good first day, and I hold you largely responsible for that, Miss Suzanne. Thank you." His smile came through in his voice. What else did he want from her? People didn't just talk that nice without a reason.

She studied his face a moment and shrugged.

"But before I get into that, I want to talk about Jacob staying after school."

She nodded, not sure of what to say.

"Marc told me you've never charged them for your time. I'd like to see that changed if this continues."

Of course. He felt sorry for the poverty-stricken old maid. But she didn't want his pity.

Well, that was the wrong thing to say. Mitch bit his tongue as color rose in Miss Suzanne's cheeks. She looked away and fiddled with a pencil.

"I'm not doing it for money, Mr. Sanderson. His mother asked me to help, and I've been glad to do so." Her voice quivered, and he couldn't remember when he'd last seen a grown woman look so vulnerable. "Jacob is an intelligent boy, and it has been my pleasure to give him some extra attention." She recovered vocally although her face kept its rosy color.

He didn't have the right words. But then, that had never kept him from speaking in the past. "I apologize. I didn't mean to offend you. I just thought that . . . well, it seemed like you . . ." Nothing was coming out right. "Forget I mentioned it. You are quite generous, and we appreciate it. Now I'd better not keep you from your work."

He retreated to his desk. What was that all about? When had Mitchell Sanderson ever been tongue-tied? No wonder she had so few discipline problems in her classroom—a couple of words, a gaze from those piercing blue-green eyes, and any wayward student would stop in his or her tracks. Whatever it was, it must be the needed quality to keep a capable teacher in the classroom for all these years.

And if anyone on the staff had the qualifications, Suzanne did. The other teachers were adequate, and given enough time they could become good or even great. He doubted Kortney would stick around that long. He perceived the married teachers to be in their classrooms mostly because there were openings, the school was desperate, and it made a good excuse to get away from home for a few hours each day. He hadn't figured Lana out yet. She was good with the first graders, but he sensed in her a resentment. As if she'd been designed for bigger and better things, but this was all she could get.

Suzanne? The epitome of dedication. Of professionalism and education. All blended with a palpable empathy for the teenagers.

In the short time since he'd become interested in New Vision, Mitch had found himself drawn to this poised young woman. Unlike the other teachers who gushed in his presence and vied for his attention, she maintained a dignity worthy of her profession.

Although he trusted he had God's blessing on his decision to take this position, he didn't know how many years he would continue in it. But he knew one thing—as long as he was here, he hoped Miss Suzanne would be around to hold the school together. She was a keeper.

The challenge would be working with the other four teachers to bring out their strengths and polish the rough edges.

He bowed his head and prayed for wisdom.

10

Christmas came on Friday, so New Vision's last day before Christmas break was December 18. As usual, Suzanne's class had a casual morning in their room and a big party in the afternoon. As uncool as it is for teenagers to get excited about something planned by their teacher, they were pretty wound up. She realized it was not just the party, but the whole Christmas spirit. And the prospect of sixteen school-free days.

Each year she chose a different theme for the food, keeping it simple this year with dips and dippers. Mexican dip with ground beef, beans, cheese, and salsa warmed in a Crock-Pot. Cream cheese and dried beef cheese ball with a hint of onion. Spinach dip in a hollowed-out loaf of sweet Hawaiian bread. Piña-colada fruit dip. Tortilla chips, fresh veggies, fresh fruit, and toasted bread cubes for dipping. Two-liters of Pepsi products, mostly Mountain Dew. The caffeine aftereffects wouldn't be Suzanne's problem.

Kate, Amy, Sabrina, and Bethany were helping spread a white tablecloth on an eight-foot banquet table. Suzanne could always count on Kate to jump in and help with anything domestic, and her cohorts usually pitched in too. "Is Mr. Sanderson coming to our party?" Kate asked.

"He's certainly welcome, but I heard a couple of the other teachers invite him before I thought about it. Plus, I'm sure his grandchildren think they have first dibs. If he eats snacks from all the other classrooms, he'll be too full to eat any of ours." Suzanne winked at her. "So don't worry, we should end up having enough that way."

Kate blushed and giggled. "That's not what I meant."

Suzanne grinned and sent the girls to the kitchen for a load of food. "I marked our stuff with blue stars," she told them. "It's pretty full in there, be careful you don't knock anything over."

The rest of the class was scattered about the classroom in groups of four or five. One cluster played a game of Rook and another a rousing round of Dutch Blitz. Loud eruptions sounded from time to time from the students playing Outburst. Suzanne watched them interact with pleasant camaraderie. A sense of satisfaction and pride filled her. They tried her patience daily, and she was more than ready for a break. But they were hers and she loved them. She was blessed beyond measure.

The girls returned and set the food on Suzanne's desk, which had been cleared of all the teacher clutter. A gaggle of boys jumped up at the girls' entrance and pretended to snitch from their plates and bowls. As only teenage girls can do, they played right into their hands, squealing and slapping at the guys.

"How many blondes does it take to carry food to the party?" Clayton called across the desk to Brent, who came up with some ridiculously funny answer that had them nearly rolling on the floor.

The two tow-headed boys continued their constant barrage of blonde jokes for the sake of the hotly protesting girls. Several of the girls they picked on had black or dark brown hair, but that didn't matter. "We know they dye it. They're really blond."

As Suzanne opened packs of red and green plates and napkins, she watched Tina. Much of her former awkwardness had faded, but when Haley left the room, Tina still had that deer-in-the-headlights look.

Suzanne scanned the room and found Blake and his buddy Nathan putting away a chess game. She called their names. "Come here, please. Tina, you too." She looked up, startled, but obeyed.

"I need you three to go out and bring in the pop. It's sitting in the gravel on the north side of my car."

"Sure, Teach." Blake faked a punch at Nate, who looped an arm through Tina's elbow and then through Blake's. "We're the pop squad. Snap." He nodded at Tina. "Crackle." Then at Blake. "Pop." He shook his head and waggled his black eyebrows. "Never let us stop." He dragged them through the classroom door and then stuck his head back in. "We promise not to touch your car, Miss Suzanne. It would be too bad if it fell apart right before Christmas break."

The lovable goof. Nate and Tina were second cousins, and in years past he was the only one who could make her act slightly comfortable in a social setting. Suzanne prayed that between him and Haley, Tina would get involved enough to enjoy the party.

After the kids had polished off most of the food, they unwrapped their gifts from Suzanne and finished up the hour with a few rounds of old-fashioned circle games.

When the three o'clock bell rang, all the teachers stood in the entryway and handed out Christmas goodie bags to the exited students. Each teacher had contributed a small item. Suzanne remembered this custom from her own school days at New Vision. The items varied from year to year, though not by much. This year the red-and-white-striped paper bags contained an orange from Mr. Sanderson, a pencil from Miss Lana, a bookmark from Miss Kortney, a candy bar from Mrs. Miller, a mini notebook from Mrs. Bower, and a pocket-pack of Kleenex from Suzanne. At the staff meeting on Tuesday each teacher had signed the mini Christmas cards—all eighty-four of them.

"Merry Christmas," the teachers said, placing a sack in each waiting set of hands.

"Merry Christmas," they shouted back.

The last straggler—there was always one, even for this exciting event—snatched his prize and ran out the door. Then the teachers all walked to the front of the carpool line, shrugging into coats and gloves as they went.

This was another tradition that had been in place before Suzanne started teaching here. They stood at the edge of the drive and waved to the departing carpool vehicles, singing at the tops of their lungs, "We wish you a Merry Christmas, we wish you a Merry Christmas, we wish you a Merry Christmas and a Happy New Year."

The line of vans, SUVs, cars, and trucks left slowly, nearly every one of them with windows rolled down and arms waving back at the ensemble. A few stopped to get their annual Christmas photo of the staff.

Suzanne loved her job. This was more than an occupation. This was her life. Not the one she dreamed of as a teenager or even into her early twenties. But she had been blessed with a good life in spite of her unfulfilled dreams.

She stood staring toward the east along Chicken Bristle Road as the last car disappeared. A few lazy flakes of snow twirled around her, but she hardly noticed the cold. There was plenty of cleanup work to finish back in the classroom, but her thoughts drifted to the task that loomed before her in the next week. Moving out of her home of twelve and a half years.

Despite their long and ardent search, Joy and Suzanne had failed to come up with anything affordable. Nothing, that is, except an ancient house trailer in the less-than-desirable mobile home park on the edge of New Loveland. Joy had a fit and insisted Suzanne reconsider moving in with her parents until something suitable would show up. Reluctantly she made a trip to visit Daddy and Mother.

She was eating supper with her parents that Saturday in early December and had just brought up the subject when her sisters arrived simultaneously.

"Did you know Suzanne's getting kicked out of her house?" Mother asked them after they helped themselves to a handful of mint Oreos.

Michelle bit into a cookie. "Yeah, when?"

"She's got another month, don't she?" Carrie waited to start her cookie until she voiced her question.

"The end of December," Suzanne said.

"Where you going next? You're still teaching, right?" As if Carrie was interested in Suzanne's life.

Daddy looked up from his bowl of chili. "She wants to move in back here. You think that's a good idea?"

"She'd pay rent, wouldn't she?" This from Michelle, who'd picked up the newspaper and stood reading it. Apparently not too engrossed to pick up the conversation around her.

Carrie nodded and waved her third Oreo. "You let her come, and you better be prepared to take us all in when we get fore-closed on. I still can't believe the bank gave us that humungous loan we needed to build our house."

Daddy nudged his bowl. "Don't we have any ketchup around here anymore?"

"I just forgot it, okay? Sit still. I'll get it." Mother sighed heavily and stomped to the refrigerator, grabbed the squeeze bottle and slammed it on the table beside him. "I don't know why you need to add anything to that anyway," she muttered.

"What?" Daddy growled.

"Nothing, just contaminate your food and eat it."

What little appetite Suzanne had when she arrived was gone. If her conscience would let her, she would leave now. Instead she pushed her own chili, ketchup-free, around in the bowl.

"You know," she finally said after they had exhausted their lists of reasons why her idea was not a good one. As if it were her idea in the first place. "Don't worry about it. I'll find somewhere closer to school."

"Have you ever considered buying a house?" asked Michelle. Her used car salesman husband was doing quite well in this economy.

Suzanne silently pleaded the fifth. Nothing had changed. They didn't get it, not that she had expected them to.

"Pretty, isn't it? And so peaceful." Mr. Sanderson's voice startled Suzanne back to the present. He ambled toward her rubbing his hands together. He did that a lot. Maybe he had a problem with cold hands, or could be a nervous habit. Surely the perfect, self-confident Mitchell Sanderson was never nervous.

"Uh, yes it is." Is pretty—*was* peaceful. Suzanne shoved her hands deeper into her coat pockets, but didn't look at him.

She would wait to start packing her things until after the weekend. She'd been collecting boxes for the past month and probably had enough for her meager belongings. She could surely take everything in two loads with her car. But she hadn't figured out what to do with the furniture. Joy and Jason would help except they were flying to California to spend Christmas with her family. They had a flight out of Dayton early tomorrow morning, and Suzanne was taking them to the airport in their van.

The van. Ask to borrow their van. If Suzanne could get the seats out, her furniture would fit in. Not all at once, of course, but she could make multiple trips. She would fill it with fuel after the last trip in readiness for getting them from the airport in January.

"So. You have big family plans for the holidays, Suzanne?" He was still there. Still rubbing his palms together.

Time to get back to the classroom to close things up for the year. "It does look like a pretty busy time," she answered. Never would she admit to him that she hadn't any plans, family or otherwise, for Christmas. Daddy and Mother left last week for Florida and would be gone through February. Carrie and Quentin were going to his family's cabin in the Smokies. Michelle and Julian had made it quite clear that they were having their own *family time* this year and nobody else was invited.

"Do you all get together at your parents' place for Christmas? Or maybe at one of your sisters'? Or they could come to your place—I didn't mean you wouldn't be capable of hosting them." They reached the school door and Mitchell held the door as Suzanne walked in.

Did he have any more options for her to choose from for their family celebration? She waited.

He followed her in and to her classroom. "You did a great job on the party for your class. You must be quite a gourmet cook. I know they say, 'Never trust a skinny cook,' but I tried that hot bean dip and I'd say you can be trusted."

Thankfully he didn't press her for an answer. Still, she should have appreciated his compliment on her food, but she got hung up on *skinny*. She hated that word. She didn't want to be *skinny*. She wanted to be slim. Slender. Thin. Svelte. Willowy. Why did people think it was fine to make comments about her weight when they'd never dream of bringing up an overweight person's size to their face? Sometimes she even wished she were fat.

"You saw the entirety of my culinary abilities today, Mr. Sanderson. I'm a teacher, not a cook." Hmph, that sounded snippy. "But thank you for the compliment. I'm glad you liked it. I'd offer you more, but I'm afraid they cleaned it up. Guess I should have made more."

"Here, let me help." He took the trash bag from her. "You know, from the looks of those boys, I think they would have cleaned up whatever amount you fixed. I know my boys at that age had hollow legs. That's what their mother used to tell them. Especially Marc. He ate and ate and never put on a pound."

Get this man out of here. She grabbed the bag from Mr. Sanderson, pulled up the corners, and tied them. "Thank you. I think I can handle the rest of it."

At least she hadn't seen his nosy daughter skulking around today. Marissa probably didn't show up every day, but it seemed like it. Suzanne used to spend years without noticing the woman, and thought she had let go of the past they shared. If the sight of Marissa stirred up those memories so painfully, had Suzanne really forgiven her?

Mitch knew when he'd been dismissed. He walked back to the office and looked around to see if there was anything left to do. There wasn't. The janitors weren't coming until early next week. That meant somebody—Mrs. Bower, according to the schedule—needed to make sure the restroom faucets and lights were turned off and the thermostats for the activities room, library, and computer room were on the night and weekend setting. That the windows and doors in those rooms were closed and locked.

This was only Mitch's eighth week on the job, but already he'd learned whom he needed to check on and boost responsibility in. He strode the length of the main hall and met Mrs. Bower on her way into her classroom with a cup of coffee.

"Hey, Mitch, want some?" She nodded at the cup in her hand. "I made a fresh pot in the kitchen. Help yourself."

He shook his head. "Thanks, but I've had my quota of caffeine for the day." Before Marilyn died, he never had any trouble falling asleep at night. Now he watched the clock change for hours if he had anything caffeinated past mid-afternoon.

Linda pulled up a chair and pointed. "Have a seat. I'll show you my loot. Ronnie's coming in a few minutes to help me haul it all home. Look." She pointed out the items her students had brought her for Christmas.

"Good thing you have help with that. Merry Christmas, Mrs. Bower. Have a blessed holiday. I'm on my way out pretty soon and wanted to stop by and tell you that I'll check the boys' restrooms for you."

"What?" Mrs. Bower appeared expectably puzzled.

"You got my note about the cleaners not coming, right?" Mitch didn't know if she was stalling so he'd offer to do all her chores or if she had completely forgotten her duty. He suspected the latter. "Teacher chores. Remember?"

"But not on—" She jumped up from her chair. "Oh, right, right, right. I get it. Yes, I'm on my way to do them now."

He took care of his promised inspection at the north end of the school and then stopped next door where Mrs. Miller handed him a trash bag and pointed at the carpeting of wrapping and paper plates, cups, and napkins. He smiled and obediently gathered trash as she showed him what her students had given her. It was similar to Mrs. Bower's "loot" as she called it.

When Mitch had the rubbish collected, he offered to help carry gifts to the car. Mrs. Miller thanked him, but said she had it covered. On his way back down the hall, he found Kortney's door closed, lights out, desk empty. In the first grade room, Lana received him warmly and excitedly showed him all her gifts.

"These cute little gals and guys, they're so much fun. Some of them get a bigger kick out of watching me open what they brought than from opening what I gave them. And poor little Dina, Scot, and Felix. Their mommies just sent gift cards. They were so embarrassed because all they were giving me was this tiny little piece of plastic. They couldn't understand why I was so excited."

It was something to be excited about. Mitch had seen the paychecks one week when they came without envelopes and he had to use some from the office. These teachers were not drawing a huge salary by any means.

He wished her a blessed Christmas, took care of the restrooms at the south end, and strolled back to his desk. There was nothing to do, but he couldn't motivate himself to go home. He rearranged his own loot, which consisted mostly of homemade goodies, and patted his midsection. He did not need all this stuff. Did they want him to roll in after the New Year? He'd seen plenty of food in all the teachers' rooms. Except Suzanne's. Hmmm. And she was the only one who hadn't shown him what the kids had given her. He should take some of these cookies and cinnamon rolls to her. They certainly wouldn't hurt her waistline.

"Knock, knock." Mitch walked the length of her classroom without Miss Suzanne looking up. He was going to feel like a jerk if she jumped.

She didn't. She just looked up from a kneeling position beside her desk. "How may I help you, Mr. Sanderson?" Coolly professional.

"I don't know what to do with all this food. I thought maybe you could use—" This wasn't coming out right. He noticed how she'd stiffened earlier when he made that silly crack about skinny cooks. She must be sensitive about her size, although he couldn't see anything wrong with it. No wonder Marilyn had drilled into him "never, never, never mention a woman's size to her."

"I mean, I didn't see any stuff like this in here, and I'd like to share some with you. If I eat all this, I'll have to buy new school clothes. Or else walk to school for a couple of weeks after vacation. But that would just make me hungry and defeat the purpose. If I could—" Mitch stopped himself. Why couldn't he just stop after he'd made his point? No surprise Suzanne insisted on being so formal in his presence. She probably put him and Gerald Cook in the same category. Just shut up and let her respond.

To his relief and surprise, Suzanne smiled. "I got my share. Had the kids put it in my car before they left. I usually give most of it away. If you want to get rid of it, set it there and I'll have more to distribute in town."

Whoa. That was the most he had ever heard her say at one time. He'd have to remember what he said and try it again.

"Ouch!"

A crashing sound and her startled cry sent him backward a step. He rounded the desk as Suzanne pulled out the desk's heavy file drawer and extracted a finger. She jumped up and wheeled to face the window.

"What? What happened? You okay?" He put his hand on her shoulder, trying to study her face.

She moved away, shut her eyes, and nodded. "Fine. Just stupid."

She didn't look so fine. Nor did she open her hand. But she opened her eyes, turned back around, and sat in her chair. Not meeting his gaze.

He nudged the offending drawer into place with his knee. Then, without thinking, he leaned down and took her hand in his. "Which one got caught?"

She shook her head and pulled away. "It's nothing. I'll be okay."

He tightened his grasp and opened the slender fingers. "It's bleeding, Suzanne. You popped it open. That's not *okay*. Sit still. I'll be back with the first aid kit."

She was a tough one. Her face read agony, but she didn't flinch when he rinsed the cut with antiseptic wash. Or when he applied triple antibiotic ointment. Not even when he clumsily wrapped a Band-Aid around the injured fingertip.

"There." He wadded the trash and threw it away. "That'll hurt like crazy for a while, but by splitting out the side of the nail like that, you got rid of the pressure. Probably won't come off now. The fingernail that is. You're going to want to take some painkiller to sleep tonight. And be sure to clean it out tomorrow and change the bandage. Doctor Mitch's orders." There he went again, blabbing on and on. Mitch stopped the flow of words and tapped her upturned palm until she met his gaze. "You have some at home?"

She nodded again. "I'm sure I can find something." She yanked her hand away. Determination chased away the pain and embarrassment on her face. "Thank you."

Then as if nothing had happened, Suzanne strode across the room. She emptied a pop bottle into her cup. "Want some Sierra Mist? This is the last of the Pepsi, and those crazy boys finished off seven two-liters of Mountain Dew. I hope their parents will forgive me." Something wet glistened on her cheeks as she dropped the two-liter in the trash bag.

"Don't mind if I do. Already turned down a cup of coffee and a can of Dr. Pepper, but this sounds good. Thanks."

She handed him a cup. "I think I'm pretty much finished here. Do you need me to do anything for you before I leave?"

She do something for *him*? "No, I'm good to go too. How can I help you? Take those boxes to your car?" He reached for the biggest box beside the door.

"Actually, no. I'm going to have to store it all here for a while. But you could set them on that table, since you offered." Suzanne pointed to the conference table. "I hope it's not in anyone's way there."

Mitch followed her instructions. "Have a blessed Christmas, Suzanne. See you back here on the fourth." She hadn't answered him when he asked about her family holiday plans. Did she not want him to know? "I'll take these to your car if you really want them. Is it unlocked?" He picked up the baked goods he'd come in with fifteen minutes ago.

"No. I mean, yes, it's unlocked, but I will take them. Thank you." She reached for them, but he held them out of her reach.

He could be stubborn too. "You don't need to be bumping that finger. I'll take them."

Mitch stood on the porch and watched the green Toyota crest the hill and disappear from sight. Suzanne Bloomer was a puzzle. Her warm friendly manner with the students and other teachers was anything but artificial. So why was she always so aloof with him? Her hand and arm had trembled at his touch and her face glowed with distrust as well as pain. What had he ever done to make her so afraid of him?

"Dad!"

He flinched and whirled around. Marissa stood there glaring, arms folded tightly in front of her.

"Oh, hi. What's wrong?" He opened the school door and motioned her inside.

As if with great effort, she dropped her arms and honeyed her voice. "Just thought I'd come over and see if you needed any help. Can't I come see you without something being wrong?"

"Of course. You just looked and sounded mad." He must have read her wrong. It was cold out there, and her jacket was lightweight.

"Nope, not mad. Is there anything I can do to help?"

Mitch grabbed his briefcase and hit the light switch. "Thanks anyway, but I'm headed out right now. Something I can do for you, Rissa?"

But she was already headed out the door. He had escaped the daily supper routine, but he could still count on Marissa checking up on him.

11

Geri and Larry at the quik-mart were delighted to get a plate of homemade cookies and wouldn't believe that Suzanne hadn't made them. Two elderly men waiting in line to pay for cigarettes watched the exchange longingly. So she waited at her car and unloaded cinnamon rolls and an angel food cake on them. Taking care not to bump her bandage. "God bless you, honey. God bless you." Their cloudy eyes overflowed and for a moment, she feared they would hug her. Or worse, kiss her.

"Merry Christmas, gentlemen." She backed away, her finger throbbing to the beat of the Christmas carol blaring from the outdoor speakers.

What a klutz. She couldn't even close a desk drawer right. Just what someone like Mr. Sanderson probably expected from someone like her.

Thing was, he hadn't acted that way at all. He seemed genuinely concerned. She shivered at the memory of her finger in his hand. His gentle hand. His compassionate touch.

The staff at the New Loveland library welcomed the rest of the baked goodies, not waiting for Suzanne's departure to dig in. Finally she drove home where she was blessedly alone. Karen had already moved in with Trevor's sister and brother-in-law.

She kicked off her shoes and flopped on the olive green sofa. Brrr. Thin whispers of wind sneaked in around the windows, and she wrapped herself in her most recently crocheted afghan. It still surprised her after twelve years that she had learned to like this couch so well. It was secondhand—maybe thirdhand—and she didn't do hand-me-downs. When she moved here, the Stricklers were redecorating their living room and decided it would be easier to bring their old couch here than to haul it to the dump. Suzanne hadn't wanted it, but common sense made her take it. Her meager savings was earmarked for paying off student loans, not for respectable furniture.

The ugly green monster had served her well over the years. But the only reason she would try to take it with her was to keep Bob from withholding her deposit for leaving trash.

Thirteen days till the end of the year, when she had to be moved out. She didn't want to be here that long, but had no choice. If she moved into the trailer before the beginning of January, she would have to pay a full month's rent.

The transition had disturbed Suzanne a great deal until Aunt Eva convinced her to ask Bob for another day here. When she talked to him and explained the situation, he was more agreeable than she'd ever seen him. "Oh, sure. The remodeling crew can't get there until mid February. I got a few things to do before they come, but we got plans New Years Day and all weekend. So if you haul everything out on the first, I won't charge you any extra."

This moment was a luxury. Peace and quiet. No pressing duties. She had left school with only her purse and the baked goodies. The girls—bless their hearts—had washed up the dishes, which Suzanne had then left at school with her Christmas gifts.

She could start packing tonight, but why? No reason to start packing until the week after Christmas. What little she had would be easier to use from drawers and cupboards than out of packing boxes.

Double brrr. She snuggled deeper into the afghan and tucked her feet up under her skirt. If only it weren't so expensive to run the furnace. She ought to get up and do something to keep warm, but she couldn't think what. So she shivered and calculated.

The deposit she'd get back from Bob was more than what she already put down for the trailer. Not as much as she spent on Christmas gifts, but then the trailer rent was less than here, so she should be able to pay off the credit card bill right away. It didn't help that Karen hadn't paid her full month's share. It did help that Suzanne had received a sizeable Christmas bonus. The largest in years—a timely miracle. It also helped that she could expect a monetary gift from Aunt Eva.

In the wee hours of Saturday morning Joy called. "You up?"

"I am now. What time is it?" Suzanne rubbed the soggy bandage on her split fingernail.

"Four-thirty."

"What? Oh, right. The airport. Good thing you called. I fell asleep on the couch without setting an alarm. I'll be there at five. That's still okay, right?"

"We'll have everyone loaded and ready to go."

It was still dark when Suzanne got back home and reclaimed her spot under the crocheted blanket. But the heat she'd generated during the night had fled. She couldn't get her feet warm, so at eight o'clock she gave up and started cleaning. The couch ended up against the north living room wall. As she vacuumed where it had always set, she couldn't help noticing how much better the room looked arranged that way. And she hadn't discovered it until it was time to leave. She unplugged the sweeper and sat on the edge of the sofa.

"You're kind of like Mr. Sanderson," she told it. "When I first heard he was our new principal, I didn't like it. But he's not nearly as bad as I expected. In fact, he isn't bad at all. Nothing like I expected a Sanderson to be."

Suzanne stood abruptly and viewed the room. How pathetic. Talking to the furniture. A conversation with a cat or even herself would be better than that. She held her lips shut and went back to work thinking about Mitchell.

He was relatively pleasant to work with. A little too chatty for her taste, but extremely polite, thoughtful, and helpful. And she could still feel his touch on her hand.

She definitely got more sleep these days. She still stayed several hours past three each afternoon and tried to get to school by six-thirty or seven. But she hadn't put in a five a.m. to nine p.m. day since late October. Neither had she gotten a cold from the many that always went around. Not even a too-much-stress-not-enough-rest sore throat.

Best of all, in the weeks since he'd taken over the science and social studies classes, the class averages had come up. In every subject, which meant that Suzanne hadn't been giving sufficient teaching time when she had the whole load.

The only negative was the new frequent visitor he attracted. Every time she turned around, Marissa was there. Reminding her of that scared, stupid, little person she thought she left behind years ago.

By nightfall she had the house cleaned and wandered around trying to decide what to do. She could cut out and start sewing on a new dress. Grandma used to say, "Never cut out a dress on Saturday, or you won't live to wear it." That wasn't Suzanne's reason for not beginning a sewing project today. She didn't want to mess up her clean house. Besides, she had a couple of days next week planned for sewing.

Making her own clothes was a pain, but with her stature and weight and clothing tastes, it took less time than shopping. Early in their friendship, Joy had offered Suzanne some of her sister's outgrown clothes. Only once. Suzanne would be content with a meager wardrobe before she would wear someone else's clothes. Her hand-me-down hang-up, Joy called it.

With nothing else to do at this time of day, Suzanne retrieved her full book bag from the car. Fiction—what luxury. As much as she loved to read, she hadn't picked up a book just for pleasure since the beginning of summer vacation last May. Yesterday at the library she had filled her bag with new releases from her favorite authors.

She read while her soup heated for supper. She read while she ate. If she'd had a bathtub she would have read in a bubble bath. She read until she fell asleep with the light on.

She even read in snatches the next week between completing three new outfits. Two for school and one for dressy occasions.

Thursday evening Suzanne slipped unnoticed into the eight o'clock service at church. Christmas Eve meeting was a special family time for their congregation. She appreciated the years Joy and Jason were around and drew her in as part of their family. On the off years, she sat in a corner and tried to be thankful that everyone else had family to worship and celebrate with. If she could focus entirely on the breathtaking realization that she was part of the reason He came, it worked. Focus on the wonder of God's love in sending Jesus as a baby.

She tried not to hear when the pastor said things like, " . . . and you women know nothing surpasses the thrill of holding your newborn infant in your arms for the first time . . ."

The one-hour service ended with the children coming forward to sing their practiced songs. When they finished, she slipped out unnoticed and went home.

On Christmas Day she went to the care center in New Loveland and visited the residents who didn't have family coming. It was surprising how many of them there were. And how many of those loved to hear the reading of Luke chapter two.

On New Year's Eve Suzanne spent hours wrestling the seats out of the Moores' fifteen-passenger van and into their garage. She wasn't sure who to call for help, so it seemed easier to do it herself—a decision she questioned when the job was finally finished. Replacing the seats looked impossible, but she'd jump off that bridge when she came to it. By midnight she had crammed nearly everything she owned into the van.

Not counting the large furniture, all that remained in the house were clothes for the next two days, the unread library books, a jar of peanut butter and honey spread, a bag of pretzels, a plastic cup, and one wooden folding chair.

Before daylight on January first Suzanne scrubbed the refrigerator, unplugged it, and propped the door open. She vacuumed the insides of cabinets and drawers in both kitchen and bathroom and scrubbed them with a strong Pine-Sol solution. Even the washer and dryer with the death rattles got cleaned to within an inch of their lives.

Several inches of snow had fallen Tuesday night, so the outside of the house looked fresh and pristine. There was nothing she could do to make it look better, and she hoped the conditions of reclaiming her deposit were only on the inside of the house.

Last week she had talked to her new landlord, Ray Grubbs, and he agreed to meet her at the trailer at nine o'clock this morning. The roads were cleared and safe as she drove the five miles in the loaded van. Her aging single-wide sat wedged between two that looked even worse than her own, if that were possible, in the small mobile home court that housed about two dozen lots, some of them vacant.

She backed the van up to the rusted carport, which looked shorter than the van, so she stopped and got out to look. With an inch to spare, she eased it in until the back doors of the van lined up with the concrete steps.

No other sign of life manifested itself in the neighborhood. Suzanne sat in the van and waited until nine-thirty. No Mr. Grubbs. After warming up the van for the umpteenth time and watching the fuel gauge drop precipitously, she got out and tried all the doors. Locked.

She didn't have all day, and that was no figure of speech. Using precious cell phone minutes and battery, she called Ray Grubbs. The call obviously woke him, but she finagled directions to his house and picked up the keys.

When at last Suzanne stepped inside her new abode, she sagged against the aluminum door frame. The last tenants of the aqua and white 1960s era trailer that she now had to call home surely hadn't collected their deposit when they vacated.

If there had been anywhere else to go, any other options, she would have spun out of that snow-packed drive and never looked back. But there wasn't. So she sucked up her self-pity, wiped her eyes and nose with both mittened hands, and ran to the van for the broom.

She checked the water heater first thing and thanked the Lord when she saw the pilot light. By the time she had trash picked up and the floor rough-swept, the water was warm enough not to freeze her hands when she began scrubbing. She worked three hours to clear enough room for stacking the boxes and walking around them.

She drove the empty van back to her old house for the furniture. She'd been working on a plan, but she still didn't know exactly how she could get that sofa into the van by herself. Her twin bed wouldn't be a problem. The mattress was lightweight foam, and the frame disassembled easily. The kitchen table with both leaves removed would stand on end on the two-wheel cart she found in Jason's shop. Same with the chest of drawers and the old recliner.

But the couch. It weighed a ton and had to be turned on its side to go through the door. And she was running out of time.

Once when she was a child, Aunt Eva had told her, "Good things come in small packages." Mother heard it and hastened to add, "But so does dynamite." Suzanne took that to mean her mother considered her a destructive child, and didn't feel complimented at all. Later she learned that dynamite is used to accomplish great tasks, not just to blow things apart in destruction.

Today she had to channel that dynamitic power. In the remaining three hours of daylight.

New Year's Day loomed before Mitch like an eternity. The kids had all been at his house for Christmas. They came Christmas Eve and spent the night. It wasn't that way when Marilyn was alive. Not since Marci got married, anyway. Marilyn insisted that the kids needed to start traditions within their young families, and she and Mitch returned to having their own special Christmas Eve time.

Last year Marissa had ordered everyone back to the home place. "For Dad's sake, you can all sacrifice one evening a year. Think about what he's going through. We can't leave him there alone." This year was the same, and not until they all left Friday evening had he wondered why everyone had to abandon their family traditions. He could go to one of their homes, take turns each year, save the hassle.

He did all his shopping online this year between studying high school science and social studies lessons. He'd ordered everything gift-wrapped and paid the shipping costs to get it delivered in time.

Mitch wanted to prepare the whole Christmas dinner. His skills were improving by the week.

Marissa objected. "No way. Marci and I've already planned everything and told Kelly and Janelle what to bring too."

It wasn't worth an argument. He used the four days before Christmas to read his school textbooks. He brought all his personal and business accounting up to date.

He insisted that the kids do something with their own families for New Year's Day and recognized the weakness in their protests. Now he had the whole day and nothing much to do. He could cook, but who would eat? He could organize business files, but they were already in order. He'd already cleaned house and washed clothes. And shoveled snow and changed the oil in the truck.

This'd be a good day to stop by and talk to Jason Moore about his projections for the year. Mitch called and got a recorded greeting. They could be out sledding on the hill behind the house, so he drove over anyway. Nobody answered the doorbell at either side of the house. He checked the snow-covered hill and found it recently used but currently unoccupied.

The Moores weren't home, but a familiar green Toyota sat beside the garage. Did Suzanne live here? He tried to remember where she lived and drew a blank. The car appeared to have been parked before the snow.

It wasn't his business, so he trekked back to his truck. At the end of the lane he waited for a full-size van approaching from the east. It looked like Jason's vehicle, but made no sign of slowing for the lane. As it passed, Mitch recognized Suzanne Bloomer in the driver's seat. He waved, but she didn't look his way.

He followed her to one of Bob Hopkins' rentals. Would she be talkative or reserved today? By the time he parked the truck, she was out of the van and into the house. She didn't knock before entering, so she either lived here or felt quite comfortable with whoever did.

Mitch stood at the bottom of the chipped concrete steps. Should he knock? She had to have seen him. Would she even say hello?

He thought back to Christmas Eve at church. Martin had sent him to the car for Chloe's blankie at the end of the service, and on his way back Mitch saw Suzanne ducking out. He waved and called her name, but she hadn't responded.

It wouldn't hurt to wait a couple of minutes. He did want to know if Jason was around.

"Mr. Sanderson?" Suzanne's voice broke in on his thoughts. "Sorry. I had to run in and—well, take care of some things. Can I help you?"

So that's how it would be today. All business.

"Hi. I'm looking for Jason. Is that his van?"

"Yes. They're in California until next Wednesday. Do you need the van?"

He explained why he had gone to their house. How he'd seen her drive past and followed her here.

Then he realized she was pacing the four-foot square porch. "I am so sorry, Suzanne, you must be freezing and here I stand running my mouth. Do you live here?"

"Not really. Come on in." She held the door and motioned him in.

Not really? You either lived in a house or you didn't.

The house was bare save a pile of furniture in the middle of what might have been a living room. The kitchen cabinets and the refrigerator hung open, revealing their emptiness.

"You moving in?"

She gave a dry chuckle. "Don't I wish. I'm moving out."

Mitch looked outside. "Today? Who's helping you?"

Her expression faltered. Then she straightened her shoulders. "It's not a big deal. I don't have much."

"That all stays here?" He nodded at the furniture.

"Um . . . no, it goes. I need to have everything out by dark. So I'd better get busy, if you'll excuse me." She picked up a wooden rocking chair and carried it to the door.

Instead of asking if she was out of her mind, he propped the door open and raced to the van, opening the rear doors. He didn't take the chair from her, but she wouldn't carry another load like that alone.

A thousand questions popped onto his tongue, but he swallowed them all. Not now. He followed her back into the house and put his hand up when she reached for the bed frame.

"If we're going to get this sofa in, it'd better go first." He stopped and read her face. "Don't you think?"

"That's the problem. I didn't think. Or maybe I thought too much. You're right." Suzanne squatted in readiness to lift the end of the monstrosity nearest the door.

He stooped and took his end. Whoa. Way too heavy. Not to mention ugly. He put it down and reached for his phone. "There's no way you and I can load this. I'll call—" *Marc,* he almost said, but remembered how Suzanne had stiffened at that name. "My son Martin. He'll be over in a jiff. Sit down a minute, will you. You look all worn out."

She started to protest, then dropped limply onto the couch. Mitch closed the outside door and put in the call to a willing Martin. After pacing the floor for a minute, he perched on the other end of the long couch. She unzipped her coat and peeled off her gloves. "It's warm in here for the furnace not having run all day." She offered a shaky smile.

"So . . . where are you moving to?"

"Not far. About five miles. I'll be a little farther from school, but it's not too bad."

He tried again. "How long did you live here?"

"Twelve years last August."

"Too bad it took you that long to find something nicer. I mean, I'm sure you had it fixed up nice in here, but this isn't Bob's best-kept rental house. Is your new place in the country? Or is it in New Loveland? Farmersburg? Or maybe—" There he was, doing it again. It used to drive Marilyn crazy. "Do I have any other choices?" she'd ask.

"It's on the south edge of New Loveland. West side of Clayton Road." She stood, apparently reenergized, and propped the door. "There's a car. That was fast."

"He and the twins were out looking for deer a couple of miles from here. Tell you what, if you can keep the boys out of our way, we'll take this thing out. It'll have to go out sideways." How in the world had she planned to do it alone?

In no time he and Martin had the van loaded with the largest pieces of furniture. Mitch didn't want to pile too much stuff together and get something scratched, but Suzanne assured him a few more scratches would never be noticed. He sent his son and grandsons to their Tahoe. They'd follow and help unload before going back to stalk wildlife.

"You want me to drive? Keys in the van?"

"It's okay. I'll drive. I know the way."

He buckled into the front passenger seat without a word. She handled the van expertly, and his mouth dropped open when she pulled into a trailer park. Surely she wasn't stopping here.

The trailer she pointed to resembled an enormous rusty soup can. "Suzanne Bloomer! You're not moving here, are you? This is not better than where you came from."

"Never said it was, but I'll have lots of opportunity to witness for the Lord here, won't I? Anyway, I'll just park on the street so we can maneuver the furniture.

Martin pulled up facing the van, an incredulous look on his face.

Mitch stepped out. "Suzanne, how about you go sit with the boys while we put this stuff in. Then you can come tell us where everything goes."

The inside didn't look much better than the outside. But it smelled like somebody had cleaned recently.

"Hey, thank you so much, Mr. Sanderson and . . ." Suzanne looked at Martin and his sons. "Mr. Sanderson, Mr. Sanderson, and Mr. Sanderson, for coming to my rescue. I'd still be over there wrestling with that monster." She looked around. "Everything will be fine right where you put it for tonight anyway. So, thanks again. I'd offer you a drink, but as you can see, I'm not quite settled in yet. Happy New Year." She opened the door. "I'll see most of you at school next week."

Martin and his kids took off as if under teacher's orders. Mitch wouldn't be dismissed so easily. "If I can't talk you out of living here, at least let me help you get some things situated." He walked to the kitchen area. A chubby ancient refrigerator, a two-burner gas range over a narrow oven, and half a dozen cabinets with a peeling linoleum countertop huddled beneath a layer of dust and grime.

"No. You've done too much already. There's not much left to do, and I'll probably wait until tomorrow to get started anyway. I need to go back over and do a final sweeping at Bob's place and take the van back to Jason's and get my car." Once more she opened the door. This time she stepped out, and he had no choice but to go. She locked the door and walked to the van. He followed.

She frowned. "You don't have to—oh right, your truck's back there."

At the empty rental house, he tried once more to help. But she insisted she could do it herself. As he drove toward home, his stomach growled. Moving was hard work. What had Suzanne eaten? What would she eat this evening? *He* certainly wouldn't eat out of that kitchen until it had been thoroughly disinfected.

12

Suzanne smiled at Mr. Sanderson when he got to school an hour after her five-thirty arrival on Monday morning January fourth. Now she felt like she actually knew him and appreciated him for more than being an efficient principal. Last Friday night she hadn't been so sure. Embarrassment didn't begin to cover how she felt to have the Sandersons see that dump of a trailer. But what else could she do? She'd prayed for help with the couch, and that's who God sent.

Martin didn't matter so much, but she saw Mitchell every day. She had hoped she was rid of him that afternoon when he left her in peace to finish vacuuming her old house.

She drove Jason's van back and started to park it in the garage. There sat the seats. If she'd had any energy left, she would have cried. No way could she get them back in. Removing them had been nearly impossible, but gravity was in her favor. Well, it wouldn't happen today. She parked, locked the garage, and took her car to the trailer where it fit nicely in the carport. If the rickety structure fell apart, at least it couldn't make her car look any worse.

Only the cold seeping through the car motivated her into the trailer. She hadn't seen inside this place when she signed the papers two weeks ago. Too late now. At least it didn't smell like smoke, and among all the foul odors, she hadn't detected animal waste. It just needed a good cleaning. Everything was old, but intact, and the electric and gas were hooked up.

Suzanne sat on the dear, familiar old couch and made a plan. Not a good plan because she was too hungry, too tired, too dirty to think, and she couldn't find the peanut butter. She'd drive into town for a chicken sandwich and fries from the dollar menu. Her keys were still in her jacket pocket, but when she went for her wallet, it was as lost as the peanut butter.

She turned up the furnace. As the warm air circulated around her, she curled up on the couch and fell asleep in the deepening twilight.

Gentle knocking at the door pulled her from an awful dream. "Suzanne?" The muffled voice came through the door. She sat straight up, heart pounding furiously. Where was she? Who was out there? Her feet landed on the floor, and she tried to look around to get her bearings in the inky darkness.

"Suzanne?" More knocking. "Suzanne!" She recognized the voice. Mr. Sanderson was back. Now what?

"Coming." She stubbed all her toes twice trying to find the door.

"Pizza delivery."

She found a light switch and peered out the grimy window. He held a large, flat box in one hand and a Pepsi bottle under his arm. "Hmmm, where should I put this?" He looked around and found the kitchen table. "This works. Don't go anywhere. I'll be right back." He returned with a pack of bottled water and napkins.

He set up chairs and they ate from the bare wooden table. Food had never tasted so good.

Before they stopped, they consumed most of the large deluxe pizza. She tried not to meet Mr. Sanderson's eyes. But in her peripheral vision she saw lots of questions on his face. He waited until they had swallowed their last bites and drained their bottles, and the questions began.

"Why here, Suzanne? Why now?"

She explained Trevor's upcoming marriage and need for the house. Mr. Sanderson didn't look impressed. "I'm trying to be thankful for the years I had there. It sounds like I may have set a record for renter longevity with him. It is his house. He can do with it what he wants."

"But why here? This is no place for a decent girl like you to live."

"It'll be better once I get everything cleaned up. I didn't expect it to be so awful. You should have seen it when I got here this morning." She held her hand under the table to hide the unsanitary condition of her bandaged finger.

"Have your parents been here?"

"No, they're in Florida for the winter. But it's okay. I'm a big girl, I can take care of myself." She laughed so he would know she was trying to lighten things up. "If you can see beyond the dirt, Mr. Sanderson, it's not so bad in here."

"Please, enough of that Mr. stuff. We're not at school. But even sparkling clean, I wouldn't sleep at night knowing my daughter lived in this neighborhood."

But she wasn't his daughter, and her father could sleep through anything. She stood and gathered up the greasy napkins. "Thank you so much, Mitchell. Now I have my second wind."

"I'll take this trash to the truck, but I'll be back. You can't get rid of me that easy." A minute later he was back with a new plastic trash can filled with cleaning supplies of all kinds. "Sanderson cleaners at your service."

Protests wouldn't stop this man, so she swallowed them and chose to welcome his help.

They dug through boxes and came up with a couple of tablecloths and sheets to cover the windows. There were no curtain rods, so she dug some more and found her pink-flowered hammer and a handful of tacks.

At six-thirty they began cleaning in the kitchen. Right after he took a fresh bandage from his wallet, applied it to Suzanne's partly healed finger, and pulled a rubber glove over the whole hand.

Suzanne would have been satisfied with a one-hour scrub job. But not her boss. When they finished, everything shone, including the refrigerator.

"Let's do the bedroom and bathroom next and call it quits for today," Mitchell suggested. He loaded up the supplies. "Lead the way."

By ten-thirty both rooms were as clean as they would get. After he left, Suzanne locked the doors, propped chairs under the knobs, and slept on the bed without sheets.

Mitchell returned Saturday morning with breakfast burritos and orange juice and helped clean the living room and the other room she'd use as library and sewing room.

"I'd stay and help you unpack, but I have an appointment at noon. See you at school next week."

In her limited experience with men, she had never met one as nice as Mitchell Sanderson. She basked the rest of the day in the warmth of his compassion.

Now, on this first day after Christmas vacation, it was great to see him. They were friends. He couldn't have known anything about how cruelly his two oldest children had treated her years ago. But he couldn't have missed how coolly she had treated him when he first started at school.

She wasn't big on making New Year's resolutions, but she made one this year: resolve to show appreciation to Mr. Sanderson for his kindness.

"Good morning, Mr. Sanderson," she said when he walked into her classroom.

"Good morning, Miss Suzanne. All ready for another year?"

"I'm going over the lesson plans, but I had everything prepared before break. How about you?"

"Yep, the vacation was nice, but I'm glad to be back. Is that a new dress?"

She nodded, glad he noticed. Had a man cared what she wore?

"Didn't see you at church yesterday. You weren't still unpacking, I hope."

"Nope, finished Saturday. I came late and sat in the back. My alarm didn't get set Saturday night, and I overslept. Probably the first time I've ever slept past nine in the morning."

"Good. You needed it. Did you prop the chairs under the door like I showed you?"

She laughed. "Worrywart. But yes, I did. I don't think there's anyone dangerous living there. They're mostly just poor. If they did get in, wouldn't find anything valuable. No computer, no microwave, no television. I don't even have a coffee maker."

"You still need to be careful. I'll get you deadbolts to put on both doors. I probably have some lying around at home somewhere."

"The chairs have worked fine so far." She turned back to her plan book. Mr. Sanderson was here early for a reason, and it surely wasn't to make sure she was safe. "Anything you need me to do for you today?"

"Uh . . . uh . . . no. I guess I'll move on and let you get back to your work." He turned to go, then wheeled back on his heels. "One more thing?"

She looked up and lifted her eyebrows. "Yes?"

"You had breakfast this morning?"

"No, I normally don't."

"How do you keep going? I've seen how little you eat."

"I know I should, but my appetite doesn't wake up as early as I do. Then I'm here with too much to do to stop and eat."

He shook his head and left the room this time. A minute later he reappeared with a small bag and an orange bottle. "Is your appetite awake now?" He set it on her desk and left.

It was. Wide awake and thrilled with the scrambled egg and ham bagel sandwich.

Mitch sat at the principal's desk and nibbled his bagel. If the other teachers had needed food, he would have brought for them as well. But none of them ever got to school in time to eat anything before the students arrived. He certainly was not showing favoritism. His responsibility included keeping the school running efficiently and proficiently. Things were coming together nicely. He thanked the Lord every day for leading him into this new phase of life.

He prayed too for wisdom to deal with Marissa. She still hadn't come to grips with his new schedule. Still seemed to think she needed to monitor his every move. When she heard how he helped Suzanne move on New Years Day, he'd been afraid she would hyperventilate.

"She asked you to help her move? Dad! That's absurd for her to expect a man your age to do her heavy lifting. Just because you're her boss doesn't give her the right to start running your life. Don't you see what she's doing? I'm going to call her and—"

"Whoa, whoa, whoa, there." Mitch was holding the phone six inches from his head out of respect for his eardrum. "No. She did not ask me to help her. And I think I resent that jab about my age. You'd better not call her. Listen a minute and I'll tell you how it all came about."

Even after his explanation, he could tell Marissa wasn't happy. She was so much like Marilyn in that way, transparent with her feelings. Never had to wonder what either of them was thinking. But, like her mother, she was also sure to get over it soon and laugh at herself for over-reacting.

The school phone rang, calling him back to the present. "New Vision, Mr. Sanderson."

"Oh, hi, Bister Addersud. I'be really sick. Cad you call a sub for be?" This teacher, whoever she was, was either in pretty bad shape or an excellent actress.

"Who is this?"

"Biss Kortney. Do you bide?"

"No. No, I don't mind. It sounds like you need to take care of yourself. Don't worry about a thing, I'll round up a substitute for you. Do you have your lessons planned for today? Where will we find your plan book?" That was another thing he needed to add to his to-do list. Learn where all the teachers kept their lesson planners or sub teacher information.

Her nasally voice said she didn't. She didn't have anything written out for an emergency sick day. Was she supposed to? Just look at their books and see what's next. It doesn't matter for kids this age. The stuff's not hard.

Her voice got easier to understand after she got going. Mitch figured he was just getting used to it until he realized the twang was fading. Oh, well. Give her another day off. No use arguing.

"Get some rest, Miss Kortney. I'll see you in here tomorrow, okay?"

He checked the clock. Five after seven. Today he would teach second and third grades as well as science and social studies to the high school. If Suzanne could do it, so could he.

He made a few more notes on his to-do list and sprinted to Kortney's room to plan some lessons.

13

The lack of enthusiasm from her class on the first day back from vacation neither surprised nor hurt Suzanne. That the day was a Monday didn't help the teenage attitudes in the least.

Tutoring didn't resume until Thursday, so she finished all her afterschool work by four o'clock and tried to find more useful tasks. Home alone didn't sound so inviting anymore. She opened the Classroom Manual to reread the motivation chapters she'd run out of time for last summer.

Half of her pbj from lunch waited in her lunch bag, and she'd seen a bag of chips in the kitchen with a sticky note that read, *For the teacher's. Merry Christmas.* The unnecessary apostrophe almost made them unappetizing. Almost. She dumped some into a disposable bowl and took a Pepsi from the fridge.

Mr. Sanderson popped into the room. He leaned against the counter and wiped his forehead in an exaggerated gesture of exhaustion. "How did you do it? And for all those weeks. I barely made it through one day."

"So you're not ready to trade jobs with Kortney?"

"Oh, I think I might be able to teach just six second graders and six third graders each day. But covering all my classes too? If she's not back tomorrow, I'm calling a sub. I have a whole new respect for what you did in between principals, and I always thought it was a lot." He helped himself to a handful of chips from the bag.

Suzanne sat on a folding chair and opened her drink. "That was different. Seriously. High school students can be bought off pretty easily with sleep. I didn't have to watch them as much when they were at their desks and I was with other classes. I just didn't wake them up when they tried to sneak a nap. You can bribe a teenager better with promise of an extra nap than with extra play time."

"You're kidding."

"It's a fine balance. You can't tell them you're giving nap time. Nothing produces widespread wakefulness more than that. They think they'd like that, but it works better if you let them think they're getting by with it." She broke a chip and studied the pieces.

"Hilarious."

"Hardly. I'm not proud of my techniques. But I guess it did help me get through that time. It's good you came when you did, or they'd be all caught up on their sleep and I'd be dead from exhaustion."

Mitchell's cell phone rang in his shirt pocket and while he reached for it, she resumed her reading. She had finished the snack when he returned. He pulled out a chair and propped his feet on the table.

"You know more about teenagers than I do, and I raised four of them."

This surprised him? "Oh, surely not."

"I'm afraid I let Marilyn deal with all that stuff. The school stuff anyway. Did you teach any of our kids? You did, didn't you?"

"Only Marci in her senior year."

His feet hit the floor with a thud. "I should have come with Marilyn to parent-teacher conferences."

She didn't think about what she said next. "You two were really in love, weren't you?"

He nodded. "All that I am, I owe to my angel wife." He laughed shakily. "With regrets to Abraham Lincoln."

Oh-kay? Suzanne raised her eyebrows and shrugged.

"He said, 'All that I am or hope to be, I owe to my angel mother.'" He stood and paced the room.

"I've loved her since sixth grade. We both went to Farmersburg School and had known each other since first grade. Longer than that, probably. She was the most beautiful girl I ever saw. Inside and out." A tear rolled down his cheek. He took the tissue Suzanne handed him. "Thanks." He swallowed and bent his forehead into his open right hand.

"I'm sorry. I shouldn't have brought it up." What was she thinking? What did she know? What do you say to a bereaved husband?

"Really, it's all right. Didn't realize my emotions were still so close to the surface." The quaver in his voice slowed down. "Thank you for asking about Marilyn. People don't anymore as a rule. Not even my children."

"Surely you didn't get married in sixth grade?" Could she steer this conversation into a lighter vein?

Mitchell laughed. And laughed. Then he laughed again. "Practically. We married the summer after high school graduation. Last day of June on a Saturday afternoon at two-thirty in the church on Church Street. I was eighteen, but Marilyn didn't turn eighteen until September."

As Suzanne listened, she carefully closed the neglected book. What a love story. She didn't even know how her parents had met. Mother didn't like to talk about it. Every time one of the girls asked, she had told them a different far-fetched story. Suzanne sighed and propped her elbow on her chin.

Mitchell jumped to his feet. "You have work to do. So do I." He returned the chair. "I need to track down a second and third grade teacher for tomorrow."

She followed him to the door. "That reminds me, I need to call the phone company. And I forgot to notify the post office about my change of address. I hope Bob hasn't taken down that old mailbox. I don't even know my new address. I'll probably need that to activate the phone."

"1978 South Clayton Road, New Loveland, 45345."

"Yeah, right."

"That's the number on your trailer, and the road name. You can use that for the phone service, but could I make a suggestion?"

"Okay?"

"If you can get a post office box, do. Or else give the school as your mailing address. If you want to be sure to get all your mail, that is."

"I thought getting mail from that bank of boxes would be a good way to meet my neighbors. They're not dangerous, just poor. Remember?" And she fit right in. "But you probably have a point about the safety of my mail."

Mitchell waved back as she headed to her old house to check the mailbox. It should have Saturday's and today's delivery in it.

She found mail in the Hopkins's junk heap behind the barn. The rusted metal of the box crumpled around a handful of envelopes and a fabric store flyer. She collected the rest from the post office.

The last traces of daylight slipped away before she reached home and examined her treasures. A couple of bills, the usual junk mail, a letter with a hundred dollar check and a hundred dollars worth of gift cards from Aunt Eva. And a card-size white envelope addressed by hand to Suzanne Bloomer. The return address was handwritten too. KW, Muncie, Indiana.

She saved the strange Indiana piece for last. Curiosity wanted to rip it open immediately, but caution wouldn't allow it. Who did she know in Muncie? Maybe it was one of those mass-mail pieces designed to look like someone wrote them out personally for you. When she had explored all options, and there was nothing left to do but open it, she removed an attractively designed New Year's greeting card.

Her eyes dropped first to the signature. *Yours in Him, Kraig Wye.* Written in pencil. Who? Suzanne read the message printed above to find clues. *May the year to come be blessed with happiness and wonderful moments for you to treasure.* No help there. She did not know a Kraig Wye.

She grabbed an eraser and rubbed out the name. It was a nice card. If she could find an unused envelope, she'd fill it out and give it to Joy when she picked them up Wednesday night.

Jason and Joy's flight arrived on time in Dayton Wednesday night. He took the wheel and Joy the front passenger seat. Suzanne sat between Elliot and Francine on one of the seats Mitchell had kindly put back in the van. For the first twenty minutes of the drive home they all chattered animatedly about their vacation. They were almost to New Loveland when Joy clapped her hands. "Oh! Did you get moved? Here we are doing all the talking, and you haven't told us about your new place. Do you like it?"

"Yep, all settled in. You'll have to come over and see it sometime." Suzanne shook Elliot's foot. "How did you like the plane, buddy?"

After the service on Sunday, Joy rescued Suzanne from a school mother asking how to help her seventh grader get better grammar scores. "I want you to meet someone." Joy led her to the foyer where Jason had the youngest two kids and stood chatting with an unfamiliar-looking man.

Jason looked up with a conspiratorial smile. "Suzanne, this is Craig. Craig, Suzanne."

She knew enough etiquette rules to extend her hand first, as the lady. The smile on her face felt fake. "Hello. Nice to meet you, Craig."

His cool and clammy hand held the shake a split second too long. "Hello. It's a pleasure to meet you, also. How are you?"

"Fine." Puzzled, ready to get out of here. Not into returning the how-are-you volley. This was better than evaluating grammar proficiency? Suzanne sensed she should say something else, but what? Who are you? Why was it so important for me to meet you? Is that all, may I leave now? Please?

Jason and Joy stood there grinning. *Uh-oh.* Suzanne felt the red blaze up her neck and over her face.

Craig cleared his throat, folding and unfolding his arms across his chest. "I'm a friend of Jason's brother . . . I mean, I know Jason's brother's friend. That's how I found out about your church. I saw you last month when I first visited. I mean the second time I visited. But I didn't get to talk to you. Well, it was nice meeting you. I'll see you around, I hope."

"Uh, sure." She watched him walk away.

"Oh, Suzanne, isn't he gorgeous? And he's single. Thirty-five, never been married. Did you feel anything?" Joy followed her to the Toyota as Jason herded their crew to the van.

"Did I feel anything? I felt stupid. *Hello.* I've never met the man in my life. And you go dragging me over there with no warning of what you're doing. Did you think I would appreciate something like that?"

Joy grabbed her arm, tears puddling in her lower eyelids. "I know, but don't be mad. Just give it a chance. I feel it in here, Suze." She pointed to her heart.

"Give what a chance? Seeing him around?"

"I shouldn't have said that. Forget it. I better run now before we both freeze out here. I'm coming to see you and your trailer this afternoon. I'll be there after I put the kids down."

Mitch got to school at six-thirty Monday morning with two breakfast burritos.

Suzanne was standing on a chair at a bulletin board, humming "Joy to the World" when he peeked in her door. She hopped down gracefully when she saw him and joined him at her desk. "Good morning, Mr. Sanderson."

"Happy Monday." Mitch handed her a napkin-wrapped tortilla. "Got room for this?"

She leaned her cheek against her palm. "What did you like the best about her?" she asked before taking a bite.

This felt almost like a grief counseling session. Not that he'd ever done anything like that, and not that he imagined any counselor would ever get him to open up like Suzanne had. Since last Monday, she'd been asking questions. As if she sensed he needed to get those feelings out.

"Like I said, she brought out the best in me. Always supported me, always believed in my ideas. Unless they were wrong, of course. Then she made sure I saw the error of my ways. I don't say that sarcastically." He washed down a bite with coffee. It felt good to talk about Marilyn again. "I recently learned that she didn't like to cook. I never knew that. She cooked uncomplainingly all those years."

Suzanne finished her breakfast and wiped her mouth with the napkin. "You and Marilyn had a perfect life, didn't you?" Anyone else saying it might have sounded bitter or envious, but he didn't hear a trace of either in her voice.

"We did. She was the most beautiful girl in six counties and believed I was the best catch too. I never told her otherwise. My dad's death four years after we married made the only wrinkle we ever experienced in our marriage." He swallowed. "Until two years ago when I lost her."

"Oh, and also, one other thing went wrong. We both wanted four children—two boys and two girls. But we ordered them in that sequence. Somehow the two middle ones got switched around. We never could figure out how that happened."

She patted his hand. "It'll be two years next Monday, won't it?"

"You remember the date?"

"Only because it's my mother's birthday. Will you do something special with your family? Go to the grave?"

"I don't know yet." Mitch stood to leave. "Thanks again for caring enough to ask."

Thursday morning over sausage sandwiches Suzanne brought up a different topic. It took her a while to get to it. Mitch noticed she didn't have any Marilyn questions for him, and she wasn't eating much. "Something bothering you this morning?"

She shrugged. "Probably, although I don't know why I'm making such a big deal out of it."

"Student problems? Parent problems? School board problems? Something I said or did?" He stopped when he realized he was making a list. "Do you want to talk about it? Sometimes it helps, I've found."

"It isn't a school issue."

"I promise not to keep guessing. I'll just let you tell me if you want to." Mitch laid his sandwich on the table beside hers. He would eat when she did.

"I'm mostly frustrated with myself. I got introduced to a visitor at church on Sunday, and now I can't help wondering what's going on." She stopped and took a bite.

He didn't remember seeing any strangers. "Who was visiting?"

"Some man the Moores knew. A Craig somebody or other."

Ah, men troubles. Most likely a single man. She was surely used to dealing with problems like this. He watched Suzanne while she talked, but she didn't make eye contact. She laid the back of her right hand against her neck. Was she blushing? This was one of those times to wait. Silently. He sipped coffee to keep his words in and nodded encouragingly.

"Anyway, Joy insisted I meet him, and afterward acted like I was supposed to *feel* something about him. She started to say something else, but stopped, so I have no idea what's going on. Joy made sure I knew this guy is a never-been-married single and quite available." She picked at the sausage with a fingernail.

"Maybe she didn't say the available part, but she implied it. So now, I don't know what I'm supposed to be thinking. Is he interested in me? Or is Joy trying to get us interested in each other? Maybe it's none of that and it was a simple introduction of mutual friends and I'm blowing this all out of proportion." She sighed heavily and pushed the sandwich away. "Thanks for bringing this, but I can't eat it."

Huh? "Have you talked to Joy since then?"

"Not about that. She came over that afternoon to see the trailer. Had a fit about the kitchen floor and appliances. And the living room floor and walls. And . . . pretty much everything. We never got around to the incident at church. I was glad, because when it comes right down to it, I'm not sure I want to know what's going on."

"Oh . . . kay?" Thirty-three years of marriage had taught him the futility of trying to understand women. But Suzanne was obviously distressed and he sensed it went deeper than not knowing how to interpret meeting a stranger at church.

"It's awkward. I have no idea how I'm supposed to act in a situation like this. Especially when I don't know what this situation is." She blinked and rubbed her cheek against her shoulder. "I have to get busy. Mrs. Miller just drove in, and I promised to help her with a bulletin board idea."

Mitch picked up her barely-touched sandwich. "I'd like to hear more about this, Suzanne."

She shrugged and walked to her desk. Mitch took the uneaten breakfast to the kitchen, wrapped it in foil, and put it in the refrigerator.

Lunch held no opportunity to continue his conversation with Suzanne and after school wouldn't work either. She had students staying for tutoring sessions, and he had scheduled a client appointment.

Marissa called Mitch mid-afternoon. "Dad, could you bring Merry and Landon home after school today?"

"Sure. I have to leave right at three anyway, so I'll just load 'em up and drop 'em off. Everything okay? You're not sick, are you?"

"I'm fine. Just bring the kids."

He would have dropped the children off at the end of the lane and let them walk, but the lane had puddles and nobody wore boots. He didn't take the truck out of gear when he pulled up to the house.

"See you tomorrow, Grandpa." They jumped out and barreled toward the house.

Mitch let his foot off the brake and aimed it for the accelerator, but a movement caught his eye and he went back to the brake. Marissa ran from the house, waving her arms.

She arrived at the recently slammed truck door, pulled it open and leaned in on the seat. "Sorry. I tried to watch. I wanted to ask you." She stopped and caught her breath.

"You need to make it quick, Rissa. I have a client coming in less than half an hour."

"Why do you have to spend so much time at school?"

"I'm the principal, remember?"

"You talk to her a lot, don't you?"

"I'm not sure what you're getting at, honey." Mitch tapped the clock on the radio panel. "But somehow I don't think we have time for it now. I talk to a lot of people. It's part of my job. And now I need to go get ready to talk to Andrew Sims."

She backed away, but kept her face where he could see it. "Don't forget, I have two sets of eyes there between eight-thirty and three. And I know how early you sometimes go when there's only one other teacher there. Don't try looking innocent. That place isn't as safe as I thought it was."

He eased his foot off the brake. "I'm a big boy, Marissa. I think I can take care of myself."

As he pulled away, she slammed the door shut. ". . . Mom wanted . . . promise," were all that he caught of her last words.

What had her so bent out of shape? So he was going to school early to talk to Suzanne. Why was that a crime all of a sudden? And dangerous—the woman wouldn't hurt a flea. If only he could have given her something this morning to ease her pain. His own daughters never came to him anymore with their relationship issues. A good thing, but he missed those days.

The consultation appointment took less time than Mitch expected, and at five o'clock he headed back to school for a chemistry book that he *might* need to study later tonight. On the way he hatched an idea.

Suzanne was alone in the school. She looked up when he cleared his throat in her doorway. "Hi."

"You about finished?"

She gave a crooked smile. "A man works from sun to sun, but a woman's work is never done. She just reaches a good stopping point, and I'm almost there."

"You have supper planned?" He leaned against her desk.

A slender shoulder lifted. "A jar of soup and peanut butter crackers. Doesn't take much. I considered splurging tonight and fixing a hot dog."

"Could I talk you into riding along with me to Kinko's? I need to pick up a print order and could use some company. We can stop and get something to eat."

Her face brightened and she started stacking papers. "Um, sure, I guess. Now?"

"I'll be ready when you are. I'll follow you to the trailer and when we get back, you won't have to drive home in the dark."

He whistled all the way to the truck.

14

Suzanne expected Mr. Sanderson—Mitchell—to bring up their earlier conversation, and she worried about it all the way home. She had surprised herself this morning by saying anything to him about the whole deal. He was easier to talk to than any man she'd ever known. Like she always wished her father would be.

He waited in his truck as she took her things inside and visited the bathroom with the rusted sink and shower and broken mirror.

While she locked the trailer door, Mitchell had turned his truck around and stood at the passenger side which was now only feet from the end of the rough walkway. He opened the door and motioned her in.

Her stomach tightened at his kind gesture. *Like a date.* She froze at the thought. No. Nothing like a date. He was a widower and practically old enough to be her father. They were co-workers. Friends. Not to mention that she was, after all, Suzanne Bloomer. A sudden heat rose from her clavicle to her forehead.

She climbed in and fastened the seat belt, watching his face as he walked around the front of the truck. Whistling in his off-key way. Not a trace of awkwardness in his features. She consciously pulled her hands from a clasped position in her lap and tried to prop one casually on the door armrest and the other. . . . What did a person do casually with both arms? The center console was down, but that's where he would put his arm. His door opened and she tucked her left arm discreetly at her side.

Mitchell flipped the center armrest up into the seat backs. "Does your outside light work? I see there's a bulb there by the door. If all it needs is a new one, we ought to find out what kind it takes. It'd be a good idea to have that working." He turned south on Clayton Road, finally buckling his safety belt. "How do you usually go to the Dayton Mall area?"

She waited a bit before answering to make sure he wasn't going to give her a list of routes to choose from. "I don't go very often, but now that I live here, I might take 35 over to 75 and down. Especially if I were in a hurry and it wasn't rush hour."

He stepped lightly on the brake. "Hadn't thought about that. That would make sense." Then he accelerated and kept going. "Oh well, this'll work too. I don't mind seeing the countryside. We still have a little bit of daylight left."

Mitchell drove with his right hand on the steering wheel and his left hand against his left leg. For the first several miles he pointed out an occasional field. "That's a Sanderson plot. That's Cooks' land." And, "That piece belongs to the Fischels, but we farm it." Then, "That is the field where my father died."

"What happened?"

He took a deep breath. "Something went haywire with the tractor's steering. It turned over and landed on him. Since no one was there to see it, we'll never really know the details." He traded hands on the wheel and wiped his eyes.

"I'm sorry. I never knew your dad, but it must have been a hard time for you."

"It was. I still miss him. Not every day anymore, but . . ." His words drifted off.

Was his mother still living? Suzanne didn't want to come right out and ask the question, but she didn't remember ever hearing anything about his other parent. "What about your mother," she finally asked.

"Within a year of Dad's death she moved to California to live with my sister. A few years after that she married a man from there."

She didn't know what else to say, so she rode in silence. After a while she realized that she was sitting with her arms folded tightly across her chest. She dropped them again to her sides and kept watching the fields and houses flit by as they rode in comfortable silence.

"How did your day go, *Miss* Suzanne?" Mitchell broke through her reverie with a teasing note.

"Just fine, *Mister* Sanderson. And yours?"

"Good. We had an interesting discussion in biology class. What a fascinating course. Which, of *course*, you already know. It gives me a deeper appreciation of God's gift of life."

This was the final week of the quarter, so they were finishing up the disease and the human immune system chapter. Had their discussion touched on the disease that claimed the life of Mitchell's wife?

"Biology has always been my favorite class to teach. I loved getting the students excited about God's amazing creation of life." She hoped he wouldn't think she was complaining about giving it up. "But I'm glad you're enjoying it now. Because, to tell the truth, when I had all the classes, I couldn't fully enjoy any of them."

"I am. Next week we start the unit on amphibians and reptiles and origin. Should I plan a day to take them to the zoo and conservatory?"

They completed the trip to Kinko's talking about their various trips to museums and local functions. The Sanderson family had visited a live nativity scene the Saturday night before Christmas. The same one Suzanne wanted to see, but staying home had seemed preferable to going alone.

As they pulled into a parking space, she realized with satisfaction that her hands lay relaxed in her lap. She hadn't thought about what to do with them in many miles.

Picking up Mitchell's printing order didn't take long and soon they were buckled back in. He started the truck. "What sounds good for supper?"

"I'm not picky. Even a fast food drive-thru satisfies me."

"What about the Grub Steak?"

"Ugh. That's the name of an eating place? It makes me think of my landlord. Pretty grubby."

His smile became a laugh. "I never thought about it that way. Red Lobster?"

Her favorite food, but she spent that kind of money less than once a year. And she didn't have it now. He would pay, wouldn't he? She guessed if he didn't, she could use her credit card. "Sounds good."

The restaurant wasn't crowded, and Mitchell asked for a booth in the corner. "Get whatever looks good, Suzanne. I'm paying."

She followed his lead and asked for water with lemon. She waited to hear his order and it cost more than what she'd been looking at. They ordered and settled back against the cushioned seats.

"Want to talk more about what had you so agitated this morning?" He picked up his silverware and unwrapped it from the napkin.

"Probably not a lot more to say."

"I can listen if you want to talk."

Since the whole uncomfortable meeting, all Suzanne had done was stew. She should shrug it off and forget about it, but she couldn't. The invitation was too tempting.

"I have no idea how I'm supposed to feel. Part of me is excited to think that for the first time in my life, a guy might be interested in me. Another part is scared that I'll only end up looking stupid for thinking he might be. The rest of me says the whole thing was my imagination. Nothing like this has ever happened before."

Mitchell sat there, head tipped slightly sideways, frowning and blinking.

Why hadn't she kept her mouth shut?

Finally he spoke. "You can't be serious. Someone as lovely as you must have men lining up for miles to ask you out."

She lifted her hands, palms facing him. "Stop it. Don't try to make me feel good. I know who I am and how I look. I've learned to accept that. Life hasn't been all I'd hoped or dreamed for, but it is what it is. Let's not pretend otherwise." She blinked away the moisture that she hated. She was some kind of charity case. Mitchell Sanderson's help-someone-worse-off-than-yourself-so-you-can-deal-with-your-own-troubles project. What had she expected? She closed her eyes and willed the stupid tears to stop.

A rough finger touched her cheek. "Suzanne," he said softly. "I'm sorry. I didn't say that just to make you feel good. I guess I *don't* know who you are. I see you as a beautiful, poised, intelligent, woman. For real." She felt and heard the sincerity in his voice.

Their bread and salads arrived, and she dabbed her eyes with a napkin. On Mitchell's face she read genuine fatherly compassion. "Sorry," she whispered.

He laid his hand over hers. "Let's thank the Lord."

Instead of closing her eyes, she watched him pray. "Thank you, Lord, for blessing us with far more than we deserve. Thank you for making Suzanne just the way she is. Open her eyes to the reality of who she is in you."

When he said "Amen" she finally believed he meant what he was saying.

"Thank you." She took a biscuit from the basket that he held toward her. "So you have poor vision. But I know your memory isn't completely gone. You have to remember that I am Jim and Carrie Bloomer's daughter. I love them, but they've never earned a lot of respect from the community."

He broke off a piece of bread and chewed it thoughtfully. "I know. But in the past three months, I've gained a new respect for your parents. They must have done something right to have produced you."

"You don't know my sisters, do you?"

He shook his head.

"Carrie is older—thirteen months—and Michelle's the same amount younger. They were what you might call 'early Bloomers.' Looking like teenagers at twelve and nine. They both had what it took to get a guy to look at them. And want to do more than look. They earned reputations before they could drive. I don't think Daddy and Mother ever knew what all they did. My parents were ecstatic when, at eighteen, Carrie got engaged to Walt Walker. He was rich, and Carrie had succeeded in doing what real women do, get a man. A rich man, in their eyes. They never did the math to figure out how a baby born three months early could weigh eight and a half pounds.

"Michelle managed to land a wildly successful used car salesman, hated by everyone in western Ohio except my parents. All that kept her from having an overweight preemie was the abortion clinic."

He shook his head as he chewed. Finally he said, "You're sure you're not adopted?"

"I used to wish I was, but the evidence is clear. I look too much like the family, and Mother and Daddy would never have purposely gotten another child so soon after the first one." Suzanne stopped as the server came with their food.

Mitchell looked at her plate. "You want to check that steak and make sure they did it right?" He waved a shrimp-loaded fork at her like a scolding finger. "I still say I'm surprised. I thought if someone attractive and poised like you was single, you'd chosen that. And I'm not saying that to make you feel good. Okay?"

She bowed her head in mock surrender. "Yes, sir. I guess I'm just a normal woman in that regard. I've always dreamed of being a wife and mother. A good one. With a good husband and good children. Six children—although I never specified the gender or the order of their births." She winked at him, and he returned a sheepish grin. Then she watched with fascination as he ate a coconut shrimp, tail and all. What would that do to a person's throat?

With a gasping cough, he spit it out. "Ugh. Maybe I should pay attention. Guess I'm distracted wondering what in the world is wrong with all those men."

Suzanne looked around but didn't see anyone. "What men?"

"The single ones who don't show any interest in you. Why haven't they?"

He meant it. His voice and his eyes left no doubt. Opening up just a bit would be risky, but the little God-nudge in her heart provided all the courage she needed. She swallowed a bite and sipped some water. He finished his shrimp and waited.

"At first the guys were attracted to the prettier, more popular, self-confident girls. Because I never felt like I fit in, I was sure nobody liked me, and what guy would want to go out with the sourpuss I became? Now I see how Tina climbs in her shell when the other kids try to be friendly, and it makes me wonder how much of my exclusion was my own doing." Her baked potato was getting cold, so she shut up to eat for a while.

"That reminds me. Did you see Tina at lunch? She was the center of attention and appeared to be enjoying it. You're doing a great job with her." Mitchell hailed the server and ordered key lime pie. "We'll share," he said when she protested.

"Did I tell you that she and Haley won't be staying after school anymore?"

"You didn't, but they did. Sounds like they're both pretty impressed with their idea of studying at Haley's house instead of at school." He slid a credit card into the folder left by the waiter. "Now, back to what you were saying. If you want to, that is."

"Well, my own attitude accounts for my dateless teenage and early twenties years. After that, I don't know. I guess all the good ones were taken, and I buried myself in my teaching and never met any new guys." Another bite and she would pop. "Here, I'm stuffed. No more."

Mitchell set the remaining pie in the smallest take-out box. "But you went to college. There were men there—surely a few without guide dogs or white canes."

"You're right, there were. But it was too risky. I saw how my sisters had been with men, so I went overboard the other way. I've been told to get out there and make myself available in other markets, so to speak. But that's not who I am. Guess I don't want a husband that badly. Call me paranoid, but it seems worse to be labeled desperate than to be single."

"Wow. You've given me a lot to think about tonight. Ready to head on out?" He stood and helped her into her coat. Another first for Suzanne. Did men really still do that?

"That was the best meal I've had all week. Thank you."

He set the plastic sack containing three to-go boxes behind his seat. "Remind me to give those to you when we get to your house."

They were within a mile of her "house" when Mitchell cleared his throat. She was learning to interpret his tone of throat-clearing. This one sounded like a nervous clear. "You made a comment earlier, Suzanne, that I'd like to go back to for clarification."

She nodded, fully aware that it was too dark for him to see her head moving.

"You talked about meeting that man at church. That was pretty rude of the Moores, I must add. But you stressed that Joy said he was never-been-married single."

Another nod, but this time they were under the mercury light at the entrance of Mobileville and he could see the gesture.

"Is that a significant way to be single?"

"Long story. Remind me to tell you tomorrow."

15

"Today is yesterday's tomorrow." Mitch announced the next morning. He and Suzanne were eating microwaved cheddar biscuits and bacon in the school kitchen.

"So it is. Now what was the question, again?" She took a quick sip of orange juice and wiped her mouth. "Just kidding. I know the question. The answer is yes, never-been-married is significant. In two ways. I'm not interested in someone who's divorced. We know the biblical teaching on that. But if he were a . . . a . . . well, a widower, he'd also be ineligible."

Hmm. "Is that biblical?"

"No, personal. Joy knows I've vowed I'll never marry a widower. I don't want to be someone's second choice. I don't like hand-me-downs. I suffered through enough secondhand things in my life. Now I'd rather do without than settle for used."

Well. She was entitled to her opinions. "Tell me about your secondhand experiences."

"I told you about my sisters, one on either side of me in age. Carrie was always bigger than me and by the time I started school, Michelle had overtaken me in size. From then on, they looked like my older twin sisters. I was the runty little sister. That was bad enough, but until I rebelled against it in my early teens, I had to wear their outgrown clothes. For years I didn't get any new clothes at all, just had to wear what they had wanted the year before. I called them hand-me-downs and hand-me-ups. I can't tell you how much I hated those outfits."

He didn't see the correlation between clothes and husbands, but he didn't say so. She had a way of making it sound sensible. "So you're waiting for a brand-new husband."

"No. Not that I've given up, but it's easier to accept my singleness and simply go on with life. When I pray for direction, it always feels like this is where I'm supposed to be. But that doesn't stop the pain. I miss having a husband and family. Does that make sense?"

He nodded. Perfect sense. "So, about this Greg guy? Craig. Whoever. Have you heard any more about or from him?"

She shook her head. "Not really. It's Kraig. With a K."

"I'd think you either have or you haven't."

"It's not that easy. See, last Monday I got a card in the mail. A New Year's card. The only thing written inside, besides the printed message, was my name at the top and a printed signature, a man's name. Written in pencil—how weird is that? I didn't recognize the name, so I erased it and reused the card for Jason and Joy and their family."

Mitch interrupted with a guffaw he couldn't hold back. "So you don't like using things secondhand, but you're fine with giving your friend a hand-me-down card?"

She looked up, her green eyes wide and sheepish. "Oops. So this morning I'm sorting trash for pick-up, and I find the envelope. With the initials K W in the return address. I'm pretty sure I remember seeing the name Kraig Wye before I erased it. With a K."

"Ahhh." Mitch stretched out the word as he organized his thoughts. "And that means . . . ?"

"If the card was from the same man I met on Sunday, and I add that to his obvious nervousness and Joy's excitement, I come up with a man who showed interest in me."

"And?"

"Probably nothing. Once he saw me up close, he changed his mind."

"If so, he's not worth thinking about." Mitch checked his watch. "I need to button up a few things in my office. Come along if you have time. Thanks for the breakfast."

"Certainly, you're welcome. Glad I could supply it for once." She laughed. "I need to stop by the supply closet. Then I have to get busy too. Thanks for listening to my silly troubles."

They weren't silly troubles and he was sure she knew that he knew it, so he said nothing. He watched her walk away. She carried herself in such a dignified way. What a delight to see her recognize how she had grown into a lovely swan from the ugly duckling she once believed herself to be.

At his desk he worked through his list. The issues there concerned all the teachers in various ways, but his mind never left the subject of Miss Suzanne. She dreamed of being a wife and mother. And that's what she deserved to be. For years she had given her life to other people's children. With little pay, from what he could see. With no interest shown to her from eligible men.

But now there was possible interest. Mitch had no idea who this guy was, but he intended to find out. If Kraig with a K was worthy of this beautiful woman, Mitch would do his best to make it happen. If he wasn't worthy, Mitch would find someone who was. For years she had toiled on the behalf of others. Now he would be the advocate for her dreams.

Before the eight-fifteen bell rang and the children's voices shattered the peace of the morning, he had hatched yet another plan. My, my. He was becoming quite the mother hen.

Maybe Marissa was rubbing off on him. That could possibly happen with all the times she dropped by the school to check on him lately. And he'd thought it bad when he only had to show up for supper once every four or five days.

Suzanne's phone was ringing when she walked in at home. She didn't race to pick it up. If it was someone who really needed something, they could leave a message. Most likely the call was not for her anyway.

The phone stopped ringing as she pulled off her gloves. Instead of her voice coming from the answering machine, all she heard was an amplified dial tone. Five seconds later it rang again.

"Suzanne Olivia Bloomer, where have you been?" Joy's familiar voice was a relief.

"Just walked in from work. Did you call a minute ago? Why didn't you leave a message? I would have called you."

"It's not working. It rings for a while and it's like I get cut off. I tried last night too. You weren't at school, and you didn't answer here. You're not mad at me, are you?"

"So that's why I haven't had any messages. I was gone last evening, and no, I'm not mad at you. What do you need?"

"Just to know if you're there. You home for the night?" Suzanne heard little voices in the background. "Hey! Get Fran some more milk."

"Yes, Mother."

"Sorry. I was talking to Amber. Will you be there all evening?"

"Yes, Mother."

"Ha, ha. Well, that's what I wanted to know. I'm coming over." Finally Suzanne would learn more about the mysterious introduction.

Joy burst through the door twenty minutes later wearing old clothes. She lugged a paint can and a Home Depot sack. "We have to do something about that bathroom."

On Sunday, she'd had a major fit. "This sink is gross, girl. How can you stand to brush your teeth over it? And that shower stall, I'm sure you washed it, but you can't feel clean after being in there, no matter how much soap you use."

"I've been brushing my teeth at school, and if I close my eyes, the shower isn't so bad." Suzanne admitted. "It really is clean. Scrubbed with bleach and ammonia. Not mixed of course."

142

"And the carpet. I hope you don't walk on it barefoot." Joy continued her fit. "Do you think they had it cleaned before you moved in?"

When Suzanne described the state of the trailer's interior when she first saw it, Joy totally lost it. "This is not right. You can't live in a dump like this."

Now she had paint to cover the bathroom stains. And carpet shampoo and a new toilet seat. On her final trip she hauled in a rented carpet cleaner.

Suzanne wasn't worried about cleaning the carpet. But the paint? "Don't you think we should get permission before we go painting the sink and shower?"

"You really think he would care?" Joy planted her hands on her hips and huffed. "Do you think he has any idea what.the last people done? Even if he did, us painting is worlds better than that. Come on, let's get busy. Jason wants me home before midnight."

There wasn't room for two women with paintbrushes in the bathroom. So while Joy painted, Suzanne figured out the cleaner machine. After going over the entire living room area twice, she still wasn't convinced it was completely clean. But if it got any wetter, it wouldn't dry for a year. She turned up the furnace and set up both space heaters plus the one Joy had brought.

Suzanne laid down a trail of towels over the damp carpet and stood at the bathroom door watching Joy. The larger woman had started with the shower, painting every surface except the lime encrusted fixtures. Now she was working on the sink. "This looks pretty tacky. It's hard to get it on smooth. The pictures at Home Depot make you think you'll get it looking like new." She straightened up and shook hair out of her face. "Better than that awful orange and gray."

"I'm not complaining. Do you think I can squeeze in there and put on the new seat? The old one's really gross."

"Okay, here's what I'm thinking. Take that seat off, but before you put the new one on, I'll paint the toilet. Do you know how to turn the water off? See if you can, and then get it all dried out in there. I mean the whole thing."

After they finished the bathroom, Joy still had some time left. And energy. So she ran the carpet genie back the hall and around the furniture in the other two rooms. "Just keep the heat up to dry it out, and wear your shoes."

"It'll be humid as a greenhouse in here," Suzanne said. "With extra chemicals from the cleaner, of course."

"I went to the health food store and got a special product instead of the stuff that comes with the machine when you rent it. I didn't want to breathe that junk." Joy paused. "Then I went and painted in that small, unventilated space."

"I'm sorry. I should have painted. I don't mind the fumes." They had finished all the tasks Joy had planned and sat on the couch with their feet pulled up off the wet floor.

Joy smoothed back her paint-speckled hair. "No, it'll be okay. I don't mind, it's just that . . . well, I don't want to hurt . . . gee."

"Excuse me?" Maybe the fumes had messed up something in her head. Joy didn't even let her kids say *gee* or *gosh*. "They're euphemisms for taking the Lord's name in vain," she explained to them.

"A, B, C, D, E, F, and now G. We just found out this week."

Suzanne shook her head. "I'm sorry, dearie, you aren't making sense. Either that, or I'm so tired my brain shut off."

"Amber, Brandon, Carlie, Denee, Elliot, Francine . . . and now . . . G." She patted her belly.

"Oh. Wow." This was the point where Suzanne was supposed to squeal and clap and hug her friend. Instead she used the back of her hand to raise her dropped jaw. "Congratulations, I guess."

"I'm trying to be excited. I just thought we were done with this. It wasn't supposed to happen."

Suzanne didn't know why it wasn't supposed to happen, but she nodded. Maybe if they didn't want the baby, she could have it. Him. Her.

"I'm too old to go through with another pregnancy. But . . ." She breathed the word out on a sigh and stuck her feet back in her shoes. "We have a few months to get used to the idea. I know the kids will be ecstatic when we tell them. They've been bugging us about having another baby. Amber especially. You'd think she might be at the age where a pregnant mom would be an embarrassment. We didn't have the heart to tell her it was impossible now. Good thing, huh? I hope it's a boy because none of the suitable girl G names would fit in our family."

Suzanne sat with her knees pulled up to her chest, arms wrapped around them. Joy was her closest friend, and knew a lot about her. But not about her feelings. Suzanne had been careful over the years. Careful to dole out enough benign thoughts and emotions to keep the friendship viable. But never allow access to her heart.

Joy didn't know how deep the knife went each time Suzanne heard of a new pregnancy. Each time she heard of a new engagement. Each time she sat through a wedding service. Fearing her time would never come. Praying for contentment with the life that was her lot.

I can't wait till Monday to tell Mitchell about this. The thought startled Suzanne and she gasped aloud.

Joy's head jerked up. "What? Are you okay?"

"Grace. What about Grace for a girl's name? It would go well with Francine, wouldn't it?"

They discussed names for the next half hour. Joy liked Grace for their baby if it was a girl. Suzanne didn't admit it was the name she had always wanted to use for her own first daughter.

Joy left at seven minutes before midnight. "It's snowing. I hope we get enough to cover up all this mud and blah. More would be fine with me. I don't have to drive anywhere this weekend or next week according to our carpool rotation, so let it snow."

She hauled the carpet cleaner through the swirling whiteness, despite Suzanne's offer to carry it for her. "I'm just pregnant, not handicapped. Besides, this thing's probably as heavy as you are.

145

Although, maybe I shouldn't mention it, but have you gained some weight, Suzanne?" She laughed at her joke and didn't wait for an answer.

Suzanne locked the door and, as requested, called Jason to tell him his wife was headed home.

Then she curled up on the couch in the warm, humid darkness and cried herself to sleep.

16

Mitch watched the white fondant landscape and thanked the Lord for the beauty of snow. The storm had moved in early Saturday morning and continued dumping on the Miami Valley throughout the day. At least five inches. Not a blizzard, but enough to mess up the roads. According to the weather map, most of the snow had moved north and east. Only a few fat flakes still drifted lazily on the frigid breezes.

If this had come during the week, they would have surely cancelled school. Church services didn't get called off so easily. Mitch was on the parking lot maintenance committee. Which explained his Carhart coveralls, leather work boots, and a hat with earflaps. When he reached the heated tractor cab, the coffee in his stainless steel mug wouldn't be in as much danger of freezing.

He'd attached the snow blade to the John Deere 7330 to do the large areas. Jason Moore, the other committee member, had a Bobcat for the fine work.

They completed their job in good time, considering the number of parking curbs to work around. Jason waved a good-bye and headed for the exit.

"Wait," Mitch hollered. "Before you take off, I want to talk to you a little bit."

He parked the tractor and motioned Jason into the cab. "What about this man visiting church last Sunday? Did you meet him?"

The younger man nodded. "Well, that's not when I met him. I knew him from years ago. Kraig Wye. You talk to him?"

"Just heard someone talking about a visitor. I was there, but must have missed him. Friend of yours?"

"A friend of a friend of my brother's. He lives in Muncie, but he's moving here. It was supposed to happen yesterday."

"What brings him here? You said Craig, or Greg?"

"Kraig. With a K. He's a civil engineer. The company he worked for in Indiana closed, but he got hired somewhere in Middletown. He bought a really nice place over on Jamaica Road between Germantown and Miamisburg. Pretty new house, huge for one person."

"He doesn't have a family?"

"No wife or kids, anyway. Thirty-five and wildly success-ful according to my brother's wife. We talked several times last month. He's planning to make this his church home." Jason gave Mitch a conspiratorial wink. "Between you and me, I think he has his eye on a certain little schoolteacher."

Mitch stiffened. Suzanne didn't like to be referred to by her size. He didn't understand. Most women would love to have her size, but hearing Jason's words, he got a taste of insight. Somehow the word *little* felt demeaning.

It also felt wrong to discuss this in her absence, but he needed to know. Mitch sucked in a breath. "That so? Tell me."

"Sure, but not now. Need to get home to help get the kids ready for church. If you see Kraig, make him feel welcome. He seems to have missed out when it comes to people skills." Jason exited the cab with a parting comment. "Nothing a good woman couldn't fix, I'd say."

An hour and a half later, Mitch returned to church wearing his best Sunday suit with a moss green shirt and charcoal striped tie. The last clothes Marilyn had picked out before they discovered the brain tumor. Today he wore them for the first time since her death.

He scanned the foyer, looking for this Kraig guy. Suzanne blew in from the cold. Their eyes met and she lit up in a warm smile. Mitch made his way through the mob to talk to her. But she disappeared into the ladies' room, and then it was time to find a seat in the sanctuary. He headed toward his usual place, then changed his mind. He waved Marissa away when she took his arm. "Go on, I'm waiting for a friend. We'll sit back here." The look on her face was priceless.

Seconds before the service began, a tall, dark-haired stranger entered the room. Mitch approached the man. "Welcome," he said and held out his hand. "Mitchell Sanderson. And you are . . . ?"

"Kraig Wye." His cool damp hand clasped Mitch's warm one.

"Sit with me, unless you have someone else you're meeting." Mitch led the way to an empty space, his new project following close behind.

Mitch was pretty sure that Kraig Wye heard little of the minister's message. Mitch had followed the man's gaze more than once and it did not lead to the pulpit. It seemed to be fixed on a petite blond half a dozen benches ahead with the Joneses' baby on her lap and their preschoolers on either side of her.

She still hadn't been able to say no. Mitch's mind wasn't on the sermon either. Instead he recalled every word of a conversation they'd had as they cleaned her trailer.

"Were those your nephews sitting with you in church last Sunday?" He leaned out of the bathroom where he was cleaning the shower stall.

Suzanne had been scrubbing the kitchen floor. "My nieces and nephews are all older than that. And not church attendees," she called back.

"You must really like kids, if you're willing to take three in a church service. I'm impressed." He stretched his legs and walked out to where she knelt on the chipped and stained linoleum.

She wrung her rag into the bucket and twisted her neck as if to work out some kinks. "I'm not much of a little children person. I like teenagers better. I guess it's good I never had any of my own, since they don't usually come that old." She scrubbed another block. "I do love newborns, though. And I like to think that if they were my own, I'd love them at any age."

"So who sits with you in church?" He pulled a new cloth from the package and knelt to join her.

Suzanne sighed and chuckled. "Lillian and Ted's children. I don't know how it happened, but Lil got in her head that she is doing me a big favor by giving me a *family* to sit with during the services." She italicized the word with her tone. "I can't remember when I last heard a whole sermon. But I shouldn't complain. Ted and Lillian get to sit and snuggle while they listen and take it all in."

She stood and dumped chocolate brown water into the sink. "Pardon my sarcasm."

He moved away from the splashes. "Let me do that the next time." He set the refilled bucket on the floor. "It's been my experience," he began slowly, "that people can only take advantage of us if we let them. Why don't you tell them you'd rather not babysit their kids every Sunday. Or any Sunday, if that's how you feel."

She shook her head. "It's not that easy."

Mitch threw his cloth into the sudsy water. "Maybe you just need some practice. Say it after me. 'No, I won't keep your children today.' Don't need to explain, just, 'No, I'm not keeping your children today.' You try it."

She blew out a loud breath. "You don't understand. If they don't sit with me, they're all over the place."

"That's your responsibility?"

"No, but it's distracting and if I can help make everyone else's worship experience better . . . I mean, it's either I'm distracted by having them with me or everyone, including me, is distracted by having them with their parents. Did you see what all they did during the Christmas service? That baby is only ten months old, but he can walk, and they let him go wherever he manages to wander." Suzanne washed three blocks to Mitch's one.

"Don't you think someone would soon say something to them about it if you refused to be used like that? Are you helping by letting them shirk their God-given duties?"

"I don't know. Probably not. But I can't think of a nice way to get out of it. Especially since they act like they're the ones doing me a favor. I'll keep trying, I promise." She rocked back on her heels. "There, done with that. Thank you."

Then she had turned her face so he couldn't see her features. "Maybe it is a favor. It's not all that fun being the only solo worshiper in a sea of couples and families."

Mitch's thoughts jerked back to the present as a chuckle swept across the congregation. He listened to Brother Herman's words to see if he could pick up on the humor. But he couldn't find anything humorous about Paul the apostle being qualified to speak with authority on suffering. A look at Kraig's face indicated he had missed the joke too. The man's eyes were again on a trim, green-clad figure following three bobbing tots down the aisle. Suzanne's head was bowed as she hurried out, but her face was visible—and flushed. Was she sick?

He'd thought a lot about her sitting alone in church. Until Marilyn died, Mitch had never realized how family-oriented they were at Farmersburg Grace. He hadn't experienced it like Suzanne did, since his whole family supported him even in Marilyn's absence. This was the first Sunday of his widowerhood that he hadn't sat with any of his children.

The congregation had a singles ministry of sorts, but it was more of an older youth group and consisted of kids in their late teens and college students. Mitch's eyes scanned the crowd now. Pretty obvious why Suzanne chose not to join the singles' group. But did she fit in any of the other groups in the church community? Young married couples? Empty nesters? Moms with preschoolers? Over sixty couples? Widows and widowers? It was a wonder she hadn't found another church by now. One that made an effort to include her.

Surreptitiously he examined the man to his right. Well-groomed, check. Well-used Bible, check. Able to care for a wife financially, according to Jason, check. No nervous tics, check. He couldn't count the handshake texture and temperature on a day this cold, but the grip had been firm. There was only so much you could learn about a person by watching him in church. If Mitch were a handwriting analyst, he could get more. Kraig's note-taking skills seemed competent enough, but the words were hard to read.

The man could sing. More than Mitch could say about himself. Kraig joined in the singing of the hymns with gusto. Probably tenor, Mitch thought. Bass might be a better sign of masculinity, but the voice quality and volume were positive.

After the service, Mitch learned that Kraig had driven the two hours from Indiana this morning, after spending the night with his parents south of Muncie. His mother didn't want him to drive in the snow, but he'd persuaded her that the roads were clear this morning. He had to go back this afternoon after he unloaded his car at the new house.

"What are you doing for lunch?" Mitch asked when Kraig stopped for a breath.

It's not personal, Suzanne tried to tell herself, but herself didn't think that made any difference. She prayed repeatedly for grace to bear the slight and forgive the slighter. Sunday afternoon and evening stretched on for weeks. She should have gone to the nursing home to see her regulars there, but the car had only enough fuel to go to school tomorrow, and her boots had holes in the toes. So she found a book she hadn't read in a while and attempted to lose her self-pity in somebody else's troubles.

Monday morning she didn't realize Mr. Sanderson was already at school until he opened the front door for her.

"Good morning, Miss Suzanne." His perky voice ignited her last nerve.

"Hmph," she answered. Without looking him in the eye. He was probably still amused by Herman's joke yesterday. Along with everyone else in the congregation. Except herself, the object of the humor.

"Good morning, Miss Suzanne," he repeated, following her into her room. "Are you okay? I saw you leave the service yesterday, but I never saw you come back."

She hadn't come back. She'd taken Bobby and Timmy and Sammy to the restroom where she changed a diaper and supervised two potty visits. Then she snagged a sixth-grade girl and asked her to take all three boys to their parents. Then she went home.

"I'm fine." Physically, anyway. She pulled out her plan book. Couldn't he see that she had work to do? What did he want? Advice for raising children?

"What's wrong, Suzanne? You don't seem very 'fine' to me." Mitchell pulled up a chair and parked himself beside her desk.

The kindness and concern in his voice unlatched the portals of her tear ducts. She wiped her eyes and willed away the emotions. "What did you think of Brother Herman's joke yesterday?"

He wrinkled his brow in concentration. "His . . . his joke? Oh, sorry, I must confess I missed it. My mind was not on the sermon at all. At one point I thought I heard some laughter, but I have no idea what he said. Want to fill me in?"

She bowed her head and shook it. "Not really," she whispered.

He laid a hand on her shoulder and gently squeezed.

She did want to talk to someone about it. Who else would see it even remotely like she did? Mitchell might not, but if she didn't talk about it, she would explode. She raised her head, but couldn't meet his brown-eyed gaze.

"I'm probably the only one who found it offensive." Suzanne breathed deeply. "He was talking something about how Paul was qualified to talk to suffering people. Then he explained how someone in financial trouble would feel better after talking to a person who'd survived the same troubles. Then he said—"

Someone had pulled in. Who would be here this early on a Monday morning? Whoever it was, she didn't want them walking past her open classroom door and seeing her fall apart. "Can we finish this later? Someone's coming."

Mitchell stood quickly and put the chair away. "I'll go see who it is. If it's just another teacher with work to do in her classroom, I'll let you know."

He knocked on her door frame a few minutes later. "Coast clear. Miss Lana's feeling super energetic this morning, I guess. Why don't you come into my office and we'll close the door."

Mitchell recapped what Suzanne had already told him. He had the details exactly as she'd said them. "So then he said . . . ?" he prompted.

"He said, and these may not be the exact words, but something like, 'And we all know that if you want to know how to raise children, ask a single person who doesn't have children. They're the ones who think they have all the answers.' Then everyone laughed."

The room was silent. After a moment she looked up at Mitchell. His eyes were closed and he was shaking his head back and forth. Finally he looked at her. "It took me a minute to get it, but now I understand what he said. He was being sarcastic, wasn't he? I'm sorry, Suzanne. Are you okay?"

He asked for it. She unleashed her pent-up feelings and rewarded his invitation with most of them. "It's what my mother used to say. 'You ever want to know how to raise children, ask the old maids. They have all the answers.' Of course she meant they *didn't*, but they were stupid enough to *think* they did. So if anyone ever asks me for advice for their children, they have to get on their knees and beg for it, and then I try to be really careful. I mean, who am I, a nobody, childless old maid, to think I'd know a thing about kids." She stood and paced the small room.

"But that's not really the point. He was saying yesterday that just because someone is single and childless, they think they know it all. When of course, not being *real* people, they don't know anything. I resent that. Especially being the only single childless person over thirty in our congregation. It felt like everyone was laughing at me. Go ahead, say it, I was being self-centered, but why is it okay to make rude jokes about me? He'd never joke about a bereaved parent, or a single parent, or a handicapped person, or . . . or . . ." She ran out of steam and sat down.

Mitchell stood and turned toward the window. How stupid must he think her to be so upset by a simple statement? For several minutes he stood there, his shoulders twitching occasionally. He wasn't laughing, was he? Finally he turned and walked around the desk. He sat on the chair beside Suzanne and cleared his throat.

"I'm sorry," he said, and cleared his throat again in a tone she couldn't decipher. "I'm almost too angry to talk, Suzanne. Not just at Herman. What he said was bad enough, but a lot of people laughed. I heard that. As a Christian father, I should tell you that if you're offended, you should go to him according to Jesus' instruction in Matthew eighteen. Just between you and him. But I can't ask you to do that." He shook his head. "I don't know what to tell you to do about it with Brother Herman. I'll have to work on that. But there is something I want you to know." He stopped talking and waited.

"What?"

"You." He placed a finger on her chin and turned her head toward his. "You, Suzanne Olivia Bloomer are not a nobody. You are not a know-it-all. And . . ." He dropped his finger, but held her gaze. "You know more about dealing with children than anyone in that building yesterday. Maybe all of them put together. Okay?"

The sincerity of his words and tone sent a thunderbolt of clarity into her heart. This man's opinion mattered more to her than all the opinions expressed yesterday in the church sanctuary. She was overwhelmingly glad to learn that his laughter had not been among that she heard. Her head and shoulders lifted as if by invisible strings. "Okay," she said. Then wrapped him in an impulsive hug.

Impulsive, and not in the least awkward.

The phone rang and they pulled apart. Mitchell answered it and handed it to Suzanne.

She took the cordless receiver and stepped out of the office. Joy didn't waste time with a hello. "Why didn't you answer your phone yesterday? I tried calling you all afternoon. Can you come to our place for supper tonight?"

"What time? I have a student to tutor and then some grading and studying to do."

She agreed to six-thirty and returned the handset to Mitchell's desk.

When she reached her desk, she found a warm McDonald's cherry pie and a clear plastic cup of milk with a single ice cube floating in it. The hurt that had enveloped her since she left church yesterday morning was gone.

17

All morning as Mitch taught classes, the plan he'd agreed to with Jason and Joy occupied his thoughts. He wasn't used to allowing his personal life to invade his business life. But try as he might to keep his mind off the supper tonight, he couldn't. Joy had insisted on not telling Suzanne what was up. At first that sounded reasonable, but the more he thought about it, the more he didn't like it.

Hadn't the not knowing been what had Suzanne so distraught last week? It wasn't fair to let her walk into the Moores' house tonight without knowing the plan.

Mrs. Bower was blessedly absent from the teachers' table at lunch. The students stood while one of the high school boys prayed a blessing on their food. Mitch was still amazed that the kids were so comfortable praying like that. He didn't remember his children ever saying anything about having to do that when they were students here, but according to Suzanne it had been the practice since the school began thirty years ago.

What a shame that he had missed out on so much of their lives. And he had considered himself a pretty good dad. If he had been more involved, would Marissa be the control freak she'd turned out to be? She was so intent on micromanaging every facet of her children's lives and trying to do the same with her siblings' and her father's lives. What did poor Layne think about his wife's most recent conviction concerning birth control? Marissa had a *revelation* that she should have as many children as the Lord saw fit to send her. Now she had her heart set on at least a dozen. Furthermore, any couple with fewer than five, and no medical excuse for not having more, had *grieved the Heavenly Father.* That included her parents. Mitch had no idea how she knew about his "little procedure" after Marci's birth. But she did and was very disappointed that her dad had not wanted to have his "quiver full."

"Mr. Sanderson?" said Suzanne.

"Uh, sorry. I kinda spaced out there."

"I guess so. That was the third time I said your name." She held a protein bar from which she'd taken a bite. "You look a little sad. Thinking about Marilyn?"

"Not really. Well, I guess I was in a way." Mitch looked down and saw that he had eaten nearly all of his meatloaf sandwich. "Were you trying to tell me something?"

She blushed. "Another thought I had on this morning's topic. It's silly, but I couldn't get it out of my mind, even while I was teaching. I wish I could do like you men do so well—compartmentalize everything, not let your emotions spill into other areas of your life."

"Any new insights? Something else to add?"

She nodded, her eyes sparkling green against the green of her dress. "If it's so stupid for us childless singles to give advice about parenting. Not that we do very often. Definitely not any more often than childless married people do, but I didn't hear them being ridiculed for it. Anyway, if we're so out of place giving counsel on a subject which we know absolutely nothing about, why is it perfectly acceptable for married people to liberally dispense knowledge to me about how to deal with singleness? People who've been married since they were in their teens." She stopped and took a bite, chewing it rapidly.

"You're kidding." But she obviously wasn't.

"I shouldn't dump this on you. It's not your fault." Suzanne laughed and stuffed half the bar into a worn and wrinkled baggie. "Sorry."

It *wasn't* his fault, but he prayed he could be a part of relieving her of the burden of singlehood. Which was exactly what he wanted to use this lunch period to address. He touched her arm when she moved as if to leave the table. "Wait, if you can. I need to talk to you about something."

Her eyes widened and roses appeared on her cheeks. "I'm sorry. We got pretty loud this morning, I didn't have everything under control when—"

He held up a hand. "I didn't even hear it. This isn't about school. You're invited to Jason and Joy's for supper tonight."

She nodded, the blush fading. Then she frowned. "How did you know that? Oh, yes, I took the call in your office."

"I knew before that. I'm, well . . . I don't know how to explain this, but I think you should know what's going on before you get there."

Confusion lined her face until he told her he had eaten lunch yesterday with Kraig Wye. And then Jason and Joy stopped at Mitch's in the afternoon. It seemed Mr. Wye did indeed want to learn to know Suzanne Bloomer. Jason and Joy believed Kraig needed some help. So they were planning a nice dinner tonight at their house and had invited both Kraig and Suzanne. Hopefully a comfortable setting where the two could relax and learn a bit more about each other.

The remaining color drained from her face. "I am so glad you warned me. I'll be way out of my league. I feel so stupid. I never know what to say to a guy. I get all tongue-tied and sound like a total idiot. How am I supposed to act tonight?"

Maybe Joy had been right. Now Suzanne had all afternoon to stew about it. "I shouldn't have said anything. I was just remembering last week when—"

"Yes, you should have said something. This way I have time to prepare. I wish you were going to be there."

"I am."

"Oh, yes!" She grinned at Mitch. "You can do the talking for me. Plus, I'm comfortable with you." She stood. "I promised Tina I'd look at her research paper before—" The bell rang and she joined the exit flow of students.

How did she keep going on such a little bit to eat? He looked down at his own waist line. It was starting to look more like it had two years ago.

Two years ago today. This was the first it had crossed his mind today. He stared at the rest of his lunch sitting on the table in front of him. How could he have forgotten? To be fair, he had not forgotten Marilyn. He thought about her when he got up before dawn, thought about her often through the morning. He just hadn't focused on this being the day.

None of the kids must have remembered, either, or Mitch would have had a reminder before now. Not even Marissa had said anything when she strolled through at the beginning of lunch. Was Suzanne in the room when Marissa came through? If so, he was sure to hear about it. He didn't know why, but he knew it to be so. He took off for his desk, cell phone already in hand.

He reached Marissa's voice mail. "Honey, this is Dad. You didn't stop to talk when you came through. I'll call back when I get another break."

"Marci. How are you doing today?"

"I feel really gross, Dad. Kaylee must be cutting teeth, she's so crabby. I went to the doctor this morning because I thought I must have the flu. Oh, Daddy, what am I going to do? How will I ever tell Abe?"

A cold hand squeezed Mitch's heart. What terrible news had his baby gotten from the doctor on the second anniversary of her mother's death? "What, Marci? What's wrong? Do you need me to come over?" He flipped open his planner. These classes could be cancelled.

Marci giggled. "Sit down, Dad. Take a breath. You're assuming the worst as usual. You don't have to come, Abe will be home in an hour. I'm not sick, I'm pregnant."

"Oh." How could that be? She just had a baby.

"I know what you're thinking, Kaylee's still just a baby. She's only five months." Now she was crying again. "I don't know what Abe is going to say."

What kind of man went off to work and left a sick wife to take herself to the doctor? With a teething five-month-old? "He'll be excited, sweetie, you know he loves kids. He loves you too. Sure you don't need me to come over?"

She didn't need him. She probably hadn't even realized what today was. His anxiety subsided. They hadn't planned to do anything special today. None of the kids had called to insist that he eat with them tonight. With the snow on the ground, it would be fairly pointless to visit the cemetery.

Thankfully he already had plans for the evening. Not exactly matchmaking. Just making sure this Kraig was worthy of Suzanne's attention. Her own father should be checking out any would-be suitors, but since he wasn't, Mitchell Sanderson would do his part to protect this lovely lady. He hoped the end result would be the fulfillment of her dreams.

He checked on Suzanne after the three o'clock dismissal bell. She sat at her desk with the remainder of her lunch and glanced his way.

"You okay about tonight? Don't be nervous, just be yourself."

"Right, but don't be surprised if I don't say anything."

"Ask questions. Find out about his work, his family." He dropped to one knee beside her. "If it helps any, he's more nervous than you are. Fellow doesn't have a lot of self-confidence. But he seems like a good, believing man. Give him a chance, Suzanne."

"Ha. Like I'm in the habit of not giving men a chance."

He opened his mouth to protest the injustice, but Jacob's entrance stopped him. He would hear more on this subject later.

Mitch hummed as he packed his lunch for tomorrow after he returned from supper with the prospective new couple and their delighted matchmakers. That had been better than sitting at home alone this evening, of all evenings.

Kraig was smitten, and why not? Suzanne was a prize of a woman. A woman who had not appeared smitten this evening. *Skeptical* was a better word for her demeanor. But she had warmed up and shown her charming self once Mitch got her going. For a while he thought they'd spend the whole evening talking about Kraig's family, Kraig's job, Kraig's new house, Kraig's education.

Suzanne had real skill that way—knowing how to get a person to talk without letting the conversation shift toward herself. Mitch had been determined to give her a moment in the sun too. He had to be careful, though. He'd learned enough by now about her family life to know that she didn't share that with a lot of people. Instead he'd asked questions about her education, her teaching history, and her stash of interesting stories.

Now he knew that, although she did not have a state teaching license, she had a bachelor's degree in educational studies and another in child development. An amazing feat, since she had accomplished all of that in night, weekend, and summer classes. On the paltry salary she made at New Vision. That's why she lived in an ancient mobile home in the slums of New Loveland. It was all she could afford. Mitch smacked his palm against his forehead—how could he have been so dense?

He had assumed she chose the location. He had assumed she chose to be single and devoted to her students and career. He had assumed he had her all figured out.

He had assumed wrong.

18

Suzanne didn't feel the cold of the trailer or see the slapdash paint job as she showered and dressed for bed. The evening had been quite enjoyable despite her earlier trepidation. For once in her life she hadn't made a complete idiot of herself in the presence of an eligible male. She was very much on edge when she first arrived at Jason and Joy's, but Mitchell walked in the door behind her, and his presence put her at ease.

Had something like this happened to her a year ago, she would have spent the rest of the night recording it in her journal. Tonight she had only the urge to share her feelings with Mitchell. They wouldn't have much time tomorrow to talk unless they both got there extra early. She set her alarm for four-thirty, brushed her teeth, and fell asleep as her head hit the pillow.

At five-fifteen she turned off the last inside light, flipped the porch light switch, and lifted the curtain on the door to check for snow.

Her heart took a flip and sent pinpricks to the tips of her fingers. A man stood at the bottom of the steps. She dropped the curtain and fell to her knees, reaching up to turn the deadbolt.

She'd been so adamant that this place was not a threat to her safety, but now she was scared to leave her house.

Call Mitchell. She crawled to the telephone and held it in the stripe of porch light that squeezed beneath the curtain. She'd thought it was silly last week when he gave her his cell number. Now she was glad it was an easy one to remember.

He answered on the first ring. "This is Mitch."

"This is Suzanne," she whispered, backing away from the door. "Sorry to bother you, but I'm getting ready to leave for school and somebody's at my door. A man, I think."

"It's me." He chuckled softly. "I was afraid I'd scare you, but I didn't have your number so I couldn't call you."

Her stomach and heart and all the other stuff relaxed. "What are you doing?"

"It snowed overnight and got really cold. My thermometer said five below. I wanted to check on you and make sure your car starts okay and everything."

She turned on a light and grabbed her coat as he explained. She opened the door to see him on the top step, broom in one hand, cell in the other. For a moment they stood there talking into their phones. Simultaneously they put them down and laughed. "Come in," she said, replacing the handset in its cradle.

"Let me have your keys, I'll get your car warming. I already swept the steps."

The sounds coming from her car didn't sound promising. "It won't turn over. But guess what? I happen to be headed the same direction as you. Would you like a ride?"

His truck was still running and nice and warm inside. Warmer than her house. He carried her book bag, opened the truck door for her and closed it when she was situated inside. "Sleep well?" he asked as he drove away from the cold trailer and dead car.

"I did. By the way, thank you for making last evening go so well. Kraig seems nice. Did you know he was going to ask me to do something with him this Saturday?"

"No, but I'm not surprised. I think he sees the beautiful woman I know and not who you believe yourself to be."

"Yeah, well . . . I did feel different last night. Thanks to you I have to believe that I'm not the poor little retarded Bloomer freak." She hadn't been paying attention, but now she realized they weren't en route to school. "Where are we going?"

"Would you like a steak bagel from the golden arches?"

"I think you're spoiling me."

"And I think it's about time someone did." He ordered at the drive-thru and handed her the bag. "I'm sorry for my insensitivity yesterday when I insisted you give Kraig a chance. I'm still surprised you don't have men lining up for a chance to spend time with you."

He was sincere, but what could she say? Wait long enough and he would continue.

Mitchell headed the truck south. "You carry a hurt from long ago, don't you, Suzanne? More than what you've already told me."

She nodded, then realized he couldn't see it in the dark. "I've tried to forget." She had never talked about it to anyone. Had never wanted to before this moment. An overwhelming need to tell Mitchell Sanderson engulfed her. "May I tell you a story?"

"Absolutely."

"Remember, the events of this story took place years ago. Most of the characters were teenagers and no more mature than today's teens."

"If you say so."

"You don't remember how I looked and acted back then, but suffice it to say that I was a late, late, late Bloomer. At fifteen I looked like a twelve-year-old. My clothes were not in style. Neither was my hair. I had few if any social skills, and I knew it, so I didn't mingle much with my classmates. I graduated at seventeen, and could pass for thirteen. At twenty-one I had a difficult time convincing people I was old enough to drive. But size wasn't the worst. By that time I had been working at the school for a couple of years while I took classes at Sinclair. That helped boost my self-confidence, and I thought I had outgrown some of my family stigma."

This all sounded mind-numbingly boring in Suzanne's ears. "I can stop anytime you've heard enough."

"Keep going. Please."

"To make a short story long . . ." She paused for his chuckle. "I was sure I had never been accepted by my peers in school. Goodness, I had never accepted myself. I didn't have any real friends in the church youth group either. Plus, I knew my sisters' reputations. I believed the kids would respect me at least for not being like Carrie and Michelle."

The next part was almost too stupid to put into words. She watched the darkness pass for awhile, trying to get up her courage to tell it.

"Why do I get the feeling I'm not going to like what you have to say next?" He flipped on his signal and pulled in the school drive.

"I was so stupid, Mitchell. I don't know if I can tell you. I've never told anyone about this. Ever." She unfastened her seat belt. "But lots of people knew about it at the time. That's what's so embarrassing."

He stopped by the front door. "Wait, I'll be around." He helped her carry things into her room and then went to park.

He took off his coat as he sat on the corner of her class table and handed her a sandwich. "You don't have to finish, Suzanne. I'd like to hear it sometime, but only when you're ready."

She perched on the opposite corner. "It's time." She closed her eyes and covered them with her hand. "I can do this." She took a bite and accepted the cup of juice, he pushed across to her.

"I had a crush on a boy. Yes, I was old enough to be past that stage. Other girls my age and many of the boys were already married. It wasn't the first time I'd had crushes on guys, just the last time. All the kids my age considered me a real dork, and none of those guys ever asked me out. But I thought I'd moved beyond the misfit years and there was this younger boy who'd caught my eye. A couple of years younger than me. The best-looking boy in the state." She stopped talking and ate for a while. Mitchell ate too and didn't say a word. He was probably afraid she'd stop the story if he interrupted.

"Not only was he handsome, but he was rich and popular and witty and had a really nice family. It seems so stupid and immature of me, looking back, but I guess it was pretty obvious to everyone in the youth group that I had a crush on this boy."

"They told you that?"

She shook her head and swallowed the last of the bagel. "I didn't know it until it was too late. I had no clue that they knew. I never even talked to him. But I let myself dream. Silly, huh?"

"I don't suppose you were any different than any other girl."

"Remember what we used to do for Leap Year?"

"You mean when the girls asked out the guys? Did you ask him out? If he turned you down, he was an idiot and didn't deserve you."

"I would never have done that. I wasn't brave enough. However . . ." She wadded up the sandwich paper. "His sister decided to play a joke on him. His parents said he had to go to the party with the first girl who asked him. So she and some of her friends cooked up a plan. One of them called him and said . . ."

Where was all this emotion coming from? Hadn't she worked through it years ago? Mitchell picked up a napkin and silently wiped her cheek.

"She said she was me. Because they knew that would be the absolute worst thing for him to do—go to the party with me. He fell for it and had to say yes to who he believed to be the ugliest, dumbest, weirdest, most retarded dweeb in the universe. Fortunately for him, his sister didn't let him believe it for very long. Only long enough for her and her friends to get a good laugh at my expense. Unfortunately for me, he believed it long enough to let the entire youth group know what he thought of the *loser* he had to take to the Leap Year Party." She slid off the table into a chair and bowed her head.

His arm went around her shoulders. "I'm sorry, Suzanne. So sorry. Did they ever apologize?"

"No." She shrugged. "They probably didn't remember it two weeks later. But I never went to youth group again. In fact, I didn't talk to anyone outside my classroom for a very long time."

Mitchell gasped sharply and turned Suzanne around with both hands. He shook his head and blinked rapidly. "Suzanne. We were the ones who told Marc he had to go with the first girl who asked. Marilyn and I. Those were my kids. How could they have been so cruel?" Dropping his hands, he walked to the window and back.

"Sit down." She grabbed his arm. "I'm okay. I shouldn't have told you. I'm sorry, Mitchell. It really and truly doesn't have anything to do with you."

"What kind of father would have kids that mean? I don't even deserve the title." He finally met her eye. "I'm a failure, Suzanne." His shoulders slumped and he practically staggered to the door. "I have some praying to do before school starts."

Suzanne's heart was light and heavy at the same time. Light for having unloaded a sixteen-year-old burden. Heavy for what she'd done to Mitchell. What a big mouth.

It took the rest of Monday and all of Tuesday and Wednesday for Mitchell to let go of the issue. And all the explaining and pleading she had in her.

It turned out to be the best way for her to get over the long-ago incident. She found herself on the other side, making excuses for them and finally placing some of the blame on herself.

They had been young. Immature. Trying to have fun.

She had internalized it. Carried the hurt. Never truly moved past it.

But it had helped shape her into the person she was today. Because of her experiences she could empathize with Tina. She could keep an open eye on the teens' activities and attitudes, and do her part to plant compassion in their hearts.

She didn't tell Mitchell how some boy had called her dad pretending to be Marc Sanderson. Wanting the "delightful honor of courting his beautiful daughter, Suzanne." How Daddy had nearly burst the buttons off his shirt with pride that the son of the county's richest farmer wanted his ugly duckling daughter. How Suzanne had to convince Daddy that it was only a cruel joke.

Kraig talked to Suzanne Wednesday night at church and wondered if the Air Force Museum might be a good place for them to go, as he had never been there. She had gone once, and hadn't ever felt the need to return, but she agreed and suggested they meet in the church parking lot where she could leave her car. She didn't want to scare him off by letting him see the trailer park and her lowly dwelling.

The temperature rose to almost freezing midweek, but dropped again by Friday night. Mitchell had taken her home Tuesday and determined that the source of her dead car was the ancient battery. He returned an hour later with a new one which he installed, waving off her attempts to pay him for it.

Thus her Toyota jumped to life Saturday morning in the five-degree air. Kraig met her at nine and they took off for Wright-Patterson and the museum.

19

All day Saturday Mitch found himself at loose ends. He met a few clients in the morning. In the afternoon he washed clothes and made a half-hearted attempt at house cleaning.

He'd pretty much kept his promise to Suzanne to quit agonizing over the past she'd shared. It grieved him that she had carried that baggage for so many years. He hated whatever part he may have played in her pain. If only he had kept a closer eye on his teenagers. If only he had spent more time with them, taught them by example more compassion, modeled a Spirit-led life.

Suzanne was sure Marissa had forgotten the incident. But it occurred to Mitch as he folded laundry that, deep down in her controlling little heart, his oldest daughter did remember. Remembered and felt guilty. Could that be why she lurked so often around the school, trying to keep him away from Suzanne? He needed to do something to get that lurking stopped.

With an idea in mind, he called his kids and invited them for lunch after church tomorrow. All except Martin and Janelle said they'd come. That gave Mitch something to do with the rest of his evening. He shopped for ingredients for a tossed salad and lasagna. By nightfall the veggies were chopped and waiting in the fridge and the lasagna was all ready to assemble and put on time-bake before church in the morning.

How had Suzanne's day gone? On his grocery run he'd driven by the church and saw her car still there. It did seem funny that this Kraig guy wouldn't insist on picking her up at her doorstep. At nine-fifteen he could stand the suspense no longer. Now that he had her number on his cell phone, he could call her. He was ready to give up listening to the ringing when she answered.

"Hey, you're home. I just wanted to check to make sure that battery worked okay." That was true. "I hope I'm not calling too late."

"Oh, no. This is fine. We got back to my car around six. I came home, went to the Laundromat, and I'm just now getting home again."

Laundromat? Why? He tried to picture the laundry area in the trailer, but drew a blank. Didn't she have one? The Wash-O-Mat in town was no place for a lady, especially after dark on a Saturday night. "So, how was your day?"

"It was okay. Not one of my favorite places. But at least it was free. And I had an Outback Steakhouse gift card that Aunt Eva sent for Christmas. So it turned out to be a very economical day too." A yawn swallowed the last of her words.

"Okay, glad to know that battery's working. Have a good night. See you at church in the morning." Mitch pocketed his phone and finished wiping down the kitchen sink. So Kraig took her to a museum she didn't even like and then let her pay for the dinner? He should give the guy the benefit of the doubt—maybe Suzanne insisted on using her gift. She wasn't likely to eat there alone.

Sunday morning Mitch talked to Kraig and learned that he was going to eat lunch by himself. Kraig didn't have plans with Suzanne, as it seemed prudent to take things slowly. Then Mitch talked to Suzanne. She too planned to eat at home alone.

Throughout the sermon, Mitch debated his next step while keeping an ear tuned to Brother Herman's words. If the minister insulted Suzanne again, Mitch wouldn't keep his seat nor his silence. But Herman stuck to the scriptures this morning.

His idea of asking Suzanne and Kraig to join his family for lunch was falling into place. It would be a good way to show Marissa that Suzanne was not a threat. And for Marc and Marissa to see Suzanne for the beautiful, graceful woman she was.

As soon as they were dismissed and a few people began standing, Mitch made his way to Suzanne. On his way, he stopped and gave Kraig an invitation that was enthusiastically accepted. He reached Suzanne just as she jumped up and chased three small boys down the aisle. Mitch joined the chase, catching and carrying the two bigger ones. Suzanne snagged the baby and pointed. "There's Ted and Lillian."

They returned the urchins, and Mitch followed Suzanne to the foyer. "I have an idea," he told her when they found a fairly quiet corner. "My kids—all but Martin and Janelle—are coming to my place for lunch. I invited Kraig, and he's coming. Do you think you'd like to come too?" He laid his hand on her forearm. "I'd really like you to. But I understand if you can't."

She stared at her hands and bit her lower lip, swallowed several times, then straightened her shoulders. "I can do it," she said softly. Then her voice strengthened. "Yes, I would be delighted to come. Thank you for the invitation."

He caught Marissa as she and Layne hurried to close the doors of their running car. All four children grinned from their seat belts and car seats. He leaned in her door and lowered his voice. "Just so you know, it's not just family today. I invited another couple."

She frowned. "Who?"

"Kraig Wye and Suzanne Bloomer." He watched the meaning of his words register on her face. "And I expect you to be nice to them." He closed the door and ignored her call as he sprinted to his truck.

Marissa cornered Mitch in the laundry room the minute she got in the house. "What do you mean by couple, Dad?"

"Exactly what you think I mean."

Her eyes doubled in size and intensity. "You mean . . . ? Surely you're not saying that Kraig Wye is interested in Miss Suzanne." Her tone of awe when she said Kraig's name contrasted starkly with the tone for Suzanne's.

Before Mitch could form an answer, Kelly called from the kitchen. How could Marissa be so blind? He wanted to confront her with her teenage behavior, but it wasn't his to confront. Instead he added referee to his hosting duties and kept a close eye on her and Suzanne.

During lunch the guys kept Kraig busy explaining his new job and the details of his recent realty dealings. Marissa seemed uncharacteristically quiet. Suzanne was characteristically so, but calm, poised, and beautiful. Mitch knew she had to be uncomfortable in the present company, but she hid it well.

She appeared completely relaxed around the children. She said she wasn't a "little children" person, but Mitch couldn't tell it by watching her with his grandkids. They flocked to her as steel filings to a magnet, vying for a seat at the table beside "Miss Suzanne." In the end, she sat between Kraig and Jacob. They both looked like they'd won the lottery.

After lunch while Kraig fielded more questions and the women talked about next Christmas's gift exchange, Mitch watched the children cluster around Suzanne to show her their favorite Grandpa Mitch toys.

Marissa and Layne left first, then Marci and Abe. Marc and Kelly stayed a while longer until five-year-old Brooklyn threw a fit and her mother insisted they go home for a nap. That left Mitch with Kraig and Suzanne. He fed the fire in the fireplace and they settled in. After some coaxing—but not much—Kraig took Mitch's La-Z-Boy. Suzanne gracefully pulled her feet up beside her on Marilyn's recliner, and Mitch took the overstuffed chair on the other side of the room.

Nobody was talking, and he couldn't think of anything to say either. "How about a game?" Seemed like a good setting for that with snow outside, flickering fire inside.

Kraig and Suzanne both nodded, so he continued. "Let's see, we have Rook. We can play that with just three, can't we?"

He looked at Suzanne's face and read her eyes, remembering that she wasn't a fan of the game. "Scrabble?" Mitch glanced at her. Yep. He found the game in the closet and they moved back to the table to play.

Mitch won his first game of Scrabble ever, while it may have been Kraig's first time losing. "I need to get home," he said when the scores had been figured. "I told Mama I'd call her before five."

And that left Suzanne. They played another round of Scrabble. "I love word games," she said as they put the letter tiles away. "but I better head home now." She stood and stretched.

"You were okay, weren't you, being here with my family?"

She nodded. "It scared me at first. But I prayed, and it turned out not to be so bad. This was the perfect opportunity to be around them with my new-found freedom."

"You handled it quite well." Mitch followed her to the entry way and watched her take her coat from the hall tree. To go home to a cold, dingy trailer by herself? "Why don't you stay and I'll pop some corn. We can even finish up that cheesecake and bread-sticks if they're not too dried up."

"If you promise to let me help you do those dishes first."

"All I have to do is run the dishwasher and fill it back up. It's— oh well, you win." He lifted his hands in surrender as she rolled up her sleeves, turned on the hot water, and squirted dishwashing liquid into the sink.

Suzanne washed and rinsed the dishes while Mitch dried them and put them away. Neither one had any problem thinking of something to say. She commented on the décor of the house and listened while he told various stories of his and Marilyn's winter travels to flea markets in warmer southern climates.

As she worked, she asked more about Marilyn's illness and death. Mitch found that he could talk about the fast-growing brain tumor and his sweetheart's last days without a knife piercing his heart. Six weeks and a day she'd lived after returning from

Christmas shopping with a headache and a confusion that had scared him out of his mind.

Mitch walked Suzanne through the details of those awful days. He looked over to see tears running down her cheeks. "I'm so sorry," she said and pulled him close with a wet, soapy hand. "Nobody close to me has ever died. You've lost your father and your wife. It makes my petty little disappointments seem silly when I think about the contrast."

Her words touched him somewhere deep inside. "I want to address that, Suzanne." He pulled away and laid clean spoons in the drawer. "The hurts and disappointments you have shared with me recently are not petty. My father died, but we had a close relationship. He was a good man and he cared about me. What you've shared with me about your dad tells me that you've been hurt more by his living absence than I ever was by my father's death. Same for my losing Marilyn. I had thirty-three glorious years with her. You have sacrificed for others over half your life, living with disappointments nobody knew about."

She nodded mutely, finishing the last pan. "Thanks. No one ever said anything like that to me before."

"Okay, let's get the popcorn going." He threw a packet in the microwave and when it finished they returned to the fireplace. This time he took his chair. She pulled her feet up onto the smaller recliner again. He tossed a handful of popcorn in his mouth and watched her pick up one piece at a time.

"Were you okay with this morning's sermon?"

She hung her head. "What I heard was fine, but I confess I didn't try to listen. For one thing, my 'family' didn't give me much opportunity to, and secondly—well, let's just say I'm dealing with an attitude problem." She picked up a kernel and threw it into his bowl.

"Good shot." He threw one back and missed. "I did that so you would feel good."

"Right. What a teenager."

"You're the one who just admitted an attitude problem." Mitch laughed and leaned forward in his chair. "I'm guilty of that too, but I listened very closely today. If he had made one hint of a slur, I'd have been on my feet."

"That would've been fun to see."

"But I didn't hear anything related to last week's joke. There was one thing I noticed, though, and wanted to ask you if it's commonplace." He got up and put another log on the fire.

"Okay?"

"Brother Herman's closing prayer. He prayed for everyone. Emphasizing *everyone*. Every mother, every father. Every wife, every husband. All the grandparents, and all the children and youth. *Everyone*." He looked at Suzanne.

"Yes?"

"In his mind he covered everyone in the congregation. But you don't fit into any of those categories."

She sighed. "Maybe I'm still considered a child since I haven't attained adulthood through the rite of marriage."

"It hit me this morning. He's probably prayed that way for years and I never noticed it." He looked at their empty glasses. "More cider?"

"No thanks, I'm fine." She sighed again. "That is his usual prayer. I try not to take it personally. I don't think he intends to slight or insult single people. We just don't register on his people-meter."

20

The rest of January passed with a paltry two snow days and—thank you, Lord—no Marissa at school. Although Suzanne imagined her presence wouldn't be so nerve-wracking anymore

It appeared that Kraig was part of Suzanne's life for the duration. The duration of what, she didn't know. After the weekend of their Air Force Museum visit and Sunday dinner at Mitchell's house, Kraig called and asked to take her out for Friday night supper. She agreed to go and told him to pick her up at school.

Saturday morning she took her laundry to Joy's house. There was nothing wrong with the Laundromat in town, but Mitchell had insisted Suzanne not go there alone. "I just don't feel comfortable knowing you're there," he said.

"Then I don't have to let you know," she retorted. He offered the use of his washer and dryer any time she wanted. Somehow that didn't seem appropriate, so she promised him she'd go to Jason and Joy's.

"Didja have a date last night?" Joy met Suzanne at the door and grabbed her clothes hamper. "Amber, go throw these in the washer for Aunt Suzanne."

She snatched it back. "She might be your slave, but she's not mine. I'll load these myself, thank you." Suzanne managed to arrive alone to the laundry room and put the whites into Joy's front-load high-efficiency wash machine, adding the detergent she'd brought. If she took long enough in here, maybe Joy would forget her opening question.

"Come on out here and have a cup of hot chocolate with me." Joy grabbed her arm and led her to the kitchen. "Fill me in on last night."

Suzanne took the drink and sat across the table from Joy. "What is it you want to know?" She was buying time, working on a way to give Joy some of the information she wanted without too much soul-baring. Joy talked to too many people. She wouldn't intentionally betray Suzanne's confidences, but she was too free to share what was on her heart and mind. Suzanne's private life didn't need to be there.

"Come on, Suze. Details."

"We went to The Dining Table. Then we went back to the school to my car. I gave him a tour of New Vision. Then he left and I went home." Suzanne leaned forward and lowered her voice. "He opened the car door for me to get in both times. But not for me to get out when we reached our destination. I had a chicken salad and he had liver and onions."

Joy wrinkled her nose. "Liver and onions?"

"I know, that's what I thought too, but he says liver is really good for you. It does something for your . . . something. It's nice to know he's health conscious."

Sunday morning at church Kraig met Suzanne at the door. "My parents are here today and Mama's fixing lunch at my house. You'll come, won't you?"

When she pulled in at school Monday morning, Mitchell pulled in behind her. She waved as she closed her car door. "Good morning, Mr. Sanderson."

"I made these breakfast burritos myself," he said when they reached her classroom. "See how you think they compare to the drive-thru kind."

Mitchell had brought with him a stack of science books. Biology, chemistry, and general science. While they ate, he flipped through them. "These are to make me look busy," he told her after a minute or two. "Tell me about your weekend if you want to."

"We went out for supper Friday night. Sunday he asked me to come to his house and have lunch with him and his dad and mom."

"Sounds like it's getting serious, meeting the parents. I thought he said something about taking it slow." He grinned—probably at the embarrassment on her face. "That's okay. You two aren't exactly teenagers. You're old enough to make wise choices."

"I was pretty much in knots from the time Kraig invited me before church until I got to his place. Meeting his parents seemed scary, but they were nice. His mother made me feel comfortable right away. His dad reminded me a lot of you—a really classy gentleman."

"That's a good sign, isn't it?"

"I guess. Mmmm, McDonald's should take cooking lessons from you. I should too."

Mitchell closed the chemistry book, and stood up. "Any time ma'am, but I'm sure you're already quite skilled."

"I suppose if I'd ever get married, I'd have to pretend to be and learn while I act."

"Surely he hasn't proposed?"

Suzanne propped her chin in her hand. "Of course not. But he did say that he's asked the Lord to send him a wife. Oh, Mitchell, this whole thing of dating, courting, whatever you want to call it, is so foreign to me. I've been doing a lot more praying myself the past couple of weeks."

"I'm praying for you too, Suzanne." He smiled reassuringly and left the room.

The problem was, she wasn't getting clear answers. Kraig seemed so sure he had divine guidance to spend time with her. He hadn't outright said the Lord told him to marry her, but she sensed it was coming. After just three weeks of knowing him and what—three dates?

Joy and Mitchell both encouraged her to "at least give him a chance." As if Suzanne was supposed to know how to do that. Just the idea of having a . . . a . . . boyfriend would have thrilled her at one point in her life. But she was past that.

Neither did she thrive on the attention it got her. She didn't like being on display as if she were some freak finally becoming normal. Ladies at church, who in the past never acknowledged her existence, had started being friendly. This whole "boyfriend" thing left a lot to be desired.

Mitch dreaded Valentine's Day. His third without Marilyn. She had always fixed a special lunch for him, and he had taken her out to a fine dinner in the evening. Now that he'd learned about her dislike for cooking, those lunches were more special than ever.

The subject came up in staff meeting on Tuesday the thirteenth. Mrs. Miller said they didn't really do that much. He'd probably bring her some chocolates and ruin her diet, and she'd get him a card. Mrs. Bower said they had reservations at a very romantic restaurant in Middletown. Miss Kortney cried and said Forrest couldn't get off in the middle of the week, and she wasn't sure he would even send anything after the big argument they had last weekend.

Miss Lana looked at the table the whole time they talked. Finally Mrs. Bower said, "Lana, what do you do on Valentine's Day? Probably what Suzanne used to do, huh? But she surely has something big planned, don't you, Suzanne?"

Suzanne straightened her shoulders. "Okay, so what did we decide about whose class sings first in the grandparents' program?"

Way to go, Suzanne. Mitch saw the look of empathy she gave Lana. He joined forces with her, and Valentine's Day didn't come up again.

That night southwestern Ohio got the largest snowfall of the season—eight inches. School was cancelled. At daybreak, Mitch put on his snowsuit and fired up the snowmobile. He loaded up a shovel and zipped over to Clayton Road. Suzanne was valiantly shoveling snow away from her car.

He killed the engine. "You're snowed in. Relax and take the day off. You don't have to go anywhere, do you?"

"Not have to. I just thought if I could get out, I'd go over to school and get some things caught up. Work on a new bulletin board."

"Want a ride on my Ski-Doo? I'll take you."

"Fun! I've never snowmobiled. Come in while I get my stuff."

Mitch stomped his boots all the way up the steps and held the door for Suzanne. No rush of warm air greeted him as he stood inside the door. He stuffed his gloves in a pocket and rubbed his hands together. "Brrr. Do you always keep it this cool in here?"

"Not quite. The furnace isn't acting right. One more reason I want to go to school. Nice of me to mooch off the parents, huh?"

"Oh, yes. You're quite the moocher."

Aboard the snowmobile, with Suzanne's books tucked under the seat and her arms wrapped tentatively around his waist, Mitch took off carefully. Her squeals of delight echoed across the clear white landscape. They sped along beside the road in the wide ditches and sometimes into open fields, the dual tracks breaking the pristine beauty.

The trip was far too short. In no time at all he parked by the front school door and helped her to her feet. "Like it?"

"I love it! I just love winter altogether. The cold is so invigorating and then to get beauty like this. Wow." She let him shoulder her bag and waited while he unlocked the door.

Suzanne checked the thermostat in her classroom. "See? Nice and warm in here. This little computer didn't know we had a snow day. I'll turn all the other rooms down. No sense in heating the whole building today."

She thought of everything. "Let me do it." Mitch took off before she could argue.

He returned to find her sorting through a large plastic storage box. "What's a good theme for a March bulletin board?" she asked without looking up.

"You're asking the wrong person. I'm sure you'll find something that's just right." He sat on the edge of the table and watched her for a while.

"You did an excellent job of steering yesterday's conversation away from Valentine's Day, Suzanne."

"With your help. Thanks. Poor Lana, I know how she must feel. The others have never been there, so they don't realize all their chatter could be hurtful." She pulled out a ball of string. "Kites. It'll have something to do with kites."

"So now that Lana's not here, may I ask about your Valentine's plans?"

"Sure. Never hurts to ask." She jumped to her feet and headed for the door. "Be right back."

She returned with a calendar page. "Thought I remembered seeing this in the art closet. I'll start with this for a background idea." He didn't see the correlation, but said nothing.

Dropping the paper on the table, she propped a hand on a hip and turned to him. "I'm waiting. I gave you permission to ask." Mischief sparkled in her eyes and words.

He combed a hand through his hair and raised his eyebrows. And waited.

"Okay, you win. Kraig's picking me up here this evening at six-thirty. I have no idea what he has planned. I guess it's a surprise. What about you?" Her voice grew serious and she took a seat behind her desk. "What did you and Marilyn do for Valentine's? This must be another hard time to deal with."

He told her about their ritual lunches and dinners. Tears pooled in her eyes and she wiped them with a sleeve. "I'm sorry you can't do that anymore."

"Thanks for caring. Sometimes I think I'm getting used to it, then a big wave comes and knocks me over. What about you?

How have you spent the evening of February fourteenth in the past?"

She rolled her eyes and left the desk chair to inspect a poster that said, *God gave you talents as a gift. Praise God by using your talents well.* "You don't want to know."

He waited, praying instead of prying.

"I've mostly pretended it's just another day. My dad tried to instill in us that it was a pagan holiday that Christians had no business recognizing. I don't buy that, but it would have made it easier, I guess."

She ripped the talents poster from the wall. "Time for this to come down. Nobody's looking at it anymore."

Mitch bit his tongue and waited some more.

She returned to the storage box and began putting everything back in. "Probably the worst was when my sisters and church couples would ask me to babysit so they could have a date night."

"You're kidding!" Had he and Marilyn ever done something so insensitive?

"I wish." She sniffed. "I seemed to be the only one who hadn't received God's message that He was keeping me single and child-less so I could make it easier for parents to have a kid-free romantic evening."

"So you babysat?"

"For a while. Until I got fed up with it and started planning visits at the nursing home or evening classes or whatever just so I could tell them I already had plans. If it had been a paying job, I might've endured it. But somehow another memo I never got says you don't pay a single woman to babysit. Letting her keep your children is a gift you're giving to her to fill her empty arms. If anything, she should pay you for the privilege." With the contents of the box neatly organized, she replaced the lid and bent to pick it up.

Mitch covered the distance in two strides. "I'll get it. Where to?" He followed her from the room. "I know I'm guilty of not thinking about single people, but I think I can say with certainty that we never expected free babysitting. That's absurd, Suzanne. Couldn't you have charged them?"

"Up on that shelf." She pointed. "I know. You've told me before. Nobody can take advantage of me unless I let them. But it's not that easy. I tried once. Said something like, I'd keep their children, but not for free. Guess what they *paid* me?"

He descended the three-step stepladder and shook his head.

"They proudly presented me with a pack of note cards. Complete with the fifty-cent clearance sticker on the back.

"Listen to me whine. That's all ancient history. I really need to get busy with those books I want to study. Surely you have something you need to be doing too." They reached the office door and she turned toward her room. "Don't hang around for my sake. Kraig's planning to pick me up here anyway." She smoothed her skirt with her hands. "I can wear this tonight and have him drop me off at the trailer. Go on, Mitchell. Take advantage of this day off."

Exactly what he'd thought he was doing. He picked up his coat and started to put it on. Then he pulled that arm back out of the sleeve and called to her as she reached her desk. "Wait a minute. You don't really need to study, do you?" Of course she didn't. She was always on top of that. He stood beside her chair, blinked, and rubbed his chin.

"Um, well . . . it never hurts to go over it again." She shoved her hands in her jacket pocket, looking like a student caught with the test key.

"That's what I thought. Let's see if some of my grandkids want to go sledding."

21

Mitch dropped Suzanne off at the trailer mid afternoon. He had already taken his oldest six grandchildren to their respective homes. The truck didn't have that many seat belts, but it had to be safer than that enormous hill they'd sledded down a hundred times at the Germantown Reserve. But he had thoroughly enjoyed every dangerous moment. Every terrified happy squeal.

Even Marissa's disapproving look when they dropped off her kids hadn't dampened his spirits. She opened her mouth as if to speak, but Mitch cut her off. "No time to chat, Rissa, I need to get our teacher back in time for her date with Kraig."

"You need to call Mr. Grubbs about that furnace," he said as he opened the passenger door for Suzanne.

She hopped out gracefully. "I know, but maybe it's better to put up with the cold than see the character who shows up as a repairman."

"Forget I mentioned it. Dave Deaton does that kind of work, I'll call him. He owes me one." He followed her to the trailer and waited at the foot of the steps.

She turned as she slipped the key in the lock. "Thank you so much for this day. I don't know when I've had so much fun. It was great to take off the teacher hat and enjoy the kids. And the snow."

"You needed a break from responsibility. Glad we could share it with you."

Door open and key pocketed, she continued. "Too bad I have plans tonight. We could clear snow off a pond and take them skating. That'd be more fun than going out to eat." She laughed. "Maybe I ought to suggest that to Kraig. Well, thanks again. See you tomorrow."

Mitch drove home with her rosy cheeks etched in his mind's eye. And the words he wasn't positive he'd heard her say as she closed the door. Had she really said, "I wish you were going with us"?

He did too. More accurately, he wished he were going *instead* of Kraig. He parked the Silverado and shook his head with his hands.

That was a thought out of the blue. Groaning and sighing he went inside and wandered aimlessly. At the fireplace mantel he picked up the frame that held his wedding picture and one taken on their thirtieth anniversary.

"Oh Marilyn. I loved you so much. You were my life. But now you're gone, and I'm still here. My life has to go on, and she's a part of my life now. What am I going to do?"

A big part of his life. Also a part of Kraig's life. Thanks in a large measure to his own encouraging.

Mitch sank into his recliner, his train of thought chugging to nowhere. Suzanne was dating another man, and even if she weren't, where would that leave Mitch? A widowed grandfather. Practically old enough to be her father.

Like a father, Mitch wanted to protect Suzanne. Like a father, he wanted her to realize her dreams. Like a father, he could see that Kraig wasn't putting that sparkly glow on her face.

Very unlike a father, Mitch wanted to see if he could do a better job.

After Mitch left, Suzanne dressed for the evening then drove to school where she fine-tuned lesson plans until Kraig picked her up at six. They went to Chipotle for a Valentine dinner. Kraig hadn't thought about making reservations, and by the time they got to town, all the non-fast-food restaurants had huge lines. He didn't want to wait that long and neither did Suzanne, although probably for different reasons.

Soon after they sat down with their food, a middle-aged couple stopped by their table to say hello to Kraig. It was one of his colleagues from work. Kraig looked around and saw there were no more empty tables, so he invited his friends to join him and Suzanne.

If she had been enjoying the time spent alone with Kraig, she might have resented the intrusion. Instead she welcomed it. Being with him was uncomfortable. They ran out of things to say, and the ensuing silence was awkward. If this was what dating was all about, she hadn't missed much.

Surely it wasn't. She needed to stick it out, and they would become more comfortable with each other. Kraig was a fine man. A strong Christian with leadership qualities and high ideals. She liked his parents. She liked his sister, whom she'd met once. He was nice-looking. Six feet tall. Thick, well-groomed brown hair and greenish-blue eyes about the same color as Suzanne's.

At first Kraig had wanted to take things slowly, learn to know each other without being together all the time. Now he counted on Friday night suppers and Sunday after church lunches every week. If Suzanne was to learn to know this man, what better way than to spend time with him?

They visited the Wright Brothers Museum in Dayton one Saturday, and the weekend after Valentine's Day she suggested sledding at the Germantown Reserve, but Kraig begged off. He was afraid he might be coming down with a cold. Nor did he want to go skating at the Bowmans' pond the next week after they cleared the snow.

Skating was one of Suzanne's favorite pastimes. She loved the cold air against her cheeks and the sensation of flying across the ice. Her skates were old and ready to fall apart, but she wouldn't have bought new ones for anything. Their soft leather fit her feet like a second skin. The trailer park was less than a mile from the pond, so earlier in the winter, she'd often come home from school, eat a quick supper, and get her skating fix in the dark.

But Kraig was not a skater. He had tried it as a teenager and decided it wasn't for him after he fell on the ice and broke his wrist. He rubbed it protectively as he told the story.

Finding something do in their times together presented a challenge. They agreed not to spend time alone at his place, and Suzanne hadn't shown him where she lived. It was curious that he never asked about her house. So far she had met him at church on Sundays, citing the fact that coming to her place would double his route. On Friday nights and Saturdays she claimed work at school so he could pick her up there. For all she knew, he was like the kids who believed their teachers lived at school.

She was not ashamed of her home, but neither was she proud of it. Kraig's family had never seemed to want for anything, and she didn't know how he would react to her place of residence. Until she was sure, she decided not to face him with the issue.

Joy continued to ask for details. So Suzanne gave her details. She and Jason thought Kraig was perfect. Suzanne should be bouncing with enthusiasm.

"Suzanne," Joy said one Saturday as Suzanne pulled towels from the dryer, "the two of you are made for each other. It's obvious. We've wondered for years why you were still single, and here's the answer. God was keeping you for this time. Why can't you act more excited?"

Because she wasn't? But Suzanne couldn't tell her that. "You know I'm not the type to spout my feelings. I'm sorry. I'll try harder." She tried to gush as she told Joy about the pair of mittens Kraig had given her the evening before. Custom-crocheted by his mother for Suzanne.

For all practical purposes useless to her as she needed to maneuver her fingers around doorknobs, keys, books, and skate laces.

Of her co-teachers, only Miss Lana welcomed Suzanne's lack of enthusiastic details. She occasionally came for advice in working with her student who still couldn't tell the difference between d, b, and p, or 6 and 9, or 2 and 5.

Lana sat at the high school table one morning folding a sticky note. "What am I doing wrong?"

Suzanne alphabetized the stack of book reports on her desk. "It's probably not you, Lana, if all the rest of the children don't have the problem. Remember, they're first graders, and he's pretty young. If he's still mixing them up by the end of second grade, then his parents should get concerned. You said he reads okay?"

"Yeah, he reads those letters fine in words. It's just when he has to write them. What am I going to do next year when you're not here to answer my questions?"

"What makes you think I won't be here?"

"Duh. You have a boyfriend. At your age, that has to mean marriage in the near future. If you marry Kraig, you won't keep teaching. Would you?"

"I don't know. I haven't thought that far yet."

"I can tell you, if I had a chance to get out of here, I'd take it. I get so sick of hearing all about Kortney's boyfriend. At least you don't rub it in my face that I never get any dates."

Suzanne walked to the table and sat down beside her. "I'm glad you don't think I'm flaunting my relationship with Kraig. I'm sure I don't know exactly how you feel, but I've had my share of years wondering if my time would ever come."

The first grade teacher nodded. "I know, and seeing you dating gives me hope. I mean, if you can get married at your age, surely there's someone out there for me. I don't want to be here for ten years, let alone as many as you have." She returned to her room, totally clueless that her words were far from complimentary.

So if someone as hopeless as she had gained Kraig's attention, Lana ought to have a chance. Nice to know she was inspiring hope in younger women. Suzanne chuckled away her annoyance.

In all the years she'd worked at New Vision, Suzanne had lost count of the teachers she'd seen come and teach for a year, maybe two, then get a boyfriend and lose all interest in the classroom until the school year dragged to an end or they quit mid-year to get married. So she expected if she ever had the privilege of dating during a school year, she'd have a real struggle focusing on her students and their needs.

So far it was not a struggle. Maybe because Mitchell was there to unload on. Dear Mitchell. He brought Suzanne breakfast nearly every morning. Often new recipes he wanted to try such as baked oatmeal, sunshine crepes, and breakfast pizza. Other times "just the old standbys" as he liked to call sausage sandwiches and his version of Egg McMuffins. As they ate his offerings together, they chatted like old friends.

She learned all about his home life, his childhood-through-adulthood romance with Marilyn. She discovered his wife had not been perfect, but that even when a story contained a fault of hers, he was not critical.

He told her stories of trips they took with their children. Of all their emergency room visits, including his own. He had witnessed the births of all his children. Had changed diapers and given baths and enjoyed doing it.

He learned about Suzanne's younger life too. How inferior she felt for being such a shrimp. How she strove to excel in academics to make up for not measuring up physically. That she had stood on the fringes of school groups, youth groups, and even adult groups all her life without ever feeling like she belonged. That she never even seemed to belong in her own family.

She heard that Mitchell had put himself through college in winter and summer classes after the crops were brought in and after the planting was finished. That he'd even taught adult classes at the college later on. He regretted the hours he'd spent away from his family and the way he had too often taken out his frustration on them. "I spent a lot of time apologizing, Suzanne," he said with teary eyes.

"But you did apologize, Mitchell. The closest thing to an apology I ever received from my father was the time he said, 'Your mother thinks I should say I'm sorry.'"

22

March came in like a lion and roared around for a good two weeks.

Mitch considered himself comfortably settled into the principal position. He had kept up with his consulting clients and learned to cook and keep house. He and his sons had agreed to wait a year before moving the farming enterprise completely into their names. Marissa had backed off her suspicions regarding any interest of his in Suzanne. Seeing Kraig and Suzanne together at his house and in the weeks since in church had put that little family problem to rest.

Apparently she hadn't seen the moves Pam Kingsley was making on him. Pam was a fairly new widow in the congregation. Her husband had died last September after a three-year battle with lung cancer. Now everywhere Mitch turned, he ran into Pam. Her message was easy to pick up. She was in the market for a new husband. One this time who didn't smoke and could provide for her in her golden years. Mitchell Sanderson was the perfect candidate.

How Marissa hadn't homed in on Pam's intentions could only have been due to her fixation on having another baby. Which didn't seem to be happening. Marci's now-obvious pregnancy didn't help matters. Nor Janelle's impending delivery.

Since that January morning when Suzanne's car wouldn't start, Mitch had made a habit most mornings of leaving home early enough to park across from Mobileville in a vacant lot and watch for her car to pull out. Then he would wave and follow her to school. Sometimes he pulled in behind her, other times he slowed down and, seeing she got into the school drive safely, drove back home to get their breakfast.

Feeding Suzanne gave him such satisfaction. It was the only thing he could do to take care of her, and she seemed to enjoy it. Hadn't protested in quite a while. Their time together was bitter-sweet. He loved hearing stories from her life experiences. Basked in the care and concern that emanated from her to open his heart and share from his life.

But he had to guard himself. He could not fall in love with a woman who was dating another man. Every day brought him closer to that possibility. Hearing about her dates with Kraig had become painful. That missing sparkle in her face when she talked about Kraig bothered him more every day.

What could he say? Kraig Wye had everything to offer her that Mitchell Sanderson could not. From his never-been-married status to his youth to his three-letter last name.

On the second Monday of March Mitch saw Suzanne safely to school then returned home for the breakfast casserole in his oven. But her car was not the first one in the parking lot. Miss Kortney was already there. Something was wrong. Kortney never came early and the earliest she came late was never on a Monday morning.

He would have pulled in to check, but in five minutes the timer would ring and he didn't want his newest creation going up in smoke. Half an hour later he unlocked the front school door and carried a small casserole dish to his office. Suzanne's classroom door was closed and Kortney's was open revealing an empty room. Mitch put an ear against the closed door. Not to eavesdrop exactly, but to make sure they were okay. Through the fireproof panel he could hear Kortney's distressed voice followed by Suzanne's soft, soothing tone. Then angry sobs and more of the calm reassuring voice. He returned to his desk and flipped through some papers. Before he could decide his responsibility, the latch on the high school classroom door clicked and squeaked. He cocked an ear.

Suzanne's voice, low and clear. "You did the right thing, Kortney. I'm proud of you. I know you're hurting, but I'm here if you need to talk. Don't forget how we prayed. God wants to give you grace for this. If you need me to send a couple of students to take your class for a while this morning, I'll try to make it happen . . ."

Their voices grew fainter with the sound of footsteps heading toward Kortney's room. A few minutes later Suzanne appeared in his doorway, cheeks flushed and eyes red.

"Good morning, Mr. Sanderson," she said and then turned quickly and retreated.

He grabbed the covered dish and followed her to her room.

She stood at the door. "Let's not shut this," she said and took a seat at a student desk in the far corner. "I don't want Kortney to think we're in here talking about her behind closed doors."

"She okay? I heard some of what you said to her." Mitch scooped casserole onto two plates. "I forgot the juice. Sorry."

"You've met Forrest, right?"

Yep. Man troubles. Made sense.

"In a nutshell, he's not the choirboy she'd made him out to be. He visited from Virginia this weekend and demanded more than she was willing to give. It wasn't pretty, and now she thinks he's gone for good."

"Not my place to pry for details, but let her know that I do care, and if she needs any more support, I'm here." Mitch propped both elbows on the desk he'd taken and looked at her intently. "How was your weekend?"

Suzanne groaned. "Don't ask." She waved a forkful of breakfast at him. "You know, this is really good. Did you get it from one of your *Taste of Home* magazines?"

Mitch opened his mouth to respond, but she kept going.

"Or did you get it from Marilyn's recipe file?" Once more he tried to get a word out. "Or did you make it up yourself?"

What was she trying to do? How was he supposed to tell her that it came from a library cookbook when she wouldn't give him a chance to answer.

She burst out laughing. "Gotcha! I've been meaning to give you a dose of your own medicine and it finally worked. Now you know how it feels to be given a question accompanied by a list of choices and no opportunity to respond."

Mitch grinned. "Good job. But I haven't forgotten the question I asked."

Her expression sobered. "Yeah, I know. I don't know what I'm supposed to do. Here I finally have Kortney coming to me as if I'm some kind of dating expert, and I'm ready to terminate the only dating experience I've ever had."

Mitch's heart took a little flip. "Suzanne! Kraig isn't trying to take advantage of you is he?"

She shook her fork. "Nothing like that. He's very much a gentleman. I just have trouble enjoying the time I have to spend with Kraig."

"Have to spend?"

"It feels that way. I'm all mixed up." She looked at him with pleading eyes and his heart ached for her. "I've never done this before. I just thought if I was dating a man whom I might marry, I'd like to be with him. I've read enough about romance in books, that I thought it would be different. You and Joy keep telling me to give him a chance, so I guess all couples go through a time like this?"

Mitch shook his head. "We didn't—Marilyn and I. Of course, we'd always known each other, so maybe we were the exception. But I don't think so."

"Well, I have to come to some kind of decision and soon. I've been praying, but I still don't know what to do. Then yesterday . . ." Her words drifted off and she blinked rapidly.

He resisted the urge to put his arm around her. "What happened yesterday, Suzanne?"

She drew in a deep breath and exhaled slowly. "Yesterday over lunch Kraig tells me that God has shown him that I'm the one for him."

"You've known him for what, a little over two months, and he's proposing?" They weren't teenagers, but even at this age that seemed pretty fast.

"Not exactly, or so he says. He just thought I should know what the Lord has revealed to him. I was awake most of the night wrestling with that. Praying, of course. And, Mitch?" She turned to him and he noticed the dark circles under her eyes. "I don't hear God telling me that. Maybe He is and I'm not hearing it."

Mitch, not *Mitchell*. She had to hear the bass thumping of his heart. "Is Kraig expecting an answer from you now?"

"No, but I can't keep leading him on if I know it's not going to work. I wish he hadn't told me the part about God telling him. He's a godly man, has a close relationship with the Lord, maybe it's me who can't hear God's voice. I mean, it makes sense, doesn't it, for me to marry Kraig?"

Mitch blinked hard and opened his mouth to protest. Why ask him? Because she looked to him for fatherly advice. Right now he felt anything but fatherly. He hedged. "Explain how it 'makes sense,' Suzanne."

"Okay. I'm thirty-seven. All I've ever done is teach. I can barely pay the rent on a slummy old trailer. I don't even have a savings account. Mitch, I'm not getting any younger. What happens when I can no longer eke out a living in the classroom? It's not like I have siblings or nieces or nephews to take me in." She pushed the chair away and paced.

"So, here's a fine Christian man who tells me that God says he's supposed to marry me. He wants children. I want children. Probably the only chance I'll ever have in my life at marriage and motherhood. Wouldn't it be stupid to turn him away just because being with him is not the ecstatic romantic experience of my dreams?"

Mitch stacked their emptied plates. "I . . . I . . . don't know what to say."

"I'm sorry. I'm not really expecting an answer. This is something I have to work through myself. The whole situation just isn't what I'd ever envisioned. And Kraig. He's a sincere man. He's just . . ." She shrugged and sighed. "He's just not what I thought I was looking for in a husband."

"What exactly were you looking for in a husband, Suzanne?" he asked. He didn't expect an answer either. The front door rattled and opened, announcing the arrival of another teacher. "We'll talk later." As he walked past her, he would have squeezed her shoulder, but his hands were full of plates, casserole dish, and forks, so he bumped her elbow with his and smiled warmly. Wanly.

Her hopeful smile tingled all the way to his toes.

23

They didn't get a chance to talk later that day. Classes kept them both busy and Mrs. Bower had plenty to say at lunchtime.

Kortney did not call on any high school students to take her class, but at five after three she zoomed in to Suzanne's desk. "Oh, Suzanne, it's all going to be okay."

Suzanne studied her face. "Oh?"

"Yes, you'll never believe it. Forrest called me this morning. We got it all worked out." She stopped beside Suzanne's chair. She leaned down and pulled her into a hug. "You always give the best advice. Thank you." She straightened back up and winked. "Maybe we can make wedding plans together." With that parting shot, she skipped away.

Leaving Suzanne to her thoughts. And to Mitch's words ringing in her ears as they had all day.

Good morning, class, algebra homework, please. *What exactly were you looking for in a husband, Suzanne?*

Tenth grade, finish researching for your term papers this week. *What exactly were you looking for in a husband, Suzanne?*

Seniors, meet in the library to work on the yearbook. *What exactly were you looking for in a husband, Suzanne?*

What exactly was she looking for in a husband? The words bounced from hemisphere to hemisphere. She finished her grading half-heartedly, walked to the window, and stared out for a long time. Jacob's mother had decided he'd had enough math help for the year, so now her evenings were completely student free.

It was five o'clock and with the recent switch to daylight savings time, plenty of daylight remained. She trudged back and straightened her desk. Then she grabbed her jacket and headed to the playground. She needed something physical to work out her frustrations. Now that the ponds had thawed and the hills were back to mud, skating and sledding were out. She picked out a swing and settled into it.

As she pumped her legs to gain altitude, the cobwebs cleared away and she began her list. Christian. Respectful. Steady worker. Strong values. And so on . . . the first dozen qualities fit Kraig just fine. So what was her problem? She reached the peak of her leg-pumping ability and let the swing drift.

Suzanne wanted more than that. Don't marry the man you can live with, but the man you can't live without. She wanted that. What else did she want? She wanted someone who was easy to talk with. Someone who increased her heart rate by walking into the room.

She dragged her feet in the gravel to stop the swing. Then she started back up, pumping furiously. Wasn't she choosy? She wanted more. Someone she trusted with her heart and feelings and who trusted her that way in return. Someone who wouldn't judge her by her family or her house. Someone she felt safe with. Someone . . .

Her legs went limp and the swing dropped in its arc.

Someone just like Mitch.

She skidded to a stop, heart pounding at the thought. All the qualities she'd ever looked for in a husband were easily described in two words. *Mitchell Sanderson.* She jumped out of the swing and ran inside.

What was she thinking? Mitch was old enough to be her father. He *was* Marc and Marissa's father. A widower. A kindhearted man

whom Suzanne had been looking to as a father figure. And he was
. . . he was . . . she didn't recognize this feeling.

She packed her schoolbag and drove home. All evening she
paced the length of worn carpet from kitchen to bedroom. On
one trip past the sewing room she stopped to check on her bicycle. Not there. She checked the closet knowing it wouldn't fit in
there. She had brought it inside, hadn't she? She meant to. She
remembered unloading it from Jason's van and leaning it against
the end of the trailer.

But the ancient ten-speed was not inside. Suzanne ran outside
and around the house. No bicycle. As far as she could tell, the rest
of her meager possessions were accounted for. The trailer didn't
look broken into. Likely she hadn't ever gotten around to bringing
it inside, and someone had helped himself. Not a great loss, but
disappointing nonetheless. She wouldn't be cycling to school.

What would Mitch say when she told him of the theft? Mitch.
That's where her mind automatically traveled. She recognized it
now. He was the one who brightened her days. Who shared her
load, not just as principal and co-teacher, but her emotional load
by touching her heart with his heart.

But he was a widower. Suzanne stumbled at that fact. How
could she feel this way about someone who'd been married before?

She didn't touch the sewing she'd planned to finish. She didn't
touch her lesson plans. Instead she paced and didn't remember to
eat anything. Kraig Wye. Mitch Sanderson. The two men in her
life. Kraig, two years younger than her, never married, wanted
to marry her. Mitch, seventeen years older than her, widowed,
thought of her only as a daughter. Shouldn't it be a no-brainer?

Finally she sat down at the table with a piece of notebook paper
and a pen and started talking to herself. If only she had a dog. Or
a cat. Talking to a pet, even a bird or a turtle, had to beat talking
to herself. Stop thinking about Mitch. Concentrate on whether to
go forward in the relationship with Kraig. Make a list of the pros
and cons like she'd seen Mitch do so often in the past months.
When the paper was full, she read her scratches and sighed. Then

she ripped it into tiny pieces and watched them flutter into the wastebasket.

As the last piece landed, the phone rang. "Suzanne, there you are." Dear as Aunt Eva was, she didn't always have the best sense of timing. "Don't you have something to share with your favorite aunt?"

Oh, yes. Suzanne should have told her about Kraig, but she wanted to wait until she knew where the relationship was going. "Uh-oh. Who have you been talking to?"

"Your mom called me to see what I knew about you having a boyfriend. I know the two of you don't communicate the best, but isn't that something you should have told her?"

"Probably so." And if Mother wanted to know, shouldn't she have asked Suzanne? She paced the floor, trying to decide how much to say right now. "Aunt Eva, I really do want to tell you what's been going on, but I can't tonight. Call me Monday night, and I'll share the whole story."

Mitch followed her to school the next day like he always did. This morning he pulled in half a minute after Suzanne did. She was still gathering up her bags when he opened her door and greeted her with his rich voice. Her heart did a somersault, then a back flip. He took her heaviest bag before closing the door gently.

A compassionate gentleman. She smiled guardedly. She had to be careful not to make him think she had any romantic feelings toward him. She didn't, did she? The heat rose in her cheeks. Who was she kidding?

"Doing okay this morning, Suzanne?" Her heart raced hearing her name on his lips.

She nodded, searching her brain for something to say. "I think someone took my bike."

They discussed that the rest of the way into the building. Mitch was alarmed that she'd been burgled, but she convinced him it wasn't a break-in, as she couldn't remember actually dragging the bicycle into the house. He still didn't like it and reminded her—again—to faithfully lock all her doors and windows.

Over sausage biscuits, they talked briefly of Kortney's revived romance and then moved on to compare classes for the day and the upcoming final quarter of the school year. Suzanne successfully steered them away from the topic of Kraig. She hadn't made a decision and needed more time to figure it out before she could talk to Mitch about it.

Thursday morning she was ready to tell him what she had decided. For the first time in months he arrived after seven o'clock with two single-serving yogurt cartons. Coffee and strawberry, Suzanne had first choice. She took the fruit on the bottom and he grinned. She knew he knew what she'd pick.

"What's up, Mr. Sanderson? You look tired. You're not getting sick, are you?"

"Just tired. Janelle had her baby last night."

"Oh, no! I thought she wasn't due till next month." Suzanne peeled the top off her yogurt instead of grabbing his arm.

"She wasn't. But they say everything's okay. A little girl. Just over four pounds, but she seems to be doing well. They left the twins and Chloe with me on their way to the hospital. I took the kids back home, fixed them supper and spent the night there. They're with Marci now."

"Wow. If you need to be with your family, go. I'll cover your classes. Or maybe you should go home and get some rest." She scooped out the last of her yogurt and saw that he hadn't opened his. "Here." She removed the lid. "Eat."

He obeyed. "Thanks, but I'll be fine here today. There're enough folks around to take care of all that. I will leave right after school and go see the baby. They want to keep her at Miami Valley for a few days. I think Janelle comes home tomorrow. Maybe they will come up with a name for the baby by then."

The news she'd planned to share with him was going to wait. Now was not the time.

Through the dumping rain Friday morning she saw a familiar truck pull out behind her and follow closely all the way to school.

Before she could open her door, Mitch was beside the car holding an umbrella.

He carried her bag in. "Good. You look fairly dry, considering that downpour. I need to make sure we get those tornado drills set off today. Oops, you weren't supposed to hear that. I'll be right back."

He returned with huge burritos. "And here's a jar of Marissa's home-canned salsa if you want to add it."

Suzanne peeked inside at potatoes, scrambled eggs, bacon, and cheese.

He poured salsa on his burrito and took a bite as his shirt pocket vibrated. He chewed fast and grabbed the phone. "Sorry. The last couple of days have been crazy."

She tried to concentrate on eating and not hearing his conversation. After a few short answers he laid the phone down. "I've been commissioned to carpool duty this afternoon. So I'll be leaving at three." He paused until she looked at him. "Why do I get the feeling you've been avoiding me this week? Did I say something to upset you?"

Suzanne shook her head. "Just had some things to figure out on my own, I guess. It's been a pretty hectic week with third quarter exams and all."

"So . . . this is Friday. Got a date tonight?"

She finished her burrito. "Wow, I'm full. I don't know if you could really call it a date. Kraig's planning to come here as usual, but I don't think I'll go with him."

Mitch's eyes widened, but he didn't say anything. He probably got tired of hearing her sigh, but she did it again. "Tell me how you think I should handle this." She stopped, not knowing how to explain.

Still he wisely waited in silence.

Without looking up from penciling little graphs on her blotter pad, she started. "It's over between me and Kraig. I can't keep going, but I don't know how to tell him. Do I call and tell him not to come? Or do I wait until he gets here and break the news to him in person and send him away alone? Or do I go with him for supper and tell him when we get back here?" She lifted her eyes to his intense gaze.

"Any other choices?" he asked, but neither of them laughed. "I'm sure you're capable of making the right decision, Suzanne, but since you asked my opinion. If it were me, I'd rather hear it in person than over the phone. And if you're going to eat supper together, with him not knowing, wouldn't that be awkward?"

"I hadn't thought about that. That's why I asked you. You see the things I don't. I guess I could tell him when he gets here, and then if he insists on talking about it over supper, I could go. Or not. I've eaten with him enough already."

"So . . ." Mitch stood. "Would you care to share how you reached this decision? Don't answer that yet. Let me get rid of this and I'll be right back."

He was soon back with a stainless steel coffee mug. "You don't have to tell me if you don't want to."

The pencil point broke, so she grabbed a pen and shaded the squares she'd drawn. "I want to, but I don't know how to say it. I've stewed over this all week. I just wish he hadn't told me that thing about God telling him I was the one for him."

"You're breaking up with him because he thought God spoke to him?"

"Of course not. I'm only saying that it would be easier to do if he hadn't said that. This was inevitable. I should have seen that weeks ago. I don't think God is asking me to spend the rest of my life with someone it's a burden to be with."

He made a sound that almost sounded like a chuckle, but humor was not the expression on his face. "Sorry. Go on."

"I love my work here with the students. I've realized that anew this week. I'll take my chances here. If I die in the poorhouse after spending my life in a service that gave me joy and satisfaction, it will have been worth it." The pen she twirled like a baton, slipped from her fingers and hit the desk.

"I used to think the thing God wanted me to do was probably what I wanted least to do. That's how I thought you could determine His will. Do whatever seems most distasteful, and you're in the will of God. I don't believe that anymore. Now that I know God better, I realize He wants me to be happy. And not just happy because I'm sacrificing all that's pleasant to me. Does that make sense?"

He nodded, then shook his head the other way. "I don't know. Keep going, I think you're getting there."

"I guess I'm just trying to say that God's not telling me to marry Kraig. In fact, I think He's pushing me the other direction. I feel peaceful about ending our relationship. Maybe not every marriage is between two people who think they can't live without each other, but I'm holding out for more. I'm sure I *could* live with Kraig, but I know I can easily live without him. I think I'd rather stay single than marry someone I had to endure. That sounds bad, but there are so many things about him that bug me."

As Suzanne talked, Mitch nodded at the right times and *mmm-hmmmed* appropriately, reassuringly. What was he thinking? Did he think she was stupid to throw away such a good chance of marriage?

"So, after tonight, it's just me again." He still didn't say anything. She grabbed his hand. His rough, gentle hand, then let go as if it had been a snake. "Please. Tell me what you're thinking. Am I completely out of my mind?"

He took her hand back and covered it with his. Those soft brown eyes met hers. "You are a wise woman, Suzanne. It sounds like you thought this through and decided the right thing. I hope and pray that you'll find the man you described. You deserve that."

He blinked and swallowed. "I'm sorry you couldn't go to your dad with this. But I'm honored that you've wanted my humble opinion. My daughters don't come to me much anymore."

She was right. He thought of her as a daughter. She could live with that, couldn't she? Did she have a choice?

The day dragged blessedly along. If evening never came she wouldn't mind. But it came and thankfully the janitors did not. All the other teachers were gone by the time Suzanne let Kraig in at six-thirty. He followed her to her classroom and took the chair she offered him across the desk. Somehow this arrangement made her feel more like a teacher giving disappointing news to a student than a woman telling a man she didn't see him in a romantic way.

Sitting there in front of her, he looked like a teenager despite his size. That was another thing. He brought out her motherly and teacherly instincts. She didn't think they would ever develop into the feelings a woman should have toward her husband.

As advised by Mitch, Suzanne didn't try to explain it all to Kraig. And as predicted, he wanted a full explanation. She repeated simply, "It's just not going to work." In the end he accepted her refusal with surprising grace and even prayed with her before he left.

Kraig left and Suzanne cried. Had she exchanged her only chance at wedded life and swaddled babies for debating surly teens and grading half-heartedly written reports?

24

Mitch sat in Martin and Janelle's family room a week later cradling his newest granddaughter in his hands. So tiny. So perfect. Little Susanna Elizabeth Sanderson, with a name longer than she was from the top of her fuzzy head to the tips of her dainty toes. If only Suzanne could be here to hold her.

He shifted the baby to the crook of his arm and rubbed his forehead. *Suzanne?* What about Marilyn? If only they were both here, but at this point only Suzanne was possible. She had told him how much she loved to cuddle little babies.

He'd watched her face when he told her the baby's name, so close to her own. She was pleased. "But it's such a long name. Like mine, but she has an even longer last name. She may hope as I always have that she can marry someone with a short last name. Every time I go to write a check or sign my whole name, I have to go through S-U-Z-A-N-N-E, B-L-O-O-M-E-R. And it's even worse if I have to use my middle name. I used to say I wouldn't marry a man with more than three letters in his last name. Amy Ely and I used to do things together occasionally. It took her less than half as long to sign in anywhere. Maybe little Susanna will go by Sue."

Mitch looked again at the tiny pink bundle of life. "I guess that puts me out of the running, huh, sweetie? My last name is longer, not shorter. Nowhere near three letters," he whispered.

That Suzanne was no longer spending time with Kraig was a great relief. To her too, from all Mitch could see and perceive. He had resisted the urge to take her somewhere for supper tonight or to invite her to spend Sunday afternoon with him. Although if he did, she'd probably view it simply as a fatherly gesture. And she had been clear that she wasn't interested in someone who'd been married before, although he thought he could talk her out of that one. What if the school had some policy against a relationship between them? Maybe he would just wait till school was out for the summer. What a coward.

Three-year-old Chloe ran into the room, followed by her seven-year-old brothers. "Gwampa, I hold her?" She held out her arms.

"Grandpa, you should've heard her. She called the baby Miss Suzanne," one of the boys said. "That's so cute," the other one added.

Mitch pointed to the couch and Chloe hopped up and seated herself. He knelt in front of her and laid Susanna in her arms. He didn't have time to stand before Chloe started to get up. "All done."

Janelle came in and took the baby and sent the other children to set the table for supper. Mitch returned to the kitchen to check the casserole in the oven. It was one he made a few weeks ago and put in the freezer. He had made biscuit dough after school and pulled out a bagged salad and bottled dressing. Who ever thought a man couldn't learn to put a good meal together for a family after a day at work?

Suzanne should be here. This would be the first Friday night she'd spent alone in quite a while. The more Mitch thought about it, the more he wanted her here. He had his hand on his phone to call and invite her when Janelle came in. She rewrapped the baby and laid her in the infant seat on the counter. "What's this I hear about Kraig and Suzanne breaking up? I expected them to announce their engagement."

He concentrated on keeping his face from showing surprise at Janelle bringing up the very person already on his mind. "That didn't take long to spread, did it?"

"Well, what do you expect. Someone with Kraig's standing comes in and starts getting serious with a lifer old maid, and then it breaks up."

Mitch wheeled around from his salad prepping. "*What* did you call her?" His voice came out harsher than he intended, but he couldn't let the term go unchallenged. He realized he was waving the carrot-slicing knife and put it down.

Janelle laughed, not seeming to notice his tone. "That's what some of the church ladies call her. We certainly never thought a wealthy, educated man like Kraig would see anything in her. It's like, she's been around forever lurking in the corners. They say she's a really good teacher, so New Vision better hang on to her. Goodness knows our boys will need all the good teachers they can get to make it through school. If she's so great at dealing with teenagers, I hope she's there for a long time." The baby let out a wail, and Janelle picked her up again.

During her monologue, Mitch had turned back to the carrots, blood boiling. His Suzanne was not an old maid. That awful moniker brought up images of harsh, sour, stubborn, inflexible, ugly women. How unfair of people to refuse to see Suzanne's beauty and grace. They could see it if they'd only give her a chance. In a flash of insight tinged with anger, he voiced an idea.

"Janelle, I was just thinking. Miss Suzanne loves little babies, and she's going home to eat alone tonight. Would you mind very much if I called and asked her to eat with us?"

"Mind? No. That'd be really sweet, Dad. Maybe she could help the boys with their homework."

Or *not*. If he had any say in it.

He checked the clock and the timer on the casserole. Six-thirty. "Let's see, Martin said he'd be here around seven. I'll set this in the fridge and be right back."

Phone to his ear, he stepped outside. Suzanne answered at school, and it didn't take long to convince her. Back inside he patted out the biscuit dough and cut it into squares which he placed on a baking tray. Then he rearranged the table setting to include another place.

Janelle needed an opportunity to see Suzanne up close. To see her beauty—inner and outer. To see that *lifer old maid* didn't fit her in the least. Janelle and Martin were the only ones not at his place back in January with Suzanne. Kelly and Marci had both commented after that meal about what a delightful person Suzanne was, they'd never learned to know her, but they should. Apparently they had not passed the observations on to Janelle.

Nor had they followed through with their intentions of learning to know her. Mitch hadn't told Suzanne their comments, but he poked around with some casual questions. Neither Marci nor Kelly had made any moves to befriend her.

Ten minutes after the call, Suzanne arrived looking apprehensive. He met her at the end of the walk. She rewarded him with a tentative, but heart-warming smile and followed him into the family room. The boys were on the floor wrestling over who had to re-stack the Jenga blocks. She leaned down and patted a head. "Hey Miles, how did the kickball game go today?"

Miles released his death grip on Carter and looked up in surprise. "Miss Suzanne! I didn't know you were coming. Wanna play Jenga with us? See we stack them like this. Then we take turns pulling out blocks without it falling down." He proceeded to stack without complaint.

Carter joined in. "He don't want to tell you about the kickball game cause we won. We beat the stuffin' outta them."

Mitch took Suzanne's elbow. "First she's going to see your new sister, guys. Then your dad should be here and we'll eat." To Suzanne he continued, "You know these two apart? I'm impressed. I'm not even always sure."

She turned up her palms in a what-can-I-say gesture and followed him to the kitchen. Janelle looked up from her magazine with a less than welcoming wave.

"Hi, Janelle," Suzanne said. "Thanks for having me tonight. I hope it's not a problem."

Janelle shrugged. "No problem. Dad's doing the cooking. I figure he'll be glad for the help in cleaning up afterward, so if he fixed enough, he can invite whoever he wants."

To avoid bringing up Suzanne's recent breakup, Mitch hopped in. "Is it okay for us to hold the baby now?"

"Sure. Help yourselves. She doesn't seem to mind what goes on when it's time for her to sleep. During the day, anyway." Janelle rolled her eyes. "Night's a different story."

He walked to the counter and lifted Susanna from the seat. Suzanne was at his elbow, eyes glowing. He laid the tiny girl in her arms and wished with all his heart that he were a doctor presenting her with her own newborn child.

She took the baby and walked to the sink, away from Janelle. She expertly shifted the bundle with one arm and pulled the blanket away from Susanna's face with the other hand. "So beautiful," she breathed.

The look of tenderness on Suzanne's face took Mitch's breath away. *So beautiful.* Both of them.

His cell phone vibrated. "Text from Martin," he announced. "He's in the lane. I'll put the biscuits in." As he performed the rest of his culinary tasks, refusing Suzanne's offer to put the baby down and help, he sneaked sideways glances at the two of them.

What an amazing woman. She deserved a child of her own like she'd dreamed. That was one of the reasons he could never let her know about his feelings for her. He could provide her with so much, but what she seemed to want the most, he would never be able to supply.

Martin came in and they called to the children, who all wanted to sit beside Miss Suzanne. "What's this, guys? You'd rather sit beside her than your grandpa?" Mitch faked a sad face and they all giggled. He put a boy on either side of her and seated himself between Miles and Chloe.

Susanna squirmed and fussed in Suzanne's arms and Janelle invited her to lay the baby back in her seat. Suzanne tipped her pink cheeks downward and back at Janelle. "Is it okay if I hold her while I eat?"

"Sure. If you don't mind. She'll be quieter that way, since she's awake now. But you don't have to."

Suzanne didn't mind. Mitch could tell from the look on her face. She stilled the crying during the prayer and bounced her gently throughout the meal, gracefully eating and conversing politely all the while.

What an amazing woman. She helped clear the table and dry the few dishes that didn't fit in the dishwasher—one-handed. When everything was cleared away, she joined the twins in the family room for two games of Jenga. The only time she relinquished the little pink bundle was when Chloe begged again to hold her. For a whole minute this time.

After letting each boy win once, she reluctantly handed Susanna to Janelle and retrieved her sweater and purse. Mitch walked her to her car. "I'd see you home, but I told them I'd stay and watch the kids until Martin gets back from getting groceries."

"Oh, no, that's fine. I need to stop at school and finish up a couple of things." She tipped her head sideways and looked up at him. "Thank you, Mitch. You can't know how much that meant to me. It's been a long time since I held a baby. She's so precious. Thank you." She opened the car door and slid behind the wheel. "The food was great too. I enjoyed visiting with Martin and Janelle and the kids. And you."

She didn't know how much it meant to him either. He swallowed hard. "You're very welcome. I'm glad you came." When she put her key in the ignition, he gently closed her door and waved as she drove away.

What an amazing woman. As surely as Marilyn had captured his heart all those years ago, Suzanne had captured it now. And there was nothing he could do about it.

When he could no longer see or hear her car, he sprinted back to the house. At Janelle's request, he bathed Chloe and put her to bed. Then he corralled Carter and Miles and supervised their homework. They had time for a game of Chinese checkers before bedtime. He had just finished praying with them and tucking them in when Martin returned.

Mitch helped carry in the bags and unload them. Janelle pointed out where to put the items and the men obliged her. "Are you sure that's the same Miss Suzanne we used to know, Dad?" Martin asked, throwing him a box of spaghetti. "It's funny, how she's nothing like she used to be and I never noticed it." He glanced at Janelle. "Not that I'm in the habit of looking at other women, honey."

"I know what you mean." She nodded emphatically. "Dad about had a stroke when I called her a lifer old maid. I guess he's learned to know her over at the school. Now I'd really like to find out why Kraig broke up with her."

"That's not how I heard it." Martin closed the cabinet doors and sat beside his wife, taking the baby from her. "It was her. And now I understand why. You ladies all seem to think he's some classy hunk, but she's got way more class than he'll ever have. And it proves she's not desperate."

Point proven. Mitch glowed with satisfaction.

25

True to the old saying, March left lamblike. The crocuses in front of the school bloomed and faded and the daffodils put in an early appearance. Some even peeked up around Suzanne's trailer in a noble attempt at bringing cheer. School days flew by in an expected pattern.

Suzanne went home on weeknights with enough energy left to spruce up the small yard around her home. Weekends she took the time to find some lovely outfits at the Goodwill and Salvation Army stores. Secondhand clothes. It wasn't so bad after all. Miraculously, she had finally begun to put on some much-needed weight and her dresses didn't fit so well anymore. Mitch continued to bring breakfast and provide a sounding board for her joys and frustrations.

Every day she cautioned herself against becoming emotionally involved with this caring man. Somehow the widower status no longer mattered either. She discarded that notion with her outgrown clothes. When she'd vowed never to marry a widower, she didn't know Mitch. He didn't fit the picture she'd had of a man desperate to find a woman—any woman—to watch his kids, fix his meals, clean his house, warm his bed.

But what was she to do with these newfound emotions? She certainly wouldn't make the first move. If Mitch wanted more than friendship and a co-worker relationship, it would be up to him to initiate it. In the meantime, Suzanne planned to treasure each moment with him.

At staff meeting on the last Tuesday in April she suggested they start thinking about activities for the last day of school. It was four weeks away, but experience showed the wisdom of planning ahead.

The married teachers sighed and Kortney studied her left ring finger. Mitch turned a page in his binder and cleared his throat. "Last day of school? What kind of planning does that take?"

"I move we keep it simple this year." Mrs. Bower started before Suzanne could answer.

"I second that," Mrs. Miller said.

"Simple's fine, but you know the students expect something really fun." Lana leaned forward with a determined look in her eye. Good for her. For once Suzanne didn't have to be the bad guy. She understood it had to be hard for Linda and Patrice to be wives, mothers, and grandmothers on top of being teachers. And hard for Kortney to put her heart into her job when all she could think about was Forrest, but it frustrated Suzanne that teaching sat at the bottom of their priority list. It didn't seem fair to the students.

It was different for Suzanne. Teaching was her life. No other forces vied for her attention, or if they did, she didn't hear them. It wasn't the life she would have picked, but since she had it, she intended to give it all she had.

Mitch cleared his throat authoritatively and they all looked at him. "This will be my first last day. I'll have to confess my ignorance on the subject. What do you usually do?"

Of all the things the two of them had talked about over the past four months, this topic had never come up. Too bad Suzanne hadn't thought of it and campaigned ahead of time. She sat back and let Lana lead.

She explained that there wasn't a *usual*. Each year they came up with different activities. "The teachers always have lots of fun scheduled. When I was in school, it was my favorite day. They could've just had a boring day since we were all excited that summer vacation was about to start. But they didn't. It was a special gift they gave us to end the year. My first graders have been asking what we'll do for the last day almost since the first day.

"One year we had Summer Olympics as our theme. Another year they made little Conestoga covered wagons with plastic pipes and sheets. Each team had to maneuver their wagon through all kinds of trails. The teachers hid in the woods as Indians. Once we had a big bonfire and wiener roast." Lana's eyes glowed as she relived the memories.

Mitch made notes. "So . . . any ideas for this year?"

Suzanne had some, but decided not to show her hand until someone else came up with something. Maybe if she didn't always take the lead, others would dredge up some creativity. So they all sat and stared at each other.

"We still have time. Think about it this week, and next week we'll brainstorm and come up with something. Can't drop the tradition on my watch." Mitch closed the subject, and they moved on.

Wednesday was the perfect spring day. By afternoon all the high school classroom windows were open and birdsong threatened all focus on iambic pentameter and elliptical clauses. At one-thirty Suzanne gave up. She left the students studying and stood in the doorway of Mr. Sanderson's classroom. He looked up and she beckoned to him.

"This weather's too much to fight against. Think you can forfeit your last class of the day with my students?" She told him her plan and he agreed enthusiastically.

Back in the doorway she stood and watched the semi-studious room. In her get-your-attention voice she announced, "Class, let's go play a quick game of softball."

Whistles and applause erupted across the classroom.

She pulled a list of teams from her top drawer. Desks banged and papers shuffled. Within minutes the students from Suzanne's room and Mitch's had converged and gathered balls, bats, and gloves. They sauntered teenage-speed toward the ball diamond. Suzanne slipped a whistle around her neck, more from habit than necessity, and followed. Mitch fell in step with her. "Good idea, Suzanne."

"Will you play with us? With Denver gone today, we have uneven teams."

"Why not you?" His bantering tone implied that he didn't expect her to.

"Well, I can hardly play on both teams, now can I?" She watched him scratch his chin and try to decipher her words. "There's no way I'd get past this crew without being on a team. You'll be surprised to find that I'm not too bad with a ball or with a bat. I'm not that good either, but the kids say I'm not bad. For a girl."

The team that got Mr. Sanderson obviously thought they had the advantage. But to their credit, Suzanne's team acted like they had the best adult player. "You guys don't know when he might have last hit a ball," they teasingly taunted. "At least we know Miss Suzanne's not rusty."

They were all a bit rusty. It took a couple of innings to get their act together. From now to the end of the school year, she should work in a couple of impromptu games a week. Games like this were as valuable as the academics. Fresh air, physical exercise, competition, working together.

Suzanne's team was ahead eight to six when she hit a double in the third inning instead of making the third out. Tina was up next and made it to first, chatting comfortably with the first baseman, who even happened to be a boy. Way to go, Tina. Everyone cheered when Jed stepped to the plate. If anyone could hit a home run, it was Jedidiah Jones. But they hadn't yet seen Mr. Sanderson's skill in outrunning a ball.

Suzanne was running from second to third to home and missed the show of the mighty catch. But as their teams exchanged sides of home base, impressed students rehearsed the details. He ran so fast with his eye on that ball the whole time. Then he slid ten feet and caught it lying on his side. Mitch passed her and grinned. The rub he gave his grass-stained left shoulder made her wonder if he'd hurt himself. She'd have to make sure he took care of that injury. He would also need the formula she kept handy for grass stains.

Taking her place at third base, Suzanne didn't see much activity from their first three players. Laurel got to second, David hit a fly easily caught by the pitcher, and Rayna made it to first in the nick of time. Mr. Sanderson was up next. "Home run. Home run. Home run," chanted his team in support.

His first hit went to Suzanne's right. Foul ball. She stopped it with her glove and returned it to Brent. If that was the direction he was hitting, she'd be ready. Brent wound up and hurled the ball. Mitch swung.

She could catch this one. She stepped left and lifted her glove.

——∞——

Mitch swung at the pitch. It was right on. He wasn't the savviest of softball players, but if he could keep it inside, he could hit a pretty good line drive between the pitcher's mound and third base. Low enough and fast enough to escape Suzanne's glove. The Louisville Slugger connected with the ball and as he took off for first, he noted that it wasn't near as low as he'd intended.

He ran forward and looked sideways. She was going to catch it. No. The ball veered and—he stopped short. It bounced on the ground as his favorite high school teacher landed on the grass.

"Somebody call 911!" Laurel screamed, and Mitch forgot the knifing pain in his shoulder.

When he reached Suzanne, the students stood in a ring around her. "Get back," he ordered. Laurel continued to scream, and Tina crept forward to pull Suzanne's skirt over her legs before retreating obediently with the others.

Mitch's hands went cold and his heart thundered. Was she alive? He dropped to his knees, picked up a wrist, and searched for a pulse. Stomach clenching at the goose egg rising above her right eye.

Come on, Suzanne, where's your radial artery? Maybe he could feel the carotid better. He unbuttoned her collar and placed two fingers beside her neck. They'd practiced this in health class last week. Why couldn't he remember how to find it?.

"Mitch? Mr. Sanderson?" At first the voice sounded like a student calling him. Maybe one of them could find her pulse. But, it was Suzanne's voice. She struggled to sit up. "What happened?"

"Hey, she's fine. Everybody back to the game." Zack, an athletic senior who had yet to learn the skill of tact. "Come on, guys, we only have twenty-five minutes left."

Mitch laid one hand on Suzanne's forehead and the other on her shoulder with enough pressure to keep her still. His gaze swung from Zack to the rest of the group and back to Suzanne. Then he stared in amazement as Tina stepped up to the uncaring jock.

"No way, idiot. We're not doing anything until we make sure Miss Suzanne is going to be okay. She got knocked out, you jerk. Look at her face." Tina used a few more forbidden words. "If you don't care anymore than that, I don't know why we call you human." The rest of the girls joined in, supporting Tina. Even most of the boys took Tina's side.

Mitch was proud and shocked at once, but for now Suzanne needed his attention. "Tina, get an ice pack from the freezer, please."

Tina jabbed a finger in Zack's chest for good measure and followed Mitch's order, followed by a handful of girls.

"Let me sit up, please," Suzanne said in a small voice. "I'm okay. Really." She rubbed her forehead and turned up the corner of her mouth. "But I think I'm going to have a whopper of a headache."

Most of the students still hunkered in a circle around him and Suzanne. Zack and Evan played catch, but they were far enough away it didn't seem to be any danger. Laurel continued to whimper, "You gotta call 911."

Suzanne pushed Mitch's hand off her head and shoulder. "Please?" Her eyes looked okay and she wasn't complaining of neck pain, so he helped her up, a hand behind her for support. The girls returned with six icepacks. Suzanne grimaced when they pushed one against the still-growing lump. She took the frozen blue bag and held it away.

She stood suddenly and Mitch put a protective arm around her shoulder. "Why don't I go behind the backstop with this ice, and you all can finish your game. You at least have to finish the inning." She gave a wobbly smirk. "Unless you want to concede the game to us."

The blow hadn't affected her thinking. Or her sense of humor. "She's right," Mitch said. "Finish the game without us. We're going inside." He looked down at Suzanne. The color was returning to her cheeks. But could she walk the fifty yards to the school? With her independent spirit, she was sure to try. He didn't want to risk her collapse on the way, so he yielded to impulse. He scooped her up and carried her.

She didn't resist. Instead she put her right arm around his neck and settled comfortably into his arms. He could get used to this.

At the school door he set her on her feet and led her to his office. She hadn't used the icepack much. "It needs a towel wrapped around it. No, not your shirt. We'll get one from the kitchen." After the secretary returned with a towel, he insisted she lie on the sickroom cot and he held the cool cloth against her forehead.

After the three o'clock bell rang and the carpools all left, Mitch followed Suzanne back to the high school room. "I'm fine, Mr. Sanderson," she said. "It looks like I'm growing a horn, but other than that, I feel fine. I need to get busy grading papers for—"

"The papers can wait. Or I can grade them. You need to rest."

She dropped into her chair, shaking visibly. "Thank you. Probably a good idea." Her face twisted in pain and she laid her head down on the desk against the now-warm icepack. Her eyes closed and she took shallow breaths.

He pulled up a chair and sat beside her. If only he hadn't hit that ball so hard. He'd knocked her out, for heaven's sake. She insisted it was just a bruise, she'd be fine with a couple of ibuprofen. But he wasn't convinced. What if she had a concussion? What if something was damaged in the fall? He took a mental inventory of his schedule for the rest of the day and discovered it free. He'd thought about offering to run the tractor and planter for a while for the boys, but it wasn't as if they needed or expected him.

He had to take care of Suzanne.

"How's your shoulder, Mitch?" Her eyes were open and shiny. "You fell on it when you caught Jed's ball. And that green stuff on your shirt. I can take care of it." Near the end of her sentence her words faded and she closed her eyes again.

He walked to the kitchen where the other teachers stood around discussing head injuries. They had all rushed to him after the dismissal bell to find out what happened. He gave them a condensed version of the events which seemed to satisfy them. The opinions he picked up now ranged from "Ow, that had to have hurt. Is she okay?" to "Oh, it's just a bruise. She might get a black eye, but a softball can't do much damage."

He ignored their chatter. Their opinions didn't matter. What mattered was how he could help Suzanne. Back in her room, he lifted her head, taking care not to jostle it, and replaced the ice-pack. "Suzanne, I know you say you'll be okay. But I think you need to have this checked out. I'm going to take you to see a doctor."

She lifted her head. "I can't, Mitch."

"Can't?"

"I don't have insurance, and I can't afford a bunch of tests. I'll be fine."

No insurance? How could he have worked with her for seven months without knowing she was uninsured? "That's the last thing you need to be worrying about right now. I'd feel so much better if you let me take you in. I feel pretty responsible, you know. Please?"

"It wasn't your fault any more than mine. Oh, grab that trash can." She leaned forward and heaved into it. He put a steadying arm around her quivering frame and reached for the Kleenex as she sat up again, teary eyed.

"Sorry. I know that's disgusting." She took the tissues. "Thanks. I wondered if my chicken sandwich got too warm before lunch. Could you get me some water, please?"

He raced to the drinking fountain and filled her glass. "Here." He lifted it to her lips. "That settles it. You've had a head injury and now you're vomiting. I'm taking you to the emergency room."

Forty-five minutes later they sat in Kettering Hospital's emergency room. Suzanne wanted to sleep on the way, but Mitch had asked her questions to keep her awake. She sat beside him now with her head against his right shoulder. He hoped she wouldn't have to wait long. He'd first parked on the street in front of the medical center in Farmersburg and run in. "We can't do anything here," they told him and sent him on.

Mitch didn't like this place. He hated it. Why hadn't he taken her to Sycamore? It was probably closer and still a hospital, but it might not have had the same effect on him. This was where he'd taken Marilyn.

And left without her.

A shudder traveled the length of his body. That wasn't going to happen this time. *Oh, Lord, keep her safe.* But wasn't that the same prayer he'd used two and a half years ago?

"Mitch? You okay? You never answered my question about your shoulder." Suzanne reached behind him with her left hand and softly patted his shoulder.

He covered her hand with his. "It's fine. I'm just not comfortable in this place." Every instinct told him to put his arm around her and hold her close. What would she think? That he'd been hit in the head instead of her? Instead he bowed his head and covered his face with his hands. He looked up when Suzanne pulled back and folded both arms across her chest. She was blinking rapidly as if to blow away tears with her eyelashes.

"Your head hurts pretty bad, doesn't it?"

She shrugged. "It's no worse. Better maybe. I just feel bad that you have to give up an afternoon for this. I saw the ball coming, I should have been smart enough to either catch it or get out of its way. Now you have to come in here and be reminded of losing Marilyn. I'm sorry, Mitch."

How did she do that so often? Know what he was thinking and feeling? It was almost eerie. It was how Marilyn had become after they'd been married for years.

Mitch lightly touched the bruise above her eye. "It wasn't your fault. How 'bout we settle this—I won't blame myself if you don't blame *yourself*. Deal?"

She smiled and held out her right hand. "Deal."

He took it, shook it, and held on to it. "It is not a burden for me to be here with you. You're very important to me, you know."

A slight nod. "High school teachers are pretty hard to replace, huh."

Replacing her as a teacher hadn't entered his mind. He opened his mouth to say that when the buzzer in his hand went off with vibrations and lights. He took her arm and helped her stand. "Do you want me to go back there with you, honey?"

The term of endearment slipped out before he could stop it. Her cheeks reddened immediately and she nodded. "If you don't mind. I've never been in the ER before. I don't know what to expect. Your presence would be calming for me, I think."

A young man in turquoise scrubs led them down a hallway to a curtained area. "Miss Bloomer, you can sit up there." He pointed to a gurney-like bed. Your father can sit on the chair if he wishes. The doctor will be right in."

He left and Suzanne giggled. "My father. Right. You don't look old enough to be my dad. Has anyone ever told you that you and Marc look like brothers?

"I guess I don't look my age either," she continued. "Joy wanted me to get her a bottle of wine for a recipe a couple of weeks ago and the clerk asked me for ID. I can finally appreciate being mistaken for a teenager." She swung her legs against the edge of the bed and continued on in a manner that told Mitch she was extremely nervous and uncomfortable in these surroundings. "Now I wish I could go back and tell the scared little girl that was me for so many years that it's okay. There's nothing wrong with being petite. I know that now, but then I thought I was a freak. If only I could have believed then that God loved me just the way I was. It seems like . . ." Her words trailed off and she looked around the room as if studying every detail.

Mitch stood and reached for her hand. She took it and held onto it. "You don't have to be scared, dear. You're going to be fine." This time he didn't even try to keep the word in. She was dear. She needed him. Maybe almost as much as he needed her. "I just couldn't take the risk of not making sure."

She nodded and a doctor strode in. "Suzanne," he boomed. "Doctor Rohr." She cringed and covered her eye and her bruise with a hand briefly before extending it to the doctor. He shook Mitch's hand instead. "Mr. Bloomer?"

"Mitchell Sanderson. Do you need me to tell you what happened?"

Dr. Rohr asked half a million questions, shined his light in Suzanne's eyes, held his pen out for her to track, and bumped into every noise-making object in the room. After four and a half minutes of examination, he stood quickly, sending the wheeled chair across the room to crash into a stainless steel waste can. "I think she's fine, Mr. Sanderson. Her thinking's clear, pupils normal, heart rate satisfactory. We could do a CT scan or an MRI if you insist, but I can tell you it won't show anything. That goose egg's going to be sore for a while and she'll have a headache. But resting would be better than waiting here for an inconclusive test. If you want, I'll get you a scrip for some high dose acetaminophen."

"Thank you doctor. But it's fine if you talk to Suzanne. If your assessment is correct, she would understand it as well as I do. What do you think, Suzanne? Want me to get you out of here? I assume you heard everything the good doctor said?"

She smiled and winked at Mitch. "You don't have to write the prescription, Dr. Rohr. I have plenty of Tylenol at home. Although, may I use ibuprofen instead? Tylenol isn't usually effective on my headaches."

The doctor approved and within minutes they were back in the waiting area. Suzanne insisted she could walk with Mitch to the truck. "Just get me out of here," she said. He was willing to comply.

Mitch started the truck and checked his watch. "It's after seven o'clock. Are you hungry?"

She patted her stomach through the seat belt. "I hadn't thought about it, but yes, I am." She turned in the seat, tucking a leg beneath her. "But you don't have to get me anything. Just take me home. I've inconvenienced you enough already today."

"I may faint from hunger before we reach home. You wouldn't want that. I won't eat unless you do too." He laid a hand on her dress-covered knee. "How about we go to a drive-thru and find a park? That should be quieter. We have Arby's, McDonald's, KFC, and Taco Bell right here, or we could go past Burger King, White Castle, or Fazoli's. I think they have a pick-up window, but it's not very fast."

Suzanne voted for chicken from the Colonel, and Mitch drove to a small park not far from the hospital. "Marci found this when we were coming down here every day a couple of years ago. It looks a lot nicer with grass and flowers than it did under the snow. Looks like we have it to ourselves." He carried the food and drinks to a stone table and returned to the truck where she waited obediently. He opened her door and held out a hand.

God help him, she was beautiful. Could he go through this evening without telling her how much she meant to him?

26

Suzanne's head started throbbing monstrously again by the time they sat down to their chicken dinners. But she had to eat something before another dose of Advil. She didn't know how to interpret Mitch's behavior. He was not his usual comfortable self, and her heart ached for him. Between his shoulder and reminders of Marilyn at every turn, he must be miserable.

He hurried around and opened her door, and a light breeze wafted the scent of cherry blossoms through the truck. She took his outstretched hand and hopped out. "That air might be chilly. Here, I'll bring my jacket." He reached behind her vacated seat and pulled out a zippered fleece sweatshirt. Then he took her hand again and led her to the table.

Instead of going to the other side, he sat beside her. He took the two covered plates from the sack and arranged them and the drink cups. "Let's pray," he said and again held out his hand. She took it, but her mind was not on the prayer. His hand was so much like him. Calloused and rough to the initial touch, yet gentle and loving with its care.

When his voice broke a few words into his prayer, she turned her attention to that. ". . . 'thank you, Lord for protecting my Suzanne . . ." *His Suzanne*? "I pray that her head will heal with no more problems. And . . . Lord, help me to make up to her for all the losses she's had in life. Show me what to do . . . Amen. Oh, yes, thank you for this food. Amen."

He lifted his head and looked at her and it was not the look of a principal. Suzanne didn't have any experience along this line, but in her heart she knew it. This pulse would have put her in ICU an hour ago. Could he hear it? "Mmm, looks good. I'm hungrier than I thought." She willed her hand to steadiness and picked up the fork he unwrapped for her.

"Good choice. You must be starved." He took a bite of mashed potatoes at the same time she did. Then they both picked up a chicken leg and bit into them.

In her peripheral vision, she could see him sneaking looks her way. The food was good, but she wasn't tasting it, and she had a strong feeling that Mitch wasn't either. She laid the drumstick back in the plate after the third or fourth bite. "I think I can take those pills now." She swallowed two with a drink of Pepsi. "There. I think my head feels better already. Or maybe it's the food and the caffeine."

She didn't want to blather, but it kept coming out. "I haven't had KFC in a long time. Not that I don't like it. Really I do. It sounded good and it is good." She clamped her mouth shut and speared a few green beans.

Mitch stopped eating. His next move was sudden, but it didn't surprise her. He put his right arm around her waist and pulled her closer to him. "I'm glad you're here, Suzanne." His words were warm and damp against her cheek.

She shivered. Not from cold, but from a flame that ignited in the pit of her stomach and spread to her fingers and toes. Not a feeling she'd ever been on speaking terms with, but she recognized it. She turned and wrapped her arms around him.

"Suzanne. Oh, hon. I was so scared. When I saw you lying there unconscious, I was afraid I'd lost you before I ever got to tell you how much I care for you." A tear dropped onto her forehead. "I know I'm an old widowed grandpa, but I have to tell you how much you mean to me." He stopped talking and held her against him.

Finally he had made the first move. If only she could stay here. She rested her ear against him and relaxed. His heart beat in rhythm with her own. Then his stomach growled. She pulled away and looked up at him. A glistening line streaked each tanned cheek, but the sunshine of his smile could have made a rainbow.

She picked up a napkin and dabbed his tears. "You'd better eat, Mr. Sanderson. I can't have you fainting from hunger on me here."

"Look who's talking." But he took a drink and resumed eating.

She picked up her biscuit. "I discovered something a few weeks ago, Mitch."

"Mmm-hmm?"

"I had this wacko stereotype of widowers. But I discovered that you don't fit it. When I made up my mind about—well, years ago when I thought I needed to keep my distance from widowers, I wasn't picturing someone like you." She took a too-big bite of biscuit to stop the flow of words.

His eyes crinkled—and leaked a little—as he thoughtfully chewed. He covered her left hand with his slightly greasy right one.

She washed down the bread with some pop. "You're not old either. As for the grandpa part, you're a wonderful grandpa. I'd never take that away from you."

He squeezed her hand and they finished their chicken dinners in silence. She didn't know what all this meant, but a warm blanket of love and security stilled her soul.

When the food was gone, he made her sit while he gathered the trash. As he stuffed plates back in the bag the outline of his cell phone showed through his grass-stained shirt pocket. "Does your family wonder where you are, Mitch?"

"Probably not. If they had needed anything, they would've called." He patted the pocket. "Was there someone you should have called?"

"Oh, sigh. Joy's probably having a fit trying to find me. Amber's sure to have told her I got knocked out."

"Speaking of Joy. Do you think she'd let you spend the night with them? I know what the doc said, but I'd feel much better knowing you weren't home alone. Anything could happen in the night, and your neighbors aren't exactly the kind you should call in an emergency. I insist on that, dear."

He was probably right. "If that keeps you from lying awake worrying, okay."

He made the call for her. Told Joy what the doctor said, and made arrangements for Suzanne to spend the night. Then he took her home long enough to pack a bag and delivered her to the Moore farm. "You don't need to be driving until at least tomorrow," he said to her protests. "I don't think anyone will take your car if it sits at school. I'll pick you up at seven in the morning with breakfast and lunch." He brushed a curl from her darkening bruise. "Take care of yourself tonight. If you need anything, don't be afraid to ask. I know Joy wants to help. If you're not up to going to school tomorrow, I'll take you home. Or to a doctor if you need it."

As he turned off Havermale Road into the Moores' lane, he picked up her hand and squeezed it. Then he lifted it and pressed the backs of her fingers against his lips. "Good night, Suzanne."

27

Joy would think that the dorky grin on her face came from being smacked in the noggin with a speeding softball. Suzanne wouldn't try convincing her otherwise.

Suzanne rested well on the Moores' couch and woke feeling fine, not counting the headache. Joy asked surprisingly few questions.

Instead she talked nonstop about her plans for the new nursery. When she had learned a few weeks ago that she was carrying twins, she went bananas. All her life she'd wanted twins. The idea now consumed her every waking minute.

Suzanne was willing to egg her on. "Have you decided yet if you'll use two g names or name the firstborn with a g and the next with h?"

"Believe me, it's been a major family discussion. Most everyone likes Grant and Grace except Amber. She says Grant is a stupid name. In fact, she hates any boys' names that start with a G. But if we use G and H, we need a boy's and a girl's name of each letter depending on which one comes first. I did tell you, didn't I, that the last ultrasound showed one of each?

"Carlie and Denee think they've won the lottery. They'll each have a baby to take care of. This will be the easiest thing since the other kids are so old and love babies so much."

If Joy noticed any foreign emotions on her friend's face or in her body language, she probably chalked it up to Suzanne being as thrilled about the twins as she was.

At school several of the girls and even some boys questioned Suzanne at length about her injury. Clark's concern was more for the welfare of the class. "Does this mean we won't get to play softball anymore this year? We can get you a catcher's mask to wear in the outfield."

"Oh, guys, I'm fine. I have a headache, but I'm not that fragile. Weather and schedule permitting, we will have more games this year."

She spent Thursday night at home alone and by Friday evening her headache had subsided. The blood from the bruise drained downward and left her with a raccoon eye. It didn't hurt, and every time she saw it in a mirror, she touched it. It was a physical reminder of the day that she'd learned Mitch's true feelings and had shown him her own.

If she worried that things would be awkward between them after their lengthy hug that evening—and, the thought entered her mind more than once—it was in vain. They continued to eat breakfast together and keep up a professional front.

Marissa showed up at school twice each day, but her presence no longer held any power over Suzanne. Now she could offer a genuinely welcome smile, and would have even initiated some small talk if Marissa hadn't always been in such a hurry.

Mitch met his sons for breakfast Friday morning but got to school before seven with a steak and egg bagel for Suzanne. "Want to go bike riding Sunday afternoon, Suzanne?"

She swallowed. "Sounds like fun. I love to ride, but I don't have a bicycle. It still bugs me that I was so careless."

"Not a problem, there's an extra still hanging in my garage. If you don't mind a hand-me-down bike, you're welcome to it."

He answered all her questions. On the Great Miami bike route, starting out in West Carrollton. No family along. He'd go home after the morning service, load the bikes, and pick her up. Pack or pick up a lunch and eat in the park at their starting point.

Sunday afternoon's bright sunshine belied the coolness of the air. Suzanne appreciated the lightweight jacket she'd brought. After lunch and the requisite hour's rest they pedaled around the parking lot to stretch their legs—Mitch on his bike and Suzanne on Marilyn's. Hers looked like it had never been ridden, and Mitch had adjusted the seat perfectly.

"Ready to head out?" He stopped and waited for her. Then he licked a finger and held it up. "Wind's mostly out of the north. What do you say we head into it while we're fresh. When we get ready to come back, we'll have the air at our backs."

Conversation wasn't as easy on the trail. The fair weather had called out cyclists and walkers of all varieties. Instead of raising their voices they rode mostly in silence except for the occasional check in from Mitch to be sure Suzanne wasn't overdoing it. Almost a week had passed since she'd taken a softball to the head and she showed no further symptoms, but he still worried.

Being with Mitch was comfortable all the way around, whether conversing or musing without words. So unlike the time she'd spent with Kraig when both were awkward and stressful.

She lost track of time, but it didn't seem they'd been on the trail long when Mitch stopped and pushed his bike to the side of the paved trail. "Doing okay, Suzanne?" He wiped his brow and handed her a water bottle.

She stepped up beside him. "Absolutely. Biking a trail like this has always sounded fun. But it's not something I'd do alone. Much better than riding along the back roads around home."

He checked his watch. "Almost an hour since we started. Let's head back. You're hardly winded, but I must be out of shape."

Trail traffic had thinned and they chatted on the return trip. "You don't act like you mind too much hanging out with an old guy," Mitch said.

"You are not old." Suzanne coasted until he was a few yards ahead. He slowed and when they were side by side again she continued. "It's like age doesn't matter when I'm talking with you. Maybe the human spirit doesn't have an age. It seems we're on the same wavelength and how old we are isn't a factor."

He cleared his throat and she expected him to say something, but he didn't, so she continued. "I didn't see Abe and Marci at church this morning. She doing okay?"

"Yeah, I think so. She said they were going somewhere, but I can't remember where. Maybe something with his family."

She noticed a few weeks ago that Marci was wearing maternity clothes. Mitch hadn't said anything about it. "When's their baby due?"

He didn't answer. Probably the wind had blown her words away. She tried again. "She's pregnant, isn't she? When?"

"August."

Another half mile passed. "So . . . you have some ideas for last day of school activities, Miss Suzanne?"

Suzanne may have been more skilled at reading teens than adults, but she got the message. Mitch did not want to talk about Marci or her pregnancy. She didn't know why, but she could respect that.

"A few, Mr. Sanderson. But you'll have to wait to hear them with everyone else Tuesday afternoon."

"Yes ma'am."

They both laughed and spent the remainder of the ride commenting on the beauty of spring unfurling around them. Clouds were gathering, swallowing the sun, and as they reached the truck, a few raindrops spritzed the pavement.

Mitch set both bicycles in the truck bed and covered them with a tarp while Suzanne stretched her legs. He opened the passenger door. "Better get in before it starts to dump."

He got in the other side, put the key in the ignition, but didn't turn it. "You okay, Suzanne?"

"I'm fine. Not even a headache." She shook her head. "You can stop worrying. It was just a little bump. My head's hard enough to take that every once in a while."

"Okay, but you know what the doctor said. I have to keep checking." He put his hand on her forehead and stroked the faded bruise with a thumb.

Electricity sparked at the point where his skin touched her. He felt it too, she could tell. So far this afternoon they had not talked about their relationship. What kind of relationship was it? Suzanne had dared all week to hope it was a romantic one. That was the message she'd gotten Monday evening.

But he was holding back. She couldn't count the times today he'd been about to say something, but stopped and looked away. Even now she could tell he wanted to talk.

She turned and faced him. "What?"

"What do you mean, what?" He pulled his hand back and it joined the other hand behind his neck.

"What do you keep not saying?"

Mitch unlaced his fingers and ran them through his hair. He let out a breath. She had done it again. It must be a woman thing. Suzanne was the second woman who could tell every time he needed to talk about an issue, but held back. No sense in arguing.

But this was a tough one.

He sighed again. "You're right. I need to tell you, but I don't know how to say it." He picked up her left hand and held it gently.

Trouble flickered across Suzanne's soulful blue-green eyes. She closed her fingers around his hand, waiting.

There was no good way to begin, so he jumped in. "As you know, when I first started working with you, Suzanne, I thought you'd dedicated your life to teaching. That you'd consciously chosen to be single and fulfill a dream of being a lifelong teacher. I admired you for that, especially because you were such a fantastic teacher." He tipped her chin up with his right index finger. "*Are* an exceptionally great teacher."

She sniffed and waved away his compliment.

"Then I learned that you wanted to be a wife and mother. I've admired you even more for your ability to rise above your disappointments and give to others when you've received so little of what you wanted."

"God has given me so much," she whispered.

"I know, but let me get to my point. I think you'll agree with me that we had a . . . an . . . I don't know what you call it moment last week. We have feelings for each other. Back in February I recognized mine for you. Now you've shown me that you have for me as well. Am I right?"

She met his eyes and nodded. "Oh yes." .

He laid a hand on her shoulder. "I never thought I'd love another woman. But I was wrong. I never thought I'd even think about proposing again but—"

"What?" Suzanne's voice came out in a screech. A delighted rather than horrified sound. She clapped a hand over her mouth and stared at him. "Go on."

"I can't Suzanne. Even if I wanted to, which I do, but I don't—I mean . . ." His words tumbled all over each other, not making any sense. *Slow down, grandpa.* He stopped and took a deep breath. Tried again. "You want to be a mother. You should be. I've seen you with children, most recently with little Susanna. That's what you deserve." He ran out of words and just looked at her, willing her to understand what he was trying to say.

Her eyelids rose and she frowned. "Oh . . . kay?"

"I don't . . ." There was no delicate way to say what he had to make her comprehend. "I can't . . ." Mitch's words were drowned out by the sudden thunder of rain from the spring downpour.

After a minute or two it subsided and he started back in. "I can't have any more children, Suzanne." He explained the decision he and Marilyn had made after Marci's birth. "It is a reversible procedure, but after twenty-eight years, not usually very successful." Hours of online research provided him with this information.

Suzanne's eyes had dropped several sentences back, and her neck and face and ears were unnaturally pink. She shifted in her seat and twisted her fingers together.

"I have to let you go, Suzanne." He struggled to control the quiver in his voice. "It wouldn't be fair to lead you on. You want more than I can offer. You deserve more."

The rain had slowed and he turned the key, conscious that she sat frozen in the seat beside him. "You understand what I'm saying?"

She nodded mutely. What a jerk he had been, hugging her like that Monday evening. It wasn't like he'd just received a diagnosis this week. Why hadn't he kept control of his feelings? Let her go on believing he had only fatherly feelings for her. He wasn't blind. He'd seen the glow on her face, the hope in her eyes.

Now he had hurt her with no way to fix it.

"I'm sorry, Suzanne. I should have told you before. I should have stayed away from you." He watched the wipers clear the windshield. "I wasn't fair to you. You are a beautiful, poised, talented, young woman. Someone will come along and be all that you need him to be. I care too much about you to stand in the way of your happiness."

She sniffed, then dug in her jacket pocket and producing no tissues, wiped her cheeks with a sleeve. Mitch wanted to pull her close and dry those tears, but he couldn't. Wouldn't.

"I think we better go home now. Are you okay?"

Her reply was so soft he might have only imagined it. "I guess."

The eleven and six-tenth miles between West Carrollton and Mobileville had never seemed longer. Neither of them talked. Mitch didn't know what to say, and Suzanne was silent too. The moisture blurring his vision wasn't affected by the wipers.

By the time he parked in front of the dilapidated mobile home, the sun was peeking through the clouds and a brilliant rainbow mocked them from the east. If only she would say something, but what? He'd been so cruel. He expected her to bolt from the truck as soon as he stopped, but she didn't.

She unbuckled and turned to him, eyes still wet. "Thank you for the lunch and the bike ride, Mitch. I had a wonderful time." She blinked and took a deep breath. "And thank you for being honest with me. I know that wasn't easy for you." She reached over and took his hand. "You're the best man I've ever known."

Then she released his hand and waited for him to come around and open her door. She headed toward the trailer. "Good night. See you tomorrow."

"Wait, there's one more thing." He walked to the truck bed, unhooked the tarp strap, and set the woman's bicycle on the gravel drive. "This is yours."

"Mine?"

"Yours. I saw it at Target yesterday and it looked like you, so I bought it."

Her hand flew to her mouth. "I thought it looked pretty new. Mitch, you didn't have to do that. I don't know what to say."

"Don't need to say a thing. I didn't do it because I had to. I wanted to. Hold the door and I'll set it inside for you."

He carried it up the steps and wheeled it, as directed, into her sewing room. "I better go now."

By the time Marc and Kelly, Martin and Janelle, and Marci and Abe arrived at the farm shortly after six-thirty, Mitch had composed himself. Marissa and family were absent, and nobody asked if something was bothering him.

See, he always knew he could have gone into acting if the farming hadn't worked out.

28

Mitch left, and Suzanne crumpled onto the dear old second-hand couch, expecting to overflow with the rest of the tears. What a day. What a week. What a year.

What a man.

A loving, generous, selfless man who had just graciously dumped her.

When the sun set she was still sitting in the living room. She showered and dressed for bed. It would be a long night, and she knew herself well enough to know sleep would be a long time coming—if it ever came. Before her consciousness faded sometime after the alarm glow read 2:34, she filled a legal pad with her thoughts.

When the alarm beeped her awake a couple of hours later, she considered hitting the snooze. Until she remembered why she was so sleepy.

For the first time in months, Mitch didn't follow her to school. She could make the drive alone, but she missed him. Surely nothing had happened to him. She panicked at the thought and called his cell phone from the office as soon as she got in the school door. No answer.

She slammed down the phone in frustration. Then turned around to see him walking through the door. "Oh, Mitch." Without thinking, she flung herself into his arms. "Are you okay?

You weren't there when I pulled out and I was so scared something had happened."

He pulled away. "You were already gone when I got there." Exhaustion lined his face. "Are you okay, Suzanne? You haven't had breakfast yet have you? Do you hate me for being such a jerk?"

"Yes, yes, no, and no."

"Don't go away." He turned and raced back outside, returning with breakfast burritos and grape juice. "I should have called you last night, but the kids stayed way too long and I didn't want to wake you. Can you ever forgive me for toying with your feelings, for selfishly throwing myself on you last week? The last thing I ever want to do is hurt you, and I know I have."

Suzanne put a finger to his lips, bowed her head, and thanked the Lord for their food and asked a blessing on it. "And open Mitch's ears to hear me out, amen."

While he peeled the foil from their breakfasts, she retrieved her notes. "Unless you were thinking of calling between two-thirty and five, you wouldn't have woken me."

Pain filled his eyes and he set down his coffee cup. "Suzanne, I'm so sorry. I should get away from you before I do any more damage."

"You slept more than that?" she asked with a mouth full of sausage and scrambled egg.

He shook his head.

"Excuse my manners. This is *eggcellent*, and I'm making a pig of myself. Why don't I finish this, then I'll talk. I have something to say."

He nodded and began to eat too.

She ate faster than usual and started in while he finished. "First of all, I have to know if your confession yesterday was just a polite way of telling me you made a mistake, that you're really not interested in me . . . that way?"

"Wh-what?" He sputtered and spewed a mouthful of coffee. "That's what you thought?"

She tossed him her napkin. "I asked first."

"Of course not. I—"

"Me neither. So now that I've put that imagined doubt to rest.
. . ." She pushed her chair back, leaned her elbows on the conference table, and rested her chin in her palms. "What you said
there in the truck caught me off guard, Mitch. All I heard was you
telling me that I didn't have—couldn't have—what I thought I'd
found. What I'd had for less than a week."

He groaned and shook his head. He opened his mouth, but she
shushed him.

It was true. Her tears yesterday had nothing to do with him
not having more children. She heard what he was saying about
her being a mother and all that, but she hadn't gone there yet.
Maybe that told her how dedicated she *wasn't* to her dreams. In
the weeks since she realized that what she'd always looked for in
a husband was Mitchell Sanderson, not once had she seen him as
an answer to her childlessness.

Now she tried to explain that. "So when you left yesterday, I
was hurt. Angry too. Because I couldn't have *you*. Not because
you can't have more children.

"Through the evening and into the night I thought about it
from every angle at least a dozen times. Since we don't have nine
and a half hours to go over it all, I'll give you a condensed version.
Okay?"

Mitch nodded, hands over his face. "I'm listening."

"If you thought you could get rid of me that easily, mister,
you're sadly mistaken." She sat back and folded her arms across
her chest.

After several weighty silent moments, he slowly raised his
head. His eyebrows were nearly hidden in his hairline. "That's it?"

"That's it. You were unselfish enough not to make me choose.
But at the risk of sounding like I'm throwing myself at your feet
with a proposal . . ." She paused until he waved her to finish. "If I
get to choose between spending the rest of my life without biolog-
ical children and spending the rest of my life without you, I'll take

you." She surprised herself with the forthrightness of her words. Sleep deprivation can do that to a person.

"But . . ." Mitch stood and walked to the door and back. "I can't ask you to . . . It's not fair to you, Suzanne."

The crunch of tires sounded on the gravel drive. Of all mornings for another teacher to come early. She grabbed his hand, pulled him into the windowless office, and hugged him tightly and quickly. "We're going to figure this out," she whispered. "Can I take you out for supper tonight?"

He pulled back from the hug, in which he had eagerly taken a part. "No. Can *I* take *you* out to dinner tonight?"

And that's how they found themselves in a cozy corner of The Grub Steak that night ordering filet mignon. Despite its name, the restaurant turned out to be quite classy.

Mitch seemed determined to change her mind. "I've seen you hold my newborn granddaughter. You were made to be a mother."

"So we don't live in a perfect world. We don't get everything we want." Suzanne buttered a steaming dinner roll and handed him half. "Eat this while I explain."

"Yes'm."

"I've dreamed of having children of my own, yes. But face it, I'm going on thirty-eight years old. I know, women older than that have babies and do fine. However, it occurred to me that right now I feel more sadness at not having a ten-year-old son or daughter than at not having a baby." She paused as the server approached with their entrees.

"Besides, who knows if I would even be physically able to bear children."

"You don't know that you couldn't, do you? I just don't think you should throw away all your chances for a dried-up old man like me."

"All my chances. Ha. I lived for nearly four decades without a man looking twice at me. You want me to wait another thirty years for a man who'd be willing to father my children? I'm not Sarah."

Mitch grabbed her wrist and held it firmly. "Don't talk like that. You are an attractive woman. If you'd give the guys half a chance, you'd have them lining up at your door."

"Thank you very much, but the only man who's stood at my door is you. And you are worth more to me than dozens of children." She sliced a bite of steak and sipped iced tea. "May I borrow your phone?"

He handed it over and, tongue in cheek, she started tapping the screen. "But since you insist, I think I still know Kraig's number." After a pause she started talking. "Kraig? Hi, this is Suzanne. Remember me? Well, I think I may have changed my mind. Uh-huh, right. Oh, I wasn't thinking clearly. Right . . . Yes . . . You're not out with someone else tonight, are you? You are? Sorry. Maybe I can catch you another time then. Okay, right. What? Oh, yes, I recently got to thinking that I could put up with you as a husband as long as we could have children right away. You do? Oh, good. And also, it's because you have such a short last name. Did I ever tell you how important that is to me? Well, I'll let you get back to your date. Tell her I said hi." She tapped again and slid the iPhone across the table. "How'd I do?"

He touched take out and viewed the screen. "You goof. You could have been an actress."

"You're saying I'm not?"

"You almost had me going there. But that's silly, Suzanne. There are other men. Younger men who can give you what you want. What you deserve."

She shook her head. "Not true. Nobody else is you."

"I don't deserve you."

"Maybe not. I'm not saying you have me. But we need a chance to decide, not based on physical abilities. Okay?"

"Okay."

"Good. I thought I could get you to see it my way. You're a good man, Mitchell Sanderson. Now, can we talk about something else for the rest of the evening? Something that doesn't involve reproduction?"

29

Early Friday morning Mitch woke up thinking about Mother's Day. This would be his third one since Marilyn's death. It wasn't as hard to get through as Christmas, Thanksgiving, or their anniversary, but difficult in its own way. When the children were small, he'd made Mother's Day special for Marilyn. She was a deserving mother and he taught the children to show their appreciation, not only, but especially, on the second Sunday of May. Maybe they had focused on her because her mother wasn't living and his lived so far away.

Now that she was gone, the kids had moved seamlessly to Mother's Day celebrations within their own homes. Marissa had dutifully included him the first two years. She called last night to invite him for this Sunday as well. Janelle had called two hours earlier with the same invitation. "Martin's grilling," she explained. So he told Marissa that he already had an invitation. Now if Marissa didn't talk to Janelle to learn he'd turned down her invitation too, he'd be home free.

Suzanne hadn't mentioned any family plans for Mother's Day. He asked her at school Friday morning over sausage and egg casserole.

"I wish I could ignore it," she said. "I shouldn't even go to church on that Sunday. The sermon is always about mothers. I'm thankful I have a mother, but she's not a mother to celebrate with.

I usually send her a card and a gift, and that's it. So I sit there in the sermon reminded that I'm not one of those awesome, praise-worthy, unselfish, superhero women. I vow not to go the next year, but somehow I always end up there anyway."

"I have an idea. Let's both play hooky from church this week. We'll hitch up my boat, drive to the lake and put in. How's that sound?"

Her smile kept him energized all day.

She was waiting on the top step Sunday morning at seven-thirty. "Happy Mother's Day," he said as he ran from the truck and greeted her with a hug. "Relax, nobody's awake around here this time of morning. And, yes, you have dozens of children. So that makes you a mother as much as if you'd birthed them physically. All ready? I have lunch. If you haven't had breakfast yet, we'll stop at a Bob Evans on the way."

Suzanne settled into the truck, sighing happy sounds. "Thank you for rescuing me from this day."

"My pleasure. But just the thought of Mother's Day reminds me how much I'm taking away from you."

"Oh, no you don't." She reached for her seat belt clasp. "If that's how it's going to be all day, you can let me out right here."

"You win. I promise I won't bring it up again today." He gave her a sideways grin. "It's too bad you aren't a mother, though. You'd make a great one."

"Mitch!"

"Sorry. But it's true."

"You do realize that if I were a mother, I wouldn't be sitting here with you anticipating a day at the lake, don't you? Oh no, instead I could be sighing with frustration at some mediocre guy I'd been stupid enough to think I should marry. You know, in case he was the only chance I'd ever get at marriage and motherhood." She patted his shoulder. "No thank you. Besides, I keep hearing women say if they'd known grandchildren were so much fun, they would have had them first. Maybe I can learn from their wisdom and have grandkids first."

"Remind me not to argue with you, I'll never win." He grabbed her hand and stroked the inside of her wrist with his thumb. "I'm not complaining."

The water was high from the recent rains, but the winds had settled to a pleasant breeze. Mitch purposely kept the conversation light throughout the morning. He regaled her with tales of family trips to the lake both when he was a child and when his own children were at home. She said this was the first time she had ever been out in a boat. When the sun was overhead, he pulled out a cooler. Shrimp cocktail, grilled steak salad with extra homemade croutons, and praline brownies. Iced tea to drink. They ate on the water and Mitch held her hand when they finished.

"I'm not sure how to go about this." He cleared his throat and tried to remember his rehearsal last night. "I don't have a way with words like you do. But, Suzanne, I'd like to court you. Date you. Woo you. Whatever you want to call it. I want to spend time with you." He wiped the sweat from his neck. He was forty years out of practice.

The sunburn on her cheeks increased stunningly. She nodded him on.

"I don't know what kind of policy the school has about dating between staff members, but school's almost out and then we wouldn't have to worry about that for a while."

She nodded again. Her lips moved, but the sound was carried away by the scream of a gull. He dropped to his knees beside her and cocked an ear.

"I'd like that, Mitch. Very much."

His heart soared with the raucous birds. They talked for a while about their escape from hearing a Mother's Day sermon. Then Suzanne fell asleep to the rocking of the waves. He headed the craft toward shore. They stopped for ice cream on the way home. He wanted to be home fairly early in case the children came for their usual Sunday evening popcorn.

He dropped her off at home, kissing her fingertips before helping her from the truck. Lips tingling, he hurried home and backed the boat into the shed. He was parking the truck in the garage when Marissa and Layne pulled in.

"Dad! Where have you been all day?" Marissa asked in lieu of a greeting. "You weren't at church this morning, and Janelle said you weren't going to their place."

"I took the boat out on the lake today. And no, in case you're wondering, Pam Kingsley did not go with me." He smirked at the horror that crossed his oldest daughter's face. "Oh, yes. I've been seeing a good bit of her around lately. But don't worry, she offers not the least temptation."

She accepted the diversion and the suspicion almost left her face. "Thank goodness. Mom would roll over in her grave. I'm glad she made you promise so often. I can't imagine how it would feel to see you replacing my mother."

Mitch hugged Marissa. "Nobody ever could or would replace your mother. That's a fact." Soon he had to have this discussion in full. But not tonight.

30

The last day of school dawned long after Suzanne awoke. At four-thirty she quit pretending to sleep and got up. Mitch wouldn't be here to escort her this early, and that was fine. She had a few things to do at school in the peaceful predawn hours, so she set out alone.

Between five and six she wrote notes of encouragement and appreciation to each of her students. Their desks were empty now except for the small envelopes.

Mitch came a few minutes after six. "Good. You're here. I guess I wasn't really surprised to find your car gone this morning. You should have called me, I would have come earlier. I set the coolers of ice on the north side of the building. Do you think that's a suitable place?"

She nodded and told him about her sleepless night and activities so far this morning.

"Wow. You must be a valuable teacher. Don't suppose I could talk you into teaching at my school next year, do you?"

"I'm sorry, Mr. Sanderson, but I've already promised to stay at New Vision another year."

By eight-fifteen the students started pouring in. They milled around the school, trying to figure out what the teachers had planned for the day. Except the high school students, who were of course, much too cool to show their curiosity.

Devotions began as usual after the eight-thirty bell and roll call, which revealed perfect attendance school wide. Gerald Cook directed the short devotion period with the day's reading from *Our Daily Bread*, a song, and a rambling prayer. Then he turned it over to Mr. Sanderson.

Suzanne settled back into her chair when Mitch took the podium. She loved to hear him speak. He had such a tactful way of holding an audience's attention. Not even Mr. Garber could hold a schoolful of children spellbound like this new principal.

"I won't take up much of your time this morning, young ladies and gentlemen. I can see some of you are already drooling in anticipation of some pretty good-looking treats in the kitchen. This is my opportunity to tell each one of you thank you for enriching my life in the past eight months. I teach some classes here, but you have taught me far more than I've taught you. This would be a good time to hand out ninety-one excellent teacher awards." He stopped and pretended to count on his fingers. "That's not right. I only counted the people under eighteen. Your amazing teachers deserve that award as well. That would be ninety-six."

He turned and looked at the row of teachers. His eyes met Suzanne's and he winked.

"I thank God every day for the opportunity to learn to know each one of you." He pulled out a white handkerchief and wiped his eyes. "My prayer is that everyone will have a joyous and safe summer, and that we will see all but seven of you back in here next fall."

He stepped around from behind the podium. "Now, I have a short challenge to meet. A certain young man, whose name shall remain anonymous—huh, Jacob?—bet me last week that I couldn't call all ninety-one students by name. So now, in front of you all, I intend to win that bet." He walked to the front row of students and pointed to each child as he said their names.

"An award of excellence to Toby, Lily, Carter, Miles, Savannah, Joanie . . ." He didn't miss a name as he went through the rows, ending up with the high school. "Zack, Tina, Amy, Kate, Amber, Bethany, Andy, Nathan, Blake, Brent, and Sabrina."

Sabrina started clapping when he said her name and the whole school joined in. A couple of boys employed their two-finger whistles and everyone cheered. Mitch walked back to the podium and the noise died away. "To each person whose name I just said, I love you. Now let's close with prayer."

It was a typical Mitch prayer. Rich and heartfelt and prayed by a man who knew the God to whom he prayed. ". . . through the name of your Son, our Savior. Amen."

Suzanne kept her head bowed for a few extra seconds while she wiped her cheeks, missing the exact words he used to dismiss the kindergarteners and first graders for donuts. She jumped up and speed-walked to the kitchen where she spent the next ten minutes handing out Texas-sized glazed donuts.

Half an hour later everyone gathered on the basketball court and waited for Mr. Sanderson's instructions. He was such a good sport. Far better than the other married teachers. This was his first last day of school but he joined in like a pro.

Mitch had become so involved that he knew what was going on as well as Suzanne did. He quieted the mob with an ear-splitting whistle. "Ladies and gentlemen! Welcome to the First Annual Magruder-Stansberry-Fleckenstein-Brandenberg-Winkleman-Pennybackerson Family Reunion! We're so glad all of you could travel from points across the continent to join us as we bring our families together on this momentous occasion.

"When I call your names, please go to the teacher who will be in charge of organizing your family. Mrs. Miller will be in charge of the Magruder family." He listed fifteen students, who crowded around that teacher. "Mrs. Bower needs to see the Stansberry clan." Again fifteen names. And so on through the list.

As they gathered their groups of fifteen or sixteen students of various ages, each teacher handed out name tags. Suzanne had the Pennybackersons. Great-grandpa Verne, Grandpa Finley and Grandma Bertha, Great Uncle Charlie, Great Aunt Effie, Uncle

Cornelius and Aunt Gertrude, Cousins Hattie, Elias, Willard, Ira, Amelia, Viola, Minerva, and Della. Laughter filled the playground as they assumed their new identities.

Each teacher, including Mr. Sanderson, had set up a "reunion center" somewhere in the school or on the playground. Each family needed to visit the stations in turn and complete the activity scheduled there.

At Miss Lana's, they worked together to wash the family car. Of course you wouldn't want to take a dirty car to the family reunion. At the day's end, all the teachers would have clean vehicles.

Miss Kortney had marked off fifteen-foot-square areas of grass on the playground, and family members took turns with an old-fashioned reel mower until they had the landscape groomed for the relatives to come.

Mrs. Miller, the school camera bug, instructed each group in the art of portraiture. She supplied large sheets of paper and the students worked together to draw their family portrait. Then she arranged them as a family and snapped a digital image. These she planned to have printed for each student before dismissal. Her husband had volunteered to run the CD of edited photos to the nearest Wal-Mart when she was ready.

Mrs. Bower had planned a few old-fashioned games at her "house." Bobbing for apples, an egg toss—with hardboiled eggs, pass the donut on popsicle sticks held in the mouth, and various other relay-type competitions.

Mr. Sanderson was overseeing the ice cream churning production. Dessert for the huge family reunion potluck at noon. He had scoured the county for six hand-crank ice cream freezers and generously provided the ingredients for vanilla, grape nut, double chocolate, mint chocolate chip, peach, and fresh strawberry. Each family took turns cranking a freezer until it was finished. Then Mitch packed the freezer in ice and set it back in the shade.

At Suzanne's post they began their family vacation treasure hunt. She had a suitcase decorated for each family. Inside were clothes—an article for each family member to wear. Old hats, gloves, shoes, jackets, spectacles, purses. And a clue that set them off to their first vacation stop where they would find another clue with directions to the next. And so on until they reached their final destination and the prize.

Every year they had to deal with parents who wanted to join the last day festivities. It was hard to discourage parental visits, but the staff couldn't handle the crowds if everyone stayed. Especially non-student children. So they suggested that visitors please leave after devotions and assembly. As always, most complied, but a few felt their presence necessary to the process.

Although Mitch's daughter Marissa was not a newcomer to this year's noncompliant group, Suzanne tried to give her the benefit of the doubt. She was, after all, the principal's daughter, perhaps standing in for her absent mother. Maybe he had asked for her assistance with the ice cream freezers. However, by the time Suzanne had sent the first family off on vacation, it was apparent that Marissa was no mere churn assistant. She stood to the side skewering Suzanne with her critical gaze.

Suzanne tried to say hello and act friendly, but Marissa avoided any contact with her. She racked her brain for something she might have done to offend her. Her conscience was clear. Hopefully Marissa's negativity wouldn't spread through the ranks.

The day warmed progressively and Suzanne had opportunity to check in on all the activities while her families were racing to vacation spots. One by one the cars lost their grime and sparkled in the warm sunshine. The grass was mowed with great hilarity. One of the hand-drawn portraits looked amazingly accurate. Students proudly displayed the "First Annual Magruder-Stansberry-Fleckenstein-Brandenberg-Winkleman-Pennybackerson Family Reunion" buttons they won in the relay races. The finished ice cream freezers lined up in the shade.

Suzanne breathed a grateful prayer to the Lord for blessing them with ideal weather and cooperative students.

At noon all the families had finished their tasks and gathered for the potluck. And after lunch it was ball time! They would play ball for a while, taking a mid-afternoon ice cream break. Grades one, two, and three played together, grades four, five, and six, grades seven and eight, and the high school. Each level was scheduled a time on one of the three ball diamonds. When they didn't have a diamond, they had the volleyball courts or in the case of the younger students, an area for playing dodge ball, king's base, or the like.

After the high school finished their volleyball game and cooled off with ice cream, they headed to the ball diamond. Suzanne chose to sit out. Mitch would be more comfortable if she didn't play.

She kept track of strikes, outs, and runs on a clipboard from a camp chair Mitch had carried out for her. The teams were tied midway through the game when first-grader Lily came racing into their game. A couple of the girls saw her and routed her around. "Mrs. Anne, Mrs. Anne, Miss Donna says you have a phone call. Come fast."

Suzanne smothered a grin at the little girl's interpretation of *Miss Suzanne* while her heart flip-flopped. Who? What? If it weren't an emergency, surely Donna would have taken a message. She handed the clipboard to Kate. "Can you keep track? Give it to Amber or someone on the other team when you go to outfield." With Lily's hand in her own Suzanne walked back to the office.

It was Haley's mother. Thankfully Suzanne hadn't spent energy running. Was she sure Haley passed her Spanish final? Haley said she had, but she might have been stretching it. Miss Suzanne calmed her fears. Yes, Haley passed. No, she was not required to take second year Spanish. Yes, it was a good thing she had the extra help after school. Suzanne almost said, "You're welcome." But realized just in time that she hadn't been thanked.

She lapped a long, cool drink from the water fountain and headed back to the game. Happy voices rang out across the enormous playground. Life was good. God was gracious. School was almost out and Suzanne could sleep in every day for almost three months. If it didn't look so childish, she would skip all the way back to her clipboard. She puckered up to whistle.

"Wait, Miss Suzanne." The command came as she reached the far edge of the building. The unfriendly voice of Mitch's older daughter.

"Marissa. Are you enjoying your day?" Suzanne raised her voice slightly to be heard over the thumping of her heart.

Marissa didn't answer the question, but stepped close. Into Suzanne's personal space, and she instinctively stepped back. She was against the blue-gray siding with nowhere else to go when Marissa closed the distance again. Marissa looked around and Suzanne followed her gaze. No one was near or looking. She lowered her voice and her eyes became slits. "Stay away from my dad, Miss Suzanne." The *Miss* came out in an emphatic hiss.

Suzanne blinked. "What?"

"Oh, you know, you little sneak. I can see past you. You're after my dad, and I'm telling you, leave him alone."

"I, what?"

"I'm talking about how friendly you think you are with Mr. Sanderson. You think you can prey on his vulna . . . whatever-it-is-ability and loneliness, and weasel your way into his pockets. You've been spending time with him, haven't you?"

The cornered teacher nodded.

"Well, I don't suppose he's told you about the promise he made to my mother, has he?"

Suzanne shook her head.

"He promised her many times that he would never remarry if she died first. My dad keeps his promises. Not that he would ever think of marrying you." She spat out the last two words like rotten food. "I'm telling you, *Miss* Suzanne, stay away from him. Stay away from our family. Dad would never do anything to tear our family apart unless some conniving little gold-diggin' tramp caught him off guard. I'm only warning you once. Understand?"

Another nod. The blood pounded in Suzanne's head and she hoped she wouldn't faint. Good thing she was leaning against the sturdy school wall. Not a word of defense came to mind. She shook her head. Did she understand or not? Of course not.

"You better figure it out. Here's a suggestion, *Miss* Suzanne, you can—Hi, Dad. Is your team winning?"

Mitch smiled at Marissa and gave her an answer Suzanne didn't hear. As he spoke, he looked past his daughter and smiled at Suzanne. She looked at the grass. "Uh, excuse me, I forgot something back inside."

She stumbled into the building and to the closest restroom. Passing the mirror on the way to the farthest stall, an unfamiliar face stared back at her. She locked the stall door, lowered the toilet lid and sat. The blood thundered in her head. She was a gold digger trying to get in Mitch's pockets? She had preyed on his vulnerability?

This wonderful day lay trampled at her feet.

She lost track of the time. She emptied the roll of toilet paper as she caught the cascading tears. When she finally checked her watch, they had eight minutes left in the game. The cool water on her eyes did little to erase the signs of crying from her face. She jogged through the empty halls to her room, dug for a pair of sunglasses in the lost and found, jerked them in place and made it to the camp chair in time to watch Tina catch a ball that ended the game with her team as winners.

Mr. Sanderson blew his whistle and sent them back to the school. Suzanne folded up the chair and was trying to stuff it in its sleeve when he bumped her elbow playfully. "I'll do that."

Her cheeks tightened and her eyes filled. She surrendered the chair and picked up her clipboard and water bottle. He caught up with her at third base. "You okay, Suzanne? I can't see you behind those dark shades." He tapped a lens and she grabbed them so he wouldn't pull them off.

A couple of hard swallows and a sharp command to relax her cheeks didn't release her voice. "Yeah. Fine. I guess I missed the best part of the game, huh?" Her smile felt as fake as the gold that rimmed the glasses.

"You're flushed, hon. Didn't get too much sun out here, did you?"

"Hey, I have some things I want to make sure to send home with a couple of students." She took off at a run. Just hearing his endearment and seeing his vibrant brown eyes broke her heart.

31

Something was wrong with Suzanne. Mitch could see it in the way she walked back to the softball game. In her refusal to tell him how she was. And the eyewear. He'd never seen her wear sunglasses before. Maybe her headache was back. Had she gotten bad news in that phone call?

The three o'clock bell brought unrivaled pandemonium. In the shouts and cheers and the age-old chants of, "School's out, school's out, teacher let the monkeys out," he couldn't find Suzanne. When she didn't join the rest of the teachers in the last day send off, he really started to worry.

He waved and shouted, "Have a happy summer," to Marissa's carload as they passed. Lance and Merry Lyn stuck their heads out the window and called back. "You too, Grandpa." Ah, Marissa. She'd been around all day. He was going to hear it now.

At Mitch's orchestration, all the teachers stayed and helped clean up from the day's festivities. He had assigned tasks ahead of time so Suzanne wouldn't get left with most of the work. Now he willed them to leave. He wanted a chance to find out what was wrong. The way she pitched in made him pretty sure it wasn't physical.

She was surely pleased with how the day had gone. As far as he could tell, everything had run like clockwork. He'd expected her to be bubbling with excitement at the fun they'd provided for the students and the cooperation and appreciation they'd shown in return. But she was avoiding him.

Thirty-plus years of marriage had also taught him that a woman sometimes just needs her space. What he wanted to do was gather her up in his arms and make everything right. What he had to do was back off and wait for her to come to him. When he returned from taking the last trash bags to the dumpster, her room was empty. Hearing the familiar chug of her ancient Toyota, he looked out the window.

Empty. Helpless. Frustrated. Mitch trudged back to his desk and placed a call to an answering machine. "Suzanne? I don't know what's wrong, but I can listen. Did you get bad news in that call this afternoon? If it's something I can help with, you know I will."

There wasn't much left to do here. He pushed a few stray papers around, finally jamming them into a file and locking all the drawers. On his way home he made a loop into New Loveland. Her car sat in its usual place beneath the swaybacked awning.

He could knock at her door, but no, he'd give her time. At least she made it home safely. He'd call her tomorrow, that should be enough time. A text from Marc summoned Mitch to the farm to make a run to the dealer for a planter part. He studied the school as he passed it on his way back from Middletown. Suzanne's car was there. *Yes.* He checked the clock. Marc would have a conniption if he stopped now. He'd deliver the part and come back. But when he returned, she was gone.

Neither did she answer the phone the next morning. She must be at Joy's house doing laundry. He chose not to call her there. But when he got the answering machine in the evening, he started to panic. She wasn't in church Sunday morning, and her car hadn't been at the trailer when he detoured past on his way to church.

Mitch didn't stay for the sermon. He returned to Mobileville and pounded on Suzanne's door. The only response was a few neighbors eyeing him strangely. He tried peeking in the windows, but they were still well covered.

A wiry, dark-haired man roared in on a motorcycle. He gave Mitch a scornful look, turned around in Suzanne's drive and sped away with furtive glances over his shoulder. Somebody had done something to her. He started knocking on doors. "Have you seen the lady who lives over there?" He pointed to the aqua and rust trailer Suzanne called home.

"Dude, we got no reason to go nosing around here. No, we ain't seen her."

"Huh? Didn't know nobody was in there. Sorry, bud."

"I gotta work the night shift. Don't you go beatin' my door and wakin' me up."

At the last trailer on the row, he hit pay dirt. "Hi, I'm Verda. Come on up. Sit down."

Mitch didn't want to come up or sit down, but the woman's tone suggested if he didn't, he wouldn't get her information. He sat on a plastic chair that didn't appear capable of bearing his weight.

"You're not selling something are you? I seen you around here before."

"No, I'm not selling anything. Have you seen the woman who lives in that trailer?" He pointed.

"Sure. I live here, don't I? Not much goes on around here Verda don't see. Just yesterday I seen her filling her car. Filled it clear to the brim. Then she came back later and put some more in. Haven't saw her since then. Maybe she moved out. Know what I mean?"

Mitch's stomach knotted, sending off a chain reaction to his heart and brain. Moved out? He almost forgot to be relieved that the information meant she hadn't been assaulted or abducted. Had he thanked Verda for her help?

What was going on? Had the trailer park finally gotten to her? Had she gone to Jason and Joy's house? That didn't seem likely, as she'd told him just last week that Joy was preoccupied with the idea of having twins and didn't have time for anyone else.

One more try at the school. Her car was not there, but Mitch went in anyway and looked around. Her classroom was bare. She had obviously spent some time here. Recently. He scanned the top of her desk, going so far as to peek in drawers for clues. Nothing.

It was past time that the Moores could be home from church, so he drove to their house. No, Joy didn't know where Suzanne might be. She didn't come to wash clothes yesterday. Or was that last week she didn't come? If she said anything about going anywhere, Joy didn't remember. Maybe Mr. and Mrs. Bloomer had a change of heart and asked her to come live with them.

Mitch reached home with no memory of how he got there. His head throbbed and the blade in his heart kept twisting. This was worse than when Marilyn died. At least then he knew where she was. Suzanne might be in danger. Might be lonely. Might be hurt—physically or emotionally.

Not a minute had passed since Friday afternoon that he hadn't prayed for her. Begged God to take care of her. To show him where she was. The man he saw in the mirror looked as if he hadn't slept in days. He called the kids and told them not to come for popcorn. He had a headache and wanted to go to bed early. Not that he planned to sleep much.

Before that, however, he looked up Jim Bloomer's phone number. A woman's voice came on the answering machine. "Hello, Bloomers . . ." Mitch's heart began bungee jumping in its thoracic cavity, bouncing against his diaphragm. Suzanne! "Please leave a message for Jim and Connie . . . beeeeeep."

Mitch's heart rate slowed. It was only her voice, left on their recording years ago and never changed because her parents couldn't—or wouldn't—figure out how to put on a new greeting. He started to leave a message when a man's voice interrupted. "This is Jim. Whadda ya want?"

Suzanne was not there. But she had been. Had stopped in last evening and given her mother three houseplants. Connie was pleased as punch. Her pink cyclamen died just last week and even if she already had two hundred of those spider plants, she could always use another one. But the African violet didn't look like it was going to make it. No, they didn't know where she was now. Who was calling? Sanderson? No way was Jim Bloomer going to fall for that one again.

Mitch didn't shower, didn't shave, didn't go to bed. He spent the night pacing between his recliner, his desk, and the kitchen table. Every five minutes he called Suzanne's cell phone. It only got turned on when she wanted to make a call. Maybe he could catch her with it on. If only he had carried through with the thought he'd had of getting her a new phone on his plan.

Around ten o'clock, after his millionth call, it rang. *Yes.* And rang, and rang. Six rings and an automated voice, "We're sorry, this user has not set up a voice mailbox." He threw his own cordless landline phone across the floor. It was the same thing he'd heard all evening.

He stared at the pieces of plastic strewn across the tile. But it had rung. She had the phone turned on. He raced to his office and dialed her number, blocking the caller ID.

"Hello?" There was too much static on the line and the one word broke in the middle.

"Suzanne?" He shouted into the phone. "Suzanne, is that you?"

"Who is this?" It was her voice.

"It's me. Mitch. Where in the world are you? Are you okay? What's going on?" They were too many questions for her to answer at once, but he had to know. "Suzanne?"

"I'm okay . . . worry . . . be back . . ."

"I can't hear you, my dear. You're breaking up, Suzanne. Where are you?" Then a beep in his ear said the connection had been lost. All he got when he tried back was the maddening message.

❦

Somewhere in Suzanne's back seat, trunk, or storage unit in New Loveland was her phone charger. The phone in her hand was dead. At least she had gotten the call in to Aunt Eva. The connection was poor, but hopefully her aunt could hear that she had crossed the state line and would be in Felda sometime tomorrow.

Suzanne had talked to Mitch. If she had known it was him calling, she might not have answered it. She thought it was Aunt Eva trying back.

After two days she still didn't know what she was supposed to do. How embarrassing. Hadn't she learned her lesson with the Sandersons years ago? Why did she think this would be any different? Only this time *was* different. Mitch was not Marc. Mitch was a warm, humble, caring man. He had touched her heart and she knew he felt the same about her.

But Marissa was still Marissa.

Suzanne had left school Friday afternoon with a jackhammer headache and a tangle of emotions. She couldn't think straight. If only she could talk to Mitch. But she was too scared. She had to get away. At home she cried for a couple of hours before calling to the school and getting the answering machine. She went back and checked to make sure all her year-end records were complete and filed correctly. She took the folder with student notes and copies of special poems and reports they'd written. Once, she saw Mitch's truck go past and slow down. Her heart raced and she looked for a place to hide. But the truck went on. She had to get out of there.

Before she finally fell asleep around midnight, she had made up her mind to spend the summer in Florida. Saturday morning she called a delighted Aunt Eva and then began emptying cupboards and drawers. By nine she had everything stacked by the door. At the post office she forwarded her mail. She deposited her paycheck, keeping a sizeable chunk of cash.

Finally Suzanne drove to Mr. Grubbs's house. He was out front with a hedge trimmer and surprisingly accommodating when she explained that she needed to leave now. She expected to pay the final month's rent and forfeit her deposit, but he said that wouldn't be necessary. He had someone else who was ready to move in and he'd been afraid he'd lose them if they had to wait until the end of

June. He considered her contract fulfilled and even gave her the deposit and instructions to leave the key locked inside when she left. It was fine to leave the couch, bed, and table. The next renters would probably use them. She returned to the bank and added three hundred dollars to her checking account.

At the Loc-N-Stor she rented a small storage area. It took two trips to get everything there. She could have squeezed in the bicycle from Mitch, but she worried about the security. All the rest of the stored items were fairly safe. They weren't valuable, wouldn't bring much money to a thief who wanted to resell them. But the bike meant a lot to her. She finally decided to take it to school. She parked it beside her desk.

She took three potted plants to the car. One last stop at the mobile park, and she filled a trash bag with the remaining things she didn't want to save. She made sure she had the phone company's number to call when their offices were open next Monday. Mr. Grubbs had promised to get the electric changed out of Suzanne's name, but she took that number as well. She loaded the trunk with clothes and books and the few food items from her pantry and refrigerator.

On Tuesday the trash collector would make its last visit to school until August. So she swung by school one last time and deposited her bag in the dumpster. No turning back now. Suzanne was officially on her way to Aunt Eva's. Officially homeless.

And what about Mitch? Of course he'd be worried, but right now it couldn't be helped. He was undoubtedly frantic. She wanted to talk to him, but it was better not to. He didn't consider her a gold-digging tramp. No question about that. He was sincere in his caring for her. But what about his promise? What about his family? For his sake she had to leave and give him time to reconnect with his sons and daughters. If she cared at all for his well-being, she had to get out of his life. Maybe she *had* preyed on his vulnerability. Not on purpose, but he had been vulnerable. Hungry for someone to talk to about Marilyn. For adult company that didn't make him feel guilty for still mourning after two years.

Suzanne had basked in his attention. The guilt lay with her. Her neediness had sparked in him the need to rescue poor, pathetic her. If she got out of the way now, he could transfer that chivalry, that energy to his children and grandchildren. The last thing she wanted was to hurt him, but this was best for him.

When it came down to actually leaving, though, she couldn't do it without leaving him a note. She parked her car in the grass behind the school and went inside. She pushed the bicycle into the principal's office and leaned it in the corner behind the door. Then took a piece of paper and wrote. She folded the paper in half three times, stapled it, wrote his name on the outside, and taped it to the seat of the bike.

Mitch's house was not on the way to Phillipsburg, but she drove past anyway. Praying he wouldn't see her go by. Praying he would. His pickup wasn't in sight and she sped up once she was past and headed north to see Daddy and Mother.

She didn't want to see her parents, and yet she did. Mitch had said some things over the past months that made her willing to give them the benefit of the doubt in a lot of areas. He was sure her dad couldn't have been all bad to have a daughter like Suzanne. When he said it, she had believed a daughter like her was a good thing. But was she? Mitch knew he had failed in some areas of fatherhood and was reluctant to criticize Daddy. He had also pumped her for good childhood memories and helped her to see that not everything had been negative.

So she wanted to tell her parents good-bye. When she got back to Ohio, she would work harder at building the relationship. But nobody came to the door when she knocked. There were no vehicles around, and a call to her sisters turned up no clues. How were they supposed to know where their parents might be? Suzanne set the plants on the porch with a note to Mother telling her that she wanted her to have them. She was going to be gone a few weeks and she'd call them in a day or two with details.

She stopped at Wal-Mart and bought snacks and drinks and filled her gas tank. Then she prayed for safe traveling and at six-thirty p.m. headed south. All the way through Dayton she tried to convince herself this was an adventure. By the time she reached Cincinnati, she was having second thoughts. Already she was fighting sleep, and big raindrops hit the windshield. Was it safe to set out like this in a fifteen-year-old car, alone, and prone to sleepiness behind the wheel?

She exited the interstate with the intention of heading back north. But to what? She had no trailer to go back to. Her parents had made it clear that they wouldn't be hotel service for her. Joy's house was full and soon to be fuller. She was officially homeless. Her only option back there was to pitch a tent at the school. Only she had no tent. She turned around and reentered southbound 75.

She drove into rain as she crossed the Ohio River. Seeing the road was a struggle, but she determined to keep on. Aunt Eva knew Suzanne was headed her way and expected her there in a day or two. Sleepiness, the rain, and her need for a restroom pulled her from the highway at a rest area a few miles north of Berea, Kentucky.

She parked under a light and dashed through the downpour. When she returned to the car, soaked to the skin, exhaustion overwhelmed her. Too tired to continue driving, she made sure her doors were locked, laid the seat back, and closed her eyes.

Now she was too far to think about turning back. She expected to fall asleep the moment she closed her eyes. Behind the wheel, she couldn't stay awake, but now she found herself too keyed up and uncomfortable to sleep. She dug in the back seat for a pillow, but it didn't help. Neither did trying to stretch out across both bucket seats with the cup holder sticking up in her back or stomach.

It was too scary to sleep here anyway. Suzanne gave up trying. Instead she put the driver's seat partway up and just sat there.

A loud horn and children's voices woke her. She jerked her head up from its sideways position on her shoulder. Ouch. She checked her watch. Five-thirty. She stretched the kinks out of her neck and returned to the restroom.

Then hit the highway again. Pepsi and pretzels made a sad substitute for sausage biscuits and orange juice. She hit every rest area along I-75 between Berea, Kentucky and the Florida state line. But the caffeine helped keep her awake. Restroom breaks and gas stations were her only stops until she finally wore out soon after leaving Georgia.

Suzanne's body was so stiff and sore and tired she could sleep anywhere. An exit boasted hotels and she took it. The closest hotel became her first choice. It looked like more than she wanted to pay, but that was too bad. A deserted Burger King sat across its parking lot and she drove through for a junior Whopper and onion rings, eating in her car before checking into the Green Roof Inn.

The last juice of her cell phone's battery had gone into that unsatisfactory call from Mitch. He sounded worried. Probably hadn't gotten her note yet. But she was able to tell him she was okay and he didn't need to worry, she'd be back in time to get ready for school.

His words hadn't all come through. Something about breaking up. He realized it too, although she wouldn't have called it breaking up, as they hadn't really been dating.

She wiped out the bathtub with the extra hand towel and filled it full of hot water, running every drop across the hard sliver of soap to make bubbles. Then she took a bath, not a shower, for the first time in twelve years.

The next morning she was up with the sun and took advantage of the free breakfast. They obviously didn't have Mitch Sanderson for a cook. Soon after noon she left the interstate and headed southeast from Fort Myers to the little spot on the map called Felda. This was her first visit to Aunt Eva's, a fact of which Suzanne was thoroughly ashamed.

Aunt Eva hustled out as Suzanne drove up. She opened her door before she'd shifted into park. "Welcome to Florida, Suzanne.

You're really here. Come in, come in. We can get your bags later. Come on in now for a glass of sweet tea. Have you eaten? I was going to wait until one o'clock and then go ahead and eat without you. I fixed us some ham sandwiches and potato salad. You can have some veggies and dip if you want. I have the freezer filled with ice cream." Aunt Eva's words tumbled over themselves.

They ate lunch with her chatting merrily all the while. She didn't ask why Suzanne was there, taking it for granted that she had been unable to wait any longer to travel by car alone to spend time with her aunt.

32

A pack of coyotes howled in the middle of the night. Mitch woke to their musical yips and checked the time. Quarter to five. Where was she? He slid from the bed and onto his knees.

If he could have, he would have spent every hour of the next however many days it took to find Suzanne. But he still had some year-end business to attend to at the school and some of his farming clients to meet. Most of the farmers had all their crops planted and were appreciating the rains. By noon he was free to return to the school.

He went first to the high school room. Thoroughly frustrated he trudged to his office and closed the door. He dropped into his chair and buried his face in his hands. When he lifted his head he saw the bicycle in the corner. The one he'd given Suzanne. Had it been there Saturday when he was here? A note on the seat. With his name printed on top. In his haste to open it, he ripped it down the middle. He took it to his desk and taped the two pieces together. Her graceful script stared back at him.

> Mitch, please don't be worried. I'll be back in time to get ready for school. My mail is forwarded, so send any correspondence to my New Loveland post office box. You're a strong man and your family needs you, and so we cannot date. We both know it

wouldn't have worked anyway. It's best for me not to be around this summer. Take care of yourself and I will be fine.

Suzanne

After a dozen readings he had it memorized without being any closer to finding her. But at least he got the message.

She didn't want him to find her. They wouldn't be dating. Why? He pounded the desk. Why?

Everything had been fine Friday morning, no question. She was exuberant and contagiously enthusiastic about the activities and the beginning of summer vacation. She chatted animatedly during lunch. Cheered the softball game.

Then she had been summoned to the school for a phone call. That was it. Mitch sat up and grabbed the phone. "Donna, do you remember the phone call for Miss Suzanne last Friday?"

She did. Haley's mother had called. Donna asked to take a message, but no, she had to talk to Miss Suzanne. Right away. Donna didn't know what it was about.

After the next phone call, Mitch slammed the phone down. Another dead end. Haley's mother had only asked about Haley's Spanish exam. She hadn't talked to Miss Suzanne since.

As Mitch paced the carpet between his desk and Suzanne's, an image came to mind. He left the game Friday afternoon for the restroom. Suzanne wasn't back yet, but he remembered now seeing her at the corner of the school talking to Marissa. He hadn't seen Suzanne's face, he didn't think, but he recalled her saying, "I forgot something inside," before taking off.

For this call, he used his cell phone. "You home, Marissa? Mind if I stop over in a couple of minutes?"

He didn't wait for an answer to his knock at Layne and Marissa's. The kids were playing computer games in the rec room. He found their mother crying at the kitchen table. "Daddy, I want another baby so bad. Why can't I get pregnant again? I'm so glad you're here. Nobody else understands, not even Layne." She wrapped both arms around his arm and laid her head on his shoulder.

Mitch didn't understand either. Why couldn't she be satisfied with the four beautiful, healthy children she had? This was not the point of his visit, but he would have to get through it first.

He tried to say comforting things without committing himself to anything. Finally she dried up and he got down to business.

"Did your children have fun on the last day of school?"

She assured him they did.

"You were there most of the day too, huh? What did you think? Ready to be a teacher and get in on all the fun every day?"

She shrugged. "It was okay."

"Tell me about your conversation with Miss Suzanne in the afternoon." He watched her face closely.

First she blanched, then red flames streaked up her cheeks. She rubbed her nose and blinked. "Conversation? With who?"

"With Suzanne Bloomer. I believe you know her, she's our high school teacher. I saw you talking to her."

Marissa stood and began throwing dishes into the dishwasher. "So I have to report all my conversations to you, Dad? I didn't even have to do that when I was a kid."

"Marissa." His voice held an edge that he didn't remember ever using with his children. "I want to know. What did you say to Suzanne? I won't leave here without an answer."

She slammed the dishwasher door and stared out the window, scratching the back of her very red neck. "Well . . . I asked her if she knew that you promised Mom you'd never marry anyone else." She turned around and looked at him defiantly. "Don't you think she had a right to know?"

He shook his head and clenched his teeth, determined not to lose his cool. "And?"

"I told her you were vul . . . vul-nible and lonely and she should be careful." She twisted the dish towel. "If you don't mind. I need to call in the younger kids and get them down for naps." She started for the door.

Mitch stood up and blocked her path. "I do mind. I need another minute or two of your time. I want to know word for word what you said to Suzanne." He waited the full sixty seconds it took her to meet his gaze. "I want to know."

"Well, I . . . I kind of told her to stay away from you, or something like that. That she didn't want to tear our family apart. I don't remember exactly."

Mitch slammed his hands into his pockets to keep from doing something else with them. Marissa's behavior called for a major confrontation, but he didn't trust himself to act like a Christian with this anger pulsing in his veins. Neither did he want to lose a precious minute finding Suzanne. "We will talk about this later, Rissa." He stepped around his stammering daughter and stumbled to the truck. With great effort he held himself together long enough to get home.

Oh, Suzanne. It didn't take a psychologist to recognize that Marissa's account was a greatly watered-down version. How badly Marissa must have scared her, hurt her, insulted her. She was sensitive and had already been hurt deeply by his family.

Why couldn't he have protected Suzanne from his own daughter? It was his fault for not having sat down with his children to help them see that it was time for him to move on with his life. That he could do so without being unfaithful to their mother. Why hadn't he? Had his fear of their responses resulted in Marissa chasing Suzanne away? *Suzanne, I'm so very, very sorry.*

───

It took five tries to pick out the right clothes to wear. It used to be funny when Marilyn had this problem. A suit would be too formal. Jeans and a t-shirt too casual. Somewhere in between, but the happy medium was hard to find. Mitch finally settled on tan Dockers and a blue oxford button-down shirt.

At seven-thirty he rang Jim and Connie Bloomer's doorbell. On the phone earlier they had agreed on the time Mitch suggested. He didn't want them to think he was fishing for a supper invitation. Suzanne's dad came to the door and gruffly invited him in.

Mr. Bloomer hadn't dressed up. Or maybe he had, it was hard to tell. Mitch hadn't seen the Bloomers in years. Neither of them looked old enough to have a thirty-seven-year-old daughter.

"You have a really nice place here, Jim. You do the landscaping yourself?"

He did and appeared pleased that Mitch had noticed. "Well, why don't you come on in to the kitchen. We're just getting ready to have some pie."

At the mention of food, Mitch's stomach growled. The only thing he'd consumed so far today were two cups of coffee, a bottle of water, and a roll of Tums. He took the offered chair and the piece of fresh strawberry pie. When Jim and Connie took a bite, he followed suit. After he swallowed, he chuckled. "If I ate like this every day, Jim, I'd be three times your size."

Jim's shoulders relaxed and he smiled—the friendliest smile yet. "Me too, Mitchell. Me too."

As they ate, Mitch complimented Connie on her collection of beautiful, healthy houseplants. She got up and told him a little bit about each one. He asked Jim about work and heard about his retirement, his monthly Social Security checks, his nearly non-existent pension—after working thirty years for the same place. Mitch heard about the inheritance that came Jim's way after his father's passing a couple of years ago. It all matched what Suzanne had told him.

Mitch asked the Bloomers about their grandchildren. They had four. Their pictures were on the refrigerator. He checked them out, specifically noticing they had no pictures of Suzanne.

Finally the plates and forks were cleared away. It was time for Mitchell Sanderson to present his pitch. He took a sip of coffee and cleared his throat. "You're probably wondering why I'm here." They nodded and he continued. "I had the privilege of being the principal at New Vision School this past year."

The looks on their faces showed they hadn't known. They looked at each other questioningly.

"I worked with your daughter Suzanne. First of all, I want to commend the two of you for raising such a fine young woman. I'm a parent myself and know what a difficult task it is." Mitch noted the looks of relief that crossed their faces. "Suzanne is our best teacher. You must be very proud of her."

Jim Bloomer puffed his chest out a bit. "Well, we did our best, didn't we, Connie?" She affirmed his declaration. "We never had any boys—just the three girls. Some people acted like I should be pretty disappointed with that, but we liked our girls pretty good. It's good to hear Suzanne's turned out good. Never was marrying material, you know. But it's good you think she's a good teacher."

If the man said *good* one more time, Mitch might lose control. Not "marrying material"?

"She's superb. Has touched a lot of lives in a positive way. And we at New Vision always appreciated the home training you gave her." *Had* always appreciated.

They beamed with pride. Connie refilled Mitch's coffee cup and said, "You're an influential man, Mitchell. It means a lot to us to have someone in your standing notice our efforts. If you ever need any help motivating Suzanne, let us know. She always took a lot more encouraging than our other two."

"I'll do that." Mitch laced and unlaced his fingers around the mug in his hands. "Now, you probably know that our final day of the school year was last Friday. This morning I was working on a few things at school and wanted to get in touch with Suzanne for a couple of recordkeeping questions. But I haven't been able to reach her. I'm really hoping you might have some insight that would be helpful."

"You check her house? That old rental of Bob Hopkins's?" Jim asked.

Connie punched her husband's shoulder. "She moved away from there, doofus. I think it's some apartment complex in New Loveland. The school probably has a current address."

272

"I checked there, but her landlord says she moved out. Joy Moore doesn't know either."

"Hmmm. That's interesting. Jim told you that she was by here last Saturday. We were gone for the evening, but when we came back she'd left those three plants and a note. Here, let me get that paper." But she couldn't find it in the stack of papers on the windowsill. "Jim, did you throw her note away?"

"Only because I thought you wanted me to. Women . . ." Jim looked at Mitch and rolled his eyes. "How do you know what they really want you to do?"

"Anyway, I don't think it would help you much anyway, Mitchell," Connie said, glaring at her husband. "Just something about going away for a while this summer. That she'd let us know when she had details." A thoughtful look passed through her eyes. She got up and left the room.

"Here." She held up a cordless phone handset. "When we got home this afternoon, I saw that I'd missed four calls from my sister. I guess it's possible Suzanne finally went to see her. Eva's been after Suzanne for years to visit. They have a strange relationship, those two. I can't imagine Suzanne would go that far by herself, but it's the only idea I have."

Mitch nearly jumped from the chair and grabbed the phone. It was a long shot, but the only shot so far. "Do you mind if I copy that number? If she's there, maybe I can call and get these issues cleared up."

The miles from Phillipsburg back to Farmersburg had never seemed so long.

When he got back he would call the number he'd written in his seed corn notepad. If this answered his question, it would be worth a hundred trips to the Bloomer home, but he hoped one was all he had to suffer through. Suzanne had grown up with those two people. That she became the person she was, was nothing short of a miracle.

That Mitch made it to the school without a speeding ticket was also nothing short of a miracle. His plan required the call to be made from the school's phone in case Eva had caller ID on her phone. At his desk he looked for the millionth time at Suzanne's recent school picture. "There is a portrait of beauty. A picture of the woman I want to marry," he said, looking into her face. Then he bowed his head and prayed for the success of this phone call.

With the hands of a Parkinson's victim he dialed the number Suzanne's mother had given him. The voice that answered sounded a lot like Connie's. "Keller residence."

Mitch assumed his business tone. "Uh, yes. Mitchell Sanderson calling from New Vision School. Is this Eva Keller?"

"Why, yes, it is. How may I help you, sir?" Her voice held a smile, and hope budded in his heart.

He smiled too and willed it across the line. "Mrs. Keller, I'm sorry to bother you, especially so late in the evening, but I spoke with your sister Connie today. She said I might be able to reach Suzanne Bloomer at this number?"

"Why yes, you can." She lowered her voice. "But I don't think right now's a good time. Suzanne already went to bed. Even with a three-hour nap this afternoon. She must have been really tired after that trip. Can I have her call you when she gets up tomorrow? I'm sorry, I've forgotten your name already. I used to be so good with names."

Mitch thought fast. "You know what, Mrs. Keller—"

"Oh, call me Eva. Mrs. makes me feel so old. I am old, but I'm not ready to feel that way yet."

"Okay, Eva. I'll tell you what. Let's not bother Suzanne. I had a few school questions, but I think I can get them worked out without taking any of her time. She deserves a break from school, I think."

Eva laughed long and loud. "You are exactly right, young man. If anyone ever deserved a break, it's Suzanne. I like the way you think."

"Do her a favor and don't even mention my call."

She matched his conspiratorial tone with her own. "That's exactly right. I want her to rest up as long as it takes. Mercy, I'm surprised her car made it all the way here."

"Have a good night, Eva, a good summer, and take care of Suzanne, will you?" He waited for her consent and good-bye.

"Yes! Thank you, Lord. I found her, I found her." He danced around the desk.

Then he raced to his truck and sped home.

A few keystrokes and mouse clicks later he had located Eva Keller. As Marilyn used to say—Oh. My. Goodness. Eva Keller lived around the Florida Everglades.

His Suzanne had driven eleven hundred miles in that old Toyota. Alone. And in what kind of emotional state? *Suzanne, Suzanne, what have I done to you?*

It was late. Well past the hour he appreciated getting phone calls. But he had a few he had to make. Tonight. His kids stayed up too late anyway. One by one he dialed their numbers and asked them to come for supper tomorrow night.

This meeting was not about food, although he had promised to feed them, so he ordered pizza instead of cooking. How many of his kids would notice that he'd unthinkingly bought Pepsi instead of Coke, which had long been the cola of choice in the Sanderson household?

The rain moved on, giving the grandchildren no reason not to play outside. Mitch turned down offers to help clean up the kitchen.

"I'll take care of it later," he said. Janelle had rejoined them after feeding baby Susanna, and everyone fell silent, giving him their what's-this-all-about expressions. Marissa kept her eyes down.

Mitch looked around at the faces he loved so much. Two were missing. One who could never come back. The other whom he hoped with all his heart could and would. He cleared his throat and grabbed a napkin to wipe his eyes. Finally he opened his mouth. "I need to talk to you all about something."

"Wow. I must be learning to read minds. That's what I thought was going to happen," Marc said.

Martin threw a breadstick at his brother. "Zip it, dude, let Dad talk."

"First of all, I want you to keep in mind that I will always love your mother. But your mother is gone. As much as it hurts to acknowledge, she's not coming back. I know some of you believe I promised her I'd never remarry." He looked pointedly at Marissa, who returned his gaze with smoldering eyes. All the other eyes were on him as well. He had their attention.

He swallowed hard. "I never promised her that. Maybe she did want me to—heaven knows she said it often enough." He pulled out his falsetto voice. "'Mitch, darling, I hope I don't die first. But promise me if I do that you'll never marry anyone else?' I always believed it was one of her ways of telling me she loved me. Don't you remember how I used to answer her? 'I'll promise you that, Lynnie, as soon as you promise you'll remarry the week after I die.'

"Marc? Marissa? Martin? Marci? You never heard either of us make that promise, did you?" One by one they all shook their heads.

"Okay, then. We have that cleared up. It's nice to see you all so agreeable tonight." Mitch tried to laugh, but instead the dam inside him broke.

"I want . . ." He stopped and lowered his face into his hands. "I'm sorry," he said.

A small hand wrapped around his arm. "Grandpa? Are you okay?" It was Merry's voice. "What's wrong, Mommy? Why is Grandpa crying?"

"Go outside, Merry Lyn," Marissa said. "This is for the grown-ups. Go check on your little sister. Make sure she's not on the slide by herself."

Mitch put a hand over Merry's and looked up. "I'm okay, honey. I'm just kinda sad right now, but it's going to be okay. Listen to your mother."

Merry skipped out and he continued. "Some of you have probably noticed that I've spent some time with and talked a lot about
another wonderful woman. But for the past four days I haven't
been able to find her. In some ways it hurts worse than when I lost
your mother. That's because I didn't know where she was. Didn't
know if she was safe.

"In those four days, I recognized that I love her. She is a fine
woman, a gracious lady. She fills an empty place in my life. I
won't say she fills an empty space in my heart left by your mother.
Because that spot is not empty. It won't ever be. But knowing her
has opened up another space—a new space in my heart. A space
that only Suzanne Bloomer can fill.

"Suzanne left, telling me in a note that my family needs me.
She is too generous, too self-sacrificing, too loving to make me
choose between her and you. Before she left, she was informed
that a relationship with me would tear our family apart." Mitch
took the handkerchief that Marci pulled from Abe's pocket and
handed it to him. He wiped his eyes again and blew his nose.

Everyone except Marissa looked around the table. Their eyes
asked, "Who?"

"Suzanne is not the one making me choose. I shouldn't have
to choose. I won't choose. You are my family. I love you. I'm your
father. I don't have to have your blessing to ask Suzanne to join
this family. I would like it, but it is not necessary. In no way
would I be betraying your mother. So, I'm just asking you—"

Through the downpour of tears that wouldn't subside, he
looked around the table at his beloved children.

Suddenly Marci jumped up and waddled around the table. She
threw her arms around Mitch's neck. "Oh, Daddy, it's my fault.
Mom told me to tell you and them, but I didn't want to. Now I've
hurt you, and I'm so sorry."

Marc, Marissa, and Martin and four in-laws stared at them,
straining their ears to hear the words she spoke into their father's
shirt.

33

Aunt Eva was the most trusting person Suzanne had ever met. She never questioned her niece about the impetus of her impulsive trip. To her it was enough that Suzanne had at last come to see her. She rolled out the red carpet. If the queen of England had visited her, she couldn't have shown more hospitality.

Tuesday morning Suzanne woke to bright sunshine streaming through the windows of Aunt Eva's guest bedroom that housed a queen-size bed with the most comfortable mattress Suzanne had ever lain on. It had an attached bathroom. With a tub. Before she went to bed last night she'd planned to take a bubble bath—Aunt Eva's idea. Before starting to fill the tub or undressing, she pulled back the covers on the bed and tried out the mattress. Her aunt must have come in sometime after that and turned off the light. Mitch would be delighted to hear that she had three full meals yesterday and twelve hours of uninterrupted sleep.

Mitch. The tiny shards of her heart broke into pieces. How would she survive the summer without Mitch? How could she ever go back to school and see him every day while staying away from him?

She dried her eyes and cheeks on her rumpled blouse sleeve. From somewhere in the house Aunt Eva's voice sang over the roar of the vacuum. Eight o'clock. Time to get up and give her some company.

She showered and joined the older woman in the kitchen where she was patting out some kind of floury dough. She put a hand on her aunt's shoulder and kissed her cheek. Aunt Eva returned the gesture. "Good morning. You look well rested. I bet you're starved. These'll be done in fifteen minutes and while they bake, I'll fry the bacon. My hens are laying pretty heavy these days, so I hope you like eggs. How do you like them? Oh, don't answer that—I'll do some all the ways. Then you can pick. I'm going to see if I can put some meat on your bones."

Technically, Aunt Eva's food was every bit as good as Mitch's. Being with her was wonderful too. But she wasn't Mitch. Suzanne tried to dismiss the thought and be thankful she was here at long last. She even tried to tell herself that learning the truth about their relationship and needing to leave was a blessing in disguise. How else would she have ever made the effort to drive to Florida?

Surprisingly, all those emotions didn't keep her from pigging out on the breakfast. Two biscuits—more tender even than Mitch's, half a dozen strips of bacon, one scrambled, and one sunny-side-up egg. With lots of never-from-concentrate orange juice.

"Aunt Eva, if I eat like this all summer, I'll have to make all new school clothes." Suzanne laid her napkin on her plate and pushed back from the table, patting her full stomach.

Satisfaction radiated from Aunt Eva's smile. "I'll help you sew. In fact, I'll take you shopping and help you pick out some clothes. If you gain that much weight, surely you'll finally enjoy clothes shopping. Why don't you sit on that new bench by the pond and enjoy the sunshine before it gets too hot. I'll be out in a bit to talk about what to do today." Excitement flashed in her eyes as she shooed Suzanne out the door.

Between Suzanne's naps yesterday her aunt had given her a tour of the plantation. She still wasn't sure what all Uncle Marlin had done, but it must have been successful. He had left Aunt Eva well cared for financially. She still kept an office going out in the back of the property, run now by a hired manager. She did a lot of the accounting, and that took up four to five hours of most weekdays. But she assured Suzanne that she could take off as much time as she needed. She was the boss, of course.

Suzanne found the recommended bench and an inspirational novel lying on it. The book was by an author she hadn't heard of. The first line caught her attention. *Virginia Mitchell watched her husband carve the Sunday pot roast and wondered if he was having an affair.*

Mitchell. She couldn't get away from him. Not even in the Everglades of south Florida. She sighed and continued reading. This Lynn Austin had a curious way of making a reader keep going. Immersed in the book, Suzanne looked up after an indefinite length of time.

Aunt Eva was watching from the other end of the wrought-iron bench. "I see you found the book. You'll like it, I think." She sat and propped Suzanne's bare feet in her ample lap. "What do you want to do today? Shall we go to the ocean first? Or do you want to drive along alligator alley and maybe tour an Indian village? Or would you rather just stay here and relax for another day?"

Every time Suzanne opened her mouth to answer, another suggestion came. Just like . . . there he was again. How was she supposed to get over him when he wouldn't stay away?

She laughed to keep from crying. "What other options do I have? No, I'm kidding. I don't know. I've never seen the ocean."

Aunt Eva jumped up. "The ocean it is. Here we go. Bring your book. I have another one—same author, different story. I have sunscreen too, and beach chairs. I even found these cute little water bottles with battery operated fans to mist us and keep us cool. Good thing it's waterproof suntan lotion, huh? We can sunbathe for a while, then go get a good seafood lunch and see what's happening on Sanibel Island today."

"Aunt Eva, I—"

"Hush, now Suzanne. I gave both your sisters wedding gifts. I send their children cards and even gifts sometimes. If I'm invited to their weddings, I'll take gifts. And even if it weren't for all that,

I want to do this. I can afford it. Can you accept something from someone else for once in your life?"

Suzanne pulled her aunt into a tight hug. "Thank you," she whispered.

"That's better. No more arguing. This is more fun for me than it is for you. Let me grab my beach bag and purse. You might want to get some shoes."

Neither of Suzanne's pairs of shoes were exactly beach worthy, so they stopped at a drugstore on the east side of Fort Myers and picked up a pair of jelly sandals.

The young man operating the cash register wore a name tag that read *Mitch*.

Aunt Eva said that some people didn't consider the west beach of Florida as being along the ocean. But Suzanne agreed that if the Gulf of Mexico wasn't part of the ocean, nothing was. She could have sat for hours listening to the water, the squawk of the gulls, and especially the laughter of children. All of those sounds blended in with the stories of Virginia, Helen, Rosa, and Jean and for a couple of hours she managed to not think about Mitch. Very much anyway. Only once per page. Maybe twice.

When Aunt Eva pulled the book from her hands, slipping a sliver of seaweed between the pages to mark her place, Suzanne could hardly believe it was nearing two o'clock. "My favorite restaurant is probably cleared out now from the lunch crowd. I'm glad you like seafood. I don't even try to fix it at home. It's not that far to come over here." She continued her chatter as they gathered up their things and kicked through the sand and back to the white Lincoln.

The lunch was as good as she'd promised. But it took a while to eat, then she needed to pump gas and stop for groceries. It was getting too late to go out on the island, although it was a good place to watch the sunset. They would come back another afternoon and do just that. Bring food along and watch the sun drop into the Gulf.

Back home they heated leftovers for supper around seven and watched a movie together before heading to bed. Aunt Eva walked Suzanne to the bedroom door and hugged her. "I can't tell you how much it means to me to have you here, Suzanne. Thank you for letting me spoil you today. Sleep well, dear. I'll get up around seven and work in the office for a while. Walk over when you get up if you want. You can ride the golf cart back here with me and we'll get breakfast. Oh, and pile your laundry outside right here. I'll have it done for you when you get up. No arguing. Put it all out here. Every last piece. Good night, Suzanne. See how that bubble bath feels tonight. I noticed you didn't get around to it last night." She pecked Suzanne's cheek and left her to obey orders.

"I love you, Aunt Eva," Suzanne called after the retreating figure.

True to her word Suzanne's clothes were laundered and even ironed when she woke up—sun streaming in the windows once more. She dressed and wandered through the kitchen to the porch door. After all she'd eaten yesterday she couldn't be hungry, but her stomach insisted otherwise. She strolled through the gardens and made her way to the trailer that housed the plantation office.

After another enormous breakfast—without Mitch—Suzanne assured Aunt Eva she would not feel deserted if the older woman went back to work. She picked up *A Woman's Place* and headed outside. From the looks of her face and arms and legs, she needed shade today. She spied the hammock and decided to test drive it.

Strung between two enormous leafy trees, the hammock was completely shaded. A breeze blew across the pond and while it wasn't exactly cool, it was not uncomfortable. Before she climbed aboard she ran back to the house and poured Pepsi over a tall glass of ice. She trudged back to the hammock with her drink. Okay, how was she supposed to lie in there reading and sipping Pepsi without spilling it? She should have brought the bottle and unscrewed the lid only when she needed a sip. One of these days she'd get it right.

The truth was, Suzanne wasn't used to such luxury. So much time to relax and feel pampered. The morning was nearly over when she finally got settled in the hammock with a cold two-liter of Pepsi half full of pop, half full of crushed ice. She balanced herself in the center and propped the bottle between her legs. The strip of seaweed stuck out where Aunt Eva had placed it. She opened the book and scanned the page. *Helen loved him. It was as simple as that. The hours that they spent together were the only ones that mattered in her life . . .*

She threw the book onto the ground, not caring how it landed. That's how it had become for her with Mitch. How could she live without him? She rocked back and forth, willing the sway to take away the hurt. She was too wide awake and already-rested to sleep. Too pained to read any more. Helen probably ended up with Jimmy in the end of the book. That's how they always ended. Well good for them, they didn't have to live in the real world.

Suzanne checked her watch and found a bare wrist. Aunt Eva would soon be in for lunch and didn't need to see her like this. She took a glug of Pepsi, recapped the bottle and set it on the ground. While she was tipped that way she made a lunge for the book and unbent its cover. She almost dumped out the other side as she struggled to right herself.

Back in a safe position, she wiped her eyes with her fingers and resumed swinging until the well-oiled purr of the golf cart set her up straight. She tried to stop the hammock's movement and realized that a hammock won't be stopped against its will. She listened for Aunt Eva's whistling. Instead she heard what sounded like a car door slamming.

Uh-oh. Golf carts don't have doors. She peeked over the edge of the canvas.

A basketball court length away from her hideout, parked behind the Ohio-licensed Toyota sat a lime green PT Cruiser. Someone must have gotten out of the car, but she couldn't see them. Aunt Eva hadn't mentioned any of the cousins traveling down today and a client looking for the business had to be blind not to see the sign pointing back the other lane.

She didn't want to talk to any strangers, so she sank back into the lap of her swinging bed and held her breath. A rapping sound came from the house. She didn't want to be ungrateful for Aunt Eva's hospitality, but whoever it was would have to find the office on their own.

Then she remembered the book and the pop bottle sitting accusingly beneath her. Another peek showed a man standing on the porch surveying the yard. Before he could look this way—she hoped—she grabbed the two-liter and the novel and ducked back in, causing the whole thing to bob like a piece of driftwood in the waves.

She held her breath as footsteps neared her hiding place. She closed her eyes. A salesman wouldn't wake a napping vacationer, would he?

Then came a sound that Suzanne had dreamed about.

A throat cleared. Nervously. A jolt of what felt like fear struck her solar plexus and spread pinpricks into her hands and feet.

"Suzanne?" It was his voice.

This was all a dream. She would try to sit up, but find that she had grown fast to the canvas. Try to open her eyelids only to have them too heavy to lift. Try to say his name and not have a larynx. But she had to try.

"Mitch?" Her voice worked, her eyes opened, and she sat up.

There he stood. The most beautiful sight she had ever seen.

"Mitch!"

She wasn't sure what happened with that silly hammock, but she rocked clear out of the thing, landing at his feet.

He helped her up. It was really him. Not a dream. "What are you doing here?" Her first and strongest impulse was to fling herself into his arms. But she remembered in time why she was here. Why she couldn't love him. She stepped back and folded her arms protectively across her chest.

He let her move away. "Suzanne." His whisper sounded like a prayer.

She lifted her eyes. Worry and love lined his haggard face. "Mitch, we have to talk."

"Wait. There's something you have to hear first." He slipped his phone from his shirt pocket and swiped the screen. Her eyes flickered from the phone to Mitch's eyes. He kept them glued to the phone, tapped quickly, and a montage of voices began. "This is Marc. This is Marissa. This is Martin. This is Marci." Then in unison. "Suzanne, we want you to make our dad happy. He doesn't have to choose between us and you. You don't have to choose between him and us. Please come home." There were some nervous-sounding chuckles and one strained voice. Marissa's. "I'm so sorry, Suzanne. When you get home and I can talk to you in person, I want to make it right." Mitch tapped the phone and pocketed it.

The little shards of heart inside her started marching back to their rightful places. Her legs turned to jelly and she sat down on the hammock. Bad idea. She landed against its edge and pitched toward the ground. Head first.

Mitch hurled himself down and caught her before she landed. He pulled her to her feet and wrapped his arms around her.

"Hey, now, mister. You get away from her. I have a stick." Aunt Eva's voice rang through the air. "I said, put her down. Step back. Now."

Suzanne backed away, but took Mitch's hand with her. "Aunt Eva," she hollered, "it's okay. I know him."

She walked around the golf cart dragging a huge branch. "You sure?"

"I'm sure. This is Mitchell Sanderson. He's a good friend of mine from Ohio. Mitch, this is my favorite Aunt Eva. Really, she's harmless."

Aunt Eva dropped her "stick" and held out her hand sheepishly. "I'm sorry, Mr. Sanderson. Didn't recognize you there for a minute. I should have, though. You're as good looking in person as you are on the phone."

Suzanne looked from her face to his, but neither explained.

Mitch pocketed his phone and shook her hand, not letting go of Suzanne's. "Aunt Eva. It's a pleasure to meet you. Please, call me Mitch."

"You're just in time to have lunch with us. Did you have any trouble finding us? Surely you didn't drive, did you? Oh, right, the car—it's a rental, isn't it? What kind of sandwiches do you two want? I have turkey, ham, pastrami, and roast beef. Or maybe you want some of each. That's what I'll do. I'll just set them all out and we can all make our own. I'll run along now and let you talk." She bustled into the house, dragging the branch off the grass as she went.

Mitch's cheeks twitched with humor. "And you thought I was bad!"

He took Suzanne's other hand and faced her. "I see a bench over there. It looks a bit sturdier than this hammock. Let's go over there. We do need to talk."

She sat on the bench and he sat right beside her. "Do you want to hear that message again, Suzanne?"

"I don't need to. It was pretty clear." She wanted to hear *his* voice.

He spread her right hand on his leg and covered it with his right hand. "I'm so sorry, Suzanne. I don't know exactly what Marissa said to you, but I know it must have hurt you very badly. If I could take it away, I would. Please, don't stay away from me. I need you."

"But what about your—"

He put a finger to her lips. "My promise to Marilyn. It never happened, my dear. It was sort of a joke between the two of us, and the kids heard it and wanted to take it as a vow. We also now know that before she died, she left a message for me with Marci."

Suzanne frowned and tipped her head questioningly.

"Her last words to our youngest daughter were, 'Tell Daddy, find someone else. Tell him and the others I said so.' Marci told us that last night. She wants you to know she's sorry for not relaying the message sooner."

She pulled her hand from under Mitch's and wiped a stray tear wandering down his face. He backed away and dropped to his knees in front of her, taking both her hands.

"I couldn't let you spend the summer here without telling you this." He tipped her chin up with his knuckles, not releasing his grip. "I love you, Suzanne. I know there are a lot of things we need to work out. And you don't have to give me an answer now. I love everything about you. Except, there's one thing I would change." He waited until she raised her eyebrows. "Your last name." He smiled and her toes tingled.

"So. Here's the question for you to think about. Suzanne Olivia Bloomer, will you marry me?"

34

Some girls spend years dreaming of and planning their weddings. They know exactly how many bridesmaids they'll have and what colors they'll wear. They make out guest lists before they know who the groom's family will be. Reception menus before they know of future in-laws' dietary restrictions.

Suzanne was not one of those girls. While she dreamed of marriage, she never thought a lot about the day it would begin. Hers didn't need to be a huge fanfare to accomplish the job.

Less than two months to prepare was plenty of time for her. The one wedding idea she'd carried from childhood was that of an outdoor wedding. Mitch's back yard was the perfect place, never having been used for a wedding, as both his daughters had winter weddings. The landscaping around his house was already in perfect order, all they had to do was plant some extra flowers and freshen up the mulch the week of the wedding.

She sewed her own dress and those of her soon-to-be step-granddaughters. They decided not to have any attendants. Her sisters didn't really fit into that role, and Joy was too busy with newborn twins—Grant and Grace—to notice the slight.

Simple was Suzanne's idea of a wedding, although she had a time persuading Mitch that it really was her taste. His own to Marilyn and those of his children had been elaborate affairs. He wanted his bride to have everything she wanted, holding nothing back. But simple and small were what Suanne wanted. And it didn't take long to get ready for. He liked that part a lot.

Except that it didn't give him time to achieve the building goal. Suzanne's aversion to secondhand items no doubt fueled his insistence on having a new house built for them to move into upon returning from their honeymoon. But there was no possible way to accomplish that between their arrival home from Florida and their wedding date of the last Saturday in July.

On a pleasant evening in mid-June the two of them knelt in a landscape bed planting flowers around his house.

"We can rent a townhouse in the new development north of town, Suzanne, and live there until L&L Construction finishes our house."

"Why? Are Marc and Kelly that anxious to get into the farmhouse? I thought they weren't moving in until October."

"They're not. But it doesn't seem fair for you to have to move into a house that Marilyn decorated and furnished with her tastes."

"I don't think of it that way at all. It makes much more sense for us to live here until our house is done. Really, it's what I want to do. Not for always, although that wouldn't be the worst thing in the world, but a couple of months would be fine."

"Okay, you win. But I still feel bad. And I still struggle not to feel like I'm cheating you out of being a mother. I should just get out of your way so that can happen."

Suzanne leaned back on her heels. "You know, I've thought about that some more too. You're probably right."

His head popped up and his eyes popped open. "What?" popped out of his mouth.

"I can see it when I think about how unfair I'm being to you." She watched him open his mouth to protest and put a dirty gloved finger, over his lips. "You are marrying far beneath you in social status and maturity. I should step out of the way so you're free to marry some widow your own age. Someone more on your socio-economic level. Someone you can reminisce with about the good ole days and share memories of your deceased spouses and the child-rearing days. It's not fair for me to make you give all that up." She finally allowed the grin into her eyes and lips.

"I ought to smack you, Suzanne Olivia Bloomer Sanderson. If I don't marry you, I don't marry anyone." He grabbed her grubby hands and pulled her close, rewarding her with the threatened smack. Right on the lips. After a couple of seconds he pulled back. "You're something else. But yes, now I see your point even clearer."

She removed her gloves and traced the tear paths on his cheeks. "If *I* don't marry *you*, I don't marry *anyone*. Is that settled, now?"

"Yes, Miss Suzanne. I'm sorry I've been such a slow learner."

"Speaking of slow learning. I'm not sure I've learned all those smacking techniques you were talking about earlier."

He was such a wonderful teacher. They had both agreed to another year at New Vision. That was back in early April before they admitted their feelings for each other, but after Suzanne realized she could never marry Kraig. It was a verbal agreement, not a signed contract, but she took those agreements seriously. Mitch did too after she showed him how the students would be the ones to suffer if they bailed out on them. A year should be enough time for the board to search diligently for Mitch's and Suzanne's replacements.

Her dream of marriage had not included teaching at the same time. But this reality was already so far from how she'd dreamed. Her husband would take her to school, be there while she was there, and take her home. And help with the housework too.

He claimed not to mind her inability to cook, nor to believe it. "You can do anything, Suzanne, but I'll gladly cook if you want me to."

The last Saturday of July dawned hot and humid. Suzanne had spent her last night in Martin and Janelle's basement where she'd been living since she and Mitch returned from Florida. Spent the night, not slept. She was far too excited to sleep. Probably she'd end up taking a nap later that morning on the couch in Mitch's home office. The wedding was at five-thirty and there wasn't much work left for today. The reception meal was being catered, and Aunt Eva would be back at nine to oversee the remaining preparations. When they had called her with the wedding date, she begged Suzanne to allow her to come and coordinate the event.

Mitch picked her up at six-thirty after she called him at six to tell him she was awake. They deemed it unnecessary for her to stay out of his sight until she walked down the aisle.

She ran out the walk to greet him. He picked her up in a hug, swinging her feet off the ground. "Good morning, beautiful. Shall I make one last breakfast for Miss Suzanne?"

His unshaven cheek scratched deliciously on hers as she nodded against him.

He led her into his—their—house and instructed her to sit at the table while he finished preparing the meal. The table was already spread for two. A white linen table cloth and fine china and crystal. Not Marilyn's. This was new.

"Close your eyes, and don't open them until I say so." He'd been guarding something on the counter.

She heard the refrigerator open and their glasses being poured. It smelled like orange juice. The oven door opened and closed, plates clanked, utensils against china. His lips brushed against her cheek and he whispered, "Not yet, dear." Finally he sat beside her. "Okay, I say so now. Behold, wedding day crepes."

They were gorgeous. Perfectly rolled, dusted with powdered sugar, and sprinkled with fresh blueberries. Sweetened cream cheese filling spilled from the ends. Slices of crisp bacon fanned out to the edge of each carefully arranged plate. The orange juice was freshly squeezed.

"It's too beautiful to eat."

"But not as beautiful as you." He took her hand and prayed.

"It's not too late to back out, Suzanne. You set me straight on the children issue. But we haven't talked much about my second-hand status. Are you sure you want a hand-me-down husband?"

"There is nothing hand-me-down about you, Mitchell Sanderson. I wouldn't even call you slightly used or reconditioned or refurbished or . . . or . . ."

"What we have, my darling, is a brand-new love."

Group Discussion Guide

1. Did you wear hand-me-downs as a child? Was that a good thing or a bad thing for you?

2. Have you ever said you would never do something and later had to eat your words? What made you change your mind?

3. The life Suzanne was living was not the one she had dreamed of. What are some of your unfulfilled dreams? How has life turned out different than you expected?

4. Suzanne has a fractured relationship with her family. What steps would you advise her to take to help repair that relationship? How could Mitch help? Can you relate to her family issues?

5. How could things have been different if Mitch had not procrastinated talking to Marissa about his supposed promise to Marilyn? Why do you think he kept putting it off?

6. Suzanne seems like too much of a doormat sometimes. Is there a balance between godly servanthood and codependency that is not beneficial to others? Have you ever struggled with that balance?

7. Kraig believed God was leading him to Suzanne, but she didn't get that message. What do you think was happening there? Would God tell one person something and another person something else?

8. Suzanne decided she'd rather be single the rest of her life than marry someone she had to endure being with. Obviously we know that was the right decision because Mitch was right there. But what if there had never been another man? Would marrying Kraig have been a better choice?

9. If Mitch had indeed promised his late wife that he'd never marry, would he have been bound by that promise?

10. Have you ever had a widowed parent date or remarry? How did that make you feel?

11. Mitch's children have varied personalities, and Marissa is obviously the "villain" in the story. What could be some of the underlying issues in her life that cause her to lash out more than her siblings do?

Want to learn more about Rosanna Huffman
and check out other great fiction from
Abingdon Press?

Check out our website at
www.AbingdonFiction.com
to read interviews with your favorite authors,
find tips for starting a reading group,
and stay posted on what new titles are on the horizon.

We hope you enjoyed Rosanna Huffman's *Hand Me Down Husband*. Abingdon Fiction offers a wide variety of fiction, including romances that feature heroes and heroines far beyond the typical twenty-something. In Sandra D. Bricker's *The Big 5-OH!*, Olivia Wallace tries to escape a string of bad luck, several feet of snow, and her upcoming birthday by seeking a new life in sunny Florida. But her new neighbor may have something even more interesting in mind. Here's a sample chapter.

1

Prudence leaned over the edge of the pond and gazed at her reflection.

"What's happened to me?" she exclaimed. "I looked like a perfectly normal young donkey when I left home this morning."

"The journey has taken its toll," Horatio HootOwl replied. "But just one dip in the Enchanted Pond, and you'll surely be revived."

Prudence lifted her head and closed her eyes.

"Braaaaaaaay," she whimpered. "Oh, me, oh, my. Braaaaaay."

"No, no," Horatio said, rubbing his feathered wing over the fold of Prudence's smooth ear. "One dunk in the water, and then a nap in the sun, and you'll be good as new. You'll be a new Prudence."

She chuckled at that. "Do you promise?"

"I promise," said her friend. "You'll be a brand-new Pru."

Liv dug the shovel into three inches of snow and pushed as hard as she could, then tossed it to the side of the driveway. Three more reps followed before the muscle down the back of her arm throbbed in response. It used to take much longer for her old body to react to physical labor in this way.

Time marches on, she thought. Whether we like it or not.

"Hey, neighbor!"

Liv looked across the white meadow between them and waved at her friend Hallie, who stood at the edge of her garage next door.

Three kids filed past Hallie, all of them bundled up in coats and boots, hats, scarves, and gloves. At thirteen, Jason was the oldest. He had reached the bottom of the driveway by the time Scotty, the ten-year-old, hurried past his mother. Katie, age six, scampered behind her brothers, then she turned and waved at Hallie.

"Later, Mommy."

"Later, sweetie."

"Hey, wait up, you guys," the little girl called.

"Boys, wait for your sister and walk with her all the way to the bus stop, please."

Jason didn't so much as slow down, but Scotty came to a full stop until Katie reached him. The two of them skated along the patches of ice on the sidewalk.

Liv's heart pinched a little as she watched them. She'd had more than her share of obstacles over the years that had kept her and Robert from having children of their own. Hallie was blessed to have a houseful, and Liv envied her that.

"Coffee?" Hallie called out to Liv.

"Half an hour?"

"I'll bring cake."

The thought of cake cheered Liv right up, and she returned to the chore of shoveling a channel up the driveway so that Hallie could bring it safely to her.

A few minutes later, the snow started to fall again, and Liv leaned on the shovel, breathless, and watched the path she'd just created disappear under a layer of white.

"Ah, crud."

Looking around at the colorless landscape of her suburban Ohio neighborhood, Liv realized there was a time when she had considered her hometown to be one of her greatest loves. Nestled into rolling green hills and bellied up right next to the Ohio River, it was such a beautiful and thriving town. Summers in Cincinnati were blue skies and picnics, and winters were powdered sugar-covered treetops and ice skating on Winton Lake. But all that had changed.

Five years had passed since Robert had died, but passing months on the calendar had a curious way of fogging up the glass through which she peered to try and find the time when she still had him with her. It made her head ache to work so hard at looking back for him, struggling to break through the wall of cancer that stood between present day and her beloved past.

Stage 3 Ovarian Cancer. The English language didn't hold four more terrifying words, and, on the chilly morning of Olivia Wallace's forty-eighth birthday, those words were hurled at her like a dagger with four sharp blades. She remembered it like it was yesterday; this particular glass was as clean and clear to look into as a freshly hung window pane.

Two surgeries, six weeks of chemotherapy, and exactly twenty-seven radiation treatments—all of it as translucent and visible as a neon sign on a spring morning. And now, on the other side of the monster, nothing looked the same anymore. In fact, the first snow of winter had fallen overnight, and it seemed just as dreary and dull as everything else within Liv's recent frame of reference.

As she pulled Robert's old canvas fishing hat from her head and shook off the snow, Liv glanced at the mirror hanging over the cherry buffet in the dining room. It didn't escape her notice that her tedious life and gloomy surroundings weren't the only uninspiring things in the room. Her own reflection looked rather bleak as well.

In the six months since making its original escape, her red hair had finally begun to grow back. Lackluster though it was, and despite those silver streaks all through it, at least she had hair again. Her cheeks were drawn, her green eyes seemed slightly sunken and hazeled, and her fair, freckled skin had gone somewhat ashen. Although her energy levels had finally peaked again, she still looked just as tired and drained as she had felt throughout her recent past.

Liv pressed the button to open the garage, and then quickly latched the door before the outside wind had a chance to make its way through. As she counted out scoops of ground coffee, the *thump-thump-thump* of Hallie's boots on the garage floor signaled her friend's arrival.

"*Buenos días*," Hallie called as she came through the door into the kitchen. Hallie was always learning something new. Spanish lessons on CD were the project of the moment.

"Morning," Liv returned, setting two oversized cups and saucers on the kitchen table.

"I brought coffee cake."

"What kind?" Liv hoped it didn't have anything healthy attached to it, like fresh fruit. At the moment, she just wanted a pure confection of sugar and sweet.

"Cinnamon swirl."

"Good girl."

"Still warm."

"Even better."

Liv slid across the padded leather bench and settled into the corner of her kitchen booth as Hallie grabbed plates and flatware before she took the outside chair. Liv watched her as she tangled her fingers into her blonde hair and shook off the flakes of fresh snow and then poured two cups of coffee.

"The first snow of the season," Hallie announced. "Isn't it beautiful?"

Liv tilted into half a shrug, leaned onto both elbows, and propped her face up with her hands.

"Or not," Hallie said, raising an eyebrow at her friend. "Feeling a little blue?"

"Blue and blah."

"Oh, I'm sorry. Anything I can do?"

The funny thing was Liv knew Hallie meant it. If she thought it would raise Liv's spirits to do a little barefoot jig across the linoleum floor of her kitchen, Halleluiah Parish-Dupont would certainly oblige. Her friend was a true-blue cheerleader that way. And at forty-seven years old, it seemed almost wrong that all she needed were the pom-poms to actually look the part.

Liv gave her a smile and shook her head.

"Well. There's cake," Hallie said with hope.

"There is that."

Liv took a large bite and her eyes opened wide at Hallie, and then she smiled.

"This is *sheeriously delishush*," she said through a full mouth. "Did you make *thish*?"

"No. Bender's Bakery on Compton."

After swallowing a couple of times, Liv let her fork clank to the plate. "It's kind of sad that this is the best thing that's happened to me in days, don't you think?"

"This isn't like you," Hallie observed.

"It's not, I know."

"Can't you tell me what's going on?"

Liv cringed and shook her head.

Suddenly, Hallie gasped and slid a hand over her mouth. "Oh, I get it," she said deliberately, nodding her head. "It's the birthday thing, isn't it? Next month is your birthday."

"Afraid so."

"Liv, you've got to give up the idea that your birthdays are cursed. You know that's not how our God works."

Our God. Sometimes Liv wondered if she still knew Him. But Hallie sure did, and that was a comfort somehow.

"I know it up here," she said, tapping her temple with her index finger. "But it doesn't quite make it down here." She smacked herself dead center in the chest several times.

"So what's the plan then? Just mope around and wait for a piano to drop on your head next month?"

Liv shrugged again, and then plopped forward into her folded arms. "Jimmy DiPlantis dumped me on my sixteenth."

"You dated someone named Jimmy Durante?"

Liv raised her head and grimaced. "Not Jimmy Durante. Jimmy DiPlantis. He made out with Rachel Wagner at my Sweet 16 party."

"Well, it's good to know you're not still holding a grudge."

"And on my twenty-first birthday, I slipped on the ice and fell down a flight of stairs. I had a cast on my leg and my arm for eight weeks."

"That's awful," Hallie said. "Really. That's *terrible*."

"On my thirtieth birthday, I had pneumonia, and a fever so high that I lost several days and didn't even realize I'd passed the thirty mark until my birthday the next year. When I finally discovered I was actually turning thirty-one instead of thirty, I was devastated."

"Oh!" Hallie exclaimed and covered her grin with both hands. "Honey. That's . . . horrible."

"I know. And then there was the big blizzard on my thirty-eighth—"

"Oh, no."

"—thirty-ninth and fortieth."

"All three years?"

"All three."

"Oh, my."

"And you were there for my forty-eighth."

"Yes."

"Ovarian Cancer. Stage 3. The worst day of my life."

"But you're healthy now."

"Yep, I am. And here comes my fiftieth, Hallie. Like a loco-motive chugging straight at me." Liv leaned back down into her folded arms again, and the dishes on the table rattled when her head dropped. "I'm just too young to be this old."

"You've got to do something drastic, Liv," Hallie told her. "You've got to bust out of this prison you're in. Gloomy weather, birthday blues, expectations of doom. It's just not healthy. You're acting like Prudence, the lop-eared donkey from my mother's books."

Liv raised her head and looked at Hallie curiously.

"She writes children's books, remember?"

"Yes, I remember."

"Prudence only sees the dark clouds."

"You're comparing me to a donkey?"

"Prudence is more than a donkey, Liv."

"Do tell."

"That's not my point. I think you need a vacation."

"So what are you suggesting? A trip to Club Med?"

"No. Not Club Med. But you do need a break."

"No Club Med? That's disappointing."

"But what better place to take a vacation than . . . Florida?"

"Huh?"

Hallie curled her hands into the sleeves of her blue cable-knit sweater and grinned from ear to ear. "Did I mention to you that my mom has been talking about coming to visit?"

Liv didn't respond. She just stared at her friend with narrowed eyes and a furrowed brow, trying to catch up.

"She hasn't seen the kids in a while, so Jim and I thought she should come for a couple of weeks."

"That's nice. I guess. Since she hasn't been here in a while."

"Do you remember where my mom lives?"

"Florida."

"Yep. *Flor-i-da.*"

"Okay. What are you *get-ting* at, *Hal-lie*?" she mimicked.

"While my mom comes to Cincinnati, her house on Sanibel Island will be completely empty."

"Uh huh." She still wasn't getting it.

Hallie groaned, and then she leaned in toward Liv for emphasis.

"You could go there, Liv, and lie in the sun, get away from Ohio in winter, and celebrate your birthday at the beach."

"Oh."

"It's brilliant."

"I don't think so."

"Liv."

"Hal."

"You have to do this."

"No. I really don't."

"Wait. You're right," Hallie exclaimed. "You shouldn't go lay by the pool and work on your tan and try to get back some of the strength and joy that all those months of cancer robbed from you. Instead, you should just go back to work in the O.R. Spend your time shoveling snow and getting your birthday sick on. Maybe try some pneumonia again. It's been a couple of decades."

Liv's stomach stood up and fell down again at the mere thought of going back to work. She'd always loved her job. The operating room at Providence Hospital was a well-oiled machine, and she'd always been excited to be a part of it. But now, post cancer surgeries and medical reports of doom that she'd barely overcome, it just didn't seem to be the right place for her anymore.

Becky from Human Resources had contacted her twice in the last week, her messages ripe with friendly enthusiasm. But the thought of returning to work, or even just returning Becky's calls, brought such an ominous feeling to Liv's heart that she hadn't been able to bring herself to dial the phone.

Just that morning, she had lain in bed, her eyes clamped shut and the blanket pulled tight against her chin, and she'd done something she hadn't done in a very long time. She prayed that God would guide her in what to do.

"I don't want to go back to my old life," she'd whispered. "But I can't seem to muster up the desire to move forward either."

Hallie reached across the table and squeezed Liv's hand, yanking her back to the moment. "This is the answer for you," her friend stated, as if she'd been in on every moment's thought. "You haven't had a vacation since the trip to Galveston with Robert six years back, Liv."

The memory pinched her. "I can't, Hallie."

"Yes. You can."

⸺

Liv propped the phone on her shoulder with her chin and sighed. She'd forgotten where Hallie had gotten her cheerleaderness. Josie Parish was Hallie's mother. She was Hallie times two.

"Oh, of course, you can, Pumpkin. The house will just be sitting here with nothing to do but provide you a little nesting place."

"Ms. Parish, honestly, I appreciate the offer. I really do."

"Didn't we establish when I was there visiting the last time that you were not going to call me that anymore?"

"Sorry. Josie."

"Okay then. We're on a first-name basis. As close as you are to my Halleluiah, my goodness, we're nearly family. The least you can do is come and babysit my home for a couple of weeks. Oh, do you like dogs, Pumpkin?"

Liv shook her head briskly to make the leap with her.

"Dogs? Umm, yes. I like dogs."

"Oh, that's so good, because my little baby has recently had surgery. She had a bit of a bad jump across the sofa. She's won't be able to travel, that's for certain. You wouldn't mind looking out for her while you're here, would you, Pumpkin? It would really help me out."

"Josie, really, I just can't see my way clear to take a trip right now."

"Of course, you can. In fact, from what my daughter tells me about everything you've suffered through in the last year or so, I'd say you really have no choice. Now, I'm going to make my flight arrangements, and I'll tell Missy Boofer that you'll be here the same day to look after her—"

Missy Boofer?

"—and I'm thinking of arriving on Wednesday. Would that work out all right for you?"

"Well, I—"

"Oh, good. Now I'm off to call Halleluiah and give her the good news. I'll leave you all the information you'll need on the dining room table, and the key to the house will be under the neon pink palm tree in the garden."

Neon pink palm tree?

"Josie."

"Olivia, I want you to know that I do appreciate this very much. If you weren't going to be here to take care of Missy Boofer, there's no way I could come to see Halleluiah and her family before I get tied up with my next book deadline. You're a little angel is what you are, and I know Jesus will take good care of you here on the island. I have a good feeling about it. I do. My insides tell me your whole outlook is going to change down here, Olivia. The Florida sun has a way of baking up fresh possibilities, you know. And that's all you really need, isn't it? Some new possibilities?"

Liv tossed up her hands and dropped her chin to her chest.

"Okay. Why not?" she said in surrender. "Thanks, Josie. I'll be there next Wednesday."

"Oh, that's wonderful, Pumpkin. Boofer will see you then."